NOAH'S ART

JB Dukes

All of the characters in this book are fictitious, and any resemblance to actual persons, living or dead, is purely coincidental. The names, incidents, dialogue and opinions expressed are the products of the author's imagination and are not to be constructed as real. The events in this book are entirely fiction and by no means should anyone attempt to live out the actions that are portrayed in the book.

Copyright © 2015
California Times Publishing, Los Angeles

No part of this book may be reproduced, scanned, or distributed in any printed or electronic form without permission. Please do not participate in or encourage piracy of copyrighted materials in violation of the author's rights. Purchase only authorized editions. All rights reserved.

www.californiatimespublishing.com

Prologue

IN THE FOLKLORE of all continents there is found a memory of the ancient land that sank beneath the waves and of a righteous survivor. The Babylonians called him Ziusudra or Xisuthras, son of Oliartes. The Chinese called him Yao or Fo-Hi. The Indians call him Satyavatra, the sun-born monarch. The Greeks and Egyptians called him Atlas, eldest son of Cleito and Poseidon. Others called him Prometheus, Deucalion, Heuth, Incachus, Osiris, Dagon.

Many would say that these are parallel accounts, arising from similar but not identical sources, whether those sources are ancient storytelling traditions, moralistic myths, or historical events. Anthropologists might call this an analogous phenomenon: many similar instances of a story genre arising from many analogous origins. Others would say that the traditions must share a common lineage, either a set of similar flood-survival events experienced around the world during a time of great global inundation, such as the drawing to a close of the last great Ice Age approximately ten thousand years ago; or in the extreme, a single flood-survival event, experienced before the dispersion of modern humans across the globe. This is what anthropologists might call a homologous folkloric tradition: many diverse versions shaped by a single source.

Among those tending to interpret the many flood stories as homologous are traditionalists within the three great Semitic religions: in order of appearance, Judaism, Christianity, and Islam. Among these three faiths, scholars have long been fascinated by the idea of identifying an actual geographical location for the resting place of a wooden ship supposedly built by the man we know as Noah (the revered prophet Nooh in Islam).

Since the historical or anthropological significance of this global ancient story is also thickly overlain with religious significance, the search for the Ark has been conducted with passion, often by extremists, and ironically (since all three of these religions are supposed to be concerned with truth), with not a small degree of bias. Of course, there is bound to be disagreement when religion is involved.

It is not at all far-fetched to suppose that for some at their respective extremes of various belief spectra, those disagreements may mingle with other dimensions of fanaticism to fuel extreme and hostile actions.

'There is above the country of Minyas in Armenia a great mountain called Baris, where, the story goes, many refugees found safety at the time of the flood, and one man, transported upon an ark, grounded upon the summit; and relics of the timber were for long preserved; this might well be the same man of whom Moses, the Jewish legislator, wrote.'

(Nicholas of Damascus, quoted by the Jewish historian Josephus sometime between AD 37 and 100.)

'El Judi is a mountain in the country of Masur, and extends to Jezirah Ibn 'Omar which belongs to the territory of el-Mausil. This mountain is eight farsangs [about 32 miles] from the Tigris. The place where the ship stopped, which is on top of this mountain, is still to be seen.'

(Al-Mas'udi, Muslim historian, writing in AD 956.)

'We flew down as close as safety permitted and took several circles around it. We were surprised when we got close to it, at the immense size of the thing, for it was as long as a city block, and would compare very favourably in size to the modern battleships of today. It was grounded on the shore of the lake, with one-fourth underwater. It had been partly dismantled on one side near the front, and on the other side there was a great doorway nearly twenty feet square, but with the other

door gone. This seemed quite out of proportion, as even today, ships seldom have doors even half that large...'

(Alleged quote from Lieutenant Roskovitsky of the Russian Imperial Air Force, 1916, published in the New Eden Magazine, California, 1939.)

'During the month of July, 1951 a team of Russian experts, were surveying the valley of Kaat. Perhaps they were busy in finding out a new mine. They noticed a few pieces of rotten wood ... They excavated the place with deep interest...(and found) quite a good amount of wood and many other things. They also found a long rectangular wooden plate... measuring 14" by 10"... Seven experts after eight months of research came to the conclusion that this plate was of the wood used in making Nooh's Ark and that the prophet Nooh had put this plate on his Ark for the safety of the Ark and for receiving favour of Allah. In the centre of the plate, there is a drawing of palm shape on which some words of ancient Saamaani language are written... The plate is still preserved at the Centre of Fossils Research, Moscow, Russia.'

(From a pamphlet published in December 1961 by Hakeem Syed Mahmood Gilani, professor at Osmania University, India, and allegedly reported in the London Weekly Mirror January 1954; Bathrah Najaf: Iraq, February 1954; and other newspapers.)

In the year 2000, while some are breathing sighs of relief at the safe passing of the Millennial celebrations, a sense of disquiet is rising in the intelligence agencies of the West. It would be wrong to call it organisational panic, for the cogs of the bureaucracies turn too slowly for that. But many of the more insightful are worried—very worried. Their awareness of an emerging new security risk—it cannot not yet be called an understanding—is growing by the day. It is fed by reports of mobile phone traffic, money transfers, people movements, and a new style of intelligence that they all find so difficult to evaluate—political, financial, sociolinguistic, theological, and behavioural profiling of many disparate groups of extremists. The data reveal the existence of hitherto unacknowledged and unmapped networks of grassroots fundamentalist groups with pretensions at international terrorism. That is the problem. They are organised but not organised. "Self-organising," the technical experts call it. Spontaneous; bottom up; complex-adaptive behaviour, like ants—but unlike ant colonies, not dense with activity and easily spotted, but spread widely and sparsely. Strong through diversity, resilient through decentralization, deadly and infectious through compellingly contagious ideas. It is as though a rising sun of religious fervour has concentrated the melanin of the body Islamic, and all of a sudden, a rash of malignancies has simultaneously broken out. Lying dormant for years, they have sprung to aggressive life, invisibly and spontaneously reproducing through unseen and incomprehensible connections, threatening havoc not only to their hosts, but more particularly, to their enemies.

Caught unawares at the turn of the Millennium by the surprise onset of a new security landscape that some are calling "the new Cold War," security agencies are slowly and reluctantly realigning their resource deployments to mine the overwhelming flood of chaotic data, identify patterns, and develop credible analysis and counter-terrorism strategies. Rumours abound in the year 2000: one in particular—of an imminent massive and audacious hit. But it is only one amongst many, and it is impossible to distinguish the components of one rumour from those of many others. This means that the intelligence response looks as fragmented as the phenomenon it is trying to track. But slowly and surely, some patterns have started to emerge. A few are old patterns that are already on file and have been taken out, dusted off, and examined afresh.

One in particular goes back a very long way.

PART I: The Preparation

Chapter 1

January 1950
Southwest Turkey
THE TWO YOUNG men stand like ancient seafarers on white steps roughly carved out of rock and leading down to an old stone quay. They are looking out to sea and scanning the narrow gulf for signs of a boat. They don't know what kind of boat. He hasn't told them that, only the day and the place and the flag it will be flying. It has taken them the best part of a month to make their way by foot, donkey carts, and for one grateful day, a motorised logger's truck, from the eastern border of Turkey to the Aegean coast. Now they are here. A fisherman they met in the town of Mugla, half a day's mule ride away and where they had spent the previous night, had offered to guide them down from the mountain plateau to the ruins of the ancient harbour. *Roman*, he had confided with pride. They found it hidden amongst the pine trees to one side of a tiny fishing village that he called Akyaka, meaning *white*.
    White. Pure. Most fitting.
    The original port, the fisherman said, had been destroyed by an earthquake centuries ago. Now the only vessels moored to the ancient granite blocks are a few old fishing boats. It looks less than a mile across the Gulf of Gokova, but distances are deceptive as dusk approaches. With the sun already sunk behind the high mountain they have just descended, the water is merging into the darkening shadows of the low-forested hills on the other side. Somewhere over there, perhaps, the boat is waiting. *It will have to be bigger than these tiny craft to carry us safely to our destination.*
    The taller of the two, wrapped in a roughly woven cloak against the January chill, his proud and handsome young face framed in a white headdress made of a softer fabric, turns as he catches the distant sound of their guide's

mule-cart clip-clopping back up the mountain path. He catches a breath of wind carrying the menthol scent of pine mixed with eucalyptus and laced with just a hint of mountain sage. He breathes deeply. Eyes closed, facial muscles relaxed, he nods in slow motion, as though settling some great matter.

The guide had not accepted payment. His service had been offered gladly because although his passenger is young—still in his teens—his reputation has spread far. He is a holy fighter, but not just any. He is a holy man first and a fighter second. Most unusual. Already a leader in the resistance movement, some say. The guide might have guessed that the visitors to his hidden harbour are on their way to the newly occupied Palestine. Or he may have believed them to be touring his country's coastal cities preaching the young seer's strange and potent blend of devotion and militancy.

When the seer turns back towards the sea, scanning with sharp eyes of striking turquoise, the boat is there. A heavy-looking wooden gulet with three sails of brown canvas has slipped silently into view—perhaps it had been moored in the next bay. Or perhaps it had been there all along, camouflaged by the shifting shadows of the light waves. It is making its way towards them. His friend sees it at the same time and they grip each other's arms in unspoken solidarity. Then instinctively they utter quiet prayers of thanks.

Neither of them has executed a man in cold blood before.

It will be different from killing at a distance, as they both have done alongside the Palestinians. The idea of a symbolic killing is surely more acceptable than ritualistic killing. He has had a problem with that for a while. But now that he has put a line between the two ideas, he has a peace about it.

In a way, all death is symbolic. Has not the one who gives breath drawn a line in the life of a man after which it will be taken away? Why could life not have gone on for a hundred and fifty years, or more? It is a judgement—a mercy, even, given men's propensity to go the way of impurity. So if it is the will of Allah to curtail the human span for his own purposes, why should he not ask one of his faithful to execute his will? To execute? And why should the righteous object? He knows it is wrong to doubt. It will be easy. All that Allah has ever asked him to do has been easy. There is always the strength to accompany the task. *And have we two brothers, not lived since the day our mother stopped suckling us, under the daily discipline of only doing what the Holy One asks?*

They had not chosen this way. It had been chosen for them. Who knows where it will lead? For now, all they know is that they have important people to meet and a job to do—first in Palestine, and then in Tehran.

For a moment, he lets his gaze dwell on the gathering darkness within the bay, but finds himself disturbed by the grey opaqueness of the sea. A flicker of doubt again, quickly suppressed. He looks to the west, where a few remaining gilded lines edge ribbons of sky that are still bright blue, like the golden-blue universe hidden in the eyes of an Afghan fighter he once lifted half-dead from a wadi floor. His thoughts drift to the many millions of people much farther west than where he stands, upon whom the sun is still shining from its zenith.

It will not shine on you for very much longer. When it comes, night will draw in rapidly.

With a revived sense of certainty and purposeful symbolism, he turns his back on the infidelic millions, moving a step or two so he has a clearer view eastwards, beyond the giant eucalyptus trees bordering the old harbour. The wide valley that feeds its rivers into the sea here is flanked by mountains that are now only discernible in partial silhouette. Just below the crescented moon, one snow-capped peak has the symmetrically convex profile of a volcano, and he tries to imagine the Anatolian Peninsula being shaped and reshaped by cataclysmic events. He imagines his home several hundreds of miles beyond the horizon and he thinks of the power of Allah to create and to destroy.

At the Day of Judgement, will he willingly submit when the end comes? Will he raise his hands in welcome submission as Allah's terrible devastation comes upon him? He knows that he will. Couldn't be more certain of it as his heart wells up inside him. It is as though he is not only being asked to submit to the inevitability of Judgment Day, but to share in its divine purpose. He finds himself breathing quickly, eyes moistening as his spirit is caught up in a quiet ecstasy that is now his frequent companion. As he turns to his friend, he finds himself muttering his own version of Hafiz, one of his beloved Persian poems:

Why do preachers commend penitence when they seem so disinclined to repentance? Possibly they think no Judgement Day will visit them and no judge will punish them for their fraudulence.

"They will be judged, brother," his friend says, touching his arm gently, understanding his mood perfectly. "They will all be judged."

As they turn in unison towards the approaching boat, he knows with utter conviction what he must do. The brothers who have tried to dissuade him from his present mission are misguided. What would they think of the bigger purpose he has just silently committed to? He has not seen it quite so clearly before. But now that he knows what he must give the rest of his life to he realises that he has known all along: even these, his brothers, belong to the fraudulent preachers. He will make his path without them. With them, but separated. Set apart. It is what "holy" means.

Then, as they step onto the granite quay to await a tiny rowing boat now making its way toward them, he stops, arrested by another profound and life-changing thought. Perhaps it *is* a ritual killing after all, like the prophet Ibrahim preparing to offer up his son Ishmael. And the animal that he bled in his son's place. Is not Eid ul-Adha a ritual killing ordained by Allah himself? Then another thought re-triggers his elation. Allah had used no human intervention at the time of Noah. Surely the great Flood was a ritual too, was it not? A wiping clean and starting again? Purely divine. Awesome in its scale and majesty. He looks at the blackness of the sea again and this time feels no unease, only a sense of oneness with the Divine Judge.

Chapter 2

Fifty years later
April 2000
London, England

THE PYRAMIDAL TIP of London Dockland's Canary Wharf Tower peaks through a thick blanket of toxic yellow smog. Metropolitan icons from the 1990's and 1950's, embracing in a prophetic photo opportunity.

Sitting transfixed by the photograph in the newspaper cutting is a woman with unusual eyes. Like many Asians, they are monolids, with the skin curving in gentle concavity from the ridge of the brows to the lashes without a fold. The lashes themselves, dark and strong, ride on a part of the eyelids completely concealed by a delicately sculptured almond arch of a hood, its taut curvature formed by the resolution of opposing hidden forces like the geometry of a suspension bridge. But it is the way the fold of the hoods curve down towards the inner corners of the eyes that causes young girls to stare in awe and old gentlemen to find an excuse to look again. Each side of the nose, the stretched skin of the upper lid overlaps the lower lid to form two distinctive epicanthal folds: the beaks of two birds of prey, facing each other, bowing.

And behind the wonder of these protruding curtains of delicate flesh, large ebony eyes dark enough not to be able to distinguish iris from pupil. Cassy Kim has achingly beautiful eyes, which are currently registering a deep vulnerability as she stares at the old newspaper picture that she has retrieved for reasons that are still confusing to her.

It is history, after all—torn from a newspaper on February 11, 1996, the day after an Irish Republican Army terrorist's bomb had torn the building's shiny glass city-suit into a million razor-sharp fragments. The journalist had cleverly captioned it *"Canary Wharf Air."*

Next to the cutting lies another. It, too, displays a photo; grainy and more faded than the first for it was taken almost half a century earlier—in another capital city, three thousand miles to the east of London. History too—even more so. But its violence is more personal and more menacing. The figures are indistinct in the half darkness, but Cassy has been able to make out three of them. One is turbaned and dressed in the sort of pantaloon suit worn by peasantry from Malaysia to Morocco. The other two are wearing some kind of uniform with ridiculously large peaked hats. They are standing around something that looks as though it might be a sack of potatoes, but on closer inspection is a rather more gruesome object. It could be a decapitated body if it weren't for the unnatural position of the arms and the peculiar way that the top of the head seems to emerge from the neck. It had taken a long time before she had worked out what it was. The troops of the 40th Soviet Army, who spearheaded the 1978 invasion of Afghanistan, had nicknamed it *the Afghan sweater*, and it was one of the reasons why terrified Moscow teenagers had deserted in thousands from the front line fight against the Mujahedeen. A single cut, a ruthless tear, and a man was left to suffocate under the skin of his own torso. The body is lying on a bed under a framed portrait. He had died under the watchful eye of an American president.

Cassy switches her gaze to study a set of distorted miniatures of the two newspaper cuttings, arranged like a magician's set of cards in the chrome of her brand new retro toaster. Facsimiles are often more revealing. In the world of forensics, Cassy Kim knows that real things give you the detail but abstractions make for better reflection.

She reflects as the toaster smokes, and then hits the eject button, shifting position a fraction to get a sharper image of herself in the middle of the magician's cards. She moves aside an uneven thick black fringe that she wears to hide those eyes, revealing a white dressing with a line of red seeping through in a pattern that indicates it is covering a wound secured by five medical stitches. The surrounding bruise is a little less obvious than in her bathroom mirror, and the image slightly more complimentary, but not much.

"Bastards," she mutters, in a soft but throaty, almost baritone voice.

The imprecation is not so much at the people responsible for the wound as at the whole set of unwelcome events that the incident represents. Scruffing the fringe back into place as if to signal an intention to withdraw from those events, and then for reassurance, running a hand up the short crop of her neck, she smiles. Her improbably mute Albanian hairdresser had surprised her with the oddly angled cut: longer at the front than the back. "From the rear," the Albanian's larger than life partner had told her, "the cut makes you look like an oh-so-handsome schoolboy!" And he had fondled her nape tellingly as he admired his partner's creation.

From the front, she notes, looking at her reflection in the toaster, she looks anything but a schoolboy. For, sitting on her own in the kitchen of her London house in the manner that is her habit, there is on her body not a stitch of clothing.

***

The head wound had been sustained on the way to the lab. The car had suddenly accelerated from behind and swerved sharply left in one calculated movement.

That was over a week ago and Cassy Kim is still unnerved. It is now Sunday morning and she is comforting herself with burnt toast smothered in butter. It has to be almost black. One of her lovers—she can't recall which—had told her it was because she takes everything to extremes.

Choral singing has just given way to a radio news bulletin. The singing is more than background noise for company—she has long been addicted to pre-classical

European sacred music. A daily fix seems to anchor something in her otherwise unruly soul. Now she reaches forward to turn up the volume.

"... A group calling itself the Human Extinction Front yesterday claimed responsibility for releasing a canister of oestrogen-rich chemicals into the Hamburg water supply. In a note sent to a German newspaper the HEF claims to have been experimenting with fertility-reducing compounds for the past fifteen years."

Experiments on the public. Fifteen years. Cassy turns the volume up a bit more.

"A spokesman for the Hamburg police said that a woman in her twenties, thought to be a student at a London university, had been taken into custody."

Cassy munches on a corner of carbon and ponders a world with only a handful of survivors. The idea conjures surreal images. The notion of starting again is appealing. Who wouldn't want to start again? She looks across the room to the only photo she has of the disturbed teenage girl who has so dominated her life. Next to it is another trophy to failure: Zach, the man who had been her lover and then briefly her husband. In her mind, she imagines the record of her accomplishments extending, with photos of too many partners to count, filling the gap since Zach. Or filling the gap that has forever been her secret handicap. *A fresh start for a tired planet?* The kettle clicks itself off and a cloud of steam becomes a low mist hovering above primeval rainforests of the future—on pristine islands of a new Southern Ocean. She wonders what it would be like to step deafened over the brow of a hill, to be the first human to peer into the abyss of the mighty Victoria Falls of a new era.

Whichever way you look at it, terracide, as the eco-terrorists call it, can't justify genocide.

Chapter 3

Leytonstone, East London and
Manhattan, New York
April 2000

TWO SUITED MEN are leaning over a very worn balustrade, one positioned on the stair above the other, looking down onto a scene that hasn't changed for one hundred and fifty years. Only the dress, conversation, and music have changed. The faces have not, and the character types that they have been having a game with would have been recognisable to any social diarist, journalist, or policeman in the era that the Victorian corner pub was built. It is jazz night in The Cricketers and the tiny odd-shaped lounge is full to standing room with those in the know from all walks of life, colour, creed, age, and sexuality, so much so that the latecomers have had to gather up the stairs that once led to the establishment's second business. You could tell by the grand open-plan oak stairway, and the quality of the doors and panelling, that the five bedrooms off the small upstairs landing were made for customers, not for the pub's staff.

The rather distinguished silver-haired gentleman with intelligent features standing on the higher of the stairs is named Hugo, and if he had had a counterpart in the equivalent scene one hundred and fifty years ago, it would have been perhaps someone high up in the Admiralty. Hugo has just rushed in by cab from a late meeting in MI6 headquarters in Central London.

Brushing away the froth on his mouth from the pint of IPA Best Bitter he has quickly downed, and picking up his wet umbrella that has been hooked on an old gaslight fitting, he takes a step down to the same level as his companion and leans into his ear against the discordant din.

"One more thing about this whole affair, Nigel: you've got to make it work with her. We'll never get another chance like it. Think knighthoods on retirement. For me, if not for you. Whatever's going on out there, and I'm not joking when I say it's big—big enough to change things forever—this network's our USP. The Yanks know all there is to know and more about Bin Laden's lot—more about what he's doing over here than we bloody do. This one's going to be ours. And if we've got it right, it's a lot more dangerous. See what you can do, eh?"

With this, he trots sprightly down a couple of stairs, stops, turns, and steps back up to cup a hand against Nigel's ear again. "Next time, check your sources, please, before calling me out of a meeting with the minister. It's not the first time you've given me an urgent call and then been stood up by one of your stooges."

***

"Sorry I'm a little late, Dr. Kim. What in Heaven's name did you do to your forehead?"

Cassy grimaces, instinctively touching the bruising around the scar and equally, instinctively, retaliating: "You don't look brilliant yourself."

She did not sleep on the overnight flight from London Heathrow to New York's Newark airport, but has become unusually alert sitting waiting at the little Italian bistro tucked into a basement on East 57th Street, next to the daycare centre for dogs. Nigel Buchanan, a sandy-haired Englishman in his early forties and a public school type, gives out cards identifying him as a British Council official. He also works for MI5—Britain's domestic intelligence agency—and it is the second time in a month that they have met in Manhattan like this. When he has settled into the privacy of the corner table that Cassy has selected, he leans forward, clasps his ginger-coloured hands together and whispers, "We're borrowing you for intellect—brains and attention to detail. Not to get involved in the rough and tumble!"

The skin on his hands is dry and freckled—I bet he had eczema when he was a child.

"Thanks for the compliment," she sniffs, "but how do you know I didn't fall off a ladder doing DIY?"

"Because you've probably never hung a roll of wallpaper in your life," Nigel retorts jovially while taking his jacket off and hanging it on the back of his seat. The dry hands are extending from double cuffs turned back and fastened with non-matching links.

He travels to the East. The Jade cufflink is from Northern Burma; the other is high-grade Korean amethyst.

It is true. His dossier is thorough.

"And because your friends say you're out of sorts," he adds, settling himself into the bistro chair and folding his hands neatly together again on the table. "Whatever's bugging you, you're not covering it up very well, Dr. Kim."

"What friends?" Cassy snaps suspiciously. She can't think of many friends who at the moment would be in a position to offer that kind of report. She thinks of the almost-one-night-stand she'd had after a disastrous party last weekend and wonders if Nigel had anything to do with it.

"So what happened?" he says, softening and looking her in the eye.

She does her usual thing when someone tries this on and squints to the point of closure. A huntswoman withdrawing into a concealed place, observing a dangerous quarry.

In terse, to-the-point sentences, she tells him about the car. It had been stalking her for some time. Once, about a month earlier, as she had pulled out of the garage at the rear of her Victorian-terraced house into the small alley, it had been there at the end of the lane. She had sworn, instinctively slammed into reverse, accelerated backwards out of the lane, and sped away into the London traffic. A week later she had been driving to her university office in Central London and noticed an old white Volvo in her rearview mirror. It had stayed with her for most of the journey and then disappeared.

She had thought she knew why the car was stalking her. It had to be to do with the tapes.

Just before Christmas, her house had been done over with the thoroughness of a Customs and Excise rummage team. Whoever did it had let themselves in with no sign of forced entry and left with only two ancient reel-to-reel computer tapes stored in scratched plastic covers plastered with faded sticky labels from the days before floppy and hard disk drives. They had been given to her by her doctoral teacher in Cornell, and contained novel research data of no great commercial value. Only they didn't only contain her teacher's research data. Hidden away amongst the old data, they also contained a very unusual and very valuable script of computer code. Why had she stored such a valuable piece of work on a computer tape stored on a bookshelf in her living room? Well, she had to store the original program and data trials somewhere. What is safer than the obvious?

When the car hit her, instead of whisking her off to be interrogated, her world had plunged into confusion. She had been preparing herself for the worst, but it hadn't come.

Then there is the MI5 contract she has recently signed—technical "experts" sign them all the time, she had told herself—but there was something missing from it. A Berkeley economics professor called Williamson that she had once met at a cocktail reception in LA—she can't remember his first name—had told her that all contracts are incomplete. "What counts is how you manage the resulting ambiguity," he had pronounced. She is now struggling with that—majorly.

Perhaps Her Majesty's men are softening me up. After all, although it was a deliberate hit-and-run, on reflection, it was a controlled bump.

She had not quite seen it like that before. She reruns her memory of the white Volvo, reinterpreting, and nods, recalling how exactly the car had impacted her.

Cassy has come to New York hoping that her conversation with Nigel Buchanan might make things a little less messy. She has come to clear up the ambiguity, but her thoughts make her even more confused. She senses a new reason to fear.

What do you really want from me, Mr. Buchanan?

She looks up at Buchanan, expecting an answer. Instead, his response is to quiz her on which of her recent cases at Scotland Yard might have won her enemies.

He has seen her CV. He has interviewed her on it. He had asked why she took up the part-time forensic position at Scotland Yard and he seemed to believe her, and said that he was beginning to understand her. She had believed his sincerity then, even warmed to him. And now, again, she finds him convincing. She closely observes his eyes, his minor facial muscles, and his hands as he speaks. She is good at this and concludes that he is genuine on this subject, at least: he had known nothing about the Volvo incident before she mentioned it.

Once she has made this conclusion, she switches her thoughts to the real purpose of the meeting—a breakfast appointment the next day with a man she assumes is with the CIA.

"We're grateful, of course, that you're going to help us," Nigel is saying, reaching down for his briefcase and pulling out some papers.

"Here's an English version of the air accident investigator's report on the first crash. It happened almost exactly six years ago. April 1994. Take a look at the page marked with a yellow sticky."

She takes the spiral-bound document and thumbs through.

"Two members of the Russian parliament were on board," he says casually as she reads.

Finishing the paragraph he has highlighted in pink marker, she says, "A Russian plane blown out of the sky over Northern Iran?"

"By Noah's Ark," he says, as though it explains everything.

"The toy was stained with RDX and PTN residue," she reads, understanding the acronyms very well.

"Chemicals left after a Semtex explosion."

It is probably naïve male condescension but it makes her angry. Instead of lashing out as she once would have, however, she switches off inside. She learnt the trick from her teenage psychiatrist and although it makes her less of a sociopath, she is fully aware that it only really shifts the alienation from one level to another.

"And the American International Airways disaster last autumn has been linked to a crackpot with a map of Mount Ararat pinned on her wall?" she continues flatly, scanning the report. "Sounds a tenuous connection to me."

"It wasn't just the map," Nigel counters. "Her computer was full of stuff downloaded from websites about Noah's Ark and *ark*-aeological controversies."

"And I'm the closest you have to a tame Ark specialist? Who on earth dreams up these bloody assignments?" She is in a particularly disdainful mood today, which is aggravating her growing sense that it was a big mistake to sign the MI5 contract.

"You were a scientist on the Anglo–US study."

"Five years ago, and I was employed to analyse pictures from spy-satellites."

"But you keep up with developments and you'll have as good an idea as any of who's out there taking it all too seriously."

She looks at him without saying anything for a moment. *How the hell does he know I "keep up with developments"?*

"Why would anyone interested in that kind of thing be into terrorism?" she parries dismissively.

She is now eyeing him with undisguised suspicion bordering on hostility, and in her mind she is thinking about getting up and walking out—ending it here and now. But she knows she won't do that. She needs answers from this man and those he represents; without him she will just have questions. Questions, and a split forehead.

"We want you to look at the archaeological data used by different groups," Nigel is saying. "Tell us how they might have gained access to them, how much money you think is going into their research, evidence of fanaticism of one kind or other—that sort of thing. We're looking for leads, that's all."

He had told Cassy this using exactly the same words at their first meeting with the American that they are due to meet again the following day. Nigel seems to repeat himself a lot, she has noticed. That meeting had taken place in a disused hotel restaurant on the twentieth floor of a grubby tower in uptown Manhattan. Cassy had been distracted for most of the time by a group of workmen perched perilously on the roof of the Roosevelt Island cable car. They had travelled back and forth, apparently doing nothing but chatting and pouring each other coffee from flasks. Eventually they had stripped off to their boxers and changed from blue to orange overalls. It was a bizarre but entertaining ritual that had occupied most of Cassy's attention so that she could recall very little of what the man in the suit had said.

What she *had* learnt was that a routine check of phone-tap archives had thrown up a surprise association. In a transcript taken from an East London apartment being watched in a people-smuggling case, there was a brief and ambiguous mention of American International Airways outbound flight AIA916 from JFK to Bombay via Munich—two weeks before it exploded metres above the Bombay runway, killing all on board. A raid on the apartment turned up nothing except for the occupant's Noah's Ark interest, and someone had remembered reading the report of the earlier plane crash and drawn a connection. It was an obscure one. The Noah's Ark toy in the earlier plane wreckage could easily have just been in a suitcase close to the bomb.

"The London apartment was rented by a Russian student," Nigel Buchanan continues.

"Oh?" This is new information.

"She was under investigation for Russian Organised Crime connection—ROC in the trade. People smuggling is only part of it. London's a busy place these days for my profession. Take a look at this."

He shoves a few sheets of fax paper across the table. Cassy recognises them as a copy of a report she has already received by post about some Iraqi visitors to London. She looks at Nigel as if reassessing him. More than once he had lost his train of thought in mid-sentence without seeming to notice. *Domestic or personality problems? Probably both.* She picks up the British Council business card he has courteously just passed to her—clearly a habit, like hanging a hat on a hook, since he had done the same at their last meeting.

The Council she knows to be a made-over remnant of the old British Empire machinery, marketing British culture, industry, and education all over the world. From its headquarters in Manchester it runs offices in most of the world's major cities and is widely regarded as a kind of cultural diplomatic service. In her imagination it is also a cover for all sorts of intelligence-gathering activities. She recalls that it has "desks" like the intelligence agencies—the North Africa desk, the South American desk, the Central Asian desk. Nigel, she has discovered from her preparatory research, has an administrative desk somewhere on the top floor of the building that houses the part of the Council that remained in London after most staff had been relocated to England's northern capital. From there, she imagines him managing an international network of intelligence-gatherers—British Council employees and their contacts, generating up-to-the-minute security assessments on matters of interest to MI5.

Or perhaps MI5 just rents space in the building.

"Why did you send me the report?" she asks accusingly.

"You need to know the lay of the land, Cassandra, my dear. Consider this a background briefing."

So he knows that he sent me the report already. Repetition must be de rigeur *in this business. Perhaps he monitors variations in my responses to his repetitions.*

But she is saying something different to her thoughts: "The Iraqis have something to do with the two plane crashes?"

"No. It's another case entirely. We've been working hard to keep Iraqi factions out of London. It might open your eyes to the way these people work—might help you spot some *patterns* on your new assignment."

It is a joke. Although Cassy lectures on and practises forensic archaeology, her specialism is the numerical analysis of digital image patterns. Or as one of her colleagues once put it, writing programs to find needles in digital haystacks. When she isn't at the university she is in a police laboratory secreted away in the middle of one of London's suburban forests, or at the headquarters of some European police force or other. It has become routine, and after a time, rather boring—Dr. Kim is called in when a farmer ploughs up a pile of bones, or a grave pattern needs picking out from air photos, or an unprovenanced ancient artefact turns up on the international ancient art market. She once helped locate a mass grave in Kosovo and has analysed rather too many images of the Irish and northern Spanish countryside for earth forms that might give away the location of weapons dumps.

"Thousands of overseas students study in London, as you well know, Dr. Kim," Nigel is saying. "Most are *bona fide* scholars—some are not. The British government doesn't generally concern itself with the strengths of its visitors' scholastic aptitude or motivation—it leaves that to the universities. It does, however, take an interest in who pays for their education and what else they might be getting up to while they're here. There's no better way to get a certain kind of spy, agitator, or terrorist into a Western country for a prolonged stay. Western security agencies are aware of this and deploy their resources accordingly. We have people working in the universities monitoring undesirable networks among students, you know."

"I didn't realise," she says, although she guessed this must be the case.

"Just look at the pattern in the report."

"It's always possible to find a pattern," she says pedantically. "The real skill is knowing whether it's significant or occurs by chance."

"Quite," he says, considering that technical detail for a second, "but look at the chap with a Syrian passport."

The *pattern* comprises suspicious configurations of names, acquaintances, travel histories, and London and American addresses.

"He's had two stints in France on French language courses at the same level, one in Paris and one in Marseilles. Don't all Syrians speak French anyway? He studied engineering for a year at a university in Paris and is now registered for a Masters degree in London. If he's the person we think he is, he got a chemical engineering degree from a Baghdad university in the early eighties."

He is artfully drawing me in. This is interesting. A mild shot of adrenaline associated with the thought warms her blood. Cassy has had suspicions about certain students but is sobered to hear it as directly as this. She lets go of some of the distance she has placed between them, cross with herself for her emotional volatility.

"And the Egyptian with an Iraqi father," he continues. "Who does he expect to fool with this kind of background? He's got a maths degree from Cairo and spent three years in the Egyptian army before buying himself out. Went to Florida to study artificial intelligence but according to the university had to return home for personal reasons. Then he turns up again registered for a PhD in computer security in Edinburgh and the same thing happens. He got a six-month break in studies to sort out finances. Look…"

Nigel stabs the photocopied letter from the Scottish university with the end of a dessert spoon.

"Must think we Brits have our eyes closed. I'll have the dates checked with immigration and the airlines. It's no wonder we've got foreign operatives walking in and out of our country for work experience."

She actually smiles at this and feels even more cross with herself. But she is liking the confidence that Nigel is extending to her—and the secrecy of the whole thing.

There are three other suspects in Nigel's report. All have proven connections with Osama Bin Laden during his early days in Saudi Arabia. Two are known to work for one of Saddam Hussein's intelligence networks. All have taken lodgings in the inner city London neighbourhood called Leytonstone, and two were in San Francisco during the same month last year. Three of them are post-graduate students.

"The girl in the Human Extinction Front's publicity stunt was a student in London," Cassy says abruptly, changing the subject.

"The BBC news bulletin?" Nigel looks up from the letter but continues to prod at it with the spoon. "It wasn't a publicity stunt and the girl wasn't from London."

"But the Front claimed responsibility—that makes it a PR exercise."

"That's what the newsreader said," Nigel says dryly. "The girl really did dump the chemicals—caught in the act by a water engineer. She pulled out a gun, but instead of firing at him, stuck it in her mouth."

"She's in custody?"

"No, she's in a morgue."

"She killed herself?" Cassy says, shocked. "Why would she do that?"

"That indeed is a mystery. No one has a clue who she was—she wasn't on the list of known HEF members. All we know is that she had a fake passport and a lot of money in her rucksack."

"Well, it certainly wasn't payment for doing HEF's dirty work. Contractors don't turn a gun on themselves to avoid capture. How much money?"

"Quarter of a million dollars in hundred-dollar bills."

Cassy nods, as though in approval.

"Which brings me back to the Iraqis," Nigel says. "Right now, too much money is moving around the world and landing in the hands of bad people. In the past two weeks we've intercepted two Pakistani secret service agents with Bin Laden connections trying to enter the country. That's one a week. One came in the back of a lorry on a ferry from northern Spain, posing as a Kurdish refugee. The other flew business class from Beijing via Guangzhou, Bangkok, and Frankfurt, and carried a Yemeni passport. His documents show him married to a Filipino nurse working in Belfast, Northern Ireland. Both had well-stocked British bank accounts waiting for them."

"Background briefing?" Cassy asks, in a tone requiring confirmation that this isn't something she is meant to follow up.

"Unless someone discovers that the Iraqis are into Noah's Ark too. You can keep that," he says, nodding to the fax she already has a copy of. "And you might want to study this." He reaches into his case again and produces a plastic folder, which he hands to her solemnly.

"It's the passenger list of the downed AIA flight."

His body language suggests that he has said all he wants to on the subject and it appears that the purpose of the meeting has been to introduce her to the twilight world from which her assignment has originated. She assumes she will need the insights for tomorrow's meeting. Perhaps the purpose has also been subtler than that—she feels like an *initiate*, implicated by shared confidence into something that is less than fully legal.

"There was a matter you wanted to raise?" he adds as he picks up and opens a menu.

Cassy had phoned Nigel from Heathrow to tell him that she wanted to check something out before the meeting with the CIA man.

"I want your opinion," Cassy says. "I had an email a few days after we were last here. Could be a hoax or a joke." She is awkward admitting she needs his opinion. It has always been a problem for her.

In truth, she thinks it might have come from his department or from the Americans, though she can't see why they would want to give her an anonymous lead to work from.

"Saying?"

"The one hundred-and-twenty-year warning is about to be given."

There had been a second line too, but Cassy doesn't mention it. She never puts all her cards on the table if she can help it.

He raises an eyebrow.

"Sender?"

"Untraceable."

"A name?"

"*Cleito.*"

There is an unmistakable reaction—a momentary tensing of his jaw, a microscopic flicker in a facial muscle. She had been waiting for it and it came. He had been about to wave the waiter over but puts the menu back down.

"Dramatic," he says. "Junk mail?"

"Cultish," she replies. "But not spam."

"Forget about it. Forward me a copy and I'll see if we can trace the sender. Probably one of your students playing a prank. Any of them read Plato?"

The conversation over, he flags down the lanky Italian teenager who has been keeping a discreet distance—it seems to be that sort of restaurant—and turns his attention to ordering.

A smartly dressed young couple step into the restaurant, shaking wet umbrellas as they hand coats to another waiter. Back in England it has been a funny spring. It started off unusually mild and everyone had hoped for a repeat of the April heat wave of the previous year. Instead, winter had returned with a vengeance. Unseasonable snow and floods dominated the news bulletins. People had died and normal life had been interrupted with predictably chaotic results.

Nigel Buchanan sits very still, watching Cassy Kim's low-slung hips rock hypnotically as she makes her way to the restroom at the back of the restaurant. She has removed her winter coat to reveal a figure-hugging cashmere dress with a high neck and no sleeves, dropping elegantly in one piece, without a waistband, to just above the knees. He lets his gaze shift to the pleasing curves of her bare shoulders and the two and a half wavelengths of light but firm female muscle giving shape to her arms. *So—Hugo was right about her. We're going to have to keep a much closer watch. Who the hell sent her that email?*

***

Cassy arrives back at her hotel on Park Avenue, tired, cold, wet—and curious. She is glad that she hadn't given Nigel the complete email message. The second line had read:

Queen Boudicca's London Camp, May 27th—16.00 hours.

The fiercely independent spirit that is a familiar friend from the past stirs within. In the stifling police culture of Scotland Yard's forensic team, she rarely gets the opportunity to see a problem yield to her full creativity and certainly not to her full cunning. It has got her into trouble before, but she yields to the beckoning recklessness as to a new lover of unproven provenance.

I'll be following up Queen Boudicca on my own; thank you, Mr. Nigel bloody Buchanan. So you made me like you with all the secrecy stuff. But I see through you. If it's a game, then just make sure you don't mess with my mind, okay? I can do the rest, but I need to be in control of me, okay? That's what I do. See through people. I'm guessing that's why you hired me.

Chapter 4

Great Mosque of Xi'an, Shaanxi Province, Central China
1959

TWO MUSLIM CLERICS are seated on the second tier of the pagoda in Xi'an's Great Mosque, the oldest and most famous in China, dating as it does to the eighth-century Tang Dynasty. Only they are not, strictly speaking, Muslim clerics. Muslims, yes, but clerics only for the watchful eyes of the Party faithful, and the Party faithful come in every shape and form, from the old lady seated at the entrance to her apartment block opposite the Mosque's front gate, to the junior mullah, the shopkeeper selling hot tea and the schoolmaster accompanying his children on a visit to the Mosque's gardens.

But this is not a normal period in the anything-but-normal short history of the People's Republic of China. For ten years, Mao Tse-tung's ultimate "policed state," where everyone polices everyone else, has grown, with varying degrees of economic success. The year of 1957 had been a good one, following eight years of economic restructuring under the Chinese Communist Party leadership and with help from the Russians. But from 1959, people have started to starve as Beijing imposes ever more unrealistic production quotas on factories and fields across the vast country.

And so it is that a Sufi from Persia, or was it Turkey?—men frequently debated his origin—has slipped across the border from Tajikistan in Central Asia into Xinjiang province on China's westernmost reach and thence to Xi'an. Those who two years earlier might have stopped and questioned the lone traveller, traversing the barren Muslim periphery of the Middle Kingdom, were too busy making things or pretending to make things in order to fulfil Beijing's quotas. And if they weren't doing this, then they were busy trying to keep themselves and their families alive. Long afterwards, researchers would estimate that over thirty million people died of starvation as a result of Beijing's Second Five-Year Plan for the country's controlled economy (1958–1963).

The other "cleric" has arrived in Xi'an by quite a different route. He is a guest of Mao Tse-tung's government under the Sino-Soviet Friendship Treaty, which he has proudly learnt to pronounce as *Zhōng-Sū Yǒuhǎo Tóngméng Hùzhù Tiáoyuè* in the Mandarin dialect. Being a high-ranking official in the Soviet Naval Research and Archive Service, he has been invited by local Communist Party Officials in the northern port city of Dalian to advise on a new archiving system for the Chinese Navy. Xi'an was both a convenient place to change planes and a good excuse to see the most famous mosque in history built without a dome or minaret. But neither of these are the real reason for his week-long diversion—one that he feels sure will get him into trouble when he returns to Moscow. The real reason for coming to Xi'an is that he has heard a rumour that one of the leaders of the Naqshbandi sect that people are starting to call the Nooh Brotherhood, is in Xi'an. He had sent a message out to try and track him down.

The two "clerics" are sitting deep in unobserved conversation on the mosque's unusual tower. The entire building has been constructed using Chinese architecture and building materials, and resembles the courtyard house of a nobleman more than a place for Islamic worship. The communist liberation has made little difference to the place other than filling up some of its corners, outhouses, and minor courtyards with communal living and eating spaces.

"You are from Moscow?" the Sufi cautiously enquires, fixing his companion with the turquoise eyes that he knows can both mesmerise and repel. He was once told that those who find themselves turning away or lowering their own eyes do so because they feel confronted by windows into another universe that is too pure or too threatening to contemplate. "A Muslim of high official rank? This is unusual in my understanding," he probes further.

"Indeed so," says the Muscovite. "I am from an old Muslim family in the city. One of my ancestors was a leader of the Tartar community in the Zamoskvarechye district and built one of the city's first formal mosques there in the eighteenth century—on Bolshaya Tatarskaya Street, between Paveletskaya and Novokuznetskaya metro stations, if you know the Zamoskvoretskaya Line."

"I have heard of it," the Sufi says enigmatically. "And I am honoured to make your noble acquaintance."

"And I yours. I pray that you are not offended by my request to meet like this. I do not want to dishonour my Chinese hosts but I may not have another chance to talk to the great teacher."

"And why would that be lamentable for you, my friend? There are many greater Sufis you could consult at more convenience to yourself."

"None, however, with your interests in the Qur'an's teaching about the beginning and the end."

"Ah. You have heard of my fanciful ideas."

"I am attracted by them. More than attracted."

"You are a free-thinking Muslim?"

"I worship at the Central Mosque in Moscow."

"Ah. But you are free-thinking in your own home, perhaps. What is it you wish to hear from me? We may not have much time. At some stage the Party watchers on the gates will come looking for you. They did not see me enter so they will not know that you have conversed with a stranger. But they will be concerned to make sure that you have not exited by another way."

"From you I desire nothing; you have inspired me enough already. No, it is I who brings you something in return."

"That, indeed, is a pleasant surprise, although I live simply and need very little to support my itinerant way of life."

"Not money, my friend. Something of more profound value. I have come across something deep in a Soviet Naval vault that I think you would be very eager to see."

After a long pause to take this in, the Sufi says: "It must be of very great value for an official of such high rank to interrupt such an important diplomatic visit to bring it to the attention of a humble wandering mystic."

Chapter 5

Isle of Dogs, Central London
April 2000
TWO DAYS AFTER Cassy's meeting in Manhattan, she is back in her London home, the clouds gone and a morning sun casting its light and its long shadows in equal measure—a chiaroscuro drape over a familiar view. The two newspaper cuttings are still on the breakfast table—next to a cafetiere full of stale coffee, abandoned when the taxi had called for her New York flight.

She had established long ago that the Tehran photo came from an Arabic daily published in Iran in the days before the 1979 Revolution. It was a poor taste "on the scene" picture story, common in the newspapers of developing countries. The press turns up; takes explicit pictures of blood, bodies, and handcuffed villains; and prints them for effect with minimal commentary, with the full story coming in the next day's edition if at all. The cutting is faded and frayed at the edges, with tape holding two halves together. The date at the top of the page is just discernible as the fourth day of the Islamic year, AH 1375, or November 29th, 1954 in Western time. It had mysteriously come into Cassy's possession four decades after being printed—during the second year of her abortive marriage to Zach.

With the puzzle and pain of Zach in mind, Cassy makes up a fresh cafetiere, filling the kitchen with a sharp aroma. She tries to relax her jaw, realising she has been clenching it tight for days. The radio is on and the newsreader changes his tone to sound mildly upbeat. It looks like the long-awaited deal to finally disarm the Irish Republican Army is about to be struck and politicians are making optimistic statements.

30   JB DUKES

Fools. Reining in those who've tasted the elixir of anarchy is an impossible task.

The thousand kilograms of explosives that had wrecked the Dockland skyscraper in her home neighbourhood in 1996 had been detonated by a rogue IRA cell disenfranchised by the first faltering steps of the peace process. She presses the plunge filter of the cafetiere and it jams, showering steaming coffee over the tabletop. She curses the hailstorm of coffee grounds raining down on the beleaguered Canary Wharf Tower, threatening to engulf it completely. Out of the window, the real thing sparkles sunlight from its long-reinstated mirror walls. The reflection of a low-flying plane from nearby London City Airport briefly appears and then disappears.

She gets up and retrieves a small vacuum-sealed pack from the refrigerator and a miniature clay china teapot and cups from the dresser. A fellow online tea fanatic had found the *Tie Guan Yin* plantation high in the mountains of the Fujian province, China. The buttery taste of the sample he had sent her was unbelievable, and the jade colouring perfect. She had offered fifteen hundred British pounds per kilo and bought ten kilos, which she reckons will supply her until the following year's harvest with some to spare to give away.

"*An American professor died cruelly after attending a conference at Tehran University. Our reporter arrived minutes after the police who examined the body in a hotel room, where a member of the cleaning staff found it. The manner of death indicates this is not a robbery. The young academician was well-respected in the Middle East and had been the guest of the university on previous occasions. This visit seemed destined to ill fate—he was on the BOAC flight to Tehran from Jordan last week that had to return to Amman airport after getting into technical trouble.*"

Having the caption translated was as far as Cassy had got—that, and discovering that the newspaper had been closed down with many others after Ayatollah Khomeini's return to Tehran. The envelope containing the faded piece of Iranian newsprint had since gathered dust on top of Cassy's wardrobe.

She looks out of her window at London. Like Tehran, New York, and so many other capitals, complex and powerful engines keeping national and global economies going. But uncontrollable, unpredictable, and vulnerable.

What kind of person becomes a terrorist? Same sort of reason why I said yes to MI5, I'm guessing.

She had been approached as she was leaving the university one afternoon by a humourless American in a perfectly cut but unimaginative light grey suit, and then, a day after, by appointment in her office, by a diffident young man from MI5. The combination of his awkwardness and the noble line of his jaw had evoked a complex emotion. She had wanted to reach out and touch him—like a museum sculpture of some ancient boy hero. Maybe *he* was the reason she had taken the job. Cassy had made other significant commitments on lesser whims.

The real reason, she knows, is that it had appealed to her need to always be moving on, her need to be fighting someone or something. For a while, her university job was an act of rebellion. She left the house each morning with a fresh wonder at the audacity of it: *Cassy Kim, a university lecturer. Member of the intelligentsia. Establishment. If only they knew.* But when the job no longer satisfied her deep need to prove that she was different from everyone else, she had signed up as a "retained expert" in Scotland Yard's forensic team, ratcheting up the irony. The renewed dissonance between who she knew she was and her public role had kept her going for a few more years. But it had worn off, and she had been about to give up both jobs to go travelling when MI5 came knocking. The timing had been precise.

In truth, she knows that it was neither the boy with the noble jaw nor her restless rebelliousness that made her take the assignment. She had taken it to exorcise herself from the ghost of Zach and all that he represented.

She touches her scarred forehead and winces.

Human society, like the human soul, is too bloody fragile. Cassy sighs, pressing harder to feel the pain. *We've come a long way since Plato's Republic. But in other ways not. There'll always be intrigue, plotting, and subversion— those within the system and those who for their own reasons want to keep to its margins.*

Plato.

Nigel had asked if any of her students read Plato.

Cleito is a character in one of Plato's Dialogues. What the hell am I meant to make of that?

***

Cleito was a mortal woman who, at the beginning of the world, lived on an island surrounded by rings of outer islands. She married the god Poseidon and fathered five sets of twin sons. The eldest became king of an idyllic island kingdom "no smaller than Africa and Asia joined together," later destroyed and sunk beneath the waves in a mythical or prehistoric cataclysm. Plato, the ancient Greek philosopher, learnt of the story from an even more ancient manuscript written by Solon, an Athenian lawyer in exile from Egypt— and Solon had heard it from Egyptian wise men. The chain of recantation went far back into man's prehistory.

The story is familiar to Cassy from teenage days and the smell of the great hall in the private girls school comes flooding back. The eldest of *Cleito's* sons was *Atlas* and his sunken kingdom, *Atlantis*. Plato recorded his version of the story in the dialogues *Critias* and *Timaeus*, written in the third century BC, but Solon had lived three hundred years before him and Plato estimated that Atlantis had sunk nine thousand years before Solon. *Far back, indeed.*

Three days after returning from New York, Cassy is working late in her office in Central London. She prefers it in the university at night; no one else is there. An information bulletin lies on the desk in front of her. It has arrived that morning and seems to be another attempt to initiate her into Nigel's underworld. At the top of the single page, in neatly formed handwriting, he has written simply: *Cassandra, dear—for your information...* It is headed "*March bulletin*" and contains several short reports.

"*Leeds—London Daily Telegraph, 2nd February—A team of young Pakistani Muslims was yesterday asked to leave the country within three days. A Home Office spokesman said the youths, aged between seventeen and twenty-one, are suspected of being in Britain in connection with an extreme political movement, rather than for legitimate religious reasons. Lawyers acting on behalf of the Leeds Mosque where the group has been based for the last month have lodged an appeal, claiming the government has produced no evidence to support the charge.*"

The next one has similarities.

"*Jerusalem—Reuters, London, 15th February— Fourteen members of a U.S. doomsday cult were deported from Israel early yesterday after being detained by Israeli police on suspicion that they were plotting violence to hasten Jesus' return, Israeli police said. 'The plane took off several minutes ago. They're on their way back,' a police spokeswoman said. They were being escorted to the United States by three Israeli policemen.*"

"They're all bloody at it", Cassy mutters aloud. A third item seems to have something to do with Nigel's current Iraqi case.

"*New York—The Times, London, 20th February— Algerian illegal immigrant dies in New York car crash, killing mother and baby.*"

A handwritten note adds that the Algerian's presence in New York had come to light six months earlier during the interrogation of a Yemeni being held in a Saudi prison. His identity has been linked to a Kuwaiti citizen suspected of being a double agent working for Iraq in the late eighties.

He had been put under surveillance, but seemed to be lying low. Apart from once driving slowly past a container port, there was nothing to indicate his reason for renting a midtown Manhattan apartment for six years. A surveillance team was following him when he apparently lost control of his car and had the head-on collision. It doesn't say what had triggered the assignment of the surveillance team.

Not far away, Westminster's Big Ben strikes twelve chimes for midnight. Cassy has just finished writing a lecture and is tired and ready to go home. Instead, she turns to her computer and following a hunch, types in the words "*Cleito*" and *"120 years."* She is startled by the phone. She doesn't get phone calls at work this time of the night—not anymore. She recalls the difficult days towards the end of her "experimental" marriage. Zach had eventually stopped checking up on her. They had agreed on marriage as a fun experiment one lazy Saturday morning in bed. It hadn't come naturally to either of them. Cassy grabs the receiver to stop the noise—and the memories.

"Yes, I'm still here," she answers irritably, suppressing a yawn and combing a hand slowly through her dishevelled hair.

The security guard has seen the light in her room and worked out whose office it is to save himself the climb. Cassy walks over to the window and waves blindly towards the gate lodge far below. The building is dark apart from an office-white glow from the lodge and the reflection of her window in the wing facing her. The colleges of the University of London are housed in many buildings all over the capital. This one is an awful 1960's monument to Europe's modernism project—twelve floors of low-quality glass and dull grey cladding with horribly textured concrete forming the concourse at ground level. The thought that someone had once thought it a good design depresses her.

Putting the phone down, she turns to the computer and hits return. Within half a second, billions of words, and six continents later, a result flashes up on the screen. She

NOAH'S ART   35

smiles, hunch rewarded. It is why she is a good forensic scientist—hunches don't usually travel in straight lines. There is just one occurrence found on the entire Web.

The screen has turned deep turquoise and white, bathing the room in a phosphorescent glow. The white at the top of the screen fades into the turquoise-blue like an exotic cocktail topped with an ice cream float. On this background are several lines of writing in an elaborate gold-coloured script.

"We sent Noah a long time ago to his people, and he said, O my people! Serve God. Then We inspired him, saying: Make the ship under Our eyes and Our inspiration. Then, when Our command comes and the water gushes forth, plead not with Me on behalf of those who have done wrong. They will be drowned. So the Ark floated with them on the waves towering like mountains and Noah called out to his son, who had separated himself from the rest: 'O my son! embark with us, and be not with the unbelievers!' The son replied: "I will take myself to some mountain: it will save me from the water." And Noah's son and Noah's wife were consigned to hell."

The next bit is in a larger font and fills up the lower third of the screen.

"I will not strive with man's wickedness forever, I will give him another one hundred and twenty years."

Without warning, her pulse starts racing. Cursoring down reveals more in a similar vein. Another piece emblazons itself across the screen:

"Just as it happened in the days of Noah, so it shall be in the days of the Son of Man. For the coming of the Son of Man will be just like the days of Noah. For in those days which were before the flood they were eating and drinking, they were marrying and giving in marriage, until the day that Noah entered the Ark, and they did not understand until the flood came and took them all away."

And then a paragraph in the smaller script:

"In the folklore of all continents there is found a memory of the ancient land that sank beneath the waves and of the righteous survivor. The Babylonians called him Ziusudra or Xisuthras, son of Oliartes. The Chinese called him Yao or Fo-Hi. The Indians call him Satyavatra, the sun-born monarch. The Greeks and Egyptians called him Atlas, eldest son of Cleito and Poseidon. Others called him Prometheus, Deucalion, Heuth, Incachus, Osiris, Dagon. He is a portent, a sign of the second judgement. Let those who have ears to hear and wisdom to understand; let them hear and understand. Let the prophet who was dead speak life. Abide in the good teacher. Before the time of the second judgement days of great evil will come upon the world. The light of Isa and other good prophets will seem to fade and a great shadow will rise in its place. The sign of the king has been given. We await the final sign. Then the end shall come."

There is one more paragraph, which she now is having difficulty reading, her vision blurring with rapidly swirling emotions:

"With the breaking of the Seventh Seal comes the Seventh Day. New Heaven. Eden re-created."

"Noah...again", she whispers to herself slowly, trying to calm a rising panic by breathing slow and deep, hands stretched out, palms down, slowly patting the air.

It's bloody happening again.

She is wearing a loose-fitted black cashmere sweater that comes down just short of the top of her jeans and, in a fit of determination, she grabs the waistband with both hands and wrenches it over her head, sweat beginning to trickle down the elegant spinal ravine formed by toned back-muscles. Her arm twists up behind her so that her hand can reach the scars, gently touching them, one by one. Always one by one. In the same order. And always gently.

They are the link with her past. Her known past and her unknown past. The ragged scars have long since healed, but the methodical gentle finger massage is her way of pretending that the pain lying not so very far below the reddened skin has also gone. It is a pretence, of course. The pain was the reason for signing the MI5 contract.

Chapter 6

LEANING HARD INTO the chair, a pink gingham-checked bra lying discarded on the floor on the other side of the room, with her sweater and sweat-drenched skin sticking to the chair's fabric, Cassy grips its arms until her knuckles turned white. Her head is spinning in free-fall panic and she sits, head bent, chin in her chest, eyes clenched shut, trying to focus, trying to breathe.

Scheisse! Scheisse, scheisse, scheisse! she expletes in broken out breaths.

For the second time the phone rings. It breaks the attack. She warily breathes a long, deep, slow in-breath, expecting her panic-constricted lungs to oppose her. But they don't.

"Porters lodge here again—just handing over shifts. Turn the lights off as you leave the building if you would. Don't overdo it, love."

She jumps up to look out of the window, not wanting the porter to go, and recalls another night not so long ago. She had been standing behind one of the panes of glass in the wing now facing her and reflecting the night's darkness—one floor above hers—and she had been staring across the void into her own office.

It had been in the very early hours of Christmas Eve, not long after Nigel Buchanan had called her to arrange the first Manhattan meeting. She had caught a cab back into work because she was bored at home. Turning into her corridor, she was confronted by a single slit of light framing the base of her office door. As she stood perfectly still, playing back in her mind her exit four hours earlier, certain that she had switched off the table lamp, the pencil-line of light flickered. Just once, but enough to tell her that someone was in there.

She had spun round and run silently through empty corridors, down in the lift, and up in another, and come breathlessly to the door of the seminar room that faces her office. She knew exactly where it was, because she had once taken a class in the room and been surprised to see the flowers she had brought in that morning greeting her from the facing building. Gingerly, she had opened the door and ever so slowly crept towards the window, hugging the blackboard that covered the wall so as not to silhouette herself.

In the darkness she could just make out the top of a man's head, illuminated by her computer and looking down as though writing. She blinked to adjust her night vision and when she focused again, the head had become a face. Oghel was partially silhouetted in front of the computer screen, hand poised above a sheet of paper. Oghel, her saintly Turkish PhD student. Oghel, whose attention, body, and soul she desires so much.

Transfixed, she couldn't move, and as she stood there breathing heavily, his gaze had left the screen and seemed to look out of the window. It was too far and too dark to see his eye direction, but from the movement of his head he was searching a patch of windows that included the seminar room. She knew that she must only be a dark shadow in a darkened interior one floor up in the next building, but he had sensed movement. Then the ghostly face had stopped moving and she knew that he was looking at a dark shape on a blackboard.

Instinctively she had closed her eyes, as if that would make her more invisible. Then, feeling stupid, she opened them to find that the computer screen in her office was extinguished and the face gone. Slowly she had slunk to the floor until her office was out of sight. She turned and half-crawled, half-ran to the door, stumbling into the corridor and running blindly through the nocturnal maze, down a fire escape, two, three, maybe four floors, then out into another corridor, into the first toilets that passed her by—men's. She locked herself into a pitch-black cubicle, shaking uncontrollably.

Oghel has obsessed her ever since, becoming at the same time her angel and her demon.

***

It takes two and a half hours to reach the historic settlement of Winchelsea amidst the apple orchards and hop gardens of East Sussex and Kent, London's neighbouring counties to the south and its traditional market garden. Once part of England's coastal defences against Napoleon's France, the town, still with its fortifications, now lies four miles inland, cut off by a retreating sea.

Ashraf Ghazali-Smith is an old friend—and one-time lover—who has unpredictably turned into something of a father figure. At least, that is how she now sees the relationship—Cassy is not sure what motivates the strained but close friendship from his side.

Cassy has been a regular visitor over the years not only because of Ashi, as she calls Ashraf, but also because of *the dream*.

The recurring dream is of her as a little girl playing with two other children of similar age, a boy and a girl, who seem in the dream to be cousins. They are playing on a hillside and on a beach backed by steep chalk cliffs that she feels sure is Kent.

The dream is precious to her because, before the age of twelve, Cassy Kim has absolutely no recollection or knowledge about her past.

***

Her earliest memory is of Joy, her mother, introducing her to a man named Harry who had moved in for a while. She recalls spending what seems in her memory to be endless days with him learning mathematical tricks. She has warm feelings as she recalls his praise at her amazing ability to copy manoeuvres that he thought were difficult; she cannot remember ever receiving praise from Joy. She remembers the game of cranking up the challenges, and his constant amazement at her rapidly developing skills. She had been charmed by his attention and confused by the ensuing emotions.

Then he had gone.

There had been a violent fallout between her and Joy following Harry's sudden exit, and in a drunken outburst, Joy had told Cassy that she was not her real mother.

"All I know, Cassandra Kim, my disappointing adoptive bloody daughter, is that you were taken in by a South Korean orphanage, aged exactly one year old. Don't ask what happened between then and the day I took you from a Scottish orphanage at age twelve, because I don't know, and I don't bloody well care anymore. There. I've said it."

Cassy can't remember much more of those turbulent early teenage years; she only remembers the pain and the rage, and of course, the time that she had tried to attack Joy with a kitchen knife.

Then Harry is there again. Cassy has estimated that she is just fourteen. It is a significant point in her life. She has incomplete memories of one of two premature childish sexual encounters with older boys when she must have been about thirteen. She recalls names, darkened lounges with parents out for the evening, a school playing field at night, and of course, the deeply stirred chaotic emotions—the only emotions she can recall from her past, apart from hatred for Joy. So when Harry came back, it was natural for her to try and seduce him. She did it because she liked him, because he had praised her cleverness, and because it would hurt Joy.

By the time she had woken the next morning, once more, he had disappeared.

She never saw him again.

Soon after, Joy insisted on Cassy accompanying her to Bangkok, where they lived separate lives for the best part of two years in an old-style Thai house in its own compound surrounded by high walls. Joy was a civil servant on secondment to the Thai Ministry of Commerce, and Cassy went first to Patana, the British school, and after being thrown out of that, to the American international school. She had willingly accompanied Joy to Bangkok not because she had no alternative—she had made several plans to run away for good— but because she had sensed an opportunity for a new kind of freedom that London might not offer her. And in this, she had not been disappointed.

***

Winding down the window of her cherished black Ford Escort RS Turbo, Cassy turns into the narrow shrub-lined lane that leads up to the Smith family farm—inherited from a long line on Ashi's English mother's side—and passes the small shack that has been rented to a stained-glass craftsman for as long as she can remember. There are no other cars parked on the gravelled courtyard fronting the eighteenth-century red brick and flint farmhouse. Its distinctive vernacular architecture creates a warmness that adds to the welcome she always feels here—grey and buff flint silicon nodules from the surrounding chalk beds set in traditional lime mortar, and framed with locally made red clay bricks. One of the barns has been converted by Ashi's mother—an acolyte of London's classical music scene—into a weekend retreat for schoolchildren gifted at instruments. Scattered around the grounds that include a patch of ancient woodland are half-finished works by one of America's most famous contemporary sculptors who had rented space here before gaining fame.

"Cassy, my dear—you look even more ravishing than usual! How lovely to see you!"

Ashi stands holding the car door open in characteristic gentlemanly fashion. A handsome fifty-year-old with distinguished Middle Eastern features, he has a light olive complexion of someone twenty years younger and grey-green eyes set in narrowly set deep sockets that presents a hard-wired empathetic demeanour.

Ashi and Cassy's relationship has been an odd one, starting out as lovers for precisely one long week. The age difference had added to the initial attraction for both sides, but as with so many of Cassy's almost-relationships, she hadn't been able to cope and broke contact. They hadn't seen each other for almost a year, but when he had called her out of the blue to ask if she was okay, they had started meeting for coffee every Sunday morning to talk over her problems. And that is how it now is, only they now catch up every month or so. Never once has the subject of their brief romance come up, and Ashi seems to Cassy to have settled happily, at least on the outside, with the role of father figure-cum-close friend.

He grips her shoulders, touching cheeks three times—the "Dutch way," he always likes to explain—and examines her messed-up face.

"Brawling in the clubs again? Tut-tut. You should give it up now you've almost reached thirty."

"Thirty-two, actually—but I appreciate the gesture," she says, enjoying the effect of the first proper smile she can remember for weeks, and standing back to look him up and down. "I got hit by a car. I'm just fine, though. You look good."

She had called him before setting off, to check he was in. These days he is more often at his second home, the leisure suite of a country club eight miles away. He has taken to cycling, working out, and swimming in a big way, and is looking a new man. It is two years since he was called before the dean of the Middle Eastern Studies school at the Boston university where he had briefly lectured and told that he didn't fit in anymore. Prior to that, he had lectured part of the year in London and the other part in Israel. The 1990's had turned out to be difficult years for those unable or unwilling to adjust to the modern style of university. Ashi is one of the wittiest and most cheerful people Cassy knows, and it has been hard for her to see him go downhill.

"Actually, I'm here for some of your medicine—fresh sea air and optimism," she says perkily, linking her arm in his and planting an affectionate kiss on his cheek. "I'll tell you about the accident later. It's good to be here."

It isn't so much the English Channel breeze that has revived his mental health, nor his renewed interest in what is left of the family's sheep farm on nearby ancient Walland Marsh; it is his new job. The other things came afterwards. Ashi has for years worked on and off for Scotland Yard—as an advisor on Islamic movements. Two years ago it looked as though the closing of his university career might end what he considered to be his consuming hobby, but Interpol had suddenly signed him up as a European advisor on Middle Eastern sects.

Ashi had explained to Cassy that in his field, something had been stirring rapidly in the late 1990's, something that had been gathering pace for almost a decade, and that security agencies across the West were suddenly queuing up to hire people like him.

Once again Cassy tells him that he is much better off now and that she is envious of him. It is a little routine that they like to go through.

***

"Look, there by the fallen oak! A young muntjac."

Cassy is being given the tour of the woods—glorious in their snow-soft carpet of delicate white flowers. English woods in spring are heavy with the scent of wild garlic. A pair of Britain's rarest deer have been breeding here, and Ashi wants to show her his discovery.

"A man called Nigel came down to see me last week," he says casually.

Cassy stops in her tracks, rapidly processing the implications.

"Nigel Buchanan?"

"Just thought you might want to know."

It sounds like a warning. He pauses and prods a rotting birch stump with his boot and it crumbles to dust.

"Don't tell me," she ventures, "he was asking about Atlantis and neo-Platonic cults."

Now it is he who stops to ponder.

"So there *is* something going on." He grins broadly. "He wanted everything I have. Atlantis with an Islamic slant."

The hairs on the back of Cassy's neck bristle.

"So what *do* you have?" she asks, feigning nonchalance. They have seated themselves on the six-hundred-year-old fallen oak and are playing naturalists, scanning the undergrowth for telltale movements.

"To be honest, Cass, not a lot. After all, it's a pretty tenuous focus for a sect. Even more so when you throw Noah's Ark in for good measure."

"He asked about that?" Cassy tries to conceal the edge on her voice.

Ashi knows about the military-sponsored archaeological project she had been recruited to in 1993, after being thrown out of the British government's electronic listening HQ at Cheltenham, but she has no reason to believe he knows about her current assignment.

"Yes," he says. "Although maybe it's not as tenuous as all that. Atlantis—the flooded Azores or some other submerged peak in the Mid Atlantic Ridge; Noah's Ark as a *metaphor*—you know, join the cause and escape the wrath to come. Anyway, I've dug up a report of an Ark 'find' that's got an Islamic involvement. It's old, but it's all there is. There's nothing on Atlantis as well as Islam and Noah, I'm afraid. I'll show it to you when we get back to the house."

He points to a tangle of brambles rustling some way down the forested hillside.

"There he is."

A few minutes later there is a fainter movement in a more distant patch of leaves.

You can always spot a pattern if you watch carefully and wait long enough. "We can achieve anything with patience, perception and persistence."

That was the psychologist's opening mantra on Tuesday mornings at the home where they had put her for a while after she had attacked Joy. The memory had once filled her with repulsion, but they had become skills that had served her well—in both jobs. Perversely, the mantra has now become important to Cassy. It tells her that she has reformed, that she is not special.

That a girl with no memory of her past can make it.

They get up and start walking back.

"How about you anyway, Cass? I'm sure this isn't just a pleasant way of spending a day off. Anyway, it's a weekday and it's term time. You should be working, you lazy slob. What do you want to know? Fire away and I'll try and help."

He puts an avuncular arm around her as he says this and ushers her forward along the narrow path, ever the protective back-stop.

But be careful, she can almost hear him add, picking up just a hint of a strange sort of mood in a way that only a longtime friend can.

***

The return of winter means there is plenty of mud still on the ground, and Cassy uses the old brass shoe scraper to get the worst off her boots. Ashi moves a chipped enamelled kettle onto the coal-fired range as they pass through the un-modernised kitchen.

"Grab a chair in the study—it's the sunniest room this time of day," Ashi calls down as he disappears up the grand dark oak staircase.

She pauses in the panelled hallway by a picture of a grand mansion, painted in the heavy hues and translucent glazes of the great masters. *Hambleton House, Hertfordshire*.

"You like that story," he says, trotting down the stairs, armed with a transparent binder spilling papers.

On his mother's side, Ashi is solid English establishment. He uses his mother's name in matters of business relating to the farm and house, but his greater allegiance is to his father, of whom he is intensely proud. His father, long since dead, was from an aristocratic Persian line of military generals tracing back to the 1621 Persian invasion of Iraq in the Safavid dynasty. His father had business interests in Tehran and London, and met Charlotte, Ashi's mother, in the summer of 1935 whilst escaping the Persian furnace. He had settled in the more temperate land and Ashi had been brought up as an Englishman—but an Englishman with the very best of his father's oriental ways.

"Spying is an old trade," Cassy says reflectively.

It was Ashi's mother who had told her that in the second decade of the nineteenth century there had been many issues to impassion the cohort of privileged young idealists that her forebears had belonged to. In the year before Napoleon's final downfall at Leipzig at the hands of the Prussians, Russians, Austrians, and Swedes, the Hambleton House parties had a noticeable number of guests from these countries—as well as from France.

"One of the oldest," Ashi says, giving her a considered look. "Take a read of this."

He takes what looks like a press cutting from the binder and continues down the corridor to the study. As he does, something falls to the floor—a piece of paper that must have been tucked behind the cutting. Cassy picks it up and follows him in.

He hands her a yellowing edition of the London Weekly Mirror, dated February 1st, 1954.

The same year as my Tehran photo. Cassy prickles as she takes it.

"Where did you get it?"

"Read it," he says, making for his favourite leather armchair.

Halfway down the last column of the cutting is a small headline "*Ark discovery by Russians*" and the following short piece:

"*Three years ago in July of 1951 a group of Soviet archaeologists digging in a valley in mountains of Armenia discovered scattered pieces of ancient wood, well preserved. Excavations unearthed a deposit of stony material that appeared to be petrified wood among which was a block measuring fourteen knots long and ten knots wide. Under this they found a layer of manganous ingots thought to be ancient smelter waste. The most controversial aspect of the find was an engraving on the wooden block in an ancient language. Last summer the Russian government formed a committee of scientists led by Sawlot Naoev, professor of Archaeology at Lenin Institute, which, after eight months of research, agreed that the wood is likely to be Gofa—the wood mentioned in the Biblical story of the Ark. The engraved letters were in an ancient Semitic script, which has been translated into English by a professor at Manchester University. They form a prayer in which the names of several revered Muslim prophets are mentioned. Islamic scholars gave a cautious welcome to the discovery. The ingots are thought to have been used as ballast. The inscribed block of wood is reportedly now on display in the Geological Museum of Moscow.*"

There is a folded sheet of lined foolscap paper clipped to the cutting. *Ashi's handwriting—must be a note to himself.*

Originally appeared in an Arabic magazine (Al-Zahra?). Story also appears in: Bathrah Najaf, Iraq,

(2/2/54), Al-Huda, Cairo (31/3/54), Weekly Mirror, London (1/2/54), Star of Britain, London (January 1954), and Manchester Sunlight, Manchester (23/1/54).

"Does this go with it?" Cassy asks, holding up the page that had fallen out and straightening it out to read.

"What's that?" he says distractedly, peering across the room.

"More of your notes," she replies, and reads aloud:

"Winston Gunther. Associate professor, University of Michigan. Well-networked with Islamic ancient archaeology community. Published several influential articles on the historicity of Noah's Ark story. Killed during a visit to Tehran in 1954."

"Ah," he says, shuffling in his seat, and then leaning forward to get up, but sitting back again. "I didn't know that was there. Yes... I remember—vaguely. It was a long time ago."

He is on the defensive.

"If I remember correctly," he says, recovering quickly, "the man was invited to Tehran for an archaeology conference on the Ark—Tehran University's my father's alma mata, you know—and murdered."

Cassy has never talked to Ashi about her macabre newspaper photo with the same date as the document in front of her. It has to be the same man.

"He was found in a hotel room by a maid," she says.

"What?"

"He was found in a hotel room by a maid."

"How the blazes do you know that?" he asks with astonishment, this time sitting bolt upright.

"Putting two and two together."

He looks at Cassy quizzically and then relaxes again and says, "Spot on—it's coming back now. It happened the day before he was due to catch a train out of the country, I think. The killers were never caught. They found threatening letters at his home in Ann Arbor. Buchanan tell you that?" he asks cautiously.

"No," she says. "He must have been a bit off his head to go waltzing over to Tehran under the circumstances."

"Maybe he was," Ashi nods. "It all ended rather unpleasantly, as I recall."

"That's an understatement."

"You really know about Gunther?" Now he is really curious.

"I've got a photo taken when the police found him," she says. "He died under a portrait of Theodore Roosevelt."

He sits there for a moment, carefully tapping his fingertips together and focusing past her at something outside the window. The posture warns her from taking the conversation any further. They are old friends, but not without their occasional disagreements, and Cassy isn't in the mood for another of those now. She needs his support. A tension has entered the room.

Buchanan must have been asking about the professor and bound Ashi to secrecy. I won't make it difficult for him.

"Actually, I've got the photo in the car," Cassy says, springing up from her seat. "I'll go fetch it."

1954. A dead professor and a suspect archaeological discovery. Why have they resurfaced four and half decades later—at a time when I've once again been drawn into the world of Ark fanatics?

Chapter 7

Three months earlier, January 2000
Marrakesh, Morocco

THE ENTRANCE TO the Banc Credit Agricole branch in the smart colonial district of Gueliz in Marrakesh is on a mezzanine level, accessed from two directions via a typically French double flight of steps, each symmetrically edged with a single iron balustrade, scrolled at both ends. It was no doubt designed to give the colonial bankers and their customers a sense of pre-Republican superiority over the masses passing by at ground level. The building is of a diminutive scale, however, like a miniature grand town hall, and painted canary yellow with white keystones edging the two corners visible from the street.

Oghel pauses before entering, partly to adjust his eyes to the dark interior and more to gather his disturbed thoughts. A uniformed guard stands in one corner behind a desk that looks like a reading lectern. Two rows of dark wooden chairs are arranged back-to-back in the small hallway that serves as a waiting area, and although there is only room for six people to sit, there is a ticket machine in one corner next to a cooled water dispenser. The guard is calling out the ticket number of the next customer to be served as Oghel enters, and a smartly dressed young Marrakeshi jumps out of her seat and enters into one of the two rooms leading from the lobby, smiling politely at the cashier sitting behind an impossibly small banking counter.

Oghel approaches the closed door on the other side of the waiting hall and knocks. The guard snaps something at him in Arabic, but the door opens and Oghel is being ushered in by a warm brotherly hand clasp belonging to a besuited gentleman in his late forties. Abdelazziz has a long and strikingly gaunt face and side-parted black hair fixed neatly in place by some kind of salon product. He is welcoming his old friend in fluent English, first placing his other hand on Oghel's shoulder and then drawing himself away to rummage in a desk drawer for a business card.

"It's not as grand as the last one, but it fits much more comfortably in my pocket," he says, ushering Oghel to a red leather and steel reproduction Eames chair and wheeling his own chair from behind the desk.

"New York was worse than London?" Oghel asks.

"Much worse, but we need to talk about you, not me. What's the urgency?"

"We can talk privately here?" Oghel says, looking around the room, clearly referring to the electronic sense of the word.

"You are nervous, my brother. This is not good," the banker says, picking up the phone and issuing an instruction in Arabic.

"So?" he says, settling in his chair turning it abruptly to face Oghel, who is sitting much less confidently on the edge of the red leather Eames.

"Why would someone keep an archive of emails about corporate take-overs?"

Abdulazziz looks shocked. "Now that is not what I was expecting, Oghel, my brother. We all are called to our particular line. Mine is finance; yours is science, right? What's happened?"

"That is all—I want to know why someone would keep an archive of emails about corporate take-overs. They go back over several years."

"A&M's? It's routine for serious stock investors. But your person obviously is not a trader; otherwise you would not be asking me the question."

"I am talking about board-level private conversations, not small chatter among financial journalists."

"A member of the board?"

"Over a hundred companies, and I stopped counting."

"An acquisitions and mergers consultant?"

"It is impossible."

"MBA student studying case material?"

That had been Oghel's first assumption. But then he had checked up on some of the companies.

"Some of the companies have never been subject to a merger and I can find no mention on the internet of other companies making a take-over bid for them. Others seem to have been taken over suddenly, with the financial media being shocked."

Abdullaziz considers this analysis silently for a minute.

"Then it sounds to me, brother, as though your someone is doing something rather… how do the English say? Naughty? I think you should perhaps not tell me anymore details."

And now it is Abdullaziz's turn to look surreptitiously around his sparsely decorated office. "But you might want to ask yourself a different kind of question: how did you uncover this information, and whose instructions were you following when you made the discovery?"

***

Two days later, Oghel is seated with another Moroccan, this one considerably older than the banker, though bearing an uncanny resemblance, and although they are probably no more than a hundred kilometres from the Gueliz office of Credit Agricole, they are in a different century. In a remote valley some two thousand metres up in the High Atlas Mountains that tower over the Marrakesh plain from the south, the two men are seated cross-legged around an open fire in the single room that constitutes the Berber host's simple home. The host's leathery skin blends with the unidentifiable animal skin long since denuded of hair, draped over the low wooden table on which two glasses of mint tea stand. Ancient dusty carpets are heaped upon the stone floor.

The Berber casually reaches into a battered old-fashioned biscuit tin and tosses a handful of incense onto the glowing logs. Oghel closes his eyes as he breathes in the exotic fragrance.

"You are too generous," Oghel says in French. The old man had slept elsewhere last night to give Oghel his warm hermitage.

The old man's response is in his Berber dialect. Then, in a heavily accented French, he adds: "You are welcome whenever you have a need. It is good to have Abdullaziz back, yes?"

"Indeed it is. He suggested I come here and seek your wise counsel."

"About the woman?"

"He told you?"

"She is an unbeliever? That makes her a danger to you."

"We have been thrown together and I am confused."

"Confused?"

"She flirts with me and I find her attractive. God forgive me. I am weaker than I thought. Could that be a good experience if it exposes religious pride and humbles me?"

"That is a very dangerous thought, young Oghel. Do not compromise your calling."

"I do not understand clearly what games people are playing with me, but I sense she is not like them. I think she is an innocent. Like me."

Innocent? The word echoes wildly around Oghels thoughts like a squirrel in a trap.

"How can a woman who flirts be an innocent? What counsel would you accept from me?"

"You could tell me that it is at least permissible to become her friend."

"And where will that stop?"

"I do not know. I have no experience with women. I imagine it stopping only at friendship."

"Huh! Innocent you are."

"She is not all she seems. She needs rescuing."

"Then you are in even greater danger than I had imagined."

Chapter 8

April 2000
Kent, England

ASHI IS DEEP in thought, staring at the tortured torso of Professor Gunther. Eventually he stretches out his elegant frame and throws his head back on the worn leather armchair to examine the study's ornate ceiling plaster. Still saying nothing, he sits forward, placing his hands together and assuming the pose of a counsellor.

"So what's your problem, Cass? You're not worried about Gunther, surely. He got killed before you were born, for goodness' sake."

"Why would I be?"

"He was an Ark expert."

"It's been five years."

"That long?"

"Someone knocked me off my bike the other day, and it wasn't an accident."

"You need a holiday, my dear—when did you last book yourself into a health club?"

"I've never booked myself into a health club."

"You should. How do you know it wasn't an accident?"

"The break-in at home."

"Everyone has break-ins in London. That's why I live here."

"No, it's not. You live here because you're stinking rich. Anyway, it wasn't an ordinary break-in—they only took two of my old reel-to-reels."

"Computer tapes? They contained Noah's Ark satellite images?"

"No, earlier work by my supervisor at Cornell—but whoever took them wouldn't have known that."

"You think they were after Ark images?"

"Let me tell you about the Tehran photo," she says. "It's been sitting in a box at home since Zach was around. I found it in an envelope tucked down the back of the sofa in my living room but I've no idea how it got there. It must have been late 1994—the first year of our marriage. Zach said he might have picked it up with a pile of letters—he used to chuck them onto the sofa for me to read when I got home. I'm worried, Ashi. No, not worried—scared."

"It was addressed to you?"

"No—it was in a blank envelope."

"I don't remember you mentioning it at the time."

She hadn't, and there had been a reason, but she doesn't want to remind him of it now, so she lies. "I should have."

In truth, their friendship had suffered at the time of her attachment to Zach. She had met Zach on the project; Ashi had not liked him, and had made it clear in a subtle way. Cassy had put it down to jealousy. It was only after Zach disappeared that their old friendship was restored.

"Where did you say you got the London Weekly Mirror cutting?" Cassy asks.

"The London Weekly Mirror, of course. You might scoff at my hundreds of box files, but I've got a superb filing system. I discovered it when Nigel Buchanan was here."

He obviously didn't take the cutting himself—unless he developed a hobby of cult-spotting very young.

Cassy sits down and picks up the cold beer he has produced from the classic 1960's refrigerator in the corner of the study. Like the rest of the house's content, the machine is without retro-guile—over-engineered for the high-income customer, it has simply never worn out.

Perhaps four decades is not such a long time.

Since he is obviously in the mood to listen, Cassy moves into confessional mode.

"I kept my own copies of the Ark images."

"And that was a bad thing?"

"They were classified."

"By whom?"

"Official Secrets. The RAF, the U.S. Airforce, the British Museum, Whitehall Mandarins—they were all in on the act. My salary came from a Dutch charitable Stichting company—registered in an Amsterdam warehouse."

Cassy hadn't discovered the full story until much later—via a well-placed friend.

Back in the mid-eighties, an RAF pilot had carefully planned a small detour on his way out and back from the Turkish airbase where his squadron was stationed for a NATO exercise. He had overflown the so-called *Ararat Anomaly*—the name given in Military Intelligence circles to the shady patch on an otherwise normal-looking glacier. The pilot had made the detour over the boat-looking shadow fourteen thousand feet up Mount Ararat in eastern Turkey with the permission of his senior officer—and it had emerged later, with the encouragement of various members of Britain's archaeological establishment.

Four successive exceptionally mild winters had meant a heavier-than-normal glacial thaw that spring, and someone had thought of photographing the anomaly under such conditions with state-of-the-art stereo photogrammetry.

The Turkish government meticulously monitor the flight paths of visiting aircraft, however, and weren't slow to figure out what had happened. An official was waiting to confiscate the frames when the plane landed, and a minor diplomatic row ensued. The Turks were happy with the best stereo images of the location they had seen, the commanding officer was called before the Ambassador for a dressing down, and the incident had ended amicably.

The Turks take their proprietary responsibilities seriously—as custodians of the unknown or unverified location of the world's oldest legendary relic. The ambiguous status of the relic—myth or history, religious or secular, ancient or modern—suits the Turkish government in many ways. They don't have the responsibility of the

Saudis as custodians of Islam's most sacred site. And yet there is a similar sense of looking after something precious on behalf of humanity. In fact, looking after a relatively non-contentious and non-specific sacred site that has equal significance to Christian and Muslim states is an appropriate curator role for Turkey, a country whose political and cultural aspirations look equally towards the Middle East and Europe. And there is always the possibility that one day someone will establish the truth of the legend and entire chapters of historical, cultural, and religious consensus will have to be re-written. The Turkish government knows what it is doing by strictly controlling access to *their* Ararat site.

What they hadn't bargained for was the fighter pilot's second set of stereo cameras. Back in London, a senior official in the MoD had passed on the photos to a former Oxford University colleague at the British Museum who in turn had convinced Military Intelligence that the pictures were so revealing that the problem should be revisited with the aid of cutting-edge computational science. Remarkably, he had succeeded, and the British had set up a modest research project with help from the Americans, who had their own collection of classified Ark pictures. The "*first U.S.–U.K. conference on the Ararat Anomaly*" was unofficial and bi-lateral, but this didn't stop resourceful officers from trawling a fascinating collection of photos and satellite images "borrowed" in quietly arranged quid-pro-quo favours among Military Intelligence officers from at least eight nations.

It seemed that it wasn't only the British who had amateur archaeologists in their fighter squadrons. The Egyptians and Saudis had firm believers in theirs and the Americans, of course, had believers of a different persuasion, but with the same fascination in theirs. The Dutch, apparently, had a particular obsession for archeology, and the Turkish air authorities had not always been as vigilant as they had been with the British fighter. Nor had they control over observation platforms mounted far above their air space. Indian and Chinese satellites as well as U.S. spy planes had all had a crack at photographing the remote mountainous region sandwiched between Turkey and the former USSR. Of course, most would have said that it was the military sensitivity of the area that demanded the attention, but that was belied by the remarkable consistency in the geographical co-ordinates of the spot they had chosen to photograph in such detail.

The study employed a team of three, including one of Britain's foremost Middle East antiquities researchers and his American research assistant, who had become Cassy's husband. Their job was to plough through the endless volumes of written evidence of previous finds and sightings. Cassy's job was to take precise measurements of the Ararat Anomaly from the stereo images and to establish the chance of it being a naturally occurring phenomenon. The objective was very specific. To use the dozen or so clear shots of the anomaly, each taken at a different time of year and in years with different average temperatures, in order to predict the precise shape of the shadow—which took subtly different forms in the different pictures. The simulated temporal and geometric pattern was then used as a template to search for other similar shapes in the Ararat glacier fringes—and in the glacial fringes of other mountain regions of the world. The output would be a detailed three-dimensional model of the shadow, and a statistical probability that its shape was unique.

"Why keep the pictures?" Ashi asks, but is interrupted by the doorbell. He gets to his feet to answer it. Looking over his shoulder, he calls out, "I still don't really understand why someone doesn't just climb up Mount Ararat with a hammer and take a peek. All this melodrama and huffing and puffing over contested evidence."

Cassy listens to him struggling with the lock on the front door that is rarely used and hears the sound of the heavy door scraping over the thick coconut mat that welcomes the few tradesmen and other callers who don't know to come through the kitchen.

"Ah, excellent," Ashi addresses the unseen visitor. "Quick off the mark—I'm impressed—come on through…"

Cassy gets up to look out of the window and sees a van standing in the drive.

I didn't hear it pull up.

The logo of Britain's most famous rodent control company is emblazoned on a vermilion livery, which blends with the rhododendron bushes in full bloom either side of the drive. *Contract animal killers.* Her thoughts turn to the girl from the Human Extinction Front and others of her kind.

"Back in a few minutes, Cass," Ashi calls out. "I'm just taking this gentleman to the big barn—make yourself comfortable."

She settles back into Ashi's leather chair but feels anything but comfortable.

Melodrama over contested evidence.

She has to concentrate hard to prevent the dizziness that has taken to plaguing her every time she dwells on the Noah's Ark puzzle.

***

Ashi eventually returns from the barn, banging dusty hands together and wiping a cobweb from his sweater, against the sound of the van disappearing down the drive.

"Thank goodness for that," he sighs. "I've been trying for weeks to get someone to commit a kindly act of mass killing. You'd think there would be a dozen firms chasing the job."

"Look where it's situated," Cassy says, drawing a blank stare from Ashi, who is still thinking about rats. "The Ararat Anomaly, I mean. The reason why someone doesn't just pick up a hammer and a pair of crampons and take a look is its *location*. During the Cold War the whole of the region was a kind of militarised no-go area. The Russians had sensitive installations on their side of the border, and we had our own on the Turkish side. Nowadays the problems are rebels and bandits—Kurdish separatists, local militia, bandits, and gangs running drugs, and goodness knows what from Central Asia and the old Soviet empire. The security issues are more local, but no less conducive to archaeological tourism."

"You have a point—but still, a relic as sensational as that..."

"Most of the expeditions that file for an archaeological permit are American—what do you think the Turks feel about that? Anyway, the anomaly is quite literally out of reach—it's right at the top of a thousand-foot cliff overhung by a glacier and at an altitude of fourteen thousand feet. It's completely inaccessible—you can't climb up to it and you can't get anywhere near from the top."

"What about the *real* anomaly?" Ashi says. "What might a frigate-sized vessel be doing fourteen thousand feet up a mountain?"

"That's all part of the *allure*. Think of the implications of finding that there's been a boat moored on the roof of the world for a very long time. You don't have to believe in anything other than science to be fascinated by that."

"You want to watch that attitude, Cass—empiricism can be dangerous. It's the partner of unorthodoxy—look what happened to Copernicus."

"Nothing happened to Copernicus," she snaps defensively. "It was Galileo who the Inquisition nobbled for his Copernican views."

"There you are, then—you can get other people into trouble as well as yourself."

"But he got it right, didn't he?" she says.

"You really believe there's an ark up there?" he says.

"Of course not," Cassy snorts.

Ashi is eyeing her with suspicion.

"As I said, you should watch that free-thinking mind—you could be misunderstood."

You're not entirely joking. What's going on, Ashi?

"You asked why all the huffing and puffing over contested facts? Take a look at these—it would seem that the huffing's hotting up." Cassy hands him a press cutting that is among several she has found during a quick library and internet search. Making a start on her new assignment, she has been surprised, once again, by how such an ancient legend can generate so much contemporary controversy.

Ashi spreads it on the coffee table between them. It is from the December 1996 issue of *Popular Mechanics* and is a front page article that reads:

"*Science Solves Ancient Mysteries of the Bible: Noah and the Ark*

Not too long ago, explorers claimed that they had found Noah's Ark atop Mount Ararat in Turkey. Yet, two years ago, what some believe to be Noah's Ark was found not on Mount Ararat but on a remote site about twenty miles away, near the border of Turkey and Iran. According to the American and Middle Eastern researchers who have been to the location, the remote site contains a buried, ship-like object, resting at an altitude of 7,546 ft. Some 558 ft long and 148 ft wide, the object conforms almost exactly to the 300 x 50 cubit boat that, according to the Bible, God told Noah to build. Salih Baryraktutan, head of geology at Turkey's Ataturk University, estimates the age of the 'vessel' at more than one hundred thousand years. "It is a man-made structure and, for sure, it is Noah's Ark," Bayraktutan said at the time of the discovery. An American shipwreck specialist with no religious affiliation led the investigation. He says that the subsurface radar surveys of the site have yielded good results. As might be expected, the findings have infuriated Christian Ark hunters who are convinced the Ark is on Mount Ararat."

"Interesting," Ashi mutters after reading it. "The quest goes on. So... we have a traditional Christian site—the top of Ararat—and a traditional Muslim site—Mount Judi—two hundred miles south. Then we have a 1950's sighting possibly inspired by Muslim zealots, and a new site that's convincing enough to win over the Turkish government as well as agnostic Western scientists. And the new site is sufficiently far from Ararat to get the backs up of traditionalists on both Muslim and Christian sides."

"Nicely put," Cassy smiles, "and spot on cue for the reason for coming to see you."

"And what might that be, I wonder?" he says, reciprocating with one of the generous smiles that had first captured her affections.

"An anonymous email with cult overtones. A one-liner. *'The one-hundred-and-twenty-year warning is about to be given*,' signed *'Cleito'*—Atlas' mother in Greek mythology. I did a Web search putting the phrase and the name together and struck lucky—take a look at this..."

She hands him a printout of the cult's web pages. He takes it over to the light of the window and reads in silence. After a few minutes he looks up.

"So a doomsday sect with a Web presence—nothing strange about that. Junk email distributed to millions of addresses automatically."

"No, I've checked the routing—there are ways of telling whether it's been mass distributed."

"Any idea why someone thought you might be interested?" he says, with a vagueness that could mean that he knows Cassy is working for MI5 but is unsure whether he should reveal it.

"I was hoping you could profile the cult from the information on the website."

Ashi is unrivalled in his knowledge of religious sectarianism. Cassy has seen him do it before: identify the source of an anonymous newspaper advert with threatening undertones, and on another occasion, name the perpetrators of a falsely signed public letter that had inflamed Pakistani youths throughout London. He doesn't disappoint her. In the matter-of-fact voice of an expert, examining evidence that is elementary, he pronounces: "Clearly Islamic. References to Noah and Isa—both venerable prophets in Islam. The paragraph about Noah is straight from the Koran. But the second and third paragraphs are quotes from the Bible. I'd say we might be talking about a Sufi sect."

"The mystics of Islam?"

"Many of them are free with their doctrine. Freethinkers... some freer than others."

He gives her a poignant look over the top of the printout.

"Could be Indonesian or East Malaysian—some of those tribes have their own idiosyncratic mix of Christian, Muslim, and animistic beliefs. Sub-Saharan African Sufism, perhaps—that's also a dividing line between Christian and Muslim influences. Then you've got the Iran, Iraq, Kurdistan axis. It's really difficult to make a guess with so little to go on. I'll check out the Koranic references if you want, and then we'll have tea."

Tea and scones is a necessary event at Ashi's farm, whatever the time of day. Cassy leaves him taking a large volume from a library shelf, and makes her way outside and down the lane towards the nearby salt marsh. The marsh stretches from the bottom of the hill to the sea and always smells wonderfully mellow—salted air laced with history and melancholy. She perches on the edge of the old sea wall, taking in the atmosphere for a while, and then takes another track back up the hill, returning to the farm through the wood with the muntjac deer. The path comes out of the trees at the back of the big barn, and she finds herself wandering inside, looking for signs of rats. Ashi has the gentleman farmer's romantic view of the English countryside and chooses to employ a variety of ex-hippies to carry out traditional farm practices for him. One side of the barn is filled with restored machinery from a bygone era; the other is stacked to the ceiling with old-fashioned bales of hay.

In her recurring dream about playing as a child in the English countryside, there is a part where she and her playmates are removing bales in just such a barn, to form secret passages where they hide for days from grown-ups. She shudders. How does a dream acquire such detail?

She is about to poke the long handle of a garden rake into a giveaway rat hole when there is a rustle behind her, and she turns to see Ashi standing in the doorway.

"That wasn't too difficult," he says, holding up a sheet of printed paper. "Even easier with a CD-ROM."

She walks over to join him and takes the printout. He has separated out the paragraph about Noah into several lines and added other similar quotations, giving each line a Koranic reference. It is Ashi all over—the meticulous academic.

"The detailed picture of who actually got into the Ark is rather complex in the Koran's version of the story," he explains, reverting to the university lecturer he has been for most of his life. "In Sura 66, Noah's wife is apparently assigned to Hell. Yusuf Ali's commentary implies from this that she perished in the flood. One of Noah's sons seems not to make it either, and there's much debate among Muslim scholars as to whether he was actually one of the family— that's because one of these other verses—see, that one— implies that Noah's whole family was saved."

"Fascinating," she says distractedly, stepping out of the barn and looking up at the sky. She is still thinking about the dream.

"The *'one hundred and twenty years'* line comes from God's warning to Noah in Genesis—a kind of 'you've got one hundred and twenty more years before disaster comes, chum, so get building.' Our Sufis, at a swift guess, have been meditating on lessons from antiquity and are convinced that doomsday's on the way. It's a simple formula for a sect. That's certainly the tone of the next bit about Noah—a warning to all cultures. '*The sign of the King*'—that will be a reference to the Sumerian King

Gilgamesh. He is the subject of one of the Near East's famous epic poems—he's said to have met the survivor of the Great Flood, Ziusudra, or Xisuthra by his Babylonian name. *'The sign of the King has been given. We now await the final sign. After the final sign, the end shall come.'* That seems to be a repetition of the Biblical warning—Noah as a portent. As for the final sign and the end that follows—that will no doubt be the sect's own little secret. They all have one. The whole thing's got the feel of a cut-and-paste ransom note. I guess that sums up some Sufis quite well—the cut-and-paste, I mean—a mix-and-match approach. Post-modernists, the lot of them—well ahead of their time."

"What about the ransom bit?" Cassy says. "Know of any wayward Sufis who might be tied up with the bad guys?"

Ashi looks as though he may have been about to say something. Instead he looks up at the clouds drifting in from the sea.

"Unlikely," he says, looking at his watch. "I wonder who wrote it. Let's get that tea before you have to head off back."

***

An hour later, Cassy is sitting in the car park of a motorway service station fumbling through a worn address book. She finds what she is looking for, dials, and waits.

"Professor Scholten, please—Department of Oriental Studies."

"Trying to connect you..." The Leeds University phone rings long enough to tell her that Marten isn't there. A beep tells her that she has been switched to the departmental office, and she hangs up. Her next attempt is more successful.

"Great to hear you, my dear." Marten is from the Netherlands and exudes that typically Dutch blend of warmth, sophistication, and efficiency.

"Can't talk for long, Marten—I'm on my way to a meeting. I've been landed with a riddle and immediately thought of you."

"If you're referring to my complex personality, I'm flattered." He chuckles at the other end of the phone. "What can I do for you? It's really good to hear you—it's been a long time."

"I want to fax you something I pulled off the internet," she says. "A collection of religious quotations with sectarian commentary. Nothing earth-shattering, but I'd rather like to profile the authors."

"Are you going to give some clues?" he asks with a distinctly Dutch *shome*. She is about to repeat Ashi's conclusions, but stops.

Better to get an independent second opinion.

"No *cluesh*," she says, mimicking his accent. "See what you think. Can I ring you back later tonight? I'm in a service station and need to hit the road before the crush gets worse. I'll be tied up until... say... eleven?"

They exchange fax numbers and hang up.

She sends the fax from the motel next to the service station, gets back onto the motorway, and puts her foot down, thrilling as the turbo kicks in—but hits the first jam within minutes. She stop-starts her way through the outer and inner London suburbs towards the relative peace of the very centre—like the eye of a hurricane.

What are those Iraqis in their East London apartments doing tonight, I wonder? Surveying London's points of vulnerability? Planning and plotting? Waiting? Eating pizza? Terrorists are humans too. What was the man who died in Manhattan thinking about when he smashed into the mother and her baby?

Cassy's evening meeting ends predictably late. It is 11.30 p.m. by the time she gets home, and she is disappointed to find an empty fax machine. She slings off her coat, empties last night's bottle of rioja into a champagne flute—she can't remember why there is a champagne flute on the table—and drops into the ridiculously expensive Italian designer loveseat she purchased on a whim from Heals in Tottenham Court Road in the New Year sales. What had it cost her? Eight thousand? She bought it because she liked the feel of the soft leather on her bare skin, and because it was wide enough to sit in cross-legged but narrow enough to rest her elbows on the chair's arms. No sooner has she settled than she jumps up again, turns on the central heating, and sheds the rest of her clothes, leaving on only a pair of thick hiking socks. Her feet get cold easily. Then she is back in the chair, snuggling naked against the heavily tanned and amazingly soft animal skin, and dialling her answer machine.

Good—a bleep, and then Marten's recorded voice.

"Cassandra, my friend—we must talk. You clever girl. How did you know? Perhaps that smooth-talking friend of yours, Ashi, told you about the conversation he and I had last summer. How did you stumble across them?" Again, a very Dutch *shtumble*. "... And what's a lovely girl like you doing reading evil cult web pages? It's not good for you— take it from an expert. It's a very, *very* unorthodox mystical group. Leaders are said to be Kurds—but that might just be an attempt by the Turkish authorities to slur them. They were split up and dispersed by Saddam years ago. They're into prophecy and judgement. This is the first evidence I've seen of them for a long time—I'm really excited. I'm in London on Wednesday at the British Academy. We must meet up—how about late afternoon? I know you're around because I've checked your university timetable on the Web. You've got exam committees Wednesday morning. Anyway, how are you, my friend? I wish I were looking into your lovely eyes rather than staring down a phone."

I bet you do. The efficiency, sophistication, and understated charm of the Dutch. She looks down at her nakedness and blows Marten a kiss into the phone. She throws the phone over to the sofa, curls up into a ball, and then stretches out to feel the sides of the leather womb. Ten minutes later she is asleep.

***

The next morning, Cassy retrieves Ashi's profile of the mystics from her briefcase.

Definitely economical with the diagnosis. Ashi's coyness is too much like Nigel bloody Buchanan's.

Cassy and Marten had first met at an initial briefing on the U.S.–U.K. Ark project. One of his side interests is the material culture of Palestine's ancient indigenous tribes, and he curates his university's tiny collection, housed in a glass-fronted bookcase in his generously sized office. After enthusing for a very long time about a small dark stone object, which he claimed to be the fourth oldest carving of Noah's Ark in the world, he had asked her out to dinner. When he had invited her back to his apartment, she had said yes, fully intending to go to bed with him. But when he had put a hand on her knee, the drawbridge suddenly snapped, as was so often the case. Friendship and intimacy have always been a problem for Cassy, even though she can cope with intimacy without friendship. The experience with Marten had lain somewhere between the two, and they had ended up seeing each other on and off for a period of three or four months during which time they had sex, on her estimation, about thirty times. Cassy had ended it after Zach started paying her attention.

So—Marten and Ashi are in touch with each other? No surprises there, since they share an interest in Middle Eastern religious movements. But talking about Kurdish mystics with a thing about Noah's Ark last summer?

***

Later that day Cassy is driving through London's fashionable Knightsbridge district on her way back from

Heathrow Airport, where she has dropped a visiting professor. Her mind has been on Kurdish refugees since Marten's voice message, and when the brass-plated plaque on the wall of the Burmese Embassy flashes by, she slams her foot on the break hard enough to both burn rubber and curve. The driver of the car behind holds up two fingers as he swerves past her and she remains quite still deep in thought, car half-blocking the carriageway.

A few years earlier, Cassy had a call from Chavalit, her close teenage friend from her time in Bangkok with Joy. Chav had struck up a typically odd relationship with a librarian at the English language library in the UN headquarters in the city, where he religiously went every Monday evening to read the British tabloids. Madam Harn, who was a refugee from the ethnic war in Burma's Shan State, one day asked Chav if he knew anyone in Britain who could help secure political asylum for her grown-up son who was in imminent danger of being sent "up-country" in his capacity as a Burmese civil servant. This was a euphemism for being posted on one of the Burmese government's many rebel-front lines—a promotion from which most did not return. Chav had pled with Cassy on Madam Harn's behalf, and Cassy had written to an ex-Cornell student friend who was by then working in a top London law firm. Remarkably, after a protracted process, the son got his visa. The eternally grateful Madam Harn had since moved to UNESCO in Paris and then to UNCHR—the United Nations High Commission for Refugees—in Geneva from where she had recently sent Cassy yet another "thank you" card with news of her son's accomplishments.

For very obvious reasons, the whereabouts of political refugees living new lives in receiving countries is highly confidential information. For technical bureaucratic reasons, however, UNCHR staff are less obliged to be so careful about refugees in so-called holding countries. The process of finding a permanent home for the many thousands of dispossessed is a long and arduous round of negotiations.

Some wait on borders in holding camps organised like small townships. Others are incarcerated in immigration jails. Others, the long-term *waiters* who for one reason or another no one wants, can end up in countries that have granted temporary residence until permanent citizenship is secured elsewhere. Some live in this stateless no-man's land for years. So when Cassy gives Madam Harn a call and asks about a group of Kurdish or possibly Turkish, Iranian, or Iraqi mystics, she says she "shouldn't, really," but takes down the details and promises she will get back. And she does—at about 5.30 pm on a Tuesday afternoon, just as Cassy is about to leave her university office.

"Dr. Cassy? I think I have something for you," she says, and pauses, as if referring to a document in front of her.

"This is a coincidence. I am not allowed to give you names, but we record details of political and religious affiliation on our database so it takes no time for me to do the search. We try to place refugees with similar backgrounds, lifestyle, and outlook together in holding locations. There are two groupings that fit your profile. One is in Banda Aceh, Indonesia, and the other is in Bangkok. There—I said it was a coincidence."

Well, well. Too easy. Both places cheap places to live, metropolitan anonymity, and far away from Saddam Hussein's hit squads.

"Amazing," Cassy responds. "Banda Aceh—isn't it the powerbase for a fundamentalist Indonesian faction?"

"Indeed, Dr. Cassy, and West Sumatra has close historical ties with Turkey. The fundamentalists in Banda have an almost identical flag."

"How many individuals listed?" Cassy tries.

"Now you are pushing me," Madam Harn says, but her friendly tone indicates that she doesn't mind. "Fifteen in Bangkok and seven in Banda."

"Anything else?" Cassy pushes once more.

"Um... let me see... yes, but this is all, you understand. Some of them have been in these cities for a long time. No one wants these guys—it's a real headache. What can the U.N. do? Sometimes we can get another holding country to take over while we continue looking for permanent relocation, but after a while it becomes clear that there's nowhere for them to go. Suicides are very common among these long-termers, Dr. Cassy. That's why we make sure they're together with friends—at least where that's possible. Actually, looking at this..." She pauses. "Some of these guys have been in both cities for twenty years or more. They're *de facto* citizens. That happens, you know— governments eventually stop insisting they have their U.N. documents stamped in the local police station once a month, and the refugees quietly slip into mainstream society—or into the twilight. I suppose it depends how eager the refugees are to get settled somewhere. Most with families and normal aspirations persist. Others—the ideologically or religiously committed—take a less conventional view of their life chances, and maybe even prefer to slip into the twilight."

***

"Let me think how to start," Marten pauses.

He is all Dutch: tall, big-boned, square-jawed, blue eyes and thick wavy light-brown hair, grown long and swept back in a way that emphasises his cerebral qualities. They are seated in one of Cassy's regular cafe haunts not far from Liverpool Street Station and overlooking the entrance to London's oldest public square. It used to be a marsh on the edge of the medieval city and at some point had been enclosed first by single-storey buildings and then by higher ones as the city filled up. Now it is an oval jewel of greenery, speckled with the bright colours of silk ties and blouses, and set in a frame of austere, neo-gothic office facades. At one stage Cassy would have despised the wearers of the ties and blouses for their normality. Now she envies them.

"In a word, it's a mixture of classical Christian and Islamic prophecy plus unorthodox application of the last judgement theme. The whole thing has this heavy Noah spin on it. Free-thinking Muslims—the giveaway themes of wisdom and light mark them out as Sufis. Biblical quotations are unusual in Sufi writings, for all their theological freedom—apart from early mystical Persian poetry. *Jalaluddin Rumi* used it. He was a very famous Sufi—but it's not the same type of usage. Here the Biblical prophesies are delivered... er... prophetically, not poetically. That in itself is not typical Sufi style. Having said that, it's easy to forget that Sufis are not averse to a bit of preaching."

"I thought Sufis were contemplatives."

"As well as giving the world the famous Whirling Dervishes and a multitude of paths to spiritual ecstasy, they played a huge part in spreading Islam through much of Africa and Asia—barefoot itinerant preachers wandering from village to village."

I love you, Marten—you're such a charming nerd.

"The freedom with the Bible and the Koran makes it almost certainly Kurdish in origin in my opinion," Marten continues. "There's a lot of inter-mixing in the region—ancient Christian mysticism, orthodox Christianity, Zoroastrianism—the ancient religion of Persia—and Neo-Platonism in and outside of Shi'ism. Shi'ism is itself, of course, a more mystical branch of Islam than Sunnism, though some would argue with that. There's *Naqshabandiyya* influence here, too."

You're sounding a whole lot more convincing than Ashi, my beautiful nerdish Dutch ex-lover.

"*Naqshabandiyya?*" Cassy asks. He has forgotten that she isn't one of his students.

"One of the largest Sufi Orders, founded in the fourteenth century by Khawaja Baha-ud-din Muhammad.

It's dominant in Central Asia but also traditionally strong in the countries that form Kurdistan—Turkey, Iran, Iraq, Armenia—as well as North Africa, India, and Malaysia."

"You're good at your job, Marten, I have to give you that," Cassy says, moving her chair closer to his, clipping a hand onto his arm, and looking up into his eyes.

"They're a funny bunch, the *Naqshabandiyya*," he says, reaching over and patting her hand with his and leaving it there. "They like to teach using folk tales and jokes—not always clean ones, either."

I can't believe Ashi didn't know this.

"The slightly *noir* bits," Marten continues, "are what gives it its *Uwaysi* overtones—giving the text a sinister undercurrent."

"I thought Sufis were all light and love," Cassy says, snuggling up even closer to rest her head on Marten's shoulder.

"Uwaysis are unorthodox even by Sufi standards. Mainstream Muslims tolerate their mystical Sufi brethren by and large, allowing them a certain latitude in belief and practice. When it comes down to it, the common people always vote for the religious party that gives them a more direct line to God—happens in all religions. In times of Sufi-led revival, mainstream Islam has nearly always taken steps to bring the mystics within its fold—encouraging formal training organised by the Sufi Orders, whose lines of pedigree stretch back into history; subsidising Sufi convents to keep the dervishes from wandering too far; that sort of thing. The temptations of property, pay, promotion, and prestige does wonders in quenching the flame of the idealist."

"Pope Innocent III used the same strategy with Francis of Assisi," Cassy says, twisting her face to receive a reward for this unsolicited contribution. She had once had a month-long relationship with a devout Catholic who had felt the need for a short rebellion.

He obliges by bestowing a fond kiss on her forehead.

"Yes," he says, eyeing her thoughtfully. "Idealists are a threat to the mainstream in all sorts of ways. Well, the established Sufi Orders—and there's about a hundred and seventy of them—take pretty much the same attitude towards the Uwaysi as clerical Muslims take towards the Sufis. Rather like the English telling jokes about the Irish and the Irish telling jokes about Kerrymen—every society has to have its fringe to hate or laugh at. Uwaysis do two things wrong. First, they dispense with legitimised teachers. Anyone can declare himself a Uwaysi mystic—or *herself*, come to that. It's not the only Sufi Order to be open to women. This is rather irritating for the rest of them who have to go through untold privations and disciplines to learn a Sufi Order's particular *way* to enlightenment."

"And the second problem?"

"Their occult tendencies," he says with a touch of disapproval. "At least by any normal person's standards, they're occultists. Instead of learning their mystical craft from a living master at the end of a long chain of succession, they go directly to the top—or bottom, should I say. Uwaysis continue the ancient practice of *incubation*— sleeping in some sacred spot to pick up the vibes, get a dream, see a vision. Mainstream Sufis talk of *annihilation* in their master—'*the spiritual alchemist transforms the base material of the novice's soul into purified gold'*..." he quotes. "Uwaysis take a somewhat more spooky route and *annihilate* themselves in a dead Sufi or even one of Islam's Prophets—from Adam through Noah to Mohammed. They really are considered out on the fringe by orthodox Sufis— beyond the fringe by most mainstream Muslims."

Annihilation into Noah. The idea makes Cassy shudder and Marten puts a warming arm around her.

They continue their conversation, sitting entwined side by side in the manner they might have done when their romance was in full bloom, only the subject would have surprised any passerby who might have chosen to eavesdrop.

"The last judgement stuff on the website isn't characteristic of any particular Sufi Order, but it's not uncommon for individual mystics, or even whole groups or sub-Orders, to get passionate on a pet theme from the Koran. Sufis generally have a sober appreciation of the wrath of God even though their central emphasis is divine love. I suppose it's not strange at all that a group sharing a common spiritual experience might find themselves caught up in a Jihad against ignorance or unbelief and go on the prophetic attack."

"Jihad?" Cassy had missed the first part of his point, distracted by a pigeon that had landed on their table. She shoos it away with her foot.

"Yes, a Sufi may declare Jihad—holy war—against himself—his unregenerate self, that is—but he can take the same attitude towards the uncleanness in society. That could tie in with the last judgement theme, I suppose—a final Jihadic onslaught against the Great Satan before Western civilisation finally meets its fiery end on Judgement Day."

"Which they probably think is soon approaching?"

"Maybe they see themselves as vanguards, with a handpicked role in preparing for the happy day in some way."

"So tell me why you got so excited by my mystical web page," she says, impatient to get to the point, and squeezing herself even more tightly into his manly frame.

He sighs. "Some years ago I spent time tracing the development of an obscure sect that seems to have emerged in Egypt sometime in the 1950's."

At this she pulls herself away and sits upright on her cane cafe chair, looking at Marten questioningly and then staring into the distance.

Another pointer back to the fifties.

Marten contemplates asking her what she's thinking, but decides to continue.

"The Nooh Brotherhood, the Bin-Nooh—son of Noah—network— it's known by various names. Led by three brothers, rumour has it—I mean, literally, sons of the same father. Every so often, you get a grassroots spiritual movement that gains influence way beyond anyone's predictions and quite incommensurate with its size, status, pedigree, and so on. It's an academic's dream when you come across one that's still spreading. Congenital non-conformists—oddballs or people with extraordinary spiritual experiences often start them. You mentioned Francis just now—he was like that. Danced naked out of an Episcopal Tribunal in the city of Assisi one day in 1206—a disgraced merchant-class debauchee with a questionable conversion experience. Within fifteen years his simple back-to-basics brand of spirituality had touched nearly every village in Italy."

"And the Kurdish Sufis—the Noah Brotherhood—brothers?"

"They're not in the normal mould at all—not confined to any one country, and their influence has been anything but open and public. I can only describe it as a shadowy influence within an esoteric world of mystical practices, beliefs, and rules. It might not have been noticed at all, had it only infiltrated the genuine spiritual Sufi Orders—and no one can really say how deep that influence goes. It's the impact on the guilds and more modern commercial associations that made it possible to track as a movement."

"Guilds?"

"In the medieval period when Sufism was getting established there were always two quite distinct types of Order. There were the mystical Orders proper, and there were the economic associations that adopted certain religious outlooks. These were the trades and craft guilds dominant in medieval towns throughout the world. Guilds that took a religious mantle became sort of consecrated by the spiritual authority of the mystics they chose to follow. Their purpose remained—and remains—social and commercial, but over the years they've acquired layers of religious rules and beliefs. They have their own patron saints and have elaborate initiation ceremonies. That's why Westerners have often viewed the Sufi movement as something like a mixture of Mystical Christianity and Freemasonry."

"Freemasons?" Cassy notes that her contribution to this monologue is becoming monosyllabic.

Now we're really talking conspiracy.

"The same ancient term *Taifa* is used for spiritual and commercial orders, but an order can't strictly be both. They've developed a complicated relationship over history. The *Bayyumiyya* order, which started in Egypt in 1726, for example, was closely linked to the *butchers'* guilds. Even Cairo's *dancing girls association* had a spiritual mentor—*Ahmad Al-Badawi*. He was an Arab trained in Iraqi mysticism before moving to Morocco, and then to Tanta in Egypt, where his tomb is now. Other commercial orders are little more than secretive associations for the mutual benefit of their members. Not all of them are squeaky clean."

"How on earth do you go about researching this sort of stuff, Marten?" Cassy asks, suddenly excited by the thought and snuggling up to Marten again as if to a father telling a bedtime story.

I love it! Far more engrossing than complex numbers and digital archaeological images.

"With difficulty and with patience, my dear," he replies. "I first came across the Bin-Nooh Brotherhood when a colleague of mine—lecturer in University of Xinjiang on the northwest border of China—stumbled across some kind of mystical spiritual revival that had engulfed several major Turkistani craft guilds. We soon heard of similar accounts from Indonesia right through to the Maghreb. There was a certain pattern—networks the guilds were linked to, visits to and fro, threads of subtle doctrinal innovations—and we eventually traced a line of influence to the Uwaysi band in Egypt. We could see how the thing had spread over time, too—it was gold dust for types like me."

And Ashi.

"There must be dozens of subtle doctrinal shifts and shades—what was special about this one?"

"Its dark side. Repentant moneylenders in the Maghreb and convicted ceramists in Central Asia were only part of it. For every humbled guildsman apologising to his wife for a secret mistress, there seemed to be a power-hungry leader corrupted and caught up in criminal activity or some moral controversy unworthy of any taifa order. In some cases, whole guilds had clearly been corrupted with no sign of any positive influence. In others, you had a division, with grassroots members finding a new spirituality while the wealthy and powerful became more and more corrupt. Some groups seem to have blown apart completely. There is no doubt that the influence comes from the same source—I can prove it to you if you have the time."

Cassy suddenly thinks of the Russian student in London who MI5 are monitoring for links with organised crime.

"Could a Sufi-inspired guild turn into an international criminal group?" she asks.

"Unlikely, but not impossible," he says, waving at the pigeon, which has returned to their table. "With this one it is almost as though the good comes with a built-in virus—something always gets infected and things start to go wrong. From the data I've collected—mostly interviews and anecdotes—I would say that there's something genuinely good in it, but that there's something nasty coming in close on its heels."

"A kind of Jekyll and Hyde fringe Sufi sect," Cassy suggests. She is instinctively mapping the problem onto her domain and thinking how she would write a smart computer algorithm to trace subtle patterns of words through hundreds of recorded interviews.

"Exactly. True and false, genuine and counterfeit, constructive and destructive. Beats me how such a group could start, yet alone continue—and to exert so much influence. And how they could disappear without trace! I've not had the resources to make a thorough research since their missives stopped appearing in the Arabic press. Their influence was detected by CIA Islamics experts working in Afghanistan during the Russian conflict, and then it seemed to spread rapidly with the dispersion of the Jihad fighters after the Russian retreat. It all went quiet after Saddam's army marched north of the thirty-sixth parallel into Kurdistan a few years ago. Many of the core group seemed to have left the country well before that, but those remaining were either blown apart through internal dissension or by Saddam's artillery."

"Or gone to ground elsewhere," Cassy suggests at the same moment as seeing in her mind the general shape of an algorithm that would do the job, at least in English language—even easier if there are digital newspaper reports to analyse.

"That's possible," Marten says. "Something came up last year that could have been a familiar pattern—reported in a local Indonesian anthropological journal, but I've seen no hard evidence until your fax the other day."

"They've regrouped as dissident refugees in Southeast Asia," Cassy pronounces, pleased with herself and this time not waiting for his response but swivelling round and planting a kiss on his lips.

Marten looks her in the eye, shocked by the kiss and puzzled by the assertion.

"Bangkok. They've gone to ground in Bangkok and West Sumatra—Banda Aceh. I'm going to Thailand next week. Fancy joining me?"

PART II: The Engagement

Chapter 9

Bangkok
May 2000

EVERY CITY HAS its distinctive fragrance. Bangkok's comes from its vast network of rotting canals and the fragrant water hyacinths that clog them up; the hawkers selling durian fruit and frying bananas on the roadside; the incense and the lotus seed necklaces on sale at the Buddhists' shrines; the damp, lush vegetation everywhere; and the cool moist smell of air-conditioned malls. The exotic blend suspends pungently in heavily polluted air and dominates even the kerosene fumes of the three-wheeled tuk-tuks. The power of the subtle—like the fragrant smell of jasmine rice, which outlasts the stronger smell of a fearsome Thai curry.

The Grand Italian is anything but grand. Cassy had stayed there twice, aged fifteen, the first time after being picked up in a girly bar by a young Catholic boy from Chicago not much older than her. She had been playing the role for a bet and felt sorry for Grady, who was passing through Bangkok with his parents on their way to Sydney and was clearly out of his depths with the group of local street-wise expatriate teenagers who had taken him out to see the sights. At first, she had just thought of taking him home for hot chocolate, Joy's place being just around the corner. Then she had thought of the Italian. It turned out to be his first time.

The next visit had been after a ferocious argument with Joy when Cassy had moved out. That time she had stayed for a week, renting an un-refurbished room for virtually nothing. When she returned home, Joy hadn't even realised she had gone. Since then, Cassy has enjoyed returning to the grand old lady with her musty air-conditioning, cigarette-stained furniture, and teak panelled walls. These days it is the haunt of the "business" traveller who prefers more anonymity than the larger hotels afford and is particularly popular with Arabs and Pakistanis.

Over a breakfast of bland rice porridge flavoured with sun-dried baby squid, a waitress brings Cassy a copy of the English language Bangkok Post sporting the headline "*English Police arrive in Bangkok to help Thais fight child exploitation.*" Four detectives from Northumberland in the north of England had flown in from Heathrow last night for a two-week training event on child abuse. The U.K. government had recently passed new laws to prosecute its citizens for crimes committed abroad, providing a good opportunity for a trip east for four lucky officers.

The waitress comes back. "Excuse me, madam, visitor, look for Miss Kim."

What will Chav have made of my request, I wonder?

Her old friend Chavalit is a reporter on Thai Rat—a popular national tabloid—and is something of an institution, famous in the trade for his unorthodox research methods, and famous amongst the public for his dangerous stories. It is a wonder to Cassy that he is still alive, let alone still in a job. To her, he is a loveable rogue as well as one of her oldest friends. During her teenage time in Bangkok, he had been a school friend's older brother and she, a good opportunity to learn English—he had never mastered it, but they had become fast friends. He had gone on to graduate from Thamasart University's respectable journalism department, then located in the shadows of the shimmering roofs of the King's Palace, but over the years he had grown into the quintessential tabloid journalist. She had sent him a fax just before leaving London.

Chav has followed his friend's career closely. He had sent a letter every single day when she had been institutionalised after attacking Joy, each letter being no more than a few lines of greeting, plus a Thai joke to cheer her up. Then, when that crisis was over, he had tried to offer what he thought was helpful advice as she sought to salvage what was left of her life. Remarkably Joy had taken her back, and then to everyone's surprise, she had got into Oxford to study maths a year earlier than she should have. Chav had sent her a slightly longer letter of congratulations, giving her advice on how to befriend the offspring of wealthy Thais. She immediately switched to archaeology to make the point that she was beholden to no one, including the "access" office at Oxford she suspected of easing her acceptance in order to meet their requirements for recruiting non-standard entry students. Recruiting an applicant with time in a semi-secure "home" must have looked really good—the social worker had suggested making this explicit in her CV.

After Cassy graduated, Joy had continued to surprise by paying over fifty thousand dollars a year for Cassy to go to Cornell University in upstate New York to do a PhD in computational mathematics and image analysis. For each of the three years, Chav managed a Christmas card and occasionally sent her a copy of one of his scoops. Sometimes a copy of Thai Rat would appear in her mailbox for no obvious reason. From Cornell Cassy had drifted for a few months, living in Berlin with an exiled Pakistani poet and then finding a job translating in the British Ministry of Defence office in that city. Again—a congratulatory letter from Chav. From there she slipped, almost without realising what was happening, into GCHQ, the British government's code breaking and electronic listening centre in Cheltenham, England. A book of Buddhist mantras this time from Chav. The work had excited Cass at first, but it was a disastrous move, ending in her dismissal after six months. Following a difference of opinion with her line manager, she had hacked her way into his clearance level and corrected his mistaken analysis, quoting the source. She was out of the building within an hour, but a week later had been contacted by someone from Military Intelligence. She was very lucky, she was told—a job exactly suited to her had come up. That was the Anglo–American Ark study. No letter of either condolence or congratulations from Chav this time—Cassy found out later he had booked into an alcohol rehab clinic.

Cassy makes her way to the hotel lobby and approaches a man in a shabby light grey suit standing with his back to her, cigarette dangling from a limp hand.

He spins round as she taps him on the shoulder, almost losing his balance, and then beams as he takes in the image of his old friend. He put his palms together and bows in a deep and affectionate wai.

"Adjan Cassy—welcome to Bangkok." The words do not flow but come out each with deliberate effort. The voice is gentle but shaky, and rough from years of alcohol and nicotine abuse.

"Adjan" is a term of respect reserved for teachers, but Chav always uses it with good-natured cynicism.

"Chav."

She extends her arms and draws him into the hug she knows he is shyly hoping for, and plants a full and voluptuous kiss on his shrivelled lips. Then she takes a pace back and makes her own respectful wai. Her eyes are moist; she knows that no other loves her like Chav, and that Chavalit Sonboon is not interested in her for her body.

"You're looking great—what happened?" she asks, using the back of a hand to wipe away the tear that had gathered in her epicathanthal fold.

Chav's emaciated face matches his voice, cultured by years of self-abuse under his three addictions of rough country-style cheroots, Mekhong whisky, and massage parlours. But he somehow seems fitter. She looks him over and decides it is the new haircut.

"And how are you, Cassy?" he says in his slow, faltering English.

He nods and smiles as he talks like a toy dog on the back shelf of a car. Like Indians who shake their head when they mean yes, his nods signify positive social engagement, perhaps more like a dog wagging a tail. He asks the question with wide, deferential eyes, which has forever been his manner.

A pathetic figure by any measure, but with a loveable honesty about his weaknesses, conveyed all too painfully in body language and self-effacing words.

You're pleased to see me, Chavalit, dear, but you've no idea how much your loyalty means to me.

He stands there with slumped shoulders, cigarette now drooping from the corner of his mouth, and beaming. His ambition, like many Thai men, is to become a career monk—something he will never do, of course, but it is an ambition that preserves his self-respect.

"I give up Mekhong," he says.

So it isn't just the haircut. Mekhong is a popular brand of the Thai's famously rough rice whisky.

"Good for you, Chav. How long?"

"One week," he says, smiling and nodding rhythmically.

Last time Cassy had seen him, he had just had "an operation on my stomach," which had frightened him into action. That was two years ago, and he had given up then too.

"Good for you," she says again. "You're a stronger man than I."

He laughs. Perhaps it is his habits that make him such a successful journalist on the gutter press; he will never become an editor, but he is one of the best at ferreting around Bangkok in search of stories. It soon becomes apparent that this is what he has been doing since Cassy's fax. They settle into ancient upholstered armchairs thick with dust and smelling of stale cigarettes.

"I have found the refugees," he says abruptly. "Do you want some drink?"

She follows his glance to the brightly coloured hostess hovering behind her.

"China tea for me."

"Song cha," he says—*two teas.*

"They live in two places. One is near your hotel—Tai Pong Towers Racquet Club, Sukhumvit Soi 47. The other is wooden Thai-style compound in canals across Chao Pya River in Thonburi."

Soi 47—a few blocks from the Grand Italian.

"You haven't lost your touch," she grins. "How did you find them?"

"No problem, Cassy," he says, this time shaking his head instead of nodding, but still with the same rhythm and smile. "I have friends to ask for anything. These people be here long time—easy for me to find someone who know where they live. We go see them now?"

Shit. I hadn't expected immediate action.

Rapidly inventing a plan of attack, she suggests, "How about going in as reporters?"

He looks at her for a moment, taking in the idea and nodding silently, and then says, "No problem, Adjan. We are reporters."

Conversation with Chav is always punctuated with silent pauses and Cassy has never been sure whether he is processing her English idioms or whether they are the pauses of a sage. If there is anything sagacious about him, it mostly has to do with Bangkok street life.

He looks at her in silence again and she realizes that he is giving her a chance to explain herself.

"It's a bit of a long story, Chav—I'm not sure I could tell it convincingly."

He waves a nicotine-stained hand. "We just go. My pleasure to help oldest friend—no say no more."

He needs a bit more than that, however, if he is to go visiting with Cassy, so she offers, "I just need a profile. Probe their agenda, what they do all day, connections with other groups—that sort of thing. We'll start by dropping in and saying hello."

Why the hell haven't I given more thought to a line of attack?

Chav shows no signs of noticing her consternation.

"How about story on Sufism in Bangkok? Not really Thai Rat story but could spice up," he suggests helpfully.

"Great! Good idea, Chav."

It doesn't sound very convincing but it will have to do.

Fifteen minutes later they are speeding through the streets of Bangkok on a low-powered Honda motorbike. This is a new departure for Chavalit. For as long as Cassy can remember he has driven the pale blue 1969 VW Beetle that he shares with his unmarried sister. The new elevated skytrain construction on Sukuhmvit Road had been the last straw. The two-lane road is now reduced to one lane in each direction, with some sections closed completely and traffic diverted through unbelievably narrow back streets. It seems that everyone has taken to small motorbikes, which swarm like a plague of rodents through every conceivable rat run. At every junction twenty or thirty bike taxis wait to ferry pillion passengers to their destinations in the maze of lanes—*sois*—leading from the main road.

Cassy tucks her bare legs in close as they brush past a blue air-con bus heading towards the airport. It isn't moving and its aisle is packed with standing passengers relieved at least to be out of the claustrophobic heat. It might be another three hours before some of them reach their destination. She tightens her grip around Chavalit as he mounts the pavement without warning, weaves past a line of vendors frying coconut patties, and heads for a slope dropping to an underground car park. The security guards take no notice as they speed past their barrier and on into the darkness. Other bikes are behind and in front—pests running in and out freely wherever there are openings. Cassy thinks of Ashi and his barn.

Why disclose only part of his analysis? It has been bothering her more and more.

Chav makes his way through the basements of several buildings, emerging for a minute into daylight, across a narrow alley, and down into another basement car park. Eventually they turn a corner onto a ramp and exit to a small soi; then, a little further on, they pass through a grand gate into some sort of government compound, and are speeding alongside a railway track towards Tai Pong Towers, a distinctive twin-tower condo development.

Tai Pong had once been a respectable compound—two ten-floor apartment buildings, a row of townhouses, and four villas all built around a racquet club and a palm-fringed swimming pool—and had been one of the first compounds of its kind in the city. In its heyday its security guards and private sports and restaurant facilities had offered its two hundred or so residents security and privileged luxury. Private neighbourhoods had since become an epidemic, and older ones like Tai Pong were showing their age. Many of its apartments, Chav has told Cassy, are now sublet to locals by their Japanese and Korean owners, who moved back home after the 1997 financial crash—explaining, perhaps, what a community of refugees is doing here. Chav has discovered that they rent three apartments—the whole of the fifth floor of one of the Towers. They stop and dismount under the shadow of the security gatehouse, Cassy's hair and clothes dripping with sweat.

The guard seems to recognise the name on Chavalit's press pass and calls to a friend, who comes out with a copy of Thai Rat. They turn the pages until they find one of his articles, and there is laughter that gives way to a friendly row between the two guards who try to draw Chavalit in too. He pulls out a wallet and flashes a purple five-hundred-baht note. They are practised in dealing with special requests, for he pulls out another before being waved through, with one of the guards running ahead to show Chav where to park the bike at the entrance to one of the Towers. The place is a picture of decline. The garages of the townhouses have been converted into the kind of blacked-out offices that no respectable Bangkok resident patronises. There are more offices on the ground floor of the apartment block the guard has led them to. These all seem to be open to the public and Cassy realises, approvingly, that the security guards are a joke, their only job to check the cars coming in and out.

Schmut-bags—we could have driven straight through with a nod. She smiles, silently acknowledging fellow conspirators.

An elevator takes them straight to the fifth floor. The door opens with mechanical arthritis and Cassy and Chavalit step out of Bangkok into the Middle East.

***

It is a lobby, but has been made into a living room. There is a heavily patterned rug on the floor, large carpet cushions for sitting on, posters of Islamic architecture scattered around the walls, and a scent of sandalwood in the air. Cassy inhales deeply, enjoying the evocation of Kasbahs and alleyways of Middle Eastern spice markets. There is something else in the air too that is subtler and not very pleasant—a damp, clammy, cold smell that she can't quite place. The smell of decay and ageing—like a hospital ward for elderly people, perhaps.

They both look around, not sure what to do next. The space is obviously used as a communal sitting area.

Do they take the rug and cushions in at night?

The doors to three apartments are all open and voices come from within. No one seems to have heard them enter. Quarter-tonal vocal music comes from one, and incongruously, the unmistakable penta-tonal lilt of Thai rock music competes from another.

So even Sufi communities have neighbour problems. She is eyeing Chavalit asking him silently whether they should announce themselves or remain silent.

Facing the lift entrance is a poster showing a snow-capped mountain against an azure sky with a yellow-flowered meadow in the foreground. It could be an Alpine scene but for the Turkish Tourism Authority caption at the bottom of the picture. Either side of the poster are two framed photographs: one of a snow-covered range of volcanic-looking mountains, and the other of a small primitively built dusty town set against the backdrop of distant peaks.

The mystics like their mountains.

On the floor underneath the poster is some garbage in a plastic bag.

Ink cartridge from a printer.

Chavalit and Cassy continue to look at each other wondering what to do next. It is rather more private than she had expected, rendering them intruders—an unfortunate start. In the end Cassy resorts to the English trick of clearing her throat loudly, and since that doesn't work, a louder *Sawat Dee Khun Krup*—a polite Thai *hello*—from Chavalit.

It seems to hit someone's wavelength among the competing noises, for a few seconds later a small, round and bald head appears around one of the doorways—a man of about fifty with the narrow eyes and flat face of a North Asian. He says nothing, disappears, and comes back a minute later adjusting a long buff-coloured robe. His head and neck are wet as if he has just stepped out of a shower.

Chavalit has his ID out and immediately launches into reporter mode in Thai, too rapid and colloquial for Cassy to keep up with. She hears her name mentioned and bites her lip.

Shit, why didn't we agree on another name?

The Middle Eastern music suddenly stops, as if other people in the apartment have just realised they have visitors. Three figures appear from the same door as the first and then a fourth from one of the other doorways. Two of them are clad in rough, woollen robes and are distinctively tall. Their common apparel accentuates the similarities in their handsome faces, which are long with gracious eyes and noble bone structure. It is the elegant sort of handsomeness that befits man or woman. They look to Cassy to be in their late sixties or possibly older, and to be brothers. A younger man has only a piece of white material wrapped around the waist and has a half-peeled tangerine in one hand. The one who came from the direction of the Thai music wears a pair of Nike shorts and a polo shirt. He looks Thai.

The North Asian turns to the others and says in heavily accented English, "The press pay us a visit. I think it is to do with the letter to the Bangkok Post."

Chav is living up to his inventive reputation.

Middle Eastern hospitality breaks out in a flurry of well-mannered activity. More cushions appear; a huge hammered brass plate is set on specially made legs to form a low coffee table, and little plates of nuts and almond biscuits appear. Chav and Cassy are seated on cushions and joined by the two tall men. One, on closer inspection, is older-looking than the other, and he takes the lead when all are seated. His eyes fix on Cassy's and then on Chav's. It is obvious to Cassy that he is avoiding her sodden shirt, which is stuck fast to her bra-less chest.

She flushes as he says, "You are both very welcome to our rudimentary accommodation."

His English is astoundingly refined.

"I am Isa and these are my brothers."

He says this with a gracious wave to the man sitting next to him and the others standing behind him at what looks like a respectful distance.

"How did you find us? The letter was my own humble interpretation of the crisis of economy and soul in this country. I did not think it would attract attention nor be traced here."

Cassy shoots Chav an eye signal to say that he is responsible for fielding this line of question and quickly makes an attempt to take control of the conversation.

"I am a university professor from England working with Khun Chavalit on his story."

Chav sits dumbly on his cushion avoiding eye contact with anyone, and Cassy suddenly realises that the connection with the newspaper article had not been his idea.

Okay, it's going to be up to me. Thanks, Chav...

She is helped by an interruption as a fifth man appears with a large vacuum flask smelling of Arabic coffee. He places it on the floor and arranges four tiny handle-less cups on the brass table. The standing brothers seem to take this as a sign to leave and, with hand-on-heart gestures and bows, disappear back into the recesses of the commune, doors tactfully closed behind them. Cassy sits with Chavalit, facing the two imposing figures and frantically thinking what to say next.

She doesn't have to make a decision, for Isa turns directly to her and says, "Your visit is a little earlier than I had expected but I am glad to welcome you to our home, Dr. Kim. Or do you prefer Dr. Cassandra? Please excuse the unusual surroundings..."

She freezes. His English is too precise to mean anything other than what she has heard.

He is expecting us. A dozen possible explanations tumble through her mind. None of which will do. *He's bloody expecting me.*

She looks in panic at the closed elevator door and then at Chav, who is the only possible explanation. But he is looking blank. Instead of making a run for it, in a confused daze, she mutters, "Er… please... call me Cassy."

She cautiously examines her assailant and visibly recoils as their eyes lock for the first time. Her heart palpitates as she finds herself drawn into deep, beautiful universes of turquoise-green.

***

"We are fifteen of us living here in these apartments," he says brightly, ignoring Cassy's obvious confusion. "The condominium management kindly allow us to use this communal space as an extra room."

She remains in stunned silence, too confused to think straight, pulse pounding in her temples. Chav is still staring blankly at a poster on the wall.

"You've... er, been expecting us?" is all she can manage.

"Not so much your friend here, though he is most welcome of course. No, I had planned to invite *you*, Dr. Kim." He lowers his eyes and spreads elegant hands across the floor in front of his crossed legs, his soft but authoritative voice matching the rest of his self-possessed demeanour.

"You knew I was in Bangkok?" she says, not being able to control the quiver of uncertainty in her voice.

He shakes his head slowly without looking up. "No, at some stage I would have made arrangements for us to meet. I am surprised that you are sitting before me now and would be very pleased to know how you come to be here—if, indeed, you are disposed to tell me."

He holds each of the cups, in turn, to the spout of the vacuum dispenser and purposefully presses the button on the lid. A sickly sweet aroma of cardamom fills the room and Cassy and Chav take the cups offered. Her hand is shaking and she brings the other up to the cup to hide the tremor.

"You planned to make arrangements to meet? In London? You plan to come to London?" She is fumbling and her voice has grown a little defiant. She wants to ask what he means by this bizarre statement, but is aware that it is she who owes the first explanation.

I'm the one who bloody came looking for you. What sort of trick is this?

"Alas, I am not permitted to travel freely," he is saying, soothingly. "Our meeting would have had to be in Bangkok—as indeed is now the case. I am surprised but not surprised—praise be to God!"

She throws a glance towards Chav, who hasn't stopped staring at the poster.

"But your visit is premature, my friend, and I am afraid, Dr. Cassandra, that I can offer you no explanation at this time. But I take your coming as a sign that there are preparations to be made. I think that this will be an opportunity for you to prepare your soul. If I am right, then much will be asked from you, and I am sure you will give it willingly."

The words, although softly spoken, have the effect of a blast of ice, and Cassy once again measures the distance to the lift door. She thinks of the old pistol that Chavalit used to carry—given to him by a Khmer Rouge guerrilla in the Cambodian jungle—stares at him, teeth gritted, willing him to produce it.

Isa sees the anxiety compounding her perplexity.

"Do not be concerned, my friend. The calling is practical and the preparations are spiritual. I have words to give you now. There may be more before your return. When do you fly to London?"

His words have a powerful quality and her dizziness deepens. Alarmingly, Cassy finds herself falling helplessly into them as a hostage might submit to the words of a captor. She tries shaking herself back but cannot. Instead she just says: "This Saturday... afternoon... I fly back to Singapore. Then London."

Chav darts a look at her, seeing that she isn't exercising the caution demanded by the situation. The dizziness gives way to what seems something like a drugged sense of calm and she realises with alarm that she *wants* him to ask her something else. Then comes an overwhelming sense of admiration—attraction, even—for this elegant and commanding man who exudes a fluent mixture of graces that gives such a strangely comfortable sensation.

Cassy shakes herself and takes another large gulp of the sweet coffee. She regains control but is surprised to find that the peaceful sensation and warmth towards the Sufi have not gone.

No doubting the man's power to win bloody followers.

"Then let us start," he says simply. "I will tell you a story of two women—a harlot and a sister."

Cassy gives an imperceptible shrug in answer to Chav's questioning look and they both turn obediently to face the storyteller.

A long silence follows while he moves his coffee cup in thoughtful circles on the floor in front of him; first in one direction, and then in the other. Then he begins.

"There are two women you might be familiar with, Dr. Kim. If you will let me, I would help you discern their accomplishments."

She cannot refuse, nor does she want to. Chavalit sits silently—bemused, bewitched, or suspicious, Cassy can't tell. Isa's voice softens further and drops a tone as he takes the posture of a fireside bard.

"At the window of my house I looked out through my lattice and saw a naive. I discerned among the youths a young man lacking sense, passing through the street near her corner. He takes the way to her house in the twilight in the evening, in the middle of the night and in the darkness. And behold, a woman comes to meet him, dressed as a harlot and cunning of heart."

The words *"cunning of heart"* stab her like a knife and an image of Zach passes before her. The image becomes a mirror and she is looking at herself with repulsion. A flashback to the way they started their relationship suddenly makes her wonder who had seduced whom. He had wooed her with his eyes, but she had lured him quickly to bed. She becomes acutely aware of the sodden shirt sticking to her breasts. She daren't look but she knows her nipples are as hard as nuts.

"She is boisterous and rebellious. Her feet do not remain at home. She is now in the streets and now in the squares, and lurks by every corner. So she seizes him and with a brazen face says to him: 'I have fine food to share; therefore I have come out to meet you, to seek your presence earnestly, and I have found you. I have spread my couch with coverings, with covered linens of Egypt. I have sprinkled my bed with myrrh, aloes, and cinnamon. Come

let us drink our fill of love until morning; let us delight ourselves with caresses—for the man is not at home, he has gone on a long journey; he has taken a bag of money with him. At full moon he will come home.' With her many persuasions she entices him; with her flattering lips she seduces him. Suddenly he follows her, as the ox goes to the slaughter, or as one in fetters to the discipline of a fool, until an arrow pierces through his liver. As a bird hastens to the snare, so he does not know that it will cost him... his life."

The effect is spellbinding, paralysing. He is drawing her as he speaks—into his world, into his mind.

Cassy suddenly has a vivid flashback. She is standing outside a busy Indian restaurant off the Strand in London. She has arrived almost an hour early for her lunchtime date with Zach because a meeting has been cancelled and she plans to sit down with a coffee and newspaper to wait for him. Stepping through the door and folding her umbrella, she catches sight of Zach seated in an armchair in the foyer in animated conversation with a beautiful young woman Cassy doesn't recognise. She and Zach have been a month into their marriage. He is gregarious, with many friends, and Cassy is not prone to jealousy, but on this occasion she is shot through with it. It is not the woman herself or the pretty curves revealed by the low-cut T-shirt being shared so generously with Zach over espressos. It is like glimpsing a version of his life in which Cassy doesn't figure. Like she has missed something absolutely fundamental about him. She feels excluded, unimportant, foolish, and strangely, in danger. It only lasts for a few seconds—and then he has spotted Cassy and introduces Beth. Beth is English with a Mid-Atlantic accent and had studied with him in Boston— and that was it. Cassy had never pressed him for another explanation. Beth was in town and he had invited her for a drink so she could meet Cass. Although Cassy hadn't realised it at the time, she realises now that she had never fully trusted Zach after that. She had snared him for sure with her bed of myrrh. But had she too been snared?

"For many are the victims she has cast down, and numerous are all her slain. Her house is the way to death, descending to the bed-chambers of death."

Isa has been looking down as he recites, first making patterns on the white marble floor with a hand and then with a cup, circling in opposite directions. Now he looks up straight into her eyes and says, "Do you recognise her, Dr. Kim? Her influence, I think, runs deeper than you are aware of."

Is he talking about Zach and me... or me and all the others, for God's sake?

She says nothing, heart pounding out of her chest, throat dried up and lungs constricted. Then a numbing sense of helplessness, and with it, a strangely comforting peace.

"Now let me tell you of another woman calling out on the city streets," he says, after a long pause to let the effects have their way.

"Does not wisdom call and understanding lift up her voice? On top of the heights beside the way, where the paths meet, she takes her stand. Besides the gates, at the opening to the city, at the entrance of the doors, she cries out: 'To you, O men, I call, and my voice is to the sons of men. O naive ones, discern prudence; O fools, discern wisdom. Listen, for I shall speak noble things; and the opening of my lips will produce right things. For my mouth will utter truth; and wickedness is an abomination to my lips.'"

As vividly as she had seen Zach she now sees Oghel—another beautiful face, but this time, saintly, honest, pure. She tries hard to replace the saint with a felon—huddled over her computer at dead of night invading her privacy, taking her property. But try as she might, Oghel's image remains pure.

Then the mirror returns and she sees an image of herself that is frighteningly familiar but, which when confronted face to face, she hardly recognises—vulnerable, impressionable, lost, empty, angry, isolated. It is as if Oghel is emanating an aura of all the insecurities, hurts, regrets, mistakes, and pain she has ever endured. Only in him, they have somehow been disarmed. She is being stripped bare. The effect is deeply disturbing but at the same time powerfully liberating. This time she is sure it is she who is being seduced, but whether by the mystic before her or by the thought of Oghel she cannot tell. All she knows is the power and sweetness of the experience.

He is speaking more forcefully now, placing the words as a duellist might a sword, and all the time his deep eyes are searching Cassy's.

"All the utterances of my mouth are in righteousness; there is nothing crooked or perverted in them. They are all straightforward to him who understands, and right to those who find knowledge. Take my instruction and not silver, and knowledge rather than choicest gold. For wisdom is better than jewels; and all desirable things cannot compare with her."

He pauses and as he does the effect in her is consummate—a raging appetite for something inexpressible, a yearning for purpose, a desire for purity that seems personified in an aching desire for the man sitting in front of her—or is it for Oghel? The two merge into a sea of spinning faces and the feeling of peace and the images of men pull her apart.

"I love those who love me, and those who diligently seek me will find me. Riches and honour are with me, enduring wealth and righteousness. My daughter, keep my words, and treasure my commandments within you. Keep my commandments and live, and cherish and protect my teachings as the pupil of your eye. Bind them on your fingers; write them on the tablets of your heart."

He looks up again, piercing deep within her with his startling eyes.

"Say to wisdom, 'you are my sister,' and call understanding your intimate friend; that they may keep you

from the adulteress, from the foreigner who flatters with her words."

She sits mesmerised by the contrast he has constructed: *"wisdom my sister"* and *"the foreigner who flatters with her words."* From somewhere comes the thought that it is a key to unlock some mystery in her life, a key for the future, for her destiny. She wants to remain with him. To hear more. She imagines not returning to London. And all the time, images of Zach and Oghel and her own image reflected in their characters flash alternately in her drugged imagination.

Chapter 10

March 1979
Kabul, Afghanistan

HE COULD PASS for a beggar but for the noble looks and the eyes. It is the eyes that most people notice first. They draw the unsuspecting in, and many a man afterward said that it was in that first look that they had begun to love him. For some, the experience quickly turns to revulsion; hate, even, but of themselves or of him it is hard to tell. The effect is the same. They become more wicked or they become less so.

He has an arrangement with the owner of the booth, situated at the end of a row of similar stalls occupied by spice merchants in one of Kabul's timeless market streets. On this occasion it is the start of spring and he has been in residence for many cold months. At night he draws down the heavy canvas curtain, ties it in place with a rat-gnawed rope and beds down on the only item of luxury in sight: a faded antique carpet lent by the wife of the cardamom seller in the next stall. A thick coat is his only covering. It seems that the chill of winter is his life-long discipline. On the wall is a faded poster showing a snow-capped mountain against an azure sky with a yellow-flowered meadow in the foreground. A caption at the bottom of the poster identifies the publisher as the Turkish Tourism Authority.

During daylight he prays. Prays and asks questions. Asking questions is his favourite method of teaching. On this occasion, however, the questions are his visitor's.

As with most, the early morning visitor has come bearing sustenance. On a battered brass tray he carries a roughly moulded aluminium pot steaming with strong local coffee, two small glasses, and two honey-soaked pastries wrapped in oil-stained brown paper. Most of them come by word of mouth and the word is passed on that if you want to learn something of the eternal light you need to keep the seer alive.

The deliberate tapping on the side of the tented booth had told the seer that this is not one of the many merchants who have been setting up stalls for a while already. They are his alarm clock, waking him with their shouts and curses and with the thuds of carts knocking into each other and into the corner pole of his booth. From the familiar rhythm of noises he judges that it is still dark outside—about six o'clock, he reckons.

"*Sobh beh'khayr!*"—Good morning! The visitor exclaims cheerfully after the seer has untied one of the ropes and lifted a corner of the makeshift front door. "You are Sufi Isa?" The visitor speaks in passable Farsi, the language of Persia.

"Please," the seer says, making the opening wider and standing aside to welcome him in. A waft of early-morning smells, mixed with frost, enter with him. "You are my first guest of the day and it looks as though we shall break fast together. You may speak English—it is not often in this place that I have a chance to do so."

A studious-looking man stoops to enter. His black hair is cropped short on the sides and back and combed on top into a neat side parting kept in place by a touch of hair cream. He is as tall as the seer and as lean, but considerably younger—in his early thirties, perhaps. There is a touch of Mediterranean or Hispanic in his skin and eyes—or just a tan, perhaps—but it seems to the seer from his accent that he is perhaps an Englishman, or someone who learnt early from a native.

The complex first impression is compounded by the visitor's next action. Breaking into an open smile that exudes a kind of enquiring affection and placing the breakfast on the fruit box that the seer uses as a table, he embraces the holy man like a brother—only it has the awkwardness of an Englishman's embrace.

"I have heard so much about you," the visitor says, standing back and looking at his host inquisitively as if trying to connect what he has heard with the man in front of him.

The seer moves his simple bedding to one side and replaces it with two cushions, embroidered with intricate patterns and colours faded with age, and with the dust of the market. They sit facing each other over the breakfast tray. Steam from the pot rises and twists in wisps, whitened by the crisp air.

"I have come to hear your story" is how the conversation starts.

The breath from the visitor's words blow some of the steam aside as if cutting through a fog that means to separate them.

Picking up the coffee, the seer pours it from a practised height. The steam thickens and the seer holds his hands over the glasses while contemplating the visitor's statement.

"You obviously know something of it already," he parries.

"Enough to seek you out on my travels. I, too, am a scholar, and keen to understand the Sufi *way* that you teach."

"You have the advantage then. I know nothing of you," the seer says with a twinkle in his eye.

The visitor smiles and takes the glass offered, looking into it as though deciding how to use it to his advantage.

"You have asked for my story, however." The seer hurries so as not to embarrass his guest. There are many reasons why his visitors choose not to introduce themselves. "And I shall oblige you happily. If it is pleasing to you, then you may tell me something about yourself later. May I at least know the name of the person who honours me with his company?"

"Marten," says the visitor. "My name is Marten and I'm a professor at a seminary."

Whether it is the name, the affiliation, the eagerness with which it is shared, or some premonition, the seer at that point suddenly knows that his visitor is not all that he might want to seem. In the fragile conditions of Soviet-occupied Afghanistan in the year that followed the invasion, there are plenty of foreigners moving around the country under the cover of darkness. Most are fluent in an Afghani or Pakistani dialect, Farsi, or some other regional language, and are looking for friends amongst the country's many extreme religious groups.

The seer smiles to himself, amused at the thought. The visitor has picked the wrong tent this time.

Chapter 11

May 2000
Bangkok

ISA'S COMPANION HAS not touched the coffee poured for him, nor has he uttered a word. Behind Cassy and Chav the lift rattles past steel doors, reminding them where they are—in an elevator lobby of a condominium complex. The thought weakens the spell and Cassy turns her attention to the silent figure, who has tilted his head as though about to address her. It is an unnerving gesture and she shifts uncomfortably. He watches her movement—like a predator about to strike. His gaze drops several inches from her face and then quickly returns to demand her attention with open disdain.

"The power of my brother's words will soon fade but you must feed from them." It is a deeper voice than Isa's and both smooth and harsh at the same time. His English is more accented.

"I am Nooh and I have my own story—listen, it will help you ponder your own mortality." At the mention of his name, Cassy visibly shudders.

"We Sufis are mortal too—but it is knowing how to perceive and master one's mortality that matters. Few of our movement are married, although we are, according to our custom, permitted to take a wife."

Again, she registers his gaze dropping and dwelling for a moment on her erect nipples.

"Darani, the great Sufi teacher once said, 'the sweetness of undisturbed surrender of the heart which the single man can feel, the married man can never experience.' Are you married, doctor?"

She doesn't answer.

He looks at her as searchingly as his brother, but in a subtly more sinister manner.

"Ahmadi Jam had forty-two children. He too was a very great Sufi. The sorrows and struggles of his family life were punishments for the execution of legally permitted lusts. I wonder if you are troubled by untamed lusts."

Isa's eyes shift to meet his brother's, carrying what might be admonishment.

"All that is permitted," Nooh continues, softening his tone a fraction, "is not always healthy for the body or soul. It is better to cut off a hand than to sin at its behest."

His words are delivered to threaten.

"Our animal instincts are not evil—it is the human's failure to get acquainted with that part of him that is *more* than an animal that is truly evil. Consider this fable, doctor."

He raises two hands, palms upward as if holding out something for Cassy to take.

"A teacher at a religious school in Karachi was convicted concerning the moral needs of his fifteen-year-olds. The wickedness of the big city had captured the hearts and affections of some already, and he felt it his duty to educate them about adult life rather than to leave them to the vagaries of myth or carnal experimentation. He asked a Sufi he knew to help administer the sex lesson. The Sufi was a modernist—that is why he had been thought suitable—and kept a diary. Or at least his wife kept it for him; for you see, marriage is no different in mystical circles."

The change in style leaves Cassy confused—she recognises it as a tactic used by cults to disorientate new recruits.

"Being a man who was not at peace with his mortal body and from whom self-righteousness had not yet been completely expunged—taking oneself too seriously is the failing of most spiritual teachers—he wrote in his diary, 'Talking to Majdud's boys about camel-racing.' Some time after the lesson, the teacher's wife met the Sufi's wife at the local market and said, 'I hear that the talk went very well.'

'Yes,' said the Sufi's wife, 'I can't understand why Majdud asked my husband to speak on the subject—he knows nothing at all about it. As far as I know he's only done it three times. On the first occasion he was violently sick. On the second his nerve failed him and on the third he fell off and broke his wrist.'"

With that, the storyteller's face crumples and with a thump of his knee, he lets out a long wheezy guffaw. Cassy is completely thrown and doesn't know how to react. Glancing at Chav, she can see from his expression that he hasn't a clue what is going on. If she is mystified, he is utterly lost. Then she remembers what Marten had said about the Naqshabandiyya Sufi Order.

They sometimes teach using crude jokes.

Lunging for an attack, Nooh, suddenly serious again, snaps: "Why do you laugh inside? Why is such a tale funny? It is because men and women live awkwardly with their animal bodies. They mate like animals but are made spiritually like God. The spirit lives awkwardly with the organism. When the spirit is faced with the base animal it reacts with repulsion and with laughter. The same is true of *death*, doctor."

He lingers on the word.

"Mirth generated by stories of men behaving as animals shows that even the least enlightened man is more than an animal. Our lack of ease with death is also evidence of the immortality we are created for."

This time it is a picture of the mutilated Professor Gunther that appears before Cassy, and with it the images of Zach and Oghel return, revolving slowly in a psychedelic carousel, orbiting out of control somewhere inside her destabilised mind.

"You are made in the image of the Divine. What images preoccupy you now, I wonder? I do not think they are of God."

The intensity of the attack is suddenly broken when the young man in Nike shorts opens one of the apartment doors and asks something in a guttural language that is not Thai.

Cassy takes the chance to recover her wits.

A well-practised double act—de rigeur *in a brainwashing sequence. How do they do the thing with the images? Do they really know something about my private life? "Wisdom, my sister" and "the foreigner who flatters with her words."*

The graphic choice has firmly lodged in her mind and she searches for some meaning in it.

Isa is replying to the boy in Nike shorts, who leaves, closing the door again, and then Isa takes over. "He is a young companion who has been with us just two years." His explanation is apologetic. "We try to preserve a free spirit and to tend it carefully—sometimes it is a longer route than crushing the spirit. Many of the *Ways* within Sufism—as with the rules of many other religions—crush the freedom that is God's gift. It is a risky way that lets freedom blossom, guided forward only by the caresses of divine love and a lover's discipline. But I enjoy risks, my friend. How about you?"

Cassy has had enough. She needs to leave. But before she has a chance to think how to make an exit, Isa is inviting her with bowed head and hands outstretched: "And now you must have *your* say. No doubt you came here with questions of your own. It would be rude of me to let you go without asking them. So please..."

A rush of adrenaline comes to her aid and she goes for it.

"Okay," she says, much too defiantly, concentrating hard to think and wiping away sweat that is blurring her vision.

"For a start—" She finds her composure, rubs her hands once along her folded legs to reassure herself, and slows her speech down to emphasise her rationality.

"Explain in simple terms what exactly you mean by saying you planned to invite me here."

There, back on track. A perfectly reasonable question after the way you and your bastard brother laid into me.

But Cassy does not get what she wants. "I cannot answer that, Dr. Cassy, I am afraid," Isa is saying apologetically, but with a finality that leaves her nowhere else to go. "Insha'Allah you will discover an answer in good time."

There is a silence as he waits for the next question. Cassy's battered brain is wracking itself for a way of turning the interview around.

"How about telling me something about your Order, then?" she blurts out like a schoolgirl who isn't getting her way. And in an instinctive bid to salvage some pride, adds, "Where's the third Sufi brother?"

It works.

Isa and Nooh look at each other and then at Cassy, Isa with amusement in his eyes and Nooh frowning at the floor.

"You already know something about us, I see," Isa says. "This is not surprising, I suppose, for someone who has sought us out in our exile hideaway. Since I cannot yet explain why and how I became acquainted with you, I will not do you the injustice of asking how and why you became acquainted with me. Let us merely assume that the hand of God is in it for both of us. But if it would be of interest, I will happily tell you how the Noah Brotherhood came to be. It is an unusual name for a Sufi movement but, as you will see, we are unusual Sufis and a descriptive name is most fitting. Some would say we are not true Sufis—but that has been a suffering we have had to bear. Sufism is where we started; perhaps it is not where we will end up. I seek only to live within the divine love and by my life and instruction lead others there too. You may not properly call us an Order—that implies too much. We are a loose companionship, held together by..." And he pauses thoughtfully. "By blood ties."

"That would be of great interest," Cassy says, feeling more comfortable with the line of conversation and passing on her reassurance to Chav with suitable body language.

"Many years ago, three brothers spent some months in the mountains of eastern Turkey with an elderly and secretive Sufi named Uthman Khidr."

There is a rhythm to his words, as though he has told the story many times. The narrator's tone is back but the objective subject matter feels safer to Cassy.

"I was fifteen years of age, my brother Nooh—it is the Persian for Noah—was sixteen and my younger brother Odam just twelve. Odam is Persian for Adam. Uthman read into our internment something of great significance and we remained with him in his remote mountain abode for the following winter and much of the spring. They were cold months, very cold, but the deprivation was our education. He taught us many things that we had not learnt in the mosque and many things that brought to life beloved passages from the Koran. He introduced us to the writings of mystics from other faiths—early Christian mystics and Hindu Brahman—many of whom he regarded as fellow embracers of the divine lover. Do you know much about Sufi history, Dr. Cassy? Uthman was the name of an eighteenth-century teacher who sought tutelage at the tomb of a dead Sufi master. Our tutor followed in the practices of his earlier namesake."

"A Uwaysi?" Cassy ventures.

"*So.* You are read in the history of Islam, as well as in science. This is most commendable. A willingness to be bound by the spiritual as well as the physical laws of the universe is the mark of truly great men and women of science—let us hope that you are one of them."

It is the only thing he has given away.

He knows I am a scientist. It matters to him somehow.

"Uthman had found a Way to a marvellous peace but lived under many tortuous contradictions. This has been our inheritance too," he says with a resigned smile to Nooh.

"Why the *Noah* Brotherhood?" Cassy asks.

"There is more than a single answer to this question—you shall discover its deeper significance before long. For now, let us say that we received our spiritual calling in the mountainous region believed by some to be the resting place of Nooh's Ark."

Now we're getting somewhere.

Cassy is reassured by her investigative persona kicking in like the turbo in her black RS.

"Although Uthman spent many hours warning us of the dangers of the Uwaysi ways, he became increasingly sure that this was to be our destiny too. Towards the end of our stay, we trekked for four days to the top of a glacier where we spent a night, a day, and another night in meditation. We had neither adequate shelter nor food, and unusually ferocious winter conditions had settled upon the region. We might have died in the bitter cold but for heavenly warmth that filled our spirits. It was the culmination of our internship—a graduating ceremony during which we flew into the arms of the divine spirit with a depth and intimacy we had not known before. We were drunk with the caresses of Supreme Love—and ice and time melted into one glorious defining moment. We barely survived the return journey. I suffered frostbite but had to carry Odam, who was not physically strong, for a whole day. When we had recovered, Uthman revealed what he himself had seen. It was a vision of a mighty angel, sheltering us from the icy winds with a small scroll that contained words of great power. The words were prophetic words and had significance for each of our lives. They were words about the Garden and the start of civilisation and about the final judgement and the end of civilisation. We were to change our names and each make a pilgrimage to a separate location. The sense of destiny and purpose lay heavily upon us."

His eyes close and he draws a slow and deep breath, feeding on a distant memory.

NOAH'S ART 113

"And the names?" Cassy says. "These are the ones you have introduced yourselves by?"

"Yes. Odam, Nooh, and Isa—three great prophets revered by Muslims. Adam, father of the human race and the first to drink of the divine spirit of love. Noah, father of all civilisations after the *First Judgement*—the *great Flood*. Noah—Ark-builder and lover of God. And Isa of the gospel, lover of light and love, one day to return to earth as judge."

"Muslims believe that?"

"Of course. It may be that Muslims have a keener anticipation of the second coming of Jesus than many who call themselves Christian. In our vision, the angel sent us out to learn from these our appointed mentors. Uthman's last instruction to us was to travel in search of the spirit of our prophet instructor and to abide in its presence. The Uwaysi *way* is to *abide* in the spirit of a great Sufi or prophet until the process of annihilation has been completed. Despite his misgivings, Uthman knew no other."

"Where did you go?" Cassy asks, as drawn now by the narrative as she had been by the preaching spell.

"Through Uthman's vision we were instructed to start at the closest location to Paradise—the Garden that gave birth to man. This was to be the place for Odam's abiding. We were to join him and then move on. We went to the traditional birthplace of humanity—the marshlands in southern Iraq where the great Euphrates and Tigris rivers spill silt into the Persian Gulf. There we spent many months together, each receiving secret dreams, parts of which we have kept even from each other to this day. Nooh travelled on to Mount Judi in southern Turkey—where Muslims believe Noah's Ark to have rested. I made my way to the holy city of Jerusalem. We remained at these places for a whole year before returning to our father's home."

Two trivial thoughts cross Cassy's mind.

"How does a trainee Uwaysi keep himself fed and sheltered for a year in a foreign country?" she asks.

He smiles at the practical diversion of a woman. "I could give you a pious answer to that, Dr. Cassy, but in truth, our father, peace be upon him, was a wealthy man."

"And if you graduated into Sufism in your teens," she continues, strengthened by the re-appearance of the forensic professional in her, "where did you learn your excellent English?"

It is carefully formed with an ease that shows both formal training and regular use.

"We were young, yes, but what I have described was only our initiation—the beginning. After this we went to study at university, all taking our bachelor's degrees in Tehran—being taught mostly in the medium of English. In addition, my father had hired a series of English tutors for us from early childhood. We went on to take further studies, Odam in Baghdad, Nooh at the University of Tabriz in Northern Iran, and I at the American University of Cairo."

"And then came back together to start your Order?"

"It was in 1962—after the month of fasting. By the end of the fast we all knew that the time had come. We each had developed our individual communities through our part-time travelling and teaching but there was much more to come. We resigned our positions—we were all working by then—and formed a community. Before long, others joined us and our work began to grow rapidly."

Cassy was fascinated at the insight he was giving her and thought of Marten's boyish enthusiasm in his subject.

Why is he telling me all this?

"In the early days we travelled all over the Muslim world, separately and together, not seeking influence or followers but unable to prevent either. When I spoke, it would not be uncommon for crowds of hundreds to receive new spiritual life—fathers and grandfathers weeping, calling for mercy with loud and anguished groans. This was not engineered nor cherished since it brought great opposition and hatred. Seekers after our Way would seek us out at night. Peasants would travel days to beg me return to their village. I travelled tens of thousands of miles, leaving nothing behind but hunger for purity—and suffering, amongst those brave enough to experiment with the Divine Light."

Cassy flinches as the intense emotional impact of his earlier monologue momentarily returns. She can believe his account.

"It was mainly the poor who received us—at least in the early days."

He pauses and she notices another exchange of looks with his brother.

So, Odam was corrupted by the patronage of the rich.

"By the early 1970's the three of us had settled in Northern Iran—a large house in Tabriz was made available by an old friend of Nooh's from university. Then after 1979 the Revolutionary Guards hounded us with other minorities over the border. Some of our companions were sent here to Bangkok at that time. I crossed the border into Northern Iraq, where I stayed until Sadaam's dreadful offensive against the Kurds. The United Nations brought us to Thailand in 1994."

She is watching his face carefully, memorising the details of his account and as he says *us*, she notices a hint of a nod towards Noah, as though the move to Thailand might have excluded the third brother.

"What happened to Odam?" she asks.

"Odam?" he looks at her approvingly. "Odam was already here—resettled some years earlier. He had been separated from the rest of us at the time of Khomeini's purge, and for a long time we believed Odam to be dead. It was a bloody purge. But he had escaped and made his way to the countries of North Africa. He was not tolerated in Egypt, however, and moved back to Iran. When a new wave of persecution came, the United Nations brought him here to Bangkok. Unlike the rest of us, however, he did not stay long. Odam is very different—he has many wealthy friends.

The Moroccans gave him citizenship. He comes and goes as he needs."

So Adam is not a refugee. It seems to Cassy to be significant.

"Where is he now?"

"When Odam visits Thailand, he spends his time in Surat Thani in the south, near his followers on the Malaysian border."

There is a sharp intake of breath from his brother at the mention of the town.

A secret divulged—why?

"I plan to visit the south myself soon," Isa continues, ignoring his brother's remonstration. "In two weeks I shall begin my travels. There are many with hunger in that part of this gentle country. I shall spend a month or two, maybe three, wandering from village to village encouraging those who follow our Way and rescuing those who are falling prey to the violence."

The Muslim insurgency? Or his brother's activities? Or are they one and the same?

"And the other Bangkok house?" Cassy asks, suddenly remembering the other base Chav had located across the Chaoprya River. Chav gives an imperceptible shake of the head, which she takes as a signal that he doesn't want to be drawn into the conversation.

"You know a lot, Dr. Cassy. That one is for the women—it is on the other side of this city."

Isa looks at the clock on the wall and says, "And now my friends...." At this he turns and bows his head graciously to Chav. "It is time for me to help in the care of the weakened brothers."

He notices her blank look.

"Six are nearing the end of their forty-day fast. It is time to wash and to turn them."

So that's it—the smell of bed-ridden, frail bodies, the smell of near-death.

Nodding to Chav, Cassy struggles to her feet, holding her skirt as modestly as she can. She looks around the corridor room five floors up and at the poster of the snow-capped mountain in Turkey.

Mount Judi.

"You like mountains," she says, carefully smoothing her clothes. He smiles as though pleased she has noticed.

"This is Mount Klyuchevskaya Sopke in Siberia," he explains, pointing at the snow-clad volcanoes. "The Kamtchatka peninsula is not unlike your Britain for size and latitude, but a much more hostile country, as you see."

It sounds to Cassy as though he is familiar with both places.

"And the poster is Mount Judi?" she suggests.

"You would make a good investigator, Dr. Cassy," he says, a hint of a question written into his broad smile.

"And this one—the town in the foothills of the mountains?"

"That, my friend, is in the Republic of Georgia, and that is the Ararat range that you see in the distance. Some of our brothers live there. The town is called Akhalkalaki."

As soon as he mentions it Cassy knows she has seen the name written down very recently.

It takes a split second to realise that it had been on the passenger list of the fated American International Airways flight to Bombay. One of the dead had come from the same small town. Instantly she realises the danger they are in.

She has her first result for Nigel Buchanan—a direct connection between the air disaster and the mystical Noah Brotherhood.

Chapter 12

AS THEY DESCEND the elevator, somewhere in the back of Cassy's mind the town of Akhalkalaki is jogging a deeper and more distant memory.

Something to do with Russian history.

There are doors to three apartments facing the lift as they exit to the ground floor lobby. The two to the front of the building seem to be used as offices and the door to one stands open as they step out of the lift. Above the door, a white Perspex sign with green and red lettering announces *East West Ecumenical Children's Aid Foundation*. Above it is a logo made up of the letters EWE-CAF, and under the letters, some Arabic script.

As Chav holds the door open for Cassy, a brute of a man with a bald head, heavy brows, and angry eyes barges through, knocking Chav off his balance. He is shouting something angrily to someone behind him, and then a young Thai man appears, possibly still in his teens, with bony but muscular arms and carrying a stack of brown cardboard boxes tilted against his chest and face. The big man is swinging a leather attaché case in each hand crossly as he brushes past Cassy and disappears into the EWE-CAF office, followed by the Thai. They are speaking Russian.

Chav shrugs silently at Cass as though it happens to him every day, but Cassy is looking beyond the doorway the two men have just passed through.

"Hold on a minute," she mouths, moving quickly to the office's floor-to-ceiling glass frontage and attempting to peer through the stick-on privacy film, which is peeled off in places.

"Disappeared," she mouths again, with a gesture of puzzlement.

Cautiously she pokes her head through the open door and steps inside to an empty office, sparsely furnished with two glass-topped desks with only a calendar and a vase of grubby silk orchids on each. A filing cabinet lies in one corner, and next to it a rattan sofa. Above the sofa is an assortment of posters and photos. A door is ajar behind one of the desks, through which comes the sound of someone shifting heavy boxes and someone speaking Russian on a phone.

Cassy makes a quick three-sixty-degree appraisal of the room. It is easy to see from the posters and photos what the foundation does. One appeals on behalf of children orphaned in recent flooding somewhere in South Asia. Another has the name of an orphanage in Uzbekistan with photos of children playing in a dusty compound. One is a montage of head and shoulder portraits of individual children with their names and nationalities written underneath in English. At the top of the poster are the words "EWE-CAF—Sponsoring Needy Children."

"Have you an appointment?"

Shit, where did he come from?

Cassy spins round to be confronted with a tall man, as thin as a rake, with thick black hair receding around a pale face dominated by black plastic glasses. The voice is as soft as a child's but as cold as ice, and with a curt German accent.

"Er, no, I'm sorry. I don't. I thought it was a travel agency."

"I am afraid there are no travel agencies in the compound," he says, looking her in the eyes and assuming what might be meant as a smile but which exudes no warmth at all. "But there are one or two out on the street as you leave the compound. We are an aid agency, as you can see…"

"I've not noticed you here before," she extemporizes. "You've recently set up office?"

"EWE-CAF has a long and respected history in the region," he replies with a hint of rebuke. "EWE-CAF is expanding to develop the work amongst street children in Cambodia."

"I wish you well—it sounds a good work," Cassy says, moving to the door under a sudden urge to get out of the place. Before he can respond she has backed out into the lobby and run outside to find Chav revving up his motorbike. The tabloid reporter has moved his Honda into position and has been watching the door with his hand on the throttle. She jumps on, grabbing hold of his waist, and whispers loudly in his ear, "Out of the compound and park up on the street opposite with the other bikes!"

"What going on, Adjan Cassy?" Chav asks over his shoulder after he has found a gap in the line of bikes and killed the engine. "I did not like that place. How the Sufis know you in town?"

"I had a bloody strange feeling back there."

"Sufi put spell on you. But I guard you. I have gun, see here." And he reaches for Cassy's hand and leads it inside his open jacket.

I love you, Chav.

"No, I meant the EWE-CAF place. I want to check out the Russian bear."

"Which Russian bar?"

"Russian *bear*—the one who almost knocked you over."

"Sure," Chav shrugs as he lights up a cigarette, used to taking such matters in his stride. "I go ask guards what they know."

Ten minutes later he is back, jumping on the bike and kicking the engine into life.

"They coming now—guard say they only be in building short while."

"How frequently?" Cassy shouts in his ear.

"Two times in week," he shouts back.

Fifteen minutes later Chav and Cassy are racing through the Bangkok streets in pursuit of a long wheelbase red pickup with a double-row blacked-out cab.

"Four cars ahead," Cassy shouts directly in Chav's ear as they turn a corner heading for an expressway ramp.

"We keep him now—no many cars use new road. Toll too much moneys," Chav shouts without turning his head. "What we do next?"

There is a screech in front as the pickup pulls away from the tollbooth.

"See where they stay, drive on," she shouts as they pull away from the next booth and join three other bikes.

"See then drive on," Cassy repeats for her own benefit, reaching over Chav's shoulder and into his jacket to feel the gun again.

It is almost an hour before the pickup pulls to a stop outside a small row of shop-houses somewhere in Bangkok's eastern suburbs.

Chav has stopped a good distance away and parked up in the driveway to a row of townhouses.

"Jay Forbes territory," Cassy says to Chav, who nods knowingly while watching the stationary pickup. No one has got out of it yet.

A few years ago Cassy had met an Australian named Jay Forbes when spending three summer weeks brushing up her Thai at a Bangkok language school. He had been a sad individual in his late forties who had sold up his sweet shop in Deptford, South London to move to Bangkok, and it wasn't hard to guess what kind of investment opportunity he was looking for out here. Neither was it hard to imagine why he might have uprooted from London or the string of similar moves that doubtless made up his life story. Cassy had forgotten about him until she had read in a London paper recently that a Deptford man with the same name had been killed in a Bangkok video shop. A visored gunman had followed him in, shot him point blank through the back of the head, and driven off. It would have been on a similar street: the pickup is parked outside a shop with a bright orange fascia saying Western Rentals. Next door a small green sign advertises a VD clinic and next to that a yellow sign that says "Gulf Videos."

The pickup's front passenger door flies open, and the Russian jumps out and makes straight for the office next to Gulf Videos. He produces a key, fumbles with the lock for a moment, and then disappears inside. After several minutes he reappears and signals to the car. To Cassy's surprise, it is not the Thai young man who steps out of the rear door but a woman. Even at a distance, Cassy can see that she has a gaunt face, unstyled hair, and clothes that are ill-fitted. She reaches inside the car and retrieves a bag, which she places on the pavement. Then she reaches further in and emerges, tightly holding a young child.

***

The following morning Cassy wakes late and pads down to the Grand Italian's poolside for breakfast, four floors above the Bangkok traffic. She has been up half the night drinking Tie Guan Yin tea and Thai whisky with Chavalit and has a hangover.

Lying back on a plastic lounger and surrounded by tropical plants in giant glazed planters, she falls asleep before her breakfast comes and is woken by the sound of voices—someone is asking her to sign and there is laughter in the background. It is the start of the rainy season and light clouds filter a fierce tropical sun. A respectable-looking Middle Eastern gentleman and his young Thai escort are arranging towels on two loungers on the other side of the pool. The laughter is coming from four men and four girls sitting around a table at the other end of the sun deck, and Cassy knows immediately from their accents who they must be. The team of police from the north of England have obviously brought their partners along for the ride. They are no doubt staying at the Grand Italian to check out the opposition.

Signing for the food and dismissing the waiter with a large tip, she tears off a blank bit of the receipt and writes the address of Gulf Videos with the words "check it out."

Then, as an afterthought, she writes "cover blown, boys—the haircuts give you away." She will put it in an envelope addressed to "the British Police" and leave it somewhere in the hotel lobby—a little risky, but she is in that sort of mood.

***

Later in the morning, leaving her bag with a cluster of doormen sporting faded green velvet suits that have seen better days, Cassy makes her way to reception to check out.

"You have visitor, madam," the receptionist says with a pleasant smile. "He insist you not disturb—he wait in lounge all morning."

Surprised, she settles up, returns the heavy brass key fob, and makes her way towards the lounge. The main waiting area is empty so she makes her way through a panelled corridor that leads to little-used private suites and other more discrete meeting areas. She finds him seated, book in hand, on an ancient Chesterfield tucked into a corner and partially hidden by a giant brass gong that once marked the entrance to a Chinese banqueting hall in the days when the hotel had four restaurants. She sits down next to him without turning to face him.

"You've been here all morning?"

"I am enjoying the solitude—it gets crowded in our little apartment."

"I didn't know whether you would come."

"I had no intention of interrupting your morning—travelling days are always too hectic. Perhaps you will allow me the privilege of riding with you to the airport—we can talk in the taxi. I have one waiting."

She wants to say no but finds herself following him out to the forecourt.

"After many years, Dr. Cassy, a puzzle is starting to make sense."

There is no preamble—he starts as soon as they turn out of the hotel concourse, speaking in a lowered voice and with a measured efficiency. He is altogether more urgent than he had been in the condo, but also easier and less aloof. Cassy has the feeling that he plans to share something of personal importance to him.

"The picture is not complete but the form is taking shape. I will need your help to finish it. Prophecies given to me long ago are coming to pass, dreams are finding form—a momentum is picking up."

He grabs Cassy's wrist gently but firmly. "The great Day of Judgement is not far off."

The cult leader line somehow sounds reasonable from his lips.

"A secret was entrusted to me in the marshes of Mesopotamia many years ago. The time has come. Are you a believer in the Biblical accounts of antiquity, Dr. Cassy?"

"Which ones in particular?"

"A common ancestry for the human race, a birthplace for humanity, an earlier civilisation than those documented by archaeological science, a worldwide deluge?"

"Adam and Eve and Noah? I'm agnostic," she says flatly. "I read a Scientific American article that showed we're all pretty much descended from the same stock of a hundred and fifty people migrating out of Africa, and I've looked at plenty of Noah's Ark evidence. But I'm still agnostic."

"In that case," he says, "it is well that we meet now. There will be time to prepare."

Instead of anger, Cassy feels herself slipping into a kind of complicity, as though at sometime during yesterday's conversation she had, without remembering, consented to an-as-of-yet-undisclosed purpose and plan.

I am a scientist and this is an experiment, she says to herself, rationalising her recklessness.

"I shall give you part of a puzzle and then leave you to do what you have to do, Dr. Cassy. Do not forget *'wisdom, your sister'*—she will aid if you ask her."

A pang of the same hunger returns as he repeats the mantra. This time, though, Cassy thinks she recognises it not from the encounter in the Sufi's apartment but from talking to someone else.

Oghel. I have something like this feeling in the presence of Oghel.

They are looking out at stationary traffic. The taxi is stuck at a crossroads and the lights have changed three times without a car moving in any direction. She has still not looked him in the eye.

Can hypnosis work without eye contact?

"Good," she says. "I like puzzles."

"Very well, then. Consider this. The prophet Adam walked in the garden Paradise with God and knew the Divine Love in a way that no one else has since. My brothers and I travelled to Paradise to be mentored by Adam's spirit and lived in the hut of a Marsh Arab, spending many days and nights in silence. When my own dream came, it was of an ancient man, noble in appearance and striding through ancient forests. In the distance were mountains higher than you could imagine, rising like the sky itself towards the roof of the world. The noble stopped to speak to me by a mighty waterfall, too high to see the top, and told me these things. 'Adam's Eden is not where you seek,' he said. 'It is further south—much further. I am a Sumerian and a King amongst Sumerians.'"

Cassy says nothing.

"The Sumerians were the mighty race that lived in ancient Iraq, appearing from nowhere in the archaeological record and bringing with them the art of writing, architecture, mathematics, and the legal principles that govern the modern states of our world today," he says, as if confiding a secret. "They preceded the great Babylonian and Assyrian empires of the Middle East and are the fathers of civilisation itself."

"A mystery race like the Fair People of Atlantis," she says, fighting dizziness and still looking straight ahead.

"The kingly figure in my dream gave me four Signs to aid my search for Paradise. The first was the *Story of Gilgamesh*; the second was the *List of Kings*; the third, *Lord Arrata*; and the fourth, the *March of Lugal Zagesi*—each a fragment of myth or history from the Sumerian tradition. Gilgamesh was the most famous of the Sumerian kings and in the poem that carries his name he meets Noah or Ziusudra or Xisuthras—and learns about the flood. The finest record of the poem is in your British Museum, Dr. Cassy—it would repay you to make a visit to that great institution."

She memorised all the names. *When were you in London?*

"In my vision, the Sumerian King gave me a commission:

'Many years from now,' he said, *'you will come across a Fifth and Final Sign. From the Four Signs I am now giving you, you will know where Paradise is by that time. The Fifth Sign will be your confirmation. Not long after the Final Sign, the End will come. You will become a warning of this time. Do not seek the sign—it will seek you. You cannot understand it on your own—seek help. When you have found Paradise warn the World.'*

In my dream the king's words filled the forest, drowning the waterfall and rebounding from the mighty mountains until they filled the whole earth."

"And I am to help you read the runes of the fifth sign?" Cassy ventures.

"This is my belief."

"Might I know what the final sign is?"

"All is not yet in place—it will not be long now."

"And the Sumerian myths—the first four signs?" she asks.

"They are not important anymore. They were signs for me, but perhaps they will amuse you. I do not think they are important for your part in this story. I could tell you of them—but I think you may find your own search rewarding. You are a talented researcher, Dr. Cassy—let us play a game and see what you can discern before we meet again."

"We shall meet again?"

"*From everlasting I, wisdom was established, from the beginning, from the earliest times of the earth. When there were no oceans I was brought forth, when there were no springs abounding with water. Before the mountains had settled, before the hills, I was brought forth. While he had not yet made the earth and the fields, nor the soil. When he established the clouds and the sky I was there. When he filled up the oceans, creating the horizon between sea and sky. When he stopped the rains of the great deluge and fixed the springs of the deep so that the seas stopped spreading, and the boundary of the oceans was set, so the water should not transgress his command when he marked out the foundations of the earth. During the great upheavals, I wisdom was beside him as a master workman; and I was daily his delight.*"

He stops and in the back of a Bangkok taxi Cassy can hear nothing but the welling of ocean waves and sense nothing but a drenching peace. She either can't move or doesn't want to. She doesn't know whether it is a form of sensuousness or purity.

"I see you are already enjoying her embrace, my friend. This is a good sign. She is everything—your love for her will deepen until you know there is nothing else worth living for. Her whispers are always fresh and her insights ever full of surprises. Now, if I am right, she wishes to share secrets with us—both of us. Let us determine to listen carefully."

Cassy comes to just in time to see the car in front swerve to a screeching halt. Instinctively she slams her foot on the floor, but the driver has got there first, coming to a stop with an inch to spare. There are shouts outside and baskets on the carriageway. An overloaded truck had spilled its cargo. Isa's flow is uninterrupted.

"There is something else you should know, Dr. Cassy."

"Yes?" She turns to face him for the first time.

"I have enemies as well as friends—you need to know this. Even within the Noah Brotherhood."

"Within your family?"

He raises both eyebrows.

"*Enemy* is not quite the appropriate term but you are perceptive. I have already told you that our *Way* is full of contradictions. These are getting greater all the time and I wonder where they will lead. Three great tensions afflict me my friend. The first is my life's calling."

Which is what exactly, I wonder?

"Sometimes it is more than I can bear. The second is my own waywardness."

"Your waywardness?"—*You who make others feel so wayward.*

"In truth, I am a poor Muslim. From the time of my first spiritual initiation I have been unable to keep my spirit from soaring, freely and boldly. Religious laws and rules can no longer tether it—it would die within me. Some acts of religious devotion help the spirit soar farther, but they are no longer my master; they serve the emancipated spirit. If this consigns me to Hell, then so be it. Then perhaps the religious teacher's Hell is not what it is made out to be." He pauses for a long moment.

"And the third tension?" Cassy asks, the airport slip road from the highway coming into view.

"Odam," he says without hesitation as though this is a revelation he has been leading up to. "Odam, I believe, has already been consigned to Hell."

Cassy is shocked.

Why should he be so frank about his own brother to a total stranger?

"Odam has always been different from Noah and I—since his time in Bagdad. It never mattered too much—until recent years…"

"Since his time in North Africa?" Cassy asks. "Corrupted by riches and power?"

"You are indeed perceptive."

"Those are strong words," she says. "Consigned to Hell. Why tell me?"

They pull up at the international departures building and Isa takes Cassy's hand with both of his and says with firm but almost tender resignation: "*'One day he will rise to extinguish the light—brother against brother.'* Our fragile unity, Dr. Cassy, has been rocked by an unfortunate event. I fear that it threatens the very existence of the Noah Brotherhood. Something precious has been taken that belongs to another, and Adam may have gone too far in his engagement with ungodly men."

It sounds ominously to Cassy like an admission that the cult was involved in the air disaster.

They are standing side by side as the taxi driver retrieves her suitcase from the car, and it seems inappropriate to respond to Isa's revelation. Instead Cassy asks a question she has been reserving for the appropriate moment.

"I'll tell you why I came to find you in Bangkok."

He has been about to lift her suitcase onto a trolley but stops without looking up.

"After your cryptic email introduction, I had your website diagnosed and did a bit of reading on Sufis and Noah's Ark. There's no other group in the world with quite the same profile. I don't like to turn up to meetings without first doing a bit of background research. You planned to meet me at Queen Boudicca's camp in a London forest—ancient encampment of an army that once tried to defeat decadent Greco-Roman based civilisation? I guess the place is significant to your movement. Are you planning to make the journey yourself, or is it to be one of your lieutenants? It turns out I'm one step ahead of you."

He looks up, fixing intense and searching eyes on hers.

"Dr. Cassy, if you received an introduction to the Noah Brotherhood, you have my assurance that it was not from Brother Isa."

Chapter 13

May 2000
London's East End

DAI ON THE Fringe is a most unusual little hairdressing salon located along the seedy Whitechapel Road in London's East End. Dai, pronounced *die*, is the colloquial diminutive for David in Welsh, and David daVinci is as Welsh as they come. He has the rich sonancy and deep lilt that, to other natives of the South Wales industrial valleys, marks out a man from the mining town of Merthyr Tydfil. He is standing over Cassy, doing what his name advertises. From inside the shop the name reads backwards in green, white, and red stained glass, and he has recently hung underneath, in a pink neon-lit scripted sign, the word "*international*." This is to honour his long time friend and associate Rashid whom he has just made a *full* partner after twenty-five years of loyal service and close companionship. They are now a trio since a third *artiste*, the deaf and dumb Hamid, has just arrived from a top salon in Tirana, Albania. David met Rashid all those years ago when hairdressing in Tangier on an extended visit to the marijuana-producing Rif Mountain region and had brought him back to London. Dai's great-grandfather was a Mediterranean immigrant himself at the start of the twentieth century. He arrived in the Welsh port of Cardiff with a shipload of Italian piazza floor tiles—a job-lot for the Marquis of Bute and other landowners who were busy building rows of identical terraced houses on their estates to accommodate the flow of coal and steel workers pouring into South Wales from all over the world. His grandfather and father had become miners, and like many other miners' sons of Italian descent in the South Wales valleys, David went into hairdressing.

Dai the hair, however, is also *Dai the existentialist*. And by a chance conversation he once had with a customer who turned out to be an undercover police officer, he has also become *Dai the informer*.

A Detective Inspector friend at Scotland Yard recommended him to Cassy in a confidential conversation after work one day. Of late, Dai has also turned his hand, at first somewhat unwillingly, but evermore enthusiastically, to entrepreneurism.

Back in the early seventies when he first set up in East London he had opened a reading-room in the underused floor above the salon. There, every Tuesday and Sunday night a mixed bag of like-minded thinkers would discuss chapters from Timothy Leary, Arthur Koestler, Frantz Fanon, Albert Camus, Sartre, and Nietzsche. Remarkably, the tradition survived the eighties and just when the last of the old hippies might have hung up their beads, a whole new generation of free-thinkers had resurrected Dai's Upper Room Experience. This time, however, the whole thing is a self-conscious parody—the arguments are less intense, but it is much more fun. They drink Rolling Rock lager from bottles rather than rolling joints and sometimes a nightclub-style queue forms up the street as far as the launderette. The idea of a sixties philosophy-themed salon with do-it-yourself live entertainment—a kind of thinking man's karaoke—had been noticed and featured in several magazines and newspapers, including short pieces in *Newsweek* and the *Los Angeles Times*. The result: a financial backer and two new branches—in trendy Islington and less-trendy Lewisham. He has hired appropriate staff and named the new shops *Dai Too* and *Dai Free*. Cassy had suggested he called his next one *Dai For?*, but he'd already thought of it.

Dai maintains contact with many of the alternative types who have passed through his doors over the years, and in this way is a mine of information about a remarkable variety of fringe groups. Among his old friends are animal rights saboteurs, environmental warriors, disarmament campaigners, anti-globalisation activists, anarchists, and a whole lot more. There are, of course, an equal number who have gone straight, among whom are several university professors, a wealthy political lobbyist, an American Congresswoman who graduated from the London School of Economics in the sixties, and at least two Members of Parliament, one of whom is about to be promoted to the cabinet.

Rashid is filling a pot of tea and they are in conversational mood. Cassy wonders what led such an unlikely couple to become such eager allies of the police establishment.

The conspiratorial excitement must outweigh any sense of morality—they are diehard existentialists, after all.

Their relationship might have helped too—certainly it has made Rashid something of an outcast from mainstream Arabic-speaking London society. For whatever reason, they are by all accounts a mine of information about life among their unusual clients and their clients' families, friends, and enemies.

"Sorry, Inspector Cassandra, darling," Dai says. "There's nothing out there on them at all. *Silencia.*"

On her previous visit Cassy had handed Rashid a piece of paper with a few scribbled details and asked them to see what they could pick up on some Iraqis recently arrived in East London. She had also asked about sectarian groups interested in the Noah's Ark myth, judgement, or anything they might think related.

"Hardly surprising, I suppose," she says.

"Very few keep themselves completely to themselves," Dai says, picking up a pair of surgical-like scissors, examining them with professional scrutiny and replacing them.

Rashid joins in, in a crossover Moroccan-Cockney accent. "You know how it is with efnic communities— difficault to hide. You don't have to show up to gaverings for people to know all about ya. They find a category and box ya in it."

You would know a lot about that, Rashid, I'm guessing.

She examines the poster on the wall entitled *Grapefruit* and advertising a one-time public reading session of Yoko Ono's single line poems. "Light a match and watch it till it goes out."

A short evening.

The poster next to it seems to sum up Dai even better. It advertises a performance of Samuel Beckett's *Breath*—the thirty-second play with no actors, dialogue, or props apart from a pile of rubbish. The futile gasp of human life between birth and death—*Die on the fringe*.

Dai gives his new creation a final few precision pats and preens, smiles at himself in the mirror then proceeds to remove the bib from Cassy's shoulders and the nylon cape printed with orange tulips on black. As he takes her hand to help her out of the seat, she touches cheeks in a thank-you gesture and says: "I'll pop in again next week for tea. I've got an exquisite Fujian Jade to share with you. Perhaps you could also keep an ear open for any to-ing and fro-ing of mystics travelling between London and Southeast Asia."

"Ramayana? Theravada? Rosicrucian? Templar? Eastern Orthodox? Sufi? New Age?" He says with a flourish. "We have them *all* in abundance in London, my dear. From Bangkok, we must be talking Ramayana."

"Sufi will do very nicely," she says with a laugh and turning her head in the mirror. At her request, he has removed the back-to-front incline and cut it spiky all over, with enough length on the spiked fringe to veil those eyes if needed.

They both nod nonchalantly as though it is a perfectly normal request from a customer at nine-thirty in the morning.

Outside the shop Cassy walks the short distance to the entrance to Whitechapel Tube station and stops in the doorway to scan the morning pedestrian traffic. After five minutes and no luck, she makes her way to a busy shopping street with market stalls on its wide Victorian pavements. Again, she stops and scans.

There she is. Perfect.

A young mother who can't be out of her teens is pushing a battered pushchair with one hand and dragging a crying, dirty-faced toddler by the other. Cassy slips a bulging envelope out of her handbag, walks straight up to her target, and blocks her path, hands on hips. Before the mother can articulate any abuse, Cassy thrusts the envelope at her. "Fifty thousand quid. You're a lucky girl this morning. It's clean. Make something of your life, huh?"

***

"Can we talk?" Oghel says as the elderly train carriage judders across a set of points, taking it onto the line out of Didcot Parkway to Oxford.

They are sitting opposite each other in faded blue-checked seats with a small table between them. Oghel is accompanying Cassy to a conference at Waddington College, Oxford University, and although it is now almost six months since Cassy witnessed her student's nocturnal intrusion into her office, she has not had the courage to confront him. Nor has she decided how that should be achieved. Every time they meet could be the occasion, and she has taken to being constantly prepared with a long practised list of alternative scripts, none of which seem to do.

And then the conversation with Sufi Isa had occurred. She cannot say exactly what had happened but she has this unshakable conviction that Oghel is an innocent. A pawn in someone's game. She knows it makes no sense and that she is probably wildly and naively deceived, but that is the way it is. Her objective and subjective personas are constantly in battle over the issue and the result is stalemate. But that is the way she wants it, for her heart tells her that Oghel needs rescuing. And she is, by now, totally infatuated with him.

Both secrets make conversations with him awkward: her knowledge that he has hacked into her computer, and her fantasy relationship with him.

Oghel studies the giant inverted urn-shaped concrete cooling towers of Didcot's power station that are passing slowly by, and Cassy uses the moment to study his side profile. Not so much to study as to consume. Not in any way an objective analysis of the sublimely angled jaw-bone, the faultless olive complexion, the strong but soft eyebrows framing those ever-so intelligent, bright and almost boy-like sparkling eyes of such complex hue. The ancient Greek nose and the manful neck muscles embedded into perfectly proportioned but not over-developed deltoids. No, it is a visceral look. *Lustful* does not capture the aching of the heart that accompanies the study. The aching would be there had he been far less beautiful, for she knows very well that it is his personality that she has fallen in love with.

There's something about you, Oghel, that makes me want you more than any man I have ever met. I would change anything in my sordid life if you asked.

"I would like to hear about your husband, Dr. Kim."

Oghel is no longer looking out of the window, and the line catches Cassy completely off-guard.

"Was he as clever as you?"

"I'll tell you about him if you like," Cassy says, putting aside her silent thoughts to confront yet another level of awkwardness in her interaction with Oghel.

"We were married for almost three years."

"I am sorry," he says gently. "He was English?"

"No. American. His mother was a Boston Jew and his father was Greek—from Crete."

Cassy had only met Zach's parents twice. Once was at the wedding in Orono, Maine in New England—where they now live. It had been a crisp April morning, filled with the lung-expanding scent of pine forests and melting snow. The second time was in London two years later. His father was an academic and prolific writer of obscure textual discussions about the Talmud. He was a Greek Jew originally from Thessalonica before moving to Crete. Cassy had liked him—he had a larger-than-life personality that Mediterranean Americans cultivate so easily and wear so fittingly.

"Jewish?" Oghel says, with interest. "You are too?"

"Not me—I'm your average agnostic modern Eurasian girl I'm afraid."

"Did your father not bring you up to believe in a religion?"

"I never knew my father."

"I'm sorry," he says again.

"I would rather not talk about it," she says.

"Do you mind talking about your husband?"

"Not if you want to."

"May I ask where you met him?"

"He was a research assistant on a project—and yes, he was clever, exceptionally so. He was an MIT graduate and came to the project straight from his PhD."

"A computer scientist too?" he asks.

If he is angling, Cassy hasn't the resolve to head him off. On the contrary, she has been waiting for months to find a way into the real Oghel.

If he wants to probe, let him. I'm all yours. Let's see where this ends up.

"Ancient languages. To be precise, his PhD was on the progression of cuneiform script in the Uruk IV stratified clay tablets. He also studied pre-cuneiform pictograms and an assortment of early Semitic languages. Not to mention modern Arabic—as well as Hebrew."

"Wow!" Oghel says, bright eyes shining in boyish admiration. "Clever. I think he must have been handsome too."

"Yes." Cassy says, acknowledging the implied compliment by risking the eye-to-eye lock-in she has been longing for. She rarely dwells in someone's gaze, even with the men she has slept with more than once. But with Oghel, she has waited a long time to consummate their relationship in this way. And now it has happened. It is a one-way moment of intimacy, but it satisfies her.

"Do you mind me asking what happened?" he says, in a way that gives her a glimmer of hope that he might have enjoyed the moment too.

"Between Zach and me?"

She rarely talks to anyone about the pain of the past and is surprised how therapeutic the thought of talking to Oghel about Zach feels.

"No, I don't mind," she confesses. "Actually it's good to talk."

He smiles.

"The marriage was great for about two years. I was happy. I assumed he was too. Then it suddenly went cold. It was painful."

"Yes," he says, making Cassy wonder what personal experience of suffering he might be drawing on.

"I threw myself into work," she continues. "We enjoyed the privileges of double income, no kids for a while—and then we drifted and the relationship faded."

In this she is not being completely honest. Zach drifted and she let the relationship fade to keep her sanity. In truth it had taken a long time for her to adjust and she knows in her heart that she still hasn't let him go.

"I'm afraid the rest is tragedy. I came back from the university one evening to find he'd gone. Him and everything belonging to him. The flat was literally half empty. I haven't seen or heard from him since."

The memory hurts in the retelling. Cassy has thought a lot about him in the years that followed—him, his family, his charm, and the inscrutable languages he loved. She had written to his parents a couple of times, who replied with politeness but nothing else.

"That is very sad." Oghel softens his tone further and surprises Cassy by reaching across the table and touching her hand. The effect is electric.

Half an hour later as the spires of Oxford pass into view and the desert-coloured sandstone of the half-constructed Said Business School welcomes them to the Western world's most ancient seat of learning, it is Oghel's turn to steal a glance at his travelling companion. He is well-trained and limits his range, reserving admiration only for those eyes. In the eyes one can see the true measure of a person. Only, Dr. Kim likes to guard her soul with those exotically-shaped curtains of delicate flesh. Apart from that moment as they were leaving Didcot Parkway. It had been brutal for him. Hoped for, but feared.

If only you knew as much about me as I do about you, Dr. Kim. Why does it have to be this way?

Chapter 14

Epping Forest, Essex
May 2000

FIFTEEN MILES NORTHEAST of London's Parliament Square lies a seat of power from more troubled times. In AD 60 when the Roman invaders of Britain were off fighting the Welsh, Queen Boudicca of the Iceni—ancient Britons—led Southeast England to burn London and the Roman towns of Colchester and St. Albans in reprisal for the violation of her daughters. She and her Celtic warriors killed two thousand highly skilled Roman soldiers. One of her forts lay strategically placed on the brow of what is now known as the Epping Forest Ridge. It would have provided a masterful view over the Thames Valley to the south and the low undulating woods to the north, east and west. The returning Romans defeated Boudicca and her armies, and for the next two millennia the forest around the old camp became the hunting ground for English kings and queens. Like many other playgrounds of the nobility, it is now the popular preserve of weekend walkers, bikers, and horse-riders. For all its faults, the British aristocracy has bequeathed much that is highly prized by contemporary commoners. From well-manicured vantage points along the ridge, weekend recreationists look down upon the distant buildings of the City of London and the flashing lights of Canary Wharf Tower pinpointing London's Docklands.

Cassy Kim is lying concealed in a thick patch of undergrowth, enjoying the summer scent of bracken, but alert and steeled for action. The chest-high fronded ferns form a natural canopy with plenty of space underneath to hide a person. It is a trick she has learnt from her recurring dream about the childhood she cannot remember. No children play on their own in this London Forest these days, however. It is one of the few true wilderness areas within the capital's boundaries and has long since acquired a more

NOAH'S ART 141

sinister reputation than being a good place to take a stroll. It is also a place for dumping bodies—or more usually, bits of bodies in bags, retrieved by early morning dog-walkers. She warily surveys the mulchy ground of her hiding place for the source of the putrid acidic smell that has been intensifying for the hour or so that she has been lying there. Prodding a mound of decaying leaves with a dried frond from the previous year's growth, she uncovers a single deathly-white fungal phallus, its head covered in a pungent sticky resin that has trapped a host of minute insects. A so-called stinkhorn. She gags.

It is the day of the forest rendezvous in the Cleito email. *Queen Boudicca's London Camp, May 27th—16.00 hours.*

Although common sense tells her it is highly likely that nothing will happen, the events in Bangkok tell her otherwise.

The Iron Age camp itself is a circular feature consisting of an earth mound standing three metres above the forest floor inside the camp, and on the outside, dropping away with the sides of the ridge on which it was built. It has a break at one end that would have been the site of a gate in the camp's wooden fortifications long since gone. Apart from two or three patches of bracken, growing in places where the great beech canopy thins to let sunlight in, the floor of the fort is barren—soft and springy with centuries of accumulated autumn debris. There are no trees growing on the mound itself, leaving a broken circle of sunlight that highlights the topography with theatrical effect and leaving the earthwork topped with ferns and briars. Cassy is concealed among these and has a good view of the entire camp. She is lying in a small perfectly circular depression in the top of the mound, which could be ancient but was more likely caused by an unexploded German bomb. In the Second World War the Luftwaffe used to drop their surplus payload over the Forest as they circled away from London and headed back to the Fatherland.

She had circled the site casually at some distance before approaching her spot—searching the trees for anyone else who might have arrived early. Although it is less than a kilometre from the main road, heading out of London into the rural county of Essex and on towards the university town of Cambridge, the site is rarely visited. It is marked as an ancient monument on maps, but is far from the main car parks and there are no signs to direct tourists to it. To most who pass by, it is just another undulation among the trees.

She has been in position for almost two hours before there is a movement in the trees beyond the entrance gap to the old hill fort. Someone has arrived at the furthest point from where she lies. Her location is well-chosen. She holds her breath and carefully retreats a fraction, pressing her body deeper into the damp layer of beechnuts and leaves. He is in motorcycling leathers, helmet under an arm, and sauntering into the fort with an air of familiarity. He glances around casually and lights up a cigarette before perching on the branch of a fallen tree. The branch looks too slender to take his weight—tight leathers reveal a bulging body, not fat but past its prime. He has black hair with a well-trimmed goatee beard and sits bouncing up and down on the springy bough. Slowly, he scans the rim of the earth mound. His gaze is detached but considered, and comes to a halt looking directly at Cassy's ferny hide. She holds her breath. Then his scrutiny continues along the rest of the fortification.

His leathers might have been threatening, but the bulges give more of a comical effect. He starts whistling. She recognises the tune—*Battle of Epping Forest,* a famous rock band's song about a bloody battle between rival gangs of motor-biked London youths in the 1960's. The legend of the mods and rockers lives on at the bikers' tea hut three or four kilometres from where she lies, and Cassy wonders if that is where he has just come from. Bikers old and young, original and nouveau, congregate there at weekends throughout the year. Perhaps he has made the connection between the song and the Briton camp—he doesn't look the type to have researched local history.

She is more prepared for this mission than the one in Bangkok. Digging uncomfortably into her left breast is the four-inch barrel of a Glock 19 Compact. The lightweight polymer-framed semi-automatic is licensed for club shooting and only once before has she taken it out anywhere other than to the range. She had very deliberately—solemnly, even—taken it from its locked drawer as she left the house. At five hundred and eighty six grams, it isn't exactly a handbag accessory, but it is lighter and shorter than the second-hand 1985 Gluck 17 nine-millimetre Luger Parabellum that had been her first indulgence after eventually managing to persuade the authorities that her violent teenage was well in the past. She doesn't plan to use the 19, but it makes her feel better. Not safer, just more confident.

She is wondering what she should do next when someone starts whistling somewhere below and behind her. It is the same tune.

Five minutes later voices come from within the fort—a man's greeting answered by a woman's. There is a laugh, and the man coughs a smoker's cough; then, a short silence followed by the low tones of conversation. She can make out the occasional word but not enough. Cautiously she raises her head a fraction to see better into the fort.

The woman is sitting a little way along from him on the same branch, which is moving up and down as they talk—there is a familiarity in the action, like two children chatting in a playground. Cassy can hear better now but not perfectly. The acoustics inside the fort are remarkably good, with the earth walls performing like the tiered seats of an amphitheatre.

"Anyway, we won't be meetin' like this much longer," the man says after he has finished complaining about the rain and mud. "I heard a rumour."

"I wouldn't know about that," says the girl, curtly but not unfriendlily.

She has an American accent although Cassy can't be sure she is American. She is also in motorcycling gear. The two helmets lie side by side on the ground next to a tank bag. He is a Londoner with the lazy nasal drawl that locals call *estuary*. He has Mediterranean features, however, and could be from any number of the city's long-established ethnic groups.

"Of course you bleedin wouldn't," he says with sarcasm. "I'm sure you ain't got a clue what that lot's paying for." He kicks the tank bag with his calf-length boot.

"What kind of rumour?" she says.

"Marriage is over. Never seemed a good mix to me anyway. Those religious baskets in Esweera have gone too far." He spits on the ground to emphasise his pronouncement. "I hear something important's gone missing and all-out warfare's broken out."

"I'll pretend I didn't hear that," she says, jumping up from the branch, almost bouncing him off. "Remember your place—dumb go-between."

With that she squats down, unzips the tank bag, and draws out a bound plastic bundle about the size of a parcel of A4 paper and squeezes it into a small purple rucksack.

There is no more conversation. He leaves first, by the gap where the gate had once stood, and she follows a minute or so later. There are no goodbyes, and it seems like a well-rehearsed exit routine. Cassy is just about to move when she hears the shot. It is only a small thud but it is unmistakably the sound of a silenced weapon. Against the noises of the forest she can just make out the sound of something heavy being dragged through the undergrowth, and then the noise of someone running through the low scrub in the direction of the road back into London.

She waits all of ten minutes, and then prises her stiffened limbs—first to all fours and then to a crouching stand. The forest is still and silent except for the birds. She shudders. In one swift move she scoops up the mountain bike that has been lying next to her in the bomb crater, pushes it over the edge of the mound, and races down the fortification and the forested ridge at suicidal speed to hit the forest track below, heading for the motorbike cafe in the woods.

***

"No, luv, ain't seen her today. Hey Eric, you seen that American girl? Rides a '72 Guzzi—and a Mediterranean-looking guy with a beard, you say?"

Cassy is talking to Bert, the tea hut proprietor. He has been serving tea and coffee to an ageing clientele for years. No one really knows who owns the small green shack that sits in a little clearing by the junction of three quiet forest roads. Perhaps it is a long-term squat. Eric hasn't seen the American girl today, but she was here last Saturday. As a matter of fact, she has been up here most Saturdays since early spring.

"Always comes about mid-afternoon—what, around three?" Eric recalls.

"As for Mediterranean-looking men, take your pick..." Bert says, offering her his clients with a wave of the hand. "What's yer name, luv? I'll let 'er know you're looking out for 'er."

"Don't worry," Cassy says. "I was just passing."

She hadn't expected him to be so helpful.

"What's yer name anyway? Just in case. You never know."

"Emma." she says over her shoulder as she mounts her mountain bike and slips a foot into a stirrup.

***

A week later Cassy is standing in a little frequented corner of the British Museum. Rising to Isa's challenge she has decided to see what she can find in a morning's search with an early start. The afternoon is reserved for a return trip to the bike hut, this time better prepared with Beccy's trail motorbike. Beccy is a niece of Joy's and the closest thing Cassy has to a relative. In spite of Joy's attempts to protect Beccy from Cassy's wayward influence, Beccy became fascinated by her hated aunt's unorthodox adopted daughter the first time she set eyes on her, and since then they have been fast friends. Beccy had left the motorbike in Cassy's garage while she is working in France.

Cassy sits herself down on the bottom of a grand stairway and leans against a large pillar, mock-marbled in warm earthy hues by late-Victorian artisans over a hundred years ago. The object in the glass case in front of her is a lot older but bears the same careful attention to detail. Instead of the marble's layers of swirls and glazes, there are rows of angular stylised pictures known by the experts as *cuneiform* writing. It had been one of Zach's fortes. On the wall above the display case are a number of white cards bearing commentaries on the stone tablets. The one she is examining bears the title "*The Gilgamesh Epic, The Sumerian King List and the Flood Story.*" Two out of Isa's four "signs" in one go and it is only ten o'clock—Cassy is feeling very pleased with herself as she reads.

"These tablets provide us with the only (virtually) complete version of the Babylonian poem known as 'The Epic of Gilgamesh.' They are an Assyrian version dating to the seventh century BC and have been copied from a composition made in Old Babylonian times, itself based on legends and stories from older SUMERIAN sources about a real King of the city of URUK on the EUPHRATES RIVER. The poem is regarded as the most important literary product of Ancient Mesopotamia. The story is of a hero king Gilgamesh whose mother was the goddess Ninsum and father was an unknown mortal. It is a meditation on mortality and death, recording the hero's exploits, passions and above all his humanity. Gilgamesh also appears as an

HISTORICAL FIGURE in the equally important Sumerian King List (see plate 3). When the twelve Assyrian tablets first came to light last century they generated much excitement for their account of the flood which has parallels to the Biblical account. The flood story in the Epic commences on Tablet XI column 14. Its hero is a wealthy man named Utnapishtim (an Assyrian derivation of the character Ziusudra who appears in the earlier Sumerian versions of the Epic), who escaped the deluge in a large boat (literally a 'mighty structure')."

Ziusudra—one of the names on the Sufis' web page, she notes.

"Gilgamesh goes off in search of Utnapishtim of old (the Biblical Noah) to discover his secret of immortality (which he was granted after surviving the flood). When he eventually finds him, Utnapishtim (Noah) tells Gilgamesh in great detail about the flood, which was a judgement on mankind. As with the Biblical story, life before the flood is pictured as being substantially different from life afterwards. Both accounts record the patriarchs as living for extraordinarily long life spans. The SUMERIAN KING LIST records eight dynasties before the flood. Other Babylonian accounts record ten, the same number as the patriarchs who lived before the Bible's Genesis flood. The King List is found on a single surviving clay tablet, dated by the scribe who wrote it, at around 2125 BC (in the reign of King Utukhegal of Uruk). The King List places Gilgamesh as the twenty-ninth king to reign after the great flood..."

She reads on with growing interest, enjoying the game, trying to imagine what Isa might want her to see in the narrative or in the story or in the characters of the poem. Inspiration eludes her, however, and after a while she goes to find an information point to ask about the other "signs:" the *March of Lugal Zagesi* and *Lord Aratta*. She is handed a phone by a helpful official and invited to test the art of the Museum's own Assyriologist.

"Lugal Zagesi—yes, of course. King of Uruk. Reigned towards the end of the Early Dynastic period of ancient Mesopotamia—modern-day Iraq. Between 2350 and 2150 BC. We have an exhibit if you want to see it—a copy of a vase fragment with an inscription of Zagesi's conquests."

"How about his *march*?"

"Oh, that'll be a reference to his march along the Tigris and Euphrates Rivers, conquering all the lands between the lower sea and the upper sea."

"Which seas are they?"

"Conventionally, the Persian Gulf and the Mediterranean respectively—they are terms used throughout ancient Middle Eastern literature. There's some controversy over them currently, however. Funny you should be asking, actually. Or perhaps that's why you're asking."

"No," Cassy says, "I'm *lay*. What's the controversy?"

"A fragment of clay tablet from the very earliest Sumerian period. Recently discovered—purchased from an undisclosed source by an American university. It's the earliest recorded use of the phrase *lower* and *upper seas*, and the word *lower* used in *lower* sea is said to clearly imply a sea that is *physically* lower than the upper sea. The suggestion is that it might refer to the Dead Sea."

Great controversy.

"The Dead Sea must be five hundred miles from the Tigris or the Euphrates," Cassy says.

"Quite. That's part of the controversy. It's a puzzle. But there's ancient history for you."

She moves on to Isa's fourth item. "How about the *Lord of Arrata?*"

"Quick answer or long?" he offers.

"Let's try the quick one for now."

"The full title is Enmerka and the Lord of Aratta. Its one of nine great Sumerian Epic poems—*The Epic of Gilgamesh* is the most famous. Written about five thousand years ago and found on twenty tablets and fragments now in the Museum of Ancient Orient in Istanbul. Aratta is the only major city-state of the Ancient Sumerian civilisation that has not been identified, found, and excavated. There are guesses about its location, but no one really knows. All we know is that it was a very wealthy city full of gold, silver, and precious stones, and was inundated by a flood."

***

Cassy makes her way through the vaulted corridors back to the Gilgamesh display and takes her seat again on the grand stairway to think about the four signs. Antediluvian kings living to fantastic ages, a Sumerian Noah story, an ancient march from a lower to an upper sea, and a legendary opulent Sumerian civilisation lost beneath floodwaters.

After sitting there for a while lost in thought, without any warning or conscious connection, the sound of the muted gunshot in the forest replays somewhere in her memory and, as if someone has shaken her from some deep preoccupation, she feels foolish for the way she has spent the past two hours. Why hadn't she reported the incident in the forest? She realises that Isa's puzzle is not a game. She is losing her sense of priority and knows that it has to do with the time spent with the Bangkok Sufi.

She steps out of the Museum with Isa's words ringing in her head:

Not long after that time, the end will come.

Chapter 15

July 1996
Cairo, Egypt

HE CAN'T SAY exactly when it was that he had fully *committed*. It had crept up on him. He had everything going for him—his languages, his doctorate, the high salary he always seemed able to negotiate whenever he had to move on. And his family, of course. He feels warm tears moisten his tired eyes as he thinks of them. His ageing father, whom he knows so little of but loves so much, and for whom he has cared for diligently for the last four years since the illness. And his young sister, now married to an Egyptian architect she met at Cairo University. He is happy that the man takes his religious duties seriously and that his sister is now even wearing the veil when she goes shopping. But he knows that their faith is thin and suspects that if they had lived a decade earlier, his sister and her new husband would be as worldly as the young people he had first envied, then despised, and finally learnt to pity when he lived in London. There is such a thing as fashion and trends, even in matters of religion. But he is thankful for it. Cairo is a better place for the renewed sense of pride the people have in their Islamic identity and for the greater sense of fervour in the air, even if it is too shallow.

But it is his brother, also some years his junior, whom he worries about most. Unrepentantly Western in his tastes, with posters of demonic-looking British rock stars from the 1980's decorating the room he occupies in the family's rented apartment in the old quarter of the city, all he wants to do is to make money.

It is obviously in the family. His father had been an accountant in their native Yemen before becoming ill, giving up work, and bringing the family to Cairo. His father said it was so his daughter and youngest son could be looked after by their elder brother, but he knew that it was his father's last attempt to reach out to the oldest son, who had become a stranger after the many years spent away from home. The thought mists his eyes even more.

Then a pang of remorse creases his brow—had he not himself started out like his younger brother? Not the rock music—he has always been too pious to be attracted to trivia—but the interest in business and finance. The world of international capitalism has fascinated him from an early age. He likes to think that it has been as a result of his love for the Koran. A kind of fascination with the opposition in order to understand it—and then, perhaps, to do something about it. But he knows that in reality this thought had come later. At first, if he is really honest, he just loved the challenge posed by the intricacies of capital flows, non-linear market dynamics, and improbably complex financial instruments. Derivatives were once a beautiful art form to him. Like Islamic tessellations that cleverly fill space without using any cruciform pattern elements.

Ironically, he had first learnt about currency market trading in Moscow University a few years before the fall of the Soviet Union. It was where the former socialist South Yemenese government liked to send the country's scholarship-winning high school children to university. It had given him the chance of learning how to be in the world but not of it. It had not been easy being a devout Muslim in an atheistic state university surrounded by young Russians whose dreams and aspirations left him cold.

As his faith grew stronger, he had wondered for a time if the tension between his inner beliefs and what he was becoming through his studies would be too difficult to sustain. But it had not been so. On the contrary; from those early days in Moscow he had known that this was all part of a wonderful plan.

His faith had continued to strengthen and with it a conviction about how his life should be invested. But there was no hint of contradiction. Some other brothers he has heard about live awkwardly with their day jobs. It can be difficult when their only task is to sit tight and wait—sometimes for years—for instructions. He knows of someone in a high-up position in a New York finance house and a doctor who has recently been promoted to what they called a consultant in a London hospital. They also are *committed*—but their time has not come. They are just ordinary people doing ordinary jobs. Only they aren't. They are waiting. And he knows that some get demoralised, or worse, distracted with doubts. For him, however, his interest in international finance is not a deception, though he has been taught that righteous deception is permitted. It is, quite simply, his calling. It is as though Allah has known from his very first years in kindergarten how this child can best be used. And he loves his job. Not for what his professional activities achieve for those who employ him, nor even for the sense of achievement. He loves what he does because it serves his higher calling. He silently recites prayers as he trades, and for him, the sense of worship is as real as when he is performing the *fajr* in the mosque each morning—greater, even, though he does not like to admit it, even to himself. Sometimes he wonders where his particular journey of faith will ultimately lead him. It has been his discipline for over two decades, ever since he met the teacher in a secret meeting in the courtyard of an ancient house in the centre of Jeddah. He had been on his way back from his second Umrah—the mini pilgrimage to the holy environs of Mecca.

The burden of being responsible for his family sometimes seems to weigh more heavily on him than the bigger task that Allah, in his mercy, has called him to. It is not a tension that he will have to face for much longer, however. For that bigger task is once again demanding that he move on. He is not sure how he is going to break it to his father. But he will have to, for there is no going back.

After a break of considerable time, the teacher had made contact again—through an equally elderly emissary. He has served the Brotherhood faithfully with his currency trading skills for many years in London, Shanghai, Cairo, New York, the Cayman Islands, and a few other places, but now he is being asked to do something quite different.

Actually, it was his younger brother's interest in business that, remarkably, had helped him progress the plans he had been asked to make, much more quickly than he had anticipated. His brother, who likes to window-shop in the job ads of the Financial Times and the various specialist money magazines he subscribes to, had found the advert and pointed it out. "It's tailor made for you," he said jokingly. And indeed it was. An international shipping firm was restructuring, having taken over an Asian shipping company and was setting up a new regional headquarters in Shanghai and two smaller offices; one in Dubai, and the other in the eastern Russian port of Vladivostok. Among several positions that had been created was one for someone with City of London experience in currency markets. They were looking for someone either with Arabic, English, and Russian; or Arabic, English, and Chinese. Depending on language proficiency, the successful candidate could choose which office to be based in. He has all four languages. He therefore went to the interview in Frankfurt, sensing that this was a divine appointment.

After the initial shock of the call from Frankfurt, his brother, who immediately assumed it was his fault for pointing out the advert, was not surprised that the job had been offered. He *was* surprised, however, to learn that his elder brother had not chosen to make the short move across Saudi Arabia to the company's new Dubai office. That would have been the natural choice. He could foreseeably have carried out his family duties from there, with visits home every other weekend or so. No. He had opted for Vladivostok. His older brother was moving to Siberia. And the posting was, as far as jobs in the financial sector can be, a permanent one.

Chapter 16

June 2000
London
THE TEA IS orange and strong and has come from a great steaming urn that looks as if it could have been there for as long as the hut. A fine drizzle hasn't deterred the thirty or so bikers standing around in twos and threes, making small talk about engine parts, the weather and share prices. Cassy is perched uncomfortably on a low wooden fence on the edge of the site with crash helmet on and visor up, hoping Bert hasn't recognised her from the previous weekend.

She doesn't have to wait long. A deep-throated and well-engineered roar draws a ritualistic turning of heads and she recognises the helmet before the rider takes it off. A bundle of strawberry blonde hair falls out—*assassin's hair*. She sits astride an imposing Italian Ducati with an engine the size of a small saloon car's, and brand new by the look of it. Eric had said she rides a classic Moto Guzzi—perhaps she has a collection stowed away in a garage somewhere.

What else might she keep there?

A few admirers wander over, exchange nods, and stand around while she parks up. Though Cassy has no need to hide from her, she instinctively lowers her face.

The assassin has been there for no longer than five minutes when she looks at her watch and throws a half-finished drink into a bin. Cassy gets off her perch as inconspicuously as possible and wanders towards her bike—she needs to be on the road and anticipating the American's direction before she is off. All heads in the crowd suddenly turn as a massive Gold Wing pulls up, followed close behind by a heavy-duty trail bike, together drowning the sound as Cassy ignites her puny engine into action. She is just about to slip off the muddy patch and onto the road when, by a stroke of bad luck, she finds herself looking beyond the Gold Wing towards the tea hut at exactly the same time as Bert is casting a pastoral glance over his clientele. He raises a hand and shouts something to Cassy, and then turns back to the urn to finish filling several cups expertly held in one palm. Cassy curses her carelessness and looks over to the American. She is pulling down her visor and a new rumble just audible above the Gold Wing tells Cassy that the assassin is on the move. Bert is walking towards Cassy, wiping his hands on his apron. He stops, looks at Cassy, and then at the girl, who has pulled onto the road and stopped to adjust a zip, and then at Cassy again. He shrugs his shoulders and turns back to his work.

With all eyes on the Gold Wing, Cassy slips out onto the narrow road that winds deeper into the forest. She has hardly started in pursuit when she realises which road she has taken and pulls up sharply. It is a dead end. Years ago, when the route of London's M25 circular motorway had been announced, the Forest Commissioners had closed off several roads to prevent an influx of motorway traffic to this popular resort spot. The bike in front of Cassy is speeding towards a concrete roadblock, beyond which the tarmac surface has been dug up to create a series of compounds used by foresters to store wood. The Ducati's road tyres and heavy frame means that it isn't going to cut into the forest paths. That means it will stop along the quiet cul-de-sac. As far as Cassy recalls, the road curves out in a winding detour through an open area of heath before re-entering the woods and coming to a dead end at the barrier. The bridle way that she can just see through the trees, however, takes a straight line towards the same point. She has cycled the forest trails a few times before. She slams into low gear and enters the woods, keeping as low as she can on the high-riding off-road bike and skidding through mud and leaves. There are no horses on the bridleway and it takes less than five minutes to reach the point at which it crosses the log store. Somewhere just to the left, through the trees, is the roadblock.

In a swift manoeuvre, she turns off the path and brings the bike to rest in a space shielded on three sides by piles of felled birch logs. As soon as she kills the engine she hears the roar of the approaching Ducati. The assassin will be here in one minute. A drainage ditch runs along the side of the road and continues under the concrete blocks and into the foresters' compound, covered here and there by felled trees. Cassy drops to the ground and rolls into the ditch. She crawls towards the sound of the approaching bike and clears the wood store. The bike slows to a halt, just feet from where Cassy lies half-submerged in the water at the bottom of the ditch. Engine off. Silence. Sound of boots walking on tarmac. She is walking into the wood the other side of the road. Cautiously, Cassy peers over the parapet. She could reach out and touch the Ducati. The American's back is to Cassy and she is disappearing along an overgrown path, casually looking from left to right. She has a good figure, accentuated by tight leathers. The combination of beauty and ruthlessness makes Cassy shudder. She moves along the ditch a little further, looking for a position that will keep the strawberry blonde hair in view.

What looks like a dense thicket of trees from one angle can yield clear lines of vision from another if the planting pattern is at all regular and although these are very old trees, the planting lines are still discernible. She finds one and sees the hair. The assassin has stopped and is standing on the root of an ancient tree, looking around her with the same affected casualness.

In the seventeenth century, the Royal hunters had generously granted the forest's villagers the right to cut beech branches for firewood. This explains the trees' characteristic shape of thick ancient trunk, up to the height a man can reach with his axe, and then a crown of branches growing almost vertically out of the rim of the trunk. In the centre of the crown between the branches, many trees have developed hollowed-out bowls that retained the rain, leaves, and other debris. She has found a foothold in the tree trunk and is reaching into the hollowed bowl. It is hard for Cassy to see precisely what the girl is doing at the distance but it looks as though she has taken something from the tree's hollow before stepping back down—either taking something or placing something. There is nothing in her hand, so Cassy assumes she had been placing something. She bends down and disappears for a second, and then starts to walk back.

The last thing Cassy sees as she sinks into the blackened water is a muscle tense in the assassin's tightly leathered thigh. Then, less than ten minutes after she arrived, the bike explodes into action and she pulls off, disappearing back along the road towards the cafe. Cassy raises herself cautiously to look over the edge of the ditch and scans the copse, the heath, and the road winding into the trees for signs of movement. Two horses are cantering across the rough grass in the distance but nothing else moves.

She makes a snap decision. If this is a delivery, then there will be a pick-up before very long. The assassin had looked at her watch back at the café, and that means that timing is important. Cassy identifies the tree by a large holly bush and an ancient leaning oak nearby, and then scrambles back along the ditch towards the bridle path. She emerges at a point concealed by the woodpiles. It is more difficult than she expects, but eventually comes to the old oak and turns to find herself facing the hollow-topped beech.

Many of the rotting pools of forest debris trapped six feet up would have remained undisturbed for decades or even centuries. She takes a glove off and reaches up, standing on the protruding root as the assassin had. Through the branches and in towards the centre, her hand sinks into water. She feels around the edge and then down into the swamp. It is deep and she can't touch the bottom from her perch.

Nothing.

She raises herself a fraction to search deeper and her fingers touch something.

A heavy-duty PVC bag?

She pulls at it. No movement. She looks back towards the road anxiously, ready to abandon the idea, when her hand rests on something else—more plastic but with a different feel and wedged in a crevice just below the surface of the flooded hollow. It yields to a sharp tug and Cassy jumps to the ground with a rectangular bundle half the size of an attaché case and wrapped in layers of carefully taped plastic. It is heavy for its size. Glancing around for somewhere to hide while she examines her find, she sees that the leaning oak's trunk is dead and hollowed out with age. Inside there is just enough room to crouch down. It takes her a minute to unwrap the outer plastic to find some kind of box sealed inside a clear plastic bag of the type used to store blood in hospitals. Peeling open the seal, she carefully extracts a wooden box with distinctive silver and mother of pearl inlay pattern. As she lifts it for a better look she catches an exotic scent of newly carved wood.

Carefully she lifts the perfectly-fitted lid—thick like the sides and base, and all fashioned out of a single piece of what looks like root wood. The inside is lined with red felt. It is empty.

The thud of horses' hooves on soft mud brings her to with a jolt—more than one horse, and galloping along the bridle path probably two hundred metres away, but getting louder. Quickly, she closes the box and roughly re-seals the parcel. By the time she has placed the package back in the tree-pond and ducked back into her hiding place, the horses have reached the edge of the copse. There are two and she can hear the voices of the riders—they have stopped their gallop and it sounds as if they have turned in towards Cassy. She squats in the hollowed tree in silence punctuated only by the sound of her own heavy breathing and the chirruping of woodland birds. Then a horse snorts further along the path and she realises that they have only slowed to pass through the forester's log yard. No sooner has the hooves faded, however, than another sound disturbs the forest birds. A motorbike. Cassy guesses which one even though she can't see it yet. The American girl had made a move seconds before the Gold Wing had pulled up.

Why a dead-letter drop? It allows for delays. It allows for anonymity. All terrorist organisations use rural stashes for weapons and ammunition to minimise the risk of incrimination. Or a buffer between two organisations for arm's length communication?

You're taking one hell of a risk, Kim, girl.

The bike pulls up and the crunch of heavy footsteps quickly approaches along the same path used by the American. Like the forest rendezvous the previous weekend, this is another well-practised routine—there is no hesitation in the steps. She lays concealed no more than five metres from the tree where the biker has now stopped. It is a man—with a muscular but agile shape. Cassy has an uninterrupted view through a hole in the broken trunk wall that makes her feel very vulnerable. Her hand closes too tightly around the Gluck. He lifts his visor as he repeats a familiar procedure—standing on the broken branch to reach into the rotting pool. Lifting out the plastic bundle Cassy has just handled, he jumps down and unzips a leather bag, pulling out a dirty towel. Wrapping the parcel in the towel, he places it in the bag and brings out something else also wrapped in plastic. Cassy stares transfixed.

A bone?

A foot or so in length with a double ball-shaped end like a head of femur where the leg fits into the hip socket. Up to this point he has had his back to Cassy. Now he stands up and very slowly turns, as if he has heard something but doesn't want to show it. She stops breathing, face pressed against the inside of her peephole, unable to move.

She is not expecting an Asian face. Like the bald-headed man in Isa's apartment, his features are North Asian.

The overall effect is frightening. It is shadowy in the trees at any time of day, but it is now late afternoon on a grey and drizzly day. He is wearing a red neck scarf tucked into a camouflage jacket and looks like a character from a Vietnamese war movie about to move in for some terrible kill.

Instead, he snaps down his visor, zips up the bag and moves back along the path towards the bike. When the engine roars into life and moves off, Cassy crawls out of her hole and catches a glimpse of the bike. It isn't the Gold Wing; it is the big trail bike that had pulled in at the same time. It is heading back along the road in the direction of the cafe. In another burst of recklessness Cassy runs over to the tree, fishes out the parcel that has just been placed there, and runs breakneck back through the scrub to her hidden Honda.

Avoiding the lane back to the cafe, she follows a minor trail to another road—one that leads up to the highest point of the Epping Forest Ridge and the historic hamlet curiously known as High Beach.

The original settlement would have been home to a handful of woodcutters, gamekeepers, and poachers living in scattered cottages around an old manor house, but it was the Victorians that had put High Beach on the map. A large nineteenth-century tavern of the style beloved by the London brewery companies was set artlessly in a clearing created for the day-tripping working classes from London's East End. The hamlet's commercial boom had led to a sprawl of yellow-brick late-Victorian houses that are now highly desirable residences. Judging by the name on the elaborate gatepost, the old manor house is now owned by an Arab.

The sky is darkening rapidly as Cassy weaves her way through the forest path, and when she hits the road, the heavens open. She carries on a short way towards the village before deciding to look for shelter. A subtle change in the density of the encompassing gloom tells her that she is out of the trees and in the open area beside the pub. A little further on she recognises a second drive to the manor house and then the churchyard wall. Somewhere through the wall of water she can make out a shaft of yellow light. The church door is ajar, protected from the rain by a deep porch. Slowing almost to a halt she pulls off the road, manoeuvres through an open gate into the churchyard, and drives along a path leading behind the church tower. Her headlamp comes to rest on an open shed-like structure containing an oil storage tank and a mound of fresh grass cuttings. Dead flowers taken from the graves are thrown on top and steam is rising from the damp composting vegetation. She kills the engine and sits for a minute, listening to the sound of a forest under siege from the heavens. Then, pulling up the collar of her leather jacket, she dismounts and runs through the rain and in through the open door. The warm light is coming from yellowing bulbs hanging from what were once gas chandeliers suspended from wooden beams in the roof. It smells like all old churches—mustiness and incense, the smell of history and hope—and has a cosy charm. She wanders down the aisle and sits in a wooden pew a few rows from the front, pulling up the zip of her jacket tight to stop the water that is trickling down her neck from her sodden hair.

It is her first chance to reflect on the events of the afternoon and Cassy sits deep in thought, moist warmth circulating under her sodden leathers like a wetsuit. At the forest meeting a week ago the American girl had received payment for goods delivered or services rendered. This afternoon she had apparently made another delivery—a wooden box. The second, bone-shaped object—now uncomfortably tucked into an inner pocket of Cassy's jacket—was left by the person who had also collected the box, so perhaps it was payment of some kind like the money. If the Asian biker works for the same party as the murdered biker, this afternoon's venue might simply have been a replacement arrangement. Perhaps the Londoner was too much of a loose cannon and both sides had planned last week's killing.

Or something much more complicated.

The body had been found—Cassy read it in the Evening Standard but is in no hurry to give evidence.

There is no let-up in the loud rumble of rain on the church roof and a deafening thunder-crash with simultaneous lightning tells her that the storm is directly overhead. She leans back to admire the carved ceiling and then shifts her gaze to the grand stained-glass window behind the altar. A river winds its way through the Garden of Eden behind a modestly posed naked Adam and Eve. Another intense crack of lightning brings the cameo bursting to life in a frenzied mosaic light show. The storm must be moving very fast, for no sooner have the colours faded than an altogether warmer, mellower version of Eden appears, animated this time with back-lit late afternoon sunshine from a gap in the clouds. The primeval couple stand in transparent submission to the illuminating work of nature, apple awkwardly in Eve's hand. A snake slithers in grass near their feet and in the background four great waterfalls seem to tumble into the garden from distant mountains that rise towards the sky up to the glass feet of a triumphant Christ in the next picture. Around him an emerald nimbus radiates iridescent light and the glass of his feet shine with fiery bronze ochre. He stands poised with patient beneficence above the fallen couple, hovering on a sea of glass that sparkles with flecks of rainbow diffraction.

For the silent, dripping solitary observer in the old forest church, something stirs deep within.

But before Cassy can respond to the stirring, the *son et lumiere* is interrupted by a dull clunk behind her. Someone has closed the heavy church door. She jolts round to see a man in biking leathers standing with his back to her. She freezes, aware of the hard bone-shaped object pressing the handgun painfully into tender flesh. Without turning, he methodically removes his helmet and gloves. Very slowly she unzips the front of her jacket, reaches in, and moulds her hand around the ergonomically formed Glock magazine.

In a snap pre-emptive decision, she stands up and says, "Seems to be clearing."

He swings around, clearly shocked. The face is that of an elderly man—elderly, but with a head of strong, sandy hair. The combination of features makes it difficult to guess his age—early seventies, perhaps. He is wiping a pair of wire-framed glasses with a white cotton handkerchief.

"Sorry, I didn't see you sitting there," he offered, with a cultured Cockney accent. "Clearing, but it hasn't quite stopped—I should wait a few more minutes if I were you. Interested in church music? We've got a wedding tomorrow. I'm the organist."

"I should be going," Cassy says, breathing heavily with the shock and walking quickly up the aisle towards him and the open door, but her voice is immediately drowned by another wave of heavy rain on the windows and roof.

"You stay right there," he says cheerfully. "It'll clear before long."

He hurries past her and through a little door beside an elaborate pipe organ, and then comes out with a portable CD player, which he proceeds to plug into a dangerous-looking wall socket. Fishing around in his army surplus knapsack, he produces a CD.

"People have strange tastes in wedding music these days," he calls over. "Never mind Mendelssohn—give them Meatloaf or Madonna. Heaven help us when the rap generation get old enough and wise enough to marry. Fortunately I won't be around," he chuckles loudly.

The low frequency vibrations of Albinoni's Adagio in G minor start to throb from the organ's heavy pipes. Then it abruptly changes to something lighter but still with a touch of sombreness - Vivaldi's "Autumn."

The music is relaxing and Cassy sits down again to calm her racing thoughts. A low sunlight now penetrates the windows and the setting reminds her of another time she had sat alone for a while in an English church. That was a very much older church, in the historic city of Oxford. She had entered the building, as now, in search of refuge—refuge then from an inner turmoil of screwed-up emotions. She was on an academic house party for "exceptionally bright" seventeen-year-old girls organised by one of Oxford's colleges.

A young lecturer named Ollie, who was helping teach the group of twenty girls, had followed her into the chapel. He was brilliant and ruggedly good-looking, and all the other girls were besotted with him by the first evening. He was too perfect for Cassy, who had instinctively decided not to trust him. It was autumn and outside in the college orchard the sweet and heavy fragrance of fermenting apples was in the air.

He had begun by praising her performance in the workshops and then after some small talk, turned and said, "You probably don't need me to tell you that you're quite a brilliant young mathematician. You'll be aware that this house party is about spotting exceptional talent to fast track into our college. You're already doing your A-levels a year early and I'm going to recommend that we offer you a place and a scholarship."

And that was my future taken care of. She often wonders what would have happened had she turned the opportunity down. Would she have ended up more in control of her life?

She looks up at Adam and Eve again, captivated by the immensity and poignancy of the scene. The organist stops playing, gets up from his throne, and walks towards her.

"You like our new stained-glass window? A tree fell through the old one last winter. This was donated by the manor house—they're from the Gulf but show a great interest in the church."

"Nice. Better get back on the road," she says. The objects in her inside pocket dig in deeply as she bends to get up and she grimaces.

"You all right?" he asks, looking her over as if he had missed something before.

"Fine," she answers. "Antonio Vivaldi—*il perte rosso*—the musical priest with red hair. You look quite the part."

"A Vivaldi fan?" he looks surprised.

"I bet you teach music to orphans too," she says with a nod.

Vivaldi wrote the piece for his pupils at the Ospedale della Pieta for orphaned girls. Cassy can relate to Vivaldi very well.

"Not quite orphans," he says. "These are privileged parts around here. But yes—good guess—I teach children. Violin, actually—at the local primary school."

"Vivaldi's better for a wedding than the Adagio," she says pensively. "But I hope you told the bride that 'Autumn' ends with the huntsman cornering his prey."

"Very appropriate," he laughs.

She leaves him chuckling and goes outside to retrieve the bike. The rain has stopped falling from the sky but is still falling from the trees. As she disappears into the shed at the rear of the church she hears the deep-throated rumble of a big bike approaching. It slows down to a halt somewhere close to the church gate and Cassy can feel its rider scanning the churchyard.

Then the organist's voice calls out from the open door: "Not at all a bad prologue for a marriage! Nice meeting you—come along to Hyde Park if you like Baroque; we've got an outdoor concert series starting soon."

The heavy church door shuts with a thud and Cassy realises he had thought the bike that has just pulled up was her, mounted and ready to go.

While she waits, it pulls round and roars back the way it came—towards the bikers' cafe. The Gold Wing. She waits a few more minutes. Two smaller bikes whine by in the same direction. If the stolen parcel is missing already she had been very lucky just now—and extremely foolhardy.

Cassy thinks of Vivaldi's huntsmen, the submissive stag, the stained-glass Christ, and Isa.

What must it feel like to submit oneself to death in exhaustion? Out of compassion? Or under enchantment? Only snakes kill by enchantment.

She shivers at the memory of brother Nooh in Bangkok, head on one side, waiting for the right moment to strike.

Chapter 17

June 1996
Kazan, Tartarstan

AT FIRST THE Tartar could see no particular reason for meeting here. He appreciates it being on home turf but he is sure it isn't a gesture of magnanimity. He suspects that the smartly cut black—or possibly mixed-race—Englishman might have other business here, but that is just a suspicion. Then there was the rumour recently that the owners of the large steel factory that had relocated from the Moscow region had paid Elton John forty million roubles to perform at an opening ceremony. Perhaps the Englishman has been negotiating some security issues with the local officials. That doesn't really sound likely, though—Julius Grant-Abban doesn't seem the type to lower himself to celebrity protection. But then again, at that sort of price, who wouldn't diversify?

He can see Grant-Abban's athletic figure in the distance still, walking briskly in the direction of the main road where he will pick up a taxi. GA, as he likes to be called, sent the email only two days ago. The Tartar is unnerved that the man knew he was in Kazan. It is his hometown for sure, but he is more often working out of any of four or five Russian cities or his office in Moscow. This knowledge, plus the odd location of the meeting—a German restaurant in an anonymous run-down suburb of the city—tells the Tartar that Julius Grant-Abban probably has another contact here. That, too, is unnerving, and he finds himself scanning the area for warning signs.

The suburb is like tens of thousands of others scattered throughout the cities of the former Soviet Union: grey Stalinist blocks of apartments in orderly rows with a large number painted onto the end of each to designate which sector, factory, and work unit its occupants had once belonged to. In between, the small trees that the Soviet architects had planted in the utilitarian communal yards have grown to fill the spaces and provide a shaded canopy. The effect, surprisingly, is not unpleasant, especially with the potted plants that people have installed in boxes hanging below their windows, and on the ground floor, extending into the courtyard in a gradual encroachment of many private domains into the communal.

A group of old men are playing chess on a chipped concrete table and a short way off, some babushkas sit around another, talking and sorting out contracted laundry into bundles. There are no other customers in the restaurant. Restaurant is too grand a name for it; it is a cafe that serves basic German food—pig's trotters, shin of pork, three different kinds of sausage, Saukraut, and spiced wheat beer—to the German enclave that had somehow established itself in this remote corner of the Soviet empire. Now that he thinks about it, he can see that the cafe has not been here for long. The heavy and sweetish smell of vaporised pork broth hangs in the air and the beaten up secondhand tables and chairs have a greasy film on them. The premises were once a ground floor apartment in one of the blocks, and as he looks around, he can see others like it. The sound of sawing he can hear comes from another conversion in a block across the street. Slowly but surely some of the sterile housing estates of the planned economy era are coming back to economic life. Others are dying a slow death; others still, being demolished. He hadn't noticed it when he had stepped out of the bus but this is one of the more lively ones—near the city centre and with plenty of undervalued apartments in which to grow small businesses. He seems to recall knowing someone who lived here once. Not a bad place, all in all, he muses—considering most of the others in the city.

He looks for GA but he has gone. He wonders about the business deal they have just concluded. It is repeat business—of a sort. Same place, same kind of job as the last one, but with a bizarre difference. When he had first been approached by Grant-Abban, he had asked around Moscow and discovered that the Englishman is known as a broker who represents a variety of very respectable business interests. Even the most respectable firms sometimes need to engage the services of people like the Tartar, and there is a flourishing industry of middlemen who have cultivated the skills necessary to move with one foot in respectable society and the other in the murkier side of the Russian economy. He can't be sure, but he also suspects that Mr. Grant-Abban has connections with the British Embassy in Moscow. It is the pattern of the jobs that give just a hint of an organisation with a political agenda. And the timing of some of them. He can usually build up a picture of his customers from small, nuanced bits of information he gleans in the negotiations that establish the deals. At another time, he often muses, he may have become a politician himself.

The Tartar's father had been a physics professor who had been moved to the Muslim city of Kazan as part of the Soviet's policy to Russify urban Tartar culture and society. But by the mid-1990's, his father had been reduced to subsistence vegetable farming on a small piece of land he rented on a share-cropping basis from a farming family two hours' walk from the city. For a while during the immediate post-Soviet economic crisis his father's university work had all but ground to a halt as, with hundreds of thousands of other government employees, he had had to find ways of surviving.

As the teenage son of a professor-turned-vegetable grower, the Tartar had developed an even more pragmatic view than his father on how one could or should make a living. Since his first big job organising a lorry-load of stolen refrigerators (he likes to think of it as logistics), he has used his considerable intellect to work himself up the ladder of the Tartar organised crime fraternity. Nowadays, he does very little hands-on himself. He is more of a director, albeit in a world of self-employed professionals. But the nexus of ties that bind them all together is as strong as the system of formal contracts that create a corporation and sometimes he lies awake at night counting exactly how many people he has in his "firm" and how he might expand it.

The previous job for the Englishman had not been too difficult to arrange: a theft from a government office in the northern port of Archangel. He classes it along with some other jobs he had organised—as information theft. Industrial espionage jobs are two a penny these days. The thought that he might have been complicit in political espionage worries him a little, however. But it was relatively good money— not the tops, but good enough.

He is puzzled by something, however. Through a Tartar named Mohamed he knows in Moscow, he has coincidentally heard something about the same government office. Some northeasterners had been asking questions about it. They first asked about the Russian Navy's historical archive, and were apparently confused when told what every patriotic Russian should know—that the archives are in Birzhenvaya Square, St. Petersburg, in the old Stock Exchange building that now houses the Central Naval Museum. They persisted, asking for details— location, level of security, maps—of all similar facilities in the north of the country. Mohamed heard this from his cousin who is a member of an Islamic militant group based in Kazan. The Russian gang members from the northeast were, according to Mohamed, in the business of selling weapons.

The more he thinks about this web of connections the more he thinks that perhaps he should pull back from his dealings with the Englishman. But then the email had come. Mr. GA had not been unfriendly but he had not minced words either. He had made oblique reference to a job that had not gone at all well and that he had no reason to know anything about. The threat was only implied, but since the job he is now being asked to do is so easy, he calculates that it isn't worthwhile objecting. He ignored the threat and named a price—which, for good measure, had been more or less at cost—and shook hands.

The oddest thing about the whole business is what he has been asked to arrange. The Englishman wants the item stolen from the Archangel Naval base returned: put back on the shelf it was taken from, and coated in fake dust.

Chapter 18

June 2000
Central London

"EVER HAD A doctoral student go missing, Malcolm?"

Cassy is in a dusty rock-specimen lab with Malcolm MacFenn, a strikingly tall geology professor of obviously Viking origins, and a new neighbour of hers. He has recently moved in a few doors away from her Dockland home and she has grown to appreciate his intelligent monosyllabic view of the world, which is as dry as his rocks. It is three weeks since the episode in the forest, four since her conversation with Oghel on the train to Oxford. She has not seen Oghel since and none of his fellow students know where he is.

"Only the one that hanged herself. How long?" Malcolm replies.

"Almost a month."

"Personally involved?"

Cassy is shocked at the thought of being so transparent.

"He's a respectable Muslim young man."

"Report it—cover yourself," he says, and then changing the subject, he holds up the object that he has been peering at while they have been talking.

"Manganese nodule from Pacific Ocean floor."

Cassy had gone round to Mal's the day after plucking it from its watery hollow in the tree. It was clearly a geological specimen and she was at a loss. The parcel dumped in the tree by the North Asian contained a dull browny-red metal with a surface broken into small, smoothly rounded nodules and shaped, as she had noticed when first seeing it wrapped in plastic, like a human leg bone.

"Obvious question, Cassy—where did you get it?" She had given it to him to analyse on condition of secrecy.

"In a forest."

He gives her a suspicious look and says, "You might have to do better than that..." He slaps two hands around the specimen. "It's an extraordinary find."

"Extraordinary?"

He reaches for a folder lying on the bench behind him and pulls out a digital image that looks like it has been taken by some kind of medical scanning device.

"What do you see?" he asks.

Taking it and holding it to the light, Cassy says, "A bone fragment—neck of femur? Encased."

"Marvellous. But whose head of femur?"

"Captain of the Titanic?" she suggests.

"That was the Atlantic. If it came from a wreck, then that ship had a big secret on board."

"A man with metal legs?"

"It's Neanderthal."

She looks again and recognises some telltale signs.

Now that I wasn't expecting.

Mistaking her silence for ignorance he continues, "Shallow, retreating forehead, massive ape-like ridges over eyes. Widely distributed over Palaeolithic Europe."

"Hey, I'm an archaeologist," she says. "But the coating—metallic molecules replacing organic molecules?"

"It's not a replacement fossil. The bone is real, cocooned in a manganese coating."

"How?"

"Back in the seventies, manganese nodules were the talk of the mineral trade. There are millions of tons of them sitting down there on the bottom of the sea. Manganese oxide's an important mineral in glass production, among other things, and the thought of vacuuming them up was too irresistible a dream not to pursue. Anyone who was anyone in the minerals industry invested in the project—all the multi-nationals had their own teams of scientists, prototyping seafloor vacuum cleaners. It was the new frontier of earth exploitation for the best part of a decade."

"What happened?"

"When all was designed and tested and the sums done, it wasn't cost-effective. If they were half a mile down rather than two to three, there might have been a bonanza. You can pull *anything* up from the Pacific floor at a price—but it's got to be worth the immense cost. The premiums on wrecked ships are a little higher than on little metal potatoes like this."

He taps the relic thoughtfully.

"But not this particular potato?" she ventures, flicking a small copper tag that is attached to the object by some kind of soldered seal. It has clearly been part of a collection and bears a single number, stamped onto the soft surface of the tag.

"Quite," Malcolm says. "My first guess was that it's from one of the marine aggregate or oil company collections."

"If a prospecting company found this, surely it would have got press, at least in the academic world?" she says. "Such a freakish phenomenon."

"Thought of that," Malcolm says, shaking his head. "Nothing of this description's ever been reported. Checked it out with our two palaeontologists. In confidence, of course," he added seeing her alarm. "If anyone in the world heard about it, *they* would have."

"Perhaps I should talk to them," she says.

"Not unless you want to let someone else in on your secret. They are intrigued, to say the least. They'd be drooling at your door until you divulged all."

"Yes, of course. So help me guess the meaning of a metal-coated Neanderthal leg bone. For a start: how do manganese nodules form?"

He smiles apologetically. "Until recently a nodule like this was thought to take say about eighteen million years to grow from waterborne minerals. They accrete around bits of debris lying on the seafloor."

"Until recently?"

He chuckles. "Since all the dredging activity there's never been so many samples circulating the world's geological laboratories and some nodules have been found that can't possibly be that old. We're talking very recent formation—like a few decades."

"How can they be sure?"

"One was found growing around a rusted tin can. From the writing on the base, probably jettisoned from a German U-boat."

She smiles at the thought.

"It's not uncommon to dredge up relics of prehistoric animals from certain parts of the seafloor. The Grand Banks off Newfoundland is a popular spot for hauling up things like mammoth tusks and elk bones."

In spite of the old bones Cassy has examined for Scotland Yard, this is way beyond her expertise.

"From the seafloor?"

"Remains of animal life that wandered across iced-over seas during the last ice age. Dead animals got entombed and when the ice melted they all dropped to the bottom."

"And the same could have happened with a Neanderthal hunter. So there's no mystery—apart from whose collection it comes from."

"And why such an unusual exhibit's been kept a secret—not to mention the question of how you came to be in possession."

"There must be a way of tracing the owner from the number on the tag," Cassy suggests.

He shakes his head. "Not with this number. I've checked. There are standard codes used by all the mining companies, museums, and research labs—alpha-numerics for different classes of rocks and mineral. Our number doesn't fit any of them. No, it's got to be from some private collection, or one that's not principally a geological specimen library."

She is about to leave when, following a hunch, she asks: "Can I borrow your computer for a minute for an internet search?"

She types in "Essweera," and then "Esweira," and is asked by the search, "*do you mean Essaouira?*"

Essaouira—the windy city of South Morocco.

She types in "craft" and "woodwork," and draws in her breath sharply as an image appears before her of a turbaned man working on a wooden box with a delicate chisel. He is surrounded by a roomful of boxes identical to the one she had pulled out of the forest dead-letter drop.

***

Cassy's mobile phone breaks the sanctified silence of London's Natural History Museum minerals room, where she is standing in front of a case displaying an outsized manganese nodule. A serious-looking visitor on the other side of the cabinet gives her a disapproving frown. She looks at the screen and is very glad she had not turned it off, however, for it is Oghel.

In a hushed tone that doesn't conceal her excitement she says, "Oghel? Where the hell have you been? It's been almost a month!"

The man is glaring at her now over half-rim spectacles.

"When are you coming into the university? We need to meet! Are you all right?"

There is a listlessness in his voice; he sounds depressed.

"I needed to think, Dr. Kim. Can we meet?"

"How about a walk in Hyde Park?"

It is open, public, and can be as short or long as either of us want.

"Hyde Park? Yes... maybe..." There is a pause, and then: "When?"

"Tomorrow morning? It's the start of open-air concert season. Anyway, I've got to be near Marble Arch first thing in the morning. Could you make eleven o'clock at Speaker's Corner?"

A museum security officer is walking towards her in a determined fashion. She glares back at him.

"Oghel, I'm in a museum about to get into a fight. I'll call you again outside. Where are you?"

"No... it's okay... Marble Arch, then. I'll see you tomorrow."

She makes her way to the exit and joins the throng of tourists in Museum Avenue. The phone call has reminded her that she needs to make another. She turns into a lane that leads to a service entrance for one of the museums, finds some polished granite steps, and sits down.

"James? Hello, James, it's Cassy Kim. Wondering if you can do me a favour?"

James Theodorson works at Scotland Yard in the highly specialised team that deals with art fraud. The illegal art market is second in size only to the illegal drugs market and valued at billions of dollars a year worldwide. That's why the British police, like their European partners, employ people like James. He hadn't started off as a detective; he'd been an art historian. Cassy had rubbed shoulders with him on two occasions, both involving very clever Italian art students with bad friends.

"James, I've got an object in my possession which could have been stolen from a museum. Is there any way you can check it out on a database of missing items? No, not an art antiquity this time, I'm afraid—a lump of metal."

***

Two telephone messages await Cassy when she arrives home. Nigel Buchanan wants to see her the next day at 10.00 a.m. sharp—just before her appointment in Hyde Park; and Ashi is in town—"Can we get together soon? Tonight would be ideal." Ohgel is more important to her at the moment than Nigel, so she doesn't return his call.

Ashi arrives at her home an hour later.

"You're keeping something from me, Ashi, and I bloody well need to know about it."

He spreads himself on a sofa and picks up a glass of cranberry juice. He had started drinking it for medicinal reasons, long before it became trendy.

"Go on," he parries, holding the glass in mid-air and then placing it back on the coffee table.

"You saw Nigel Buchanan earlier today."

"He told you that?"

"No, you phoned within minutes of each other. My guess is you've come round to warn me that he's gunning for me. What I'd like to know is why you were discussing me behind my back, and why you're in cahoots with an MI5 officer."

He is well prepared.

"Ever the astute one, eh? Top marks. If you must know, we met this afternoon because our Mr. Buchanan wanted to knock some sense into his dangerously headstrong expert consultant—his words, not mine. And as for hob-nobbing with MI5, you probably won't be surprised to hear it's not the first time they've come to me for advice recently."

So now it's out in the open—we are both employed by Buchanan.

"Buchanan's been out of the country for a while," Ashi continues. "I imagine he's working his way through a backlog of problems and you're one of them."

"So go on," she says flatly. "Give me the friendly warning—I can take it."

"He isn't happy about your secretive visit to Southeast Asia."

So, I was tracked. That's bad.

"I don't have to tell him where I am all the time."

"That's not quite how he sees it. He's furious, actually. You'll need to ask *him* why exactly."

He hesitates and then adds, "Making contact with some Kurdish refugees, possibly?"

"How the hell did he find that out?"

Monitoring her international movements via airline ticketing and immigration departments is one thing, but it takes time to organise a trail within a country. She is deeply shocked.

"I'm just a go-between Cassy, believe me. But I *would* like to know how this relates to our conversation at my place last month. To say I'm intrigued is an understatement."

Cassy is not convinced by his air of innocence and ignores the request.

"Why the hell does he need a go-between?" she demands. "He's summoned me to his bloody office tomorrow anyway."

"Who knows?" Ashi holds up his hands and shrugs his shoulders. "The man seems to have his inscrutable ways. But don't overdo it in the mistrust department, uh? We're all just trying to do a job, serve our beloved country, keep the pension contributions coming in, and all that. Just be careful, Cass—*really* careful, I mean."

She fixes him a glare.

"What's going on, Ashi?"

He seems serious about the warning and despite her anger she is sobered—touched, even—by his concern.

He looks her in the eye then peers into the ruby-red fruit juice. "All I know is that our Mr. Buchanan is extraordinarily edgy—especially about you."

"Why were you deliberately obtuse with me when we last met?" she asks.

"Obtuse?" He seems genuinely surprised.

"I asked you who might have created that doomsday web page. You gave an efficient and professional answer—but not a full one."

There is an awkward hesitation.

"I thought it was a pretty good diagnosis actually," he says with a smile.

"You could have told me more."

"I could?"

"You're being obtuse again."

"Look, Cassy, you followed an unauthorised hunch to another bloody country while employed on a sensitive project. What do you expect from your MI5 line manager?"

***

Cassy and Oghel are walking side by side at a measured distance, along the path that runs parallel to Park Lane under majestic plane trees planted in the time when nannies perambulated with the babies of wealthy employers. Cassy is thinking of the father she never knew. Oghel is thinking of what he has to say to Cassy. They walk without speaking for a long time. The drizzle of the summer morning has stopped and a golden sun is warming the moisture-filled air.

"Where did you get to Oghel?" she eventually asks as they walk.

"I went to stay with friends."

"Turkey?"

"Not Turkey," he says. "But away, Dr. Kim. Away."

"Cassy, please," she says.

They are approaching a park bench and she gestures to it. It is still damp but it will do. They sit down, still a few feet apart, looking out across the open grass towards the concert tent where an audience is beginning to gather. Little figures move on the stage, setting up and checking sound and lighting equipment.

"I am interested that you never knew your father, Dr. Cassy."

She is startled not so much by the change of tack as by the connection with her thoughts a few moments ago.

Oghel the mind reader. Are you aware that you do that?

Then another thought: *What is it about my father?*

"I was placed in an orphanage when I was twelve months old. I know nothing about my father or my mother."

"I'm sorry." And then adds what for him, is clearly a connected thought: "I love my father but we are too far apart."

It isn't clear if he means geographically or in their relationship.

"He lives in Istanbul?" Cassy asks, eager for a glimpse into Oghel's private life.

He laughs. "I cannot even imagine my father in Istanbul. He has never been to a big city in his whole life. He is..." He hesitates and then falls silent.

"Why do you ask about my father?" she asks.

He is watching the stage and without turning says, "I entered your office and searched your computer."

"Why?" The response is an instant and instinctive riposte.

"I was told to."

"By whom?" There is no time to stop and think.

"By the ones who threaten my father if I do not."

"Why would they do that?"

"I do not exactly know."

"Not exactly? But you know something. How did you get into my office? It is locked—always."

"I received a key."

"From who?"

"Anonymously. In the post."

"And the computer? They also gave you a password?"

"Yes."

"What were you looking for?"

"Financial transactions."

"What kind of financial transactions?"

"Anything unusual—large sums of money."

"Did you find what you were looking for?"

"I found something."
"What did they say?"
"I did not tell them."
"Why not?"
"Because…"

***

Half an hour later they are seated on Cassy's jacket towards the back of a large crowd gathered to hear the early summer concert.

He had not answered Cassy's question but instead, standing to face her, putting his hands on her shoulders to address her eye to eye, he had said quietly and firmly: "I do not know what you have done or who you are, apart from a university teacher, but I must ask you please to forgive me."

That was it. And then they had walked in silence around the park.

"Andy Booth," Cassy says, leaning towards Oghel. "The latest in cool musicians injecting pop into classics."

"He is like a schoolboy," Oghel responds.

An ear-piercing squeak of electronic feedback comes from the stage followed by the crash of symbols and a high and intricate scale on the flute as the star warms up his band with a final sound check.

"Memory of my father is not the only loss from my childhood," Cassy says, staring at the distant musician.

"I have no memory or information about me whatsoever before the age of twelve."

It is the first time she has uttered those words to anyone. Ever.

She turns to Oghel knowing that he will see her insecurity.

I have exposed myself in exchange for your confession.

She has never felt so intimate with a man in all of her promiscuous life.

"An accident?" He is gentle. His strong, confident, and caring eyes, narrow just a touch in concern.

"The shrinks couldn't tell me for sure. *Psychogenic retrospective autobiographical amnesia.* That's what they labelled it. Everything gone. The earliest thing I can remember is swearing at the woman who I thought at the time was my mother. I'm a bad one, Oghel. You wouldn't want to know much more about me, I'm afraid."

The warm drizzle suddenly returns, and Oghel puts his umbrella up and invites Cassy to move closer. But she can't. It would be easy to reach out and put her arm on his, to caress his cheek, to tuck her head into his neck as she did with Marten.

But the intimacy of exchanged secrets has transfixed her, like a shot of anaesthetic rapidly spreading warmth through the whole body. She doesn't want to move. She senses an untouchable quality to the attachment—as though it will evaporate if she acknowledges it. The rain makes the small space they are sharing very private and she realises that her feelings for him are complexly abstracted from the physical. The charm that draws her like a magnet is also keeping her at a distance.

Would I have trusted him had I not wandered into Isa's apartment?

Without warning, a distant memory comes back that is so startling that she momentarily sways and Oghel reaches out to her. It is the little town in the Republic of Georgia. She remembers when she had first heard of it.

Akhalkalaki.

The town featured in a photo on the wall of Sufi Isa's Bangkok apartment and also in the passenger list of AIA flight 916.

It had been during the Anglo–U.S. Ark study. The town had been mentioned in one of the more unlikely historical accounts in the chronicles of Ark-hunting. It was in the year 1917, when Imperial Russia was on the verge of collapse. A Lieutenant Roskovitsky in Tsar Nicholas II's

Imperial Air force had brought back an unusual story from the southwest corner of the empire—an extraordinary sighting fourteen thousand feet up Mount Ararat. So taken was the Tsar, allegedly, that he had dispatched a military expedition of three hundred engineers to verify the account. The expedition was apparently astoundingly successful and detailed measurements, drawings, and even film footage had apparently been brought back. The evidence never got to the Tsar, however. The troops had billeted at Akhalkalaki before returning to St. Petersburg and sent the finds on in advance. Somewhere between Akhalkalaki and St. Petersburg they had disappeared. Events had overtaken the Tsar and the treasure from the expedition had been lost in the maelstrom that followed. There was a rumour, however: Leonid Trotsky, first Foreign Commissar of the Soviet Government that replaced Nicholas II in the autumn of 1917, was said to have whisked the bounty away and executed its couriers.

Chapter 19

"I DON'T HAVE to remind you that you have *form*."

Nigel Buchanan emphasises the word *form* as he taps manicured fingers on the empty desk he seems to have had borrowed for the occasion. The ill-lit room belongs to a personnel officer, judging by the labels on the files stacked from floor to ceiling. It is located in the basement of an anonymous building next to the headquarters of the famous Royal Town Planning Institute, tucked away in medieval Botolph Lane, just around the corner from Pudding Lane where the great fire of London started in Thomas Farynor's bakery one early autumn Sunday in 1666.

"You could have made things *very* difficult."

He is very agitated.

"You're a highly paid consultant and you should know better. Play by the rules, Dr. Kim. Think of it as a matter of *professionalism*." His eyes go into a kind of blink-cum-twitch spasm.

He picks at his fingernails as the spasm wears off and then looks up and asks more calmly, "Perhaps you could tell me what you found in Bangkok."

He has been standing, leaning on the desk with both hands for emphasis. Now he returns to his seat and waits for a response.

Choosing her words, Cassy Kim gives a selective account of her South East Asia trip while Nigel makes neat notes with a green tortoiseshell fountain pen. After about ten minutes he asks her to stop while he changes the ink cartridge. By the time he starts writing again, there is little sign of his initial anger, as if the deliberate penmanship is a well-practised therapy for him at such times. He makes the occasional comment and is particularly intrigued at how Cassy had located the refugees. He quizzes her on her account of the three brothers and their history. She doesn't tell him that she had met Isa on a second occasion on the way to the airport, although she thinks it highly likely he might know already. She also gives only patchy detail on the parts of the conversations that had so disoriented her. She serves the best morsel last. As she tells him about the photo of the dusty Georgian town with a name that also appears on the passenger list of the AIA flight he stops writing and remains silent for some time, bent forward in concentration, face just an inch or two from the paper. She cannot see his face but from a subtle shift in the skin around his temple, she detects a hint of a smile. When he finally looks up, all he says is 'well done'.

The meeting is short and, despite the softening in mood, he shouts a final warning at her as she is escorted out.

***

Two items of mail await her at home. One is a sepia antique postcard from Beccy of la Tour Eiffel, with a massive statue of a trumpeting elephant in the foreground and the caption "*Un bonjour de Paris. Je t'aime.*" It releases a ray of sunshine as Cassy holds it in her hand. The other is a letter from the Vice Chancellor of the university and has quite the opposite effect. It respectfully points out that academics are paid by taxpayers to extend the frontiers of knowledge and to attract research money, not to subsidise public services. He would like her to make a decision: is she going to work for the university properly or work as a consultant to the police? She wonders if this has anything to do with her other extra-curricula consultancy contract.

She thinks of Ashi's forced redundancy and picks up the phone, needing to talk to someone who understands.

Besides, it might help ease the growing tension between us.

"Come on down for a weekend at the health club!" he offers after she has read the VC's letter out. "So long as we agree not to talk business." His tone isn't quite as pally as his words, however.

That would be too awkward for us both, wouldn't it now?

The conversation, like the one with Nigel, is shorter and more to the point than it should have been, and Cassy is about to finish it when he says, "Oh, and Cassy... one thing. I owe you an apology. You were right about the obtuse bit. Sorry, this business puts us in such damned awkward situations. I know about the Kurdish Sufis of course. How the devil did you find them?"

"Intuition," she says, thinking quickly about where this disclosure might be leading. "Did you tell Buchanan more about them than you told me?"

"Just filled him in on technical stuff about Sufi Orders. When you came to see me I had just come out of a long session with him and two other chaps—MI6 and an American. You breezed in asking the same sort of questions and my defences went on red alert. Know what I mean? I tried to be as helpful as I could without giving too much away. There. Hope that clears the air between us. Keep it to yourself, eh, Cass? I shouldn't have told you."

***

Cassy awakes with an inspired idea for tracing the killer and her forest victim. It is a long shot but worth a try. The old hill fort had been chosen as a meeting point by someone with local knowledge or by someone who had read up about it. It had been the murdered man who had delivered the payment, but the girl was obviously in command of the exchange, and Cassy can think of two types of published sources where an American might learn of the camp's location: local tourist pamphlets, and more serious archaeological or ancient history books.

It proves much simpler than she imagined to hack her way into London's Joint Library Services loans-management database, linking the capital's entire stock of civic and university collections. Towel wrapped around her after showering, and a tiny cup of China tea in hand, she tries searching "books on loan" for *Epping Forest*. The reply comes: *no titles found*. She tries a number of word combinations: *Roman + London*, and then *Archaeology + London*. There are many books out on the Archaeology of London, but all of them rather too general. Then she tries *Boudicca* and *Hill forts* and then several combinations of all the words. Nothing of interest.

She is about to log off when she notices the "*search on abstract*" button. That means that she doesn't have to guess the title correctly—an impossible task, now she thinks about it. It works immediately. She types in *Boudicca + Camp + Forest* and gets no less than twelve books, all taken out from the library of London University's most famous archaeology school. She checks through the names of the borrowers they are issued to: James Johannes, Sir Andrew Letherage, and various other males and two females. Lady Petula Letherage has two and four are issued to a *Belinda Ryan, post third year PhD student, Department of International Peace Studies*. This is followed by her college details and student number. Cassy follows a link to the university student record database and smiles with satisfaction as her details came onto the screen. *U.S. citizen*—bingo! Direct hit.

Post third year means that Belinda has officially timed out of her doctoral programme, and is in a grace period where she can carry on using university facilities but is no longer fee-paying. Cassy knows how these things work.

So you're pretty much a free agent and might have been for some time. Perhaps you should be on Nigel's little list.

"Okay, Belinda, you've been spotted," Cassy says out loud, logging off. "I won't do anything rash, but I know where to come when I need to."

Elated by her success, Cassy unrolls the towel, letting it drop to the ground. Then, sitting down on the towel, she brings first one leg and then the other into a full lotus position, from which she basks in the glow and prays a silent prayer to Dr. Edmond Locard.

Locard's Principle—the idea that every contact leaves a trace.

She has long learnt the power of extending the principle to the entire network of a crime's sub-scenes, which she likes to refer to as the *crime footprint*. Every perpetrator takes something out of the crime footprint and leaves something behind. The so-called *Locard's Exchange*.

After a while, she manoeuvres into to a half-lotus, gently prising one leg out of its contortioned knot to ease the tension on her hips.

She massages her calf muscles with her thumbs, enjoying their athletic bulk, shaped by walking up the two hundred steps to her office in the university at least once a day and cardiovascular exercise three nights a week in the gym. She surveys her soft pale thighs as she works the calves and cautiously starts to imagine that it is Oghel who is massaging. Her hands move up, kneading her thighs deeply, sensuously.

Her imagination goes no further, however. It is blocked, like a radio signal suddenly cut by an electronic weapon, or speech suddenly made impossible by a hypnotist's magic. She looks at her nakedness and suddenly feels dreadfully empty. So much given for so little. The adulteress. The foreigner who flatters with her words and seduces with her emotional poverty. She struggles against whatever is happening to her, digging her thumbs deep into her thigh muscle so that it bruises. Exerting all her energies, she tries to conjure up an image of Oghel. Instead, to her horror, all she sees is Sufi Nooh. She recoils. Then it is Sufi Nooh sitting on the floor facing her, with Sufi Isa next to him. They are in the Bangkok apartment. Isa is looking at her obliquely, steadily in the eye but Nooh is looking further down her body with a look of self-righteousness on his face that is only a thin concealment of the lust that shines from his thickly hooded eyes. Sufi Isa is clothing her with his kindness. Sufi Nooh is abusing her vulnerability, penetrating her with lascivious imaginations.

Frightened, she grabs the towel and wrapping it around her so tightly that she can hardly breathe, makes her way back to the computer, where she hits the space bar hard enough to break the keyboard. Frantically concentrating to shake off the hallucination, she retrieves the London Libraries search screen and finds her way to a section titled *Business Directories*.

Within minutes she has it. *U.K. Craft-Importers* is indexed by country and it takes her just under an hour of intensely focused note-taking to compile a list of all the companies importing craft goods from Morocco. Some are general import–export agents but there are forty charitable U.K. companies in her notebook. By the time she is finished she is exorcised of the panic but very disturbed. Not so much about the faces—she has experienced that before—but about the thoughts that had passed through her mind.

PART III: The Exposure

Chapter 20

Essaouira, South Morocco
July 2000
TWO WEEKS LATER a girl in her late twenties, with thick dark brown hair matted with sub-cultured neglect and woven at three points into thin beaded braids, slips out of an ancient iron bed and pulls on a baggy T-shirt. Beccy's natural look is sustained by unplucked brows, a freckly complexion, and warm brown-hazel eyes. She wanders over to a set of turquoise-blue shutters powdery with many layers of weathered paint that are filtering angled shafts of sunlight into the room, and thrusts them open to a sparkling Atlantic Ocean. She closes her eyes and slowly inhales the salt breeze scented with eucalyptus and baked sand.

Beccy and Cassy's bond started when Cassy was thirteen and Beccy just ten. They had found a common enemy to defend each other from and scheme against: Joy.

It was not that there had been anything obviously unpleasant about Cassy's adoptive mother and Beccy's aunt, at least at that stage. In fact, neither can still quite put their finger on what might have been the original event that soured the relationships. They both just recall an intense resentment; Cassy's some kind of subliminal awareness, perhaps, of the truth of the relationship—it wasn't till some time later that Cassy had discovered her adopted status. Beccy's probably came, they had often agreed, from having to stay with her aunt during those holidays when her parents, who were more or less permanently stationed in Pakistan, were travelling and couldn't have her join them from her Somerset boarding school. *Why did they have me if they were going to get on with their life without me?* she would often ask Cassy. And she projected the resentment onto her mother's sister.

Three days earlier Beccy had met Cassy at Gare St. Nazaire in Paris, where they had purchased two open return tickets on the transcontinental express to Malaga at the southern tip of Spain. From there they had taken the ferry to the Spanish outpost of Ceuta in Morocco and hired a four-wheel drive from a French company. It wasn't the fastest of vehicles so they had booked into a hotel in the city of Rabat on the way south and rolled into their destination late the following day.

"There is nowhere on earth quite so ruggedly romantic," Beccy had read out to Cassy from her guidebook at one point of the journey. "From Essaouira's fortified seawalls, a row of sixteenth-century Portuguese cannons still defy the Atlantic waves and under the arched vaults of the walls, craftsmen hand carve exquisite boxes made from the roots of an ancient olive-like tree found only in the western foothills of the Atlas Mountains."

"That's why we're going there," Cassy had explained cryptically, without explaining.

The town proved as wildly wonderful as they had pictured. At its core is a fort, built on a rocky headland that breaks up the otherwise featureless Atlantic coast running down to the desert state of Mauritania. The old fortifications contain the good part of the town and remarkably little has been added on the land side. To the north and west, the ancient town walls drop directly into the ocean, where they are pounded day and night by Atlantic waves, and to the south, in the lee of the headland, the town fronts a gentle sandy beach.

Their hotel is built into the town wall where it meets the beach. It is an old-fashioned Moroccan establishment, completely un-modernised and enchanting in every feature, including the morning pot of mint tea and plate of rich tea biscuits that have just been delivered to Beccy's room.

In the room next door, Cassy pours from her own pot of mint tea, takes it over to the bed, and lies there studying a sheet of paper she typed the night before leaving London. There has been precious little time over the past months to reflect on her afflictions and the holiday is already helping.

She reaches over to the end of the bed where she has tipped out the contents of her handbag and picks up a pen. She picks up a piece of paper and writes down six headings: *Isa*, *Bangkok*, *Ark*, *Essaouria*, *Sumerian keys*, *final key*. Then she sits back and tries to conjure the details of Sufi Isa's face and that of his brother. If she can do the conjuring she need not fear the faces, she tells herself.

There is a bang on the wall and she jumps up and returns it. A cheerful shout answers from somewhere outside her window. Opening the shuttered French doors to find a narrow Juliet balcony, she is met by the sight of Beccy, hair blowing about her face and dressed only in an oversized white T-shirt billowing wildly in the breeze. Beccy leans over the balustrade of her own balcony and blows Cassy an air-kiss.

***

Later, they are seated at an open-air cafe amidst the nets and fish remains on the quayside of the town's harbour. It smells of diesel and fish oil but provides an atmospheric breakfast spot, which seems to be a gathering place for travellers. Beccy, ever the gregarious extrovert, doesn't waste any time making friends with four Australian boys and a girl on the next table, who insist that she and Cassy join them, making Cassy feel younger and older at the same time. Being with extroverts also shrinks her further back into her shell.

"Take up their offer, Beccs," Cassy says later. "Take off with them for a day in our Jeep. I don't need to come—I have some things to do. We'll have plenty of time together later. I think the girl appreciated having another female around."

"Very generous," Beccy says, "but it's you I've come on holiday with."

She places her coffee cup carefully on its saucer and leans towards Cassy, folding her arms on the plastic table.

"Okay, Kimmy, are you going to tell me why you've brought me halfway to the Sahara to stay in a run-down hotel in a dirty little town tumbling into the Atlantic?"

Beccy smiles cutely, doing that thing with her face that some girls can do which is guaranteed to win a man's heart. She asks a series of silent questions using the subtlest of movements of her lips, eyes, and neck.

"There's some people here I need to follow up, that's all," Cassy responds. "Sort of work-related, but not quite."

She is pleading for a bit of discreet latitude and a lot of trust.

"I always did want to work on a case with you, Dr. Kim!" Beccy laughs. "What is it? Tomb raiders? I'll trust you not to get me into danger!"

Cassy acknowledges the trust by nodding out to sea. "You see that island out there... just showing beyond the harbour wall? It's the only island off this part of the African coast and has been a prison since the sixteenth century. It's only a mile or so offshore but the reefs are treacherous and there are strong currents between the island and the headland that would take an escaping man out to drown in the Atlantic."

"Conquistador treasure troves then?"

"Not exactly. I was just thinking about the history of this place—the visitors from the sea it's received over the centuries."

They are interrupted by a group of Asian fishermen walking past, arguing in a language familiar to Cassy Kim. They are dressed in rough all-in-one canvas overalls with no sleeves.

"Koreans?" Beccy asks, surprised.

"Trawlermen. They restock supplies on the way up from southern waters or unload their fish. Essaouira's an important sardine port—we can go and see the operations later."

"So what sort of visitors to Essaouira are *you* interested in, Kimmy? Not Korean fishermen, I wouldn't have thought."

"It's hard to know what to tell you, Beccs," Cassy says, as they step over a pile of stinking fish entrails buzzing with flies. "I'm not quite sure what I'm looking for myself, but I have an idea it's going to be good having you around. The first thing I want to do is to visit the woodcarvers under the ramparts. I'm trying to trace a sectarian group importing Essaouiran boxes to England."

"*Mm*. So you're with Customs and Excise on this one?" Beccy asks, feigning disappointment. "Oh well, not quite as glamorous as an international art syndicate, but it'll do. Anything else?"

"It might lead to something else but I can't say what. If the sect has a base in Morocco I'd like to pay a fact-finding visit. In fact, you might be better at that than me. Less conspicuous than a Korean."

"Aha! So that's it." She breaks into her huge open grin. "You've brought me here to do your dirty work. Well, if that's all I have to do to pay for my passage, it sounds a good deal to me. At your service, Kimmy dear!"

Cassy remains serious. She doesn't know what to expect, and Beccy's childlike fun is having a depressing effect on her.

What if things go horribly wrong? The single shot from the forest rings out in her memory, followed by the rustle of a body being dragged through the undergrowth.

They make their way through a maze of dark, cavernous streets paved with granite blocks weathered by the centuries, and leading through ancient archways.

"It's impossible!" Beccy says as they find themselves trapped in yet another dead end. "I wouldn't do this after dark."

They are following a very crude plan provided by the hotel proprietor and they eventually emerge into a small public square. There have been very few signs of

Essaouira's inhabitants in the shady passages but the square is bustling with life. Avenue Sidi Mohammed ben Abdallah, the town's main shopping street, they agree, is somewhere to their right while to their left, through a low stone arch they spot the path that runs along the inside of the great fortified sea wall. Joining a group of tourists filing through the narrow arch, they find themselves in a dark, cobbled street, lined on one side with the workshops of the famous Essaouira woodcarvers.

Cassy looks anxiously at Beccy, who is standing in front of her taking in the medieval scene.

The craftsmen occupy what would once have been gunpowder and weapons stores and barrack space—arched caverns built into the enormously thick sea walls. Some are fronted with rough wooden facades; some are shut up and others have doors open to reveal dingily lit workshops filled with pieces of wood and haphazardly displayed finished products. A few of the arches have been transformed into modern tourist shops, the wooden shutters replaced by glass windows and doors. In these, shelving has been put up on the rear walls and display cabinets stand in the space occupied by materials and tools in the working arches. A pungent scent of fresh cut wood confirms Cassy's detective work. *The same as the box in the forest.*

Tourists haggle with young boys over prices and old men sit cross-legged, applying the skills of their fathers. The sound of hammering, sawing, chiseling, and shouting mingles with the wood dust and fragrant smell. They follow the tourist trail for a while, wandering up and down the craftsmens' row, succumbing to the welcomes and venturing inside the arched Aladdin's caves.

Then, leaving Beccy watching a particularly intricate carving, Cassy makes her way to a vantage point and picks her man. Returning to collect Beccy, she makes her way to one of the modernised premises. Several of the woodworkers have gone in and out of his shop and she had seen him enter a workshop in the arch next to his to shout abuse at its occupant. He is influential—a buyer, perhaps, or landlord. She had also heard him speaking passable English to a tourist.

"Please, please, be welcomed to my shop," he effuses as he makes a fuss of ushering them in. "I am Jamil and you are my guests. Come in, come in; honour me by looking at the most unique handmade works of art. They are famous around the world. A table? I can ship to Asia. You are from Japan? A box? Which size box would you prefer? And your friend? A box for the jewellery, perhaps? Two beautiful ladies! Insha'Allah the young lady will be married before long. Now this is a box traditionally given to brides as a wedding present..."

They sit back and accept the innocuous verbal onslaught, looking around as he goes on.

"Actually we're not tourists," Cassy suddenly interrupts. "I'm from the British Embassy in Rabat and this is my secretary."

Beccy throws her a sharp look. Jamil looks momentarily confused.

"We are with the trade mission and are making a survey of British firms trading in Moroccan crafts."

Cassy draws a typed piece of paper from her pocket, unfolds it and holds it out for Jamil to read. "BRITISH EMBASSY TRADE MISSION, RABAT" is written across the top underneath an official-looking logo.

Jamil peers at it, the wind gone from his sails, and then looks around his shop, as if he might be checking that there is nothing on display that shouldn't be.

"Would you mind if I asked which of the following British companies you have ever had business with?"

"Sure, sure," he says, shrugging his shoulders and lighting a fresh cigarette from a burnt-out stub, his charm suddenly evaporated.

"You buy something from my shop—I answer your questions. It's a good bargain." Said with no smile.

Cassy begins reading through the list she had prepared in London from the trade directory. Beccy, breathing noticeably rapidly, is obliging the charade by wandering around the shop picking up items to examine in a business-like fashion. Jamil stands inhaling strong French cigarette smoke and shaking his head at each name read out. When she is halfway down the list, he reaches out and snatches the paper from her hand, finds the name she has just read, and prods it with a chubby nicotine-stained finger.

"Yes, yes, I have done business with this company. Two years ago, maybe three. What do you want to know?"

Cassy is on thin ice and improvises. "We're putting together a training package for British firms trading in Morocco and need to know which companies have been most successful in building relationships with local suppliers. Was it a successful trading relationship?"

Beccy has stopped browsing to listen with interest, giving Cassy a discreet raised eyebrow.

"I would *never* trade with them again," he says with emphasis, looking up towards the bare electric lightbulb hanging from the ceiling and opening his mouth to let a blue cloud of smoke drift upwards.

"They accused me of not supplying to the order and did not pay on time. Even then they did not pay what we agree." He snorts in contempt.

"Okay," Cassy says, "that's very helpful. Just the sort of information I'm looking for. Let's carry on down the list."

He has dealt with two others. His brother who owns one of the other modernised premises had almost struck a deal with another but hadn't followed it through. Cassy scribbles down details while he peers down the column of typed company names. Right at the bottom of the page he flicks the paper hard with his forefinger and roars: "Haaa! Now you don't need me to tell the British Embassy that Atlas Ocean trades in Essaouira!"

It is a statement that doesn't seem to demand an answer so Cassy shrugs with a nod and makes a noise as if to say "of course not."

"Everyone loves and hates them. Atlas Ocean! Ha! Now there is a perfect importer for you, my good friend from the British Embassy. You shall use them for your training book."

There is only a London address listed on her sheet that Jamil is still holding, so she asks ambiguously, "How often has a representative visited?"

He looks at her as if it is a strange question to ask.

"Good practice indeed. Every week on the same day. He will be here tomorrow. Atlas Ocean has fed our pockets well. Some would say our spirits, too. You can put that in your training books too, mademoiselle."

"Spirits?" she asks, treading carefully.

"You will know all about them—there have been many English with them over the years."

"Sorry." She improvises again. "I've only been in Rabat a few months."

"It is the small village south of Essaouira—you walk along the sand. It can be seen in the distance from the top of these walls." He pointed a finger upwards.

"We have our hippie commune in the sand for many years. Praise be to Allah, now it is within the fold of Islam. Or so some say. I am Berber, my friend. Essaouira is Berber; the Atlas Mountains is Berber. We Berbers have always given honour to the saints and prophets of Islam—there are many saints' tombs everywhere and many have chosen the Sufi way in our great religion. Rabat! You come from Rabat! Even the name of our great capital city means a *house of Sufis*. Aha! We have our own Rabat now in Essaouira. Insha'Allah it will give us prosperity and peace."

It isn't at all clear to Cassy whether or not he is being sarcastic. There is certainly some kind of edge in his sudden burst of energy. He stops and turns his attention to Beccy, who is examining an intricately worked box inlaid with mother of pearl and tiny threads of metal.

"It is silver. The pearl is from the Persian Gulf," he says with pleasure, charm returning.

Cassy has heard enough. Beccy selects a suitably expensive box and Cassy hands over the asking price without the customary haggling. When they are out of sight and climbing up a steep stone flight of stairs to the walkway above the arches, Beccy jumps round in front of Cassy, puts two hands on her shoulders and says, "Brilliant! Kimmy, you are fantastic. Absolutely brilliant! This is going to be *so* exciting! You've done this sort of thing before, haven't you? Where on earth do you learn to do *that?*"

"All in a day's work, Beccs," Cassy says, brushing her off playfully and then pulling her back for an appreciative hug.

Cassy squints to conceal the moisture in her eyes. She rarely gets praised for her skills. She realises shamefully that it is one of the reasons she loves being with Beccy.

"Come on, let's take a look from the top."

The stairs are built into a giant buttress that supports the wall—a magnificent piece of military architecture that could last for a thousand years or more. The walkway running behind the turreted parapet at the top is ten metres or so in width and seems more to be holding the town from falling into the Atlantic Ocean than holding the waves at bay. Beccy jumps up and sits astride the barrel of one of the ancient forty-pounders, peering over the edge at the sea below.

"There it is," Beccy exclaims in her endearingly childish way. "Look, over the rooftops. You can see the beach on the other side of the town."

Two, possibly three miles beyond the far side of the town, a small settlement of low white buildings is shimmering in hot sand.

Retracing their steps, they pass Jamil's shop, door shut up and no one inside. The light is switched off.

"Coincidence?" Beccy asks, a note of seriousness tempering her holiday exuberance.

"Coincidence," Cassy lies.

Chapter 21

April 1994
New Orleans, USA

THERE ARE FOUR of them seated around the oval end of a long boardroom table. At the head sits a tall and lean man with the handsome features of a high caste Indian or Central Asian nobleman and eyes of startlingly deep turquoise-green that are surveying the little group with what could be mild amusement. He has the alertness and bearing of someone not yet past the prime of life, but the sagging tanned skin at the base of his neck, visible above a collarless shirt of fine white linen, suggests he could be considerably older.

To those familiar with the Middle East, he speaks with the gently rounded soft consonants of an Iranian. The Persian linguist in the CIA's National Clandestine Service who listened in on a fragment of phone conversation a few days earlier had thought that she heard hints of a highly palatalised West Iranian dialect. It could have been the Dimili dialect common in eastern Turkey, but then again there was something quite Gilaki about it—from quite a different area altogether, near the Caspian Sea. She had been puzzled, but the fragment, which had been intercepted on a Belgian network, had been so short that it was not worth transcribing.

To the untrained ear, however, the Iranian's English is impeccable. To his left sits an American of similar build but younger and with much less handsome features made weaker by a large moustache and glasses too big for him. The American shifts in his chair uneasily, eyes fixed on a stapled sheaf of papers placed on the table in front of him. To the right of the Iranian sits a man and then a woman, both in their early thirties. The man is wearing a tight-fitting T-shirt under an expensive suit. He is thin but muscular with a shock of thick fair hair and has just spoken, using a cultured Russian accent. In one hand he holds a cigarette between his forefinger and thumb, and with the other he grips his copy of the report that sits in front of each of them. His gaze follows a trail of cigarette smoke spiralling upwards toward the giant wooden fan that revolves slowly in the room's high ceiling. The woman is a less healthy specimen altogether, with a pale face pockmarked with scarring and framed by thin mouse-brown hair. Her grey eyes are sunken, hardened, and distanced, and they are locked on the Iranian's hands as they move in carefully controlled circles on the richly polished tabletop. At the brief introductions—hers was monosyllabic—she had spoken like an American but with the hint of a European accent. The begrudged exchanges had been at the invitation of the Iranian and now he is speaking again.

"Gentlemen." Then, turning with an affected bow of the head: "And ladies. I think we all know why this meeting was necessary."

There is a pause while his hands each make a single circle in opposite directions.

"I am honoured to be your host and grateful that you have made such an effort to oblige each other. We shall not be more than half an hour at most and then, Insha'Allah, you may return to your various... ah, responsibilities."

He speaks slowly with precision and looks at each in turn. Only the Russian refuses to return eye contact.

The Iranian has made only the smallest acknowledgement of the distances they have come. He himself has travelled over the previous three days from Singapore with a flight to Paris Charles de Gaulle, a train to Brussels, and a short flight from Brussels to London's Stanstead Airport. From there he had taken two trains and a black cab to London Heathrow and flown to New Orleans with a connection at Chicago O'Hare. The Russian's journey has been no less circuitous, starting in Moscow and arriving in Louisiana via Madrid, Argentina, and Mexico. The woman has flown in that morning from LAX—Los

Angeles' International Airport—and the American with the moustache, who has had the shortest journey of them all, has driven down the day before from Chattanooga, Tennessee. It is he who has organised the venue—the clubhouse of a luxurious golfing resort at a place called English Turn, named after a decisive battle in the War of Independence. For some in the meeting, the location has ironic significance.

"We have all read our friend's report." The Iranian gives a slight wave towards the American with oversized glasses, although he is still looking at the Russian as though willing his attention. "It is intriguing, I think—I hope to everyone's approval?"

The American is the first to respond.

"May we know *anything* about the origin?" The issue has clearly been raised on some previous occasion.

The Russian carefully lowers his gaze from the ceiling to look first at the Iranian, and then, with obvious contempt, at the questioner.

"The trade embargo doesn't stretch to pieces of stone. There are many corrupt officials in Saddam's cultural bureau."

The Russian's pronunciation of "bureau" has a touch of upper class, indicating either a good English boarding school or mimickery of BBC radio presenters.

"An unprotected site in southern Iraq? Do we know which?" The American with the glasses again.

The Russian only lifts an eyebrow.

"But it's been immersed in sea water for a very long time. Look at paragraph twenty-three." The American flips over a couple of sheets, takes off his glasses, and scans the page, holding it so close to his face that it looks as if he might be trying to smell the salt.

The Russian shrugs as if the matter doesn't interest him.

"But it is authenticated to your satisfaction, I think?" The Iranian speaks, tilting his head slightly for the American's confirmation.

The American nods, putting his glasses back on, slamming the report onto the table and then, as if reconsidering something, shifting it forty-five degrees. "All the characteristics of the earliest cuneiform script but with some unaccountable differences compared to the best known examples."

"Dated." The Russian is now sitting forward, apparently moving into business mode. It is a question but comes out like a threat.

"It's all here," says the American, awkwardly fumbling his way to the middle of the report and flattening the central fold to keep it open. "Three different methods giving an average of approximately..." He looks up nervously. "Six thousand years."

A silence follows, in which each of the four seem to be calculating the significance of this information to their own particular interests.

"It's impossible," says the Russian at last, "but his results match ours. A Japanese and a Moscow lab came up with the same."

There is another long silence and the Russian resumes his interest in the ceiling fan while the others leaf through the report.

Eventually the Iranian folds his hands in a priestly gesture and looks slowly at each of his guests as if inviting dissention. Then, staring down the long table to a golfer on a green outside, golf club raised above his head, says: "Then the deal is struck?"

Immediately he turns and looks directly at the woman.

Her lips are pursed and she is staring to one side of him where one of two immaculate American flags of heavy cloth and elaborate white rope-work regale the darkly panelled walls. The second flag is on the other side of the Iranian, giving him the appearance of some senior

Washington official or perhaps a past American president in a waxwork museum.

Awkwardly, she shifts a fraction in her seat so that her back is partially turned to the Russian, although she is still looking past him at the Iranian. She glances at the American opposite her for a brief moment in what could be unspoken communication, and then nods to the Iranian. "Deal," she whispers. Then she coughs nervously.

Chapter 22

Essaouira, South Morocco
July 2000
BECCY HADN'T HAD to do much to convince the Australians to join her on an overnight excursion along the coastal trails to the south. They had driven through the sand dunes and found the commune easily enough. It was the only two-storey house in the village and stood in its own walled compound. It was locked up and a villager told them that its occupants were *en retraite*.

"Retreat to where?" Cassy asks as Beccy recounts the story. "Why would anyone need to retreat from a backwater village like that?"

"Perhaps it's like hi-fi," Beccy says. "The more you appreciate the subtleties, the more sophisticated your tastes get. They went to the mountains—they've got another centre somewhere at altitude. We had better luck on the way back today, though—the place was swamped by two coachloads of Americans on a tour from Marrakech. Back in the sixties there was a big musical party in the Roman ruins the other side of the dunes. Everyone shacked up in the village—including Bob Dylan and other icons, fans, locals—and the party drifted on for weeks. Imagine that. It's a celebrated place—if you're in the know."

"That's when the hippies moved in?"

"No, that was later, but it must have been an influence. Anyway, we met a girl. She was sitting on her own under a fig tree—about the only shade in the village—after the coaches had gone. I thought she'd been left behind. Did you ever see any of those documentaries about people who get caught up in cults and can't get out? Or people who are all twisted up but don't want to get out? That's what she reminded me of."

"Not on retreat with the rest, then?"

"It seemed like she was there by herself, from what she was saying, but a spooky sort of guy turned up right at the end—after we'd been talking. The girl said she'd volunteered to stay back to look after the building. It looked like the guy was minding her—or had come looking for her. He had a Moroccan cloak on with the hood up and was really offish—North African or Mid East, but pretty good English. It all finished when he turned up. I would say the girl had just had some sort of a bad turn when we saw her—or was on something. She was retching every so often as we talked and wasn't exactly stable on her feet. Drugged up or right on the edge."

"Did she ask for help?"

"In an indirect sort of way. Jamie and I—the Australian girl—talked to her while the boys were in the sea and we both thought she was dead scared. She came out with quite a bit about the sect after I'd told her I was interested in staying in the commune to try it out. Thought you'd be proud of me for that one—you should have seen Jamie's face. Anyway, it drew a strong reaction—this was before the guy turned up. She got all agitated and started hyperventilating—like she was going into an asthma attack. Then she started shouting at us and looking around and jerking her head. She ended up sobbing her wretched heart out—I felt desperately sorry for her and so useless! She started talking after that."

"So what did you get?"

"Quite a lot, actually, given the state the poor wretch was in."

"They're a seriously mixed-up bunch. Bonkers. They started off in the seventies as an Atlantis cult, hence the location, I guess—doesn't Atlas and the gates of Gibraltar figure somewhere in the Atlantis story? It's not the only place the sect is based. There are other groups in America and elsewhere—all over the place. Then again, she wasn't all there, so maybe she was exaggerating. It seems to have started off with something of a doomsday take on the

Atlantis story—into generating spiritual energy to avert earthquakes and natural disasters. A sort of a New Age monastery, I suppose, moving those energy lines on behalf of humankind—that sort of thing. I'm not sure exactly where Atlantis fitted in. From what I could understand, they were just obsessed with it—she didn't really make much sense on that bit. Maybe it was just a device for focusing members—cult leaders do that, don't they?"

"Where was she from?" Cassy asks.

"Dutch. Leen. That's her name. Leen. And she said she's been with them since her teens! She's probably early thirties now. Can you imagine? What a life!"

"Why on earth do the Moroccan authorities tolerate a group like that? Surely not just on the basis of their export activities? It doesn't require a whole commune to ship a few trinkets. You don't even need an office in the country."

"That's easy. They've set themselves up as a travellers' hostel and are good for the tourist trade. We could stay overnight if you want to see for yourself—it's really cheap."

"I wonder if Leen's parents know where she's been for the past fifteen years," Cassy muses.

"Anyway," Beccy continues, sounding now as though she has been an authority on the subject for years, "the Atlantis *thing* went off the boil some time ago. Remember Jamil's comments? Well, the way Leen told it, someone's come in and been working on a corporate take-over. The old gang were falling apart with in-fighting and apathy—the whole thing was getting incestuous and heading for self-destruct."

"What did she have to say about the new regime?"

"The new influence seems to have worked its way in via a Moroccan member who converted to mystical Islam—he was one of the leaders in the original set-up."

"And the old leaders?"

"They all seem to have bought in—she was paranoid about being the only one not toeing the line. I think groups like that must get to be like a family after a while. Once you've gone beyond a certain point of investing your life into it, perhaps the precise issues of creed don't matter too much. Someone came along offering a new spiritual focus and everyone's happy because the party can continue."

"Except those tipped over the edge already."

***

Three days after Beccy had met Leen a note arrives with her early morning pot of mint tea. It is in a sealed envelope, and the hotel staff inform Beccy that it was dropped into the hotel by a young lady very early that morning.

"Dear Beccy, I am glad we talked. If you want to know more about our community, please talk to Sami. He will visit to the woodworker's workshops in Essaouira tomorrow. He gets there at 8.30 in the morning. You will not miss him; he will be talking business with one of the craftsmen. Also he is almost seven feet tall."

"Sami," Beccy says, sitting cross-legged on Cassy's bed, munching a very dry biscuit. "That's the name of the Moroccan leader I told you about. How about we do this one together?"

The following morning they are standing under the arch leading from the town square into the woodworkers' street and haven't been waiting more than two minutes when, without warning, Jamil's voice sounds very close. Cassy grabs Beccy's arm and retreats behind one of the columns forming the arch at the same time as Jamil's back appears, feet away, hands on hips as if waiting for someone. He shouts to someone and then walks straight back in the direction of his shop. Cassy steps forward a few paces to peer round the corner, seeing him gesticulating in an urgent manner to a giant of a man whose hand he is holding on to as if the tall man might run away. They are standing in the entrance to one of the workshops and Jamil is now thumping a ledger book and talking in a high-pitched gabble. The other man looks down at him silently, but as Cassy watches, raises his eyes and looks over in her direction. His eyes meet Cassy's for a brief moment and then move on.

Cassy's grip on Beccy's hand tightens and she hears Beccy wince from behind the pillar. Jamil goes inside the shop, carrying on the conversation in muffled shouts while the tall man remains outside, his eyes moving slowly along the lane, hesitating at the groups of early-rising tourists, and then moving on. Cassy is about to retreat when Beccy steps out from the shadows. The giant's gaze immediately returns to Cassy and she sees him take in the picture. He has found what he is looking for. Without a word to Jamil, who still seems to be shouting at him from within the shop, he heads straight towards them with huge un-Moroccan-like strides. There is nothing they can do but wait to see what will happen next. When he reaches them, instead of stopping, he grabs both their wrists and in one swift move pulls them back around into the shadows. He turns and, looking intensely at Cassy, says in confident English with a heavy French accent: "Welcome, sister, please follow me—we will talk privately."

There is not so much as a nod of acknowledgement to Beccy. Before either of them can say anything, he is off in the direction of a little alley that disappears into the warren of passages Cassy and Beccy had navigated on their first visit to the craftsmen's quarter. They step in line, trotting to keep up. Beccy takes hold of Cassy's arm tightly and draws close as their guide leads them deep into the dark maze before suddenly stopping. He is standing outside one of the many ancient timbered doorways and extending a hand to usher them in through an open door from which a single shaft of daylight is sparkling.

Inside, the contrast with the dark, airless passages that function as streets could not be greater. They step into an expansive sunlit courtyard dazzling with terracotta pots of purple bougainvillea and scarlet hibiscus. In the centre is a low fountain gently bubbling over a cobalt and ultramarine mosaic. The rest of the courtyard is patterned in white, turquoise, and terracotta tiles and vines rise on all sides towards the open sky four floors up. Beccy stands mouth open at the sight and mouths to Cassy: *A secret garden*.

Their guide must have seen her reaction, for acknowledging her for the first time, he says, "It is a surprise to the first-time visitor, no? I am pleased that it gives you pleasure. Please come. We shall sit."

He leads them to a corner of the tiled courtyard where a rug and cushions adorned with tassels and small mirrors form an outdoor room. When they are seated he turns to Cassy and says, "So… you are a friend of Brother Isa."

Cassy is utterly speechless.

She had anticipated a number of conversation starters, but not this one. Since she cannot tell from his look or tone whether being a friend of Isa is a good thing or a bad thing, she says, "Would that make us friends or enemies?"

Beccy looks at Cassy uncertainly. Cassy's unspoken response offers no comfort. It is an uncanny rerun of her visit with Chav to the Sufis' Bangkok home.

Sami smiles a serene smile that Cassy has seen before and says, "Your cautious answer shows that you are well-informed. Forgive me, but it is important… when did you last see him?"

"About a month ago, in Bangkok," Cassy replies. "He was with Nooh and several others. He is well, very well. Apart from the weight of his role as father to many. Some of the brothers were nearing the end of the forty-day fast. He takes the responsibility upon himself."

Beccy is now staring at Cassy in astonishment. Cassy is wondering where the inspired improvising came from.

"And the apartment?" the giant enquires with cordiality.

"The old apartment," Cassy says. "It is not perfect but it is adequate. The lift lobby makes a good meeting room.

You have been there too." She says it so that it could be a question or an acknowledgement.

"Yes, I have sat in Isa's famous lobby."

There is a silence before he sighs and says, "So my friend, you are really from the British Embassy in Rabat? Have Isa's disciples achieved such success? Or was that righteous deception?"

Not wanting to commit herself on that one just yet, Cassy tries the kind of enigmatic smile she has seen used so effectively by his kind. It works, for he immediately turns to Beccy and gives her a slow and respectful bow.

While his head is down, Beccy shoots Cassy a murderous look and signals to the door with panicked eyes.

"She is my younger sister," Cassy explains, laying her hand gently on Beccy's arm. Then adds, "And an inquirer of the *way*. I won't burden you with my official reason for travelling to your country but it was a convenient opportunity. I had to come here."

Beccy's eyes are now tightly shut and it looks as if she might faint.

Drawing on Isa's revelation about his brother and the conversation in the forest Cassy cranks up the risk: "So, there are tensions besetting us all. Isa has shared some of it. How bad has it got here? And Odam…?"

The last question is asked in a way that doesn't necessarily link Isa's brother with things getting bad. She is feeling her way with scrupulous care. The gamble pays off for he starts shaking his head and tutting thoughtfully. At the same time he stretches himself out into a semi-recline, places his hands behind his head, and shuts his eyes.

"Very bad. Things have become *very* bad."

There is a long silence. Then, without opening his eyes, he says, "The envoy sent by Odam was an angel of light when he made the first visit. We found ourselves loving and fearing him."

Another silence as he screws up his face.

"And now?" Cassy asks gently.

"And now... I don't know, my friend. And now I find myself sharing a table with... with schemers. By light I was drawn to Isa. They were rescuers, redeemers, life-givers—we had all but died here. We were spiritually bankrupt. Most were wide open to the *way* of the Noah Brotherhood. We did not know that it is a way that divides quickly after the journey is started. Most take the fork that leads to... to corruption."

He sits up again and looks Cassy in the eye.

"Those who welcome darkness become slaves to darkness, *mon amie*. Most of what used to be my family here are now slaves. Perhaps they have always been so. Enslaved without knowing it. They are beyond help."

"And you have not tried to leave?"

"To answer that," he says, "I would have to tell you just how deep our depravity had become. It is hard for an outsider to understand how completely the mind and conscience can be deceived. I must bear some of the blame for what has befallen us—I cannot leave them. This is my punishment. I will also bear my portion of our shame. Besides..." He looks up at the sky above and lets his gaze wander around the courtyard.

He doesn't finish his sentence.

"When were you with Isa?" Cassy asks, relaxing into what she alarmingly realises is only half-charade.

He brightens. "He did not tell you? It was not long after Odam's disciples first paid a visit to our community. It was I who introduced them here. As a young man I once had the free-thinking Sufi hunger for love and light in my heart. Early on, the community seemed a bearable place for my personal search. Then my light went out. Once, when one of Isa's disciples came to teach in the mountains, I went to hear him. My soul was captured—re-ignited. He had everything we had lost, perhaps everything we never had. Then Odam's people came and spent a while with us. I knew... sensed... from the start. About Odam. But I had seen integrity and truth in the Sufi in the mountains and I would not let it go. Odam was still wooing us and his envoys did not refuse when I asked to visit Isa in Bangkok."

He sits silent for a while and then asks, "How was it with you when Isa spoke?"

"I too was captured," Cassy answers and, hearing herself, she knows indeed that this is not pretence. Beccy's jaw drops a fraction before she buries her head in her hands.

The silence is broken by the clink of glasses on a tray. An elderly lady in a blue and yellow floral headscarf hobbles painfully towards them with two glasses and a brass mint teapot with a traditional spout shaped like the long curved beak of a wading bird.

"There are three of us," he says firmly but kindly. "Another glass, please."

He watches kindly as she hobbles back to a door in the far corner of the courtyard, and then turns to Cassy and explains, "My mother."

He sees surprise in her eyes and explains, "My father was French. Actually half-French, half-English. His family was from Gibraltar." With an expansive gesture and a wistful smile he says, "My family home. There is no one else now, just my mother and me."

"You live here with her?" Cassy asks.

"What do you think it feels like, my friend, to give yourself to something for a quarter of a century and then to find that you have been mistaken? That you have wasted the best years of your life. Look at me; I am a middle-aged man. What do you think it feels like for a mother to lose her only son, to suffer the insult of undeserved rejection? She is crippled with a disease of the joints and her heart is weak. Withered by the bitterness and pain of my folly. For twenty years I hardly saw her, cast her out of my life, disowned her. Living a few kilometres apart but in different worlds. Allah be merciful to me."

He pauses and sips the sweet-smelling tea.

"Isa's words were my release. When I first heard him speak, they stripped me naked. They were words of cleansing and healing. They brought back my youth, dragged me from a living death. That's what most in the commune have become—living dead."

He pauses again, and then seems to realise that he hasn't answered Cassy's question and says, "No. I do not live here. That would be to leave the community, to abandon... an act of treachery. You have never lived in a community for a long time? What seems possible to those in the world beyond is not possible within. Even for one such as me, with the chains of delusion broken, the chains of fear often return to haunt and threaten. No, I cannot leave. At least not yet. Perhaps never."

He lifts the teapot and, with a graceful gesture, pours tea from a height into the empty glasses. Pungent steam drifts along the tiles turning the courtyard into a mint field.

Intrigued by the unsolicited outpouring of his soul, Cassy asks, "Are there others who feel the same as you?"

"There is one other who follows Isa's way—a Sufi in the heart, a lover of goodness. But not one of the original family—joining more lately and coming and going less constrained by the bonds that tie the rest of us."

"Leen?" she asks.

He looks up with alarm. Cassy recoils, wondering what she has said wrong.

"No, it is not Leen," he says, a note of wariness entering his voice. "But how do you know of Leen?"

For the second time in the conversation Cassy is nonplussed.

How the hell did you know we are here if it wasn't Leen who told you? And the Isa connection? What the bloody hell's going on?

Frantically suppressing a rising panic, she merely says, "Beccy here met Leen at the village the other day. She drove there with some Australian friends."

He looks at Cassy and then Beccy without speaking and then says, "So you have met poor Leen. I have not seen her recently. She has been staying away from here. Leen is ill. She is sick in the mind. There have been a few like her but they are taken care of…"

Her mind reeling to make sense of the situation, Cassy takes the offensive again. It is all she can think of doing.

"Do you mind if I ask about the community in the early days? I am interested to know who drew you all together right at the beginning."

I doubt if it's the man sitting in front of me.

"We were young and impressionable hippies; idealists, and gullible. Our founding father is a man we used to call Solon. Now we just call him Viejo Hombre—Old Man. Some of our number are Spanish. He is old and long ago lost his charisma. He enchanted us with stories of Atlantis and spun his mystical doctrines of nature and civilisation. It was simple—primitive, even. Pagan. Atlantis represented the wrath of Mother Nature, the same wrath seen in the volcano, the storm and the earthquake. By walking close to her, submitting our lives in obedience to her discipline, we believed we could intercede for the rest of humanity. As we tilled the barren slopes of the Atlas Mountains and dug salt with our bare hands, we humbled ourselves before the spirits of nature and restored the rightful balance. We did it for everyone else. We kept another Atlantis catastrophe at bay."

"Solon was interested in the archaeological quest for Atlantis?" Cassy asks.

He has been moving his glass in circles on the tray, staring at the patterns in the tea, but he stops and looks up. "Solon? Finding Atlantis? Yes. Finding other things too…"

Then he says in a quiet and purposeful voice, "I will get it now."

With that, he eases himself to his feet, straightens his djellaba, and makes his way to one of the doors that opens onto the courtyard.

As soon as his back is turned, Beccy gives Cassy another intense glare but is sensible enough not to say anything—or too petrified. He returns with a leather bag—

the sort sold in the night bazaars of every town in Morocco. It is made in the style of a small knapsack about a foot wide at the base and is secured with a single leather buckle fastener. The smell of poorly cured animal skin wafts with the mint as he places it carefully on the floor next to Cassy's cushion seat.

"May I?" she asks, laying a hand on the bag that he seems to be giving her.

"Please, but it is wrapped up, sealed. I have been hiding it here since taking it from the safe—Solon doesn't know I have the code. You should not take the seal off. It is old and would deteriorate quickly. The heat and the dust."

Sweat breaks out on Cassy's brow.

I hear something important went missing and warfare's broken out.

The Brotherhood is being broken apart by something taken that belonged to another.

She picks up the bag and places it cautiously on her lap, words of the murdered courier and of Isa playing in her mind.

"You will take it to Isa immediately?" he says.

"Immediately," Cassy says, wildly trying to think of how to get away.

It isn't going to be easy, however, for it seems that he is beginning to relish the chance to talk.

"Solon is old," he says, once again making circles on the tray with his glass. "And no more our beloved father, but he is not senile. Sometimes I think he would like people to think he is senile—but he is not. He was once a professor. In the 1960's—a young professor in an American university. There is still an inner circle he confides with, but I am no longer part of it. There are others... in America... Ukiah, Yakima... other places too."

Cassy makes a mental note of the names.

"How does Solon feel about the Sufism?" she asks.

"The old man is tolerant. More than tolerant. He knew he had lost us. He welcomed Odam's interest and the new purpose... and wealth... he offered us. He remains secure in his new prosperity—and his own paranoid delusions."

"So what keeps the whole thing together?" she asks, looking around the room and toward the door.

He smiles. "It is a reasonable question to ask, my friend, and there can be only one answer to it. Fear. Fear—we all feel it in different ways but it keeps us together one way or another."

There is a long silence, and Cassy sits summoning courage to leave; she senses the fear that he is fighting against.

"We must not overstay our hospitality," she says at last. "You have been most kind. Your mother too."

She pulls herself up to a crouching position. "Please thank her for the refreshments."

The intention to end the interview is not challenged. They all get to their feet.

"How long does the mountain retreat last for?" Cassy asks to ease the intensity of the moment. "Are you returning?"

"Leen told you about the retreat?" he says. "It will last for another week, maybe two. The Old Man and Abdullah will return here tomorrow evening and I will go back to the mountains with them the day after."

"Abdulla?"

"Abdullah leads. He is Odam's *shadow* here."

"Where is Odam?"

"Odam is everywhere and nowhere. In Iraq. In Basra in the south, where he has many under his influence. In Bagdad. In Jerusalem. In the Far East. In London..."

He brightens, stooping to pick up the leather bag and handing it to her. "You will see Isa soon then?"

This time she doesn't have to lie. Cassy has already decided she will have to make another visit to the mystic in Southeast Asia. "Yes, as soon as possible. Within the next month I would hope."

Sami's reply makes her heart miss a beat.

"I tried to speak to him on the telephone last night."

Somehow she hadn't bargained for that.

"I spoke to one of the brothers," he says. "Isa has gone away for a while, it seems. I do not have the chance to phone often."

"He's travelling through the villages of southern Thailand," Cassy explains, desperate to get out before another question exposes her. "Like his brother, he is a conscientious teacher and encourager."

"Odam and his devotees teach but do not encourage," he corrects.

At this, Sami seemed to throw off any last remaining reservation about Cassy. For the first time since they had entered the house, his eyes crease into a warm smile of gratitude tinged with a hint of sadness and without warning he stoops to embrace her with a most un-Middle Eastern bear hug, drawing her with muscular arms into his broad chest.

Cassy reciprocates, with a genuineness that shocks Beccy, who is looking on in complete disbelief. He holds the affectionate embrace, making it hard for Cassy to breathe. When Sami eventually lets her go, she turns so Beccy cannot see and wipes tears from her eyes.

"I do not want to be seen with you," Sami says in a lowered voice. "Abdullah is not the only shadow Odam possesses. You will turn left out of my mother's house and then take the next left turning and through the first arch on your right. This will take you to a small square from which you will be able to find your way back to the harbour easily enough."

As he is opening the heavy wooden door to let them out into the gloom, he stops.

"I almost forgot. Please excuse me for a minute," he says, easing the door shut again and hurrying back across the courtyard.

He returns with a piece of paper. "This is yours," he says. "I will not be rude enough to ask why you approached me in this way, but you may want it back."

Cassy takes the paper. It is the list of import–export firms she had shown to Jamil in his shop. She turns it over and there on the back in her scribbled writing are the words *Isa, Bangkok, Ark, Essaouira, Sumerian keys, final key?* The words she had idly jotted down the night she arrived in Essaouira. Jamil had handed the suspicious piece of paper to his regular visitor from the sect.

Chapter 23

"WHAT DO WE say if Moroccan or British customs search us?"

They are sat at a dirty cafe in a public square at the back of the town next to a small industrial quarter that extends out of the ancient citadel along the Rue de Mellah towards the rugged coast that leads eventually to Casablanca two hundred miles or so to the north. The familiar breakfast smell of diesel and sardines is present, only it is from buses rather than fishing boats. A charcoal burner glowing in the corner periodically bursts into flames with fish oil, choking breakfasters with smoke and adding flavour to an already earth-rough coffee.

Beccy is in uncharacteristically touchy mood. After leaving Sami's house the day before they had made their way through the dark passages of the Kasbah in silence. As soon as they emerged into the busy harbour she had turned on Cassy. First she shouted, and then cried, and then hit Cassy, and eventually laughed and cried at the same time. She had not enjoyed the experience.

"It's only a tape," Cassy says, waving a cloud of fishy smoke away.

"But what sort of tape?" Beccy says, looking around at the other customers and lowering her voice. "And what's on it? It doesn't look like it's going to be Sufi Isa's top ten sermons."

The leather bag had contained a single package, carefully wrapped against the elements in plastic and secured with heavy-duty sticky tape. Inside was an old-fashioned tin case for a film cartridge, but it was not a thirty-five-millimetre film reel but magnetic computer tape—the type that had been stolen from Cassy's apartment. It was obviously old and carried no labels.

"That, my dear Becs, we do not know. But we either take it or dump it and I intend to take it. I'll think of something to say."

"You're good at that," Beccy says with emphasis. Then she leans forward so her face almost touches Cassy's and whispers: "Please don't *ever* do that to me again, Cassy! You want to take the tape? You clear customs on your own. You've just lost a helper to cowardice."

Then she bursts out laughing as she had the day before and reaches across the table to pat Cassy's hand.

"Don't worry. I'll stop being cross with you after a bit. I'd just rather be out of this place, like hours ago." She looks around again to emphasise the point. "The tyre should be ready by now."

They had risen early to pack the four-wheel drive. It was only when they had checked out of the hotel that Beccy had noticed the flat tyre. There turned out to be one garage open, also serving as a bus service station, which is why they are eating where they are.

Looking at her watch, Cassy says, "Let's go and see. We'll hit the road and still get almost a full day's driving between us and this place."

She is as edgy as Beccy, though has been trying not to show it. They have agreed to drive to Marrakech, leave the hire car there, and catch a Royal Air Maroc flight to the South of France. They will find somewhere sunny, familiar, and safe for the second week of their holiday. Cassy's business in Morocco is done.

Fifteen minutes later they are driving back through the town. There had been no complications and the garage had even accepted American Express. As they pull onto the only main road out of Essaouira, Cassy eases back into the contours of the driving seat, a sense of relief settling in, when without warning Beccy shouts and grabs Cassy's arm, forcing the vehicle onto a sandy verge.

"Shit, Becs! What are you doing?"

"Over there! By the prickly pear cactus! Can't you see her?" The vehicle comes to an abrupt stop and Cassy looks over to where Beccy is pointing.

"Leen?" Cassy says, immediately matching the pathetic figure before them with Beccy's earlier description.

Beccy jumps out and runs over the road, to where a dishevelled European girl in a filthy and torn kaftan is on her knees leaning forward, face in the sand, like a Muslim at prayer. Beccy is kneeling too, shouting directly into her face. "Come on, Leen! Leen... can you hear me? We met the other day, remember? Leen?" Leen's eyes are open wide as she slowly sits up, staring into the distance in a trance-like state. Cassy cautiously walks around her, looking for signs of injury. Beccy shouts again, and then whispers; then she takes her by the shoulders and gently shakes her. The physical contact works. She lets out a stifled scream and looks left and right with wild, exaggerated movements. She catches sight of Cassy and freezes. Then she turns her head to stare at Beccy, her eyes trying to focus.

"Beccy?" she says, this time in a hoarse whisper.

"Yes, it's me," Beccy says. "Don't worry, you're okay. What happened? How long have you been lying here?"

"I'm coming with you. I'm leaving... need to leave... I waited for you... we must go!"

Beccy shrugs her shoulders to a mouthed question from Cassy. *How did she know when we were leaving?*

"Where, Leen?" Beccy says gently and slowly. "Where do you want us to take you?"

Leen answers by stumbling over to the vehicle, fumbling with the rear door handle and, with pained exertion, climbing in. Again Cassy and Beccy look at each other, unsure what to do. She sits there hugging her small canvas shoulder bag tightly to her emaciated chest. Cassy approaches her like a timid animal and tries again, talking as if to a child. "Leen, can we take you to a hospital? How about back to the village?"

Beccy jumps to Leen's defence with a sharp prod in Cassy's back. But the offer has the desired effect. Leen starts shaking her head in the same uncontrolled movement.

"We should have let the great earthquake come," she moans. "We were too kind." She looks up and gives what might be meant as a smile but comes out as a snarled grimace.

"Now the great harlot has been let loose there is no stopping her. Before there was Russia; now there is no power on earth strong enough. We should not have interceded; we have let the great harlot loose to roam the earth. She will devour everybody."

She looks over at Beccy. "They won't let me out... but we must try. When they let Russia join we knew they had won—for now. Wait until G13—then you will see the harlot's true nature! They will all see the monster they have unleashed. No, they will never let us out."

Cassy turns to Beccy and whispers, "Come on, Becs, let's get her out of here—she needs professional help. It'll have to be a hospital in Marrakech."

Beccy draws Cassy away from the vehicle and whispers, "Let's take her to the Dutch consulate first. There's bound to be one in a place as big as Marrakech. Or the British, if there's no Dutch. We've got to help her more than just dumping her off in a Moroccan public hospital. What are they going to make of her in a general hospital in a place like this?"

For the next two hours, Leen hardly says a word. She sits staring out of the window and refuses to be drawn into any form of conversation. Beccy tries a few times but with the same result. The road starts to wind into the foothills of the High Atlas and progress becomes very slow. There are trucks on the road carrying fish from Essaouira and sending a pungent stench through the air-conditioning as they overtake. There is another smell too. The smell of someone who has been sleeping rough and taking drugs.

As the road winds higher into the mountains, Leen becomes more and more agitated. She starts muttering and is in full swing with an incoherent monologue when Cassy suddenly hits the air-conditioning switch to be better able to catch what Leen is saying.

Did you hear that? she mouths to Beccy.

Beccy had, and nods solemnly. Then Leen says it again, quite clearly this time.

"The killings. All around, but no one noticed. No one wanted to know."

Beccy has her seat belt off and is half out of her seat, leaning towards Leen, touching her on the arm.

"Stop, Cassy... can we pull over somewhere?"

Leen is getting very upset, fidgeting and wringing her hands in a desperately pathetic gesture. She picks up her bag, pulls it open, and starts rummaging around inside.

"*Stop*, Cassy, please bloody stop. I need to try and calm her down... look... up the road there... there... a turning off... into that clump of trees... see?"

Cassy breaks hard to slow enough for the turning and manoeuvres the jeep onto a rocky track that leads into a small grove of olive-like trees. It is the only vegetation and the only shade around. The banana plantations, bamboo groves, and prickly pears of the coastal plain have been left far behind. Everywhere is a dark and foreboding bare rock, layered in great folds and coloured shades of deep brown, black, and grey. Into the distance they turn into a ruggedly undulating sea of black bare-rock mountains, rippling its way south. It is a cold and inhospitable environment.

By the time Cassy has switched off the engine, Leen is lurching towards the door, her head pressed against the window. Beccy jumps through the gap in the front seats, trying to put an arm around her, but is fought off with a violence that does not belong to her small frame. Cassy jumps out and as she opens the rear door, Leen leaps past her and dashes towards the shade of the trees, her bag falling to the ground, its contents scattering around the rear wheel. Cassy and Beccy are both running, and reach her as she is violently sick. Cassy looks away and returns to the Jeep to fetch a water bottle.

The trees in the isolated grove have yellow olive-shaped fruit hanging by slender stalks. The raw material for the Essaouiran craftsmen. The ancient *argan* tree—one of the oldest tree species on earth, found only in this small area of southwest Morocco and thought to have been growing here for eighty million years.

Looking at the trees' ancient knurled roots, it suddenly occurs to Cassy that the wooden box she had plucked from the hollow tree in the London forest must have had a false base. It had been exceptionally thick and too heavy for its size.

Beccy is walking over to Cassy. She has hardly asked anything about Cassy's odd conversation with Sami but now she says, "What's on the tape, Cassy?" She has left Leen sitting against the tree with her eyes closed. There is nowhere she can run to.

"I really don't know, Becs. I can't even guess."

"But you came to Essaouira to collect it, didn't you? You must have done."

Cassy shakes her head. "I know it's difficult to believe, but no, I didn't. I came to find out about the cult—that's all."

"But you couldn't have made all that up on the spot—about... what was his name? Isa? You do know him, don't you?"

"Yes. I know Isa—he's an elderly Sufi living in exile in Bangkok. But what happened back there was pure and inexplicable coincidence. Having waded in that far, I couldn't exactly refuse the tape."

Beccy wanders back to the Jeep, deep in thought, and starts gathering together the contents of Leen's bag.

Cassy reaches up for one of the yellow olives and turns at the sound of hurried footsteps. Beccy is running towards her with something in her hand.

"Look," she whispers with urgency and thrusts three passports into Cassy's hand. "Her name's not Leen. It's Janice. Janice Molenaar, and she's from Belgium, not the Netherlands. And... look... look at the other passports... she's got children... two children…"

***

It is another four hours before they reach the outskirts of the oasis city of Marrakech, a harmonious composition of desert-red buildings and green date palm fronds. The mountain road eventually drops down into a barren flat plain of rocks with the occasional palm tree and isolated group of single-storey whitewashed farm compounds. The setting makes Marrakech all the more majestic and enchanting. In the distance it appears as a low, reddish glow on the horizon, like Ayers Rock rising out of the Australian outback. Before they reach any buildings, the tall and slender date palms appear, first scattered thinly then thickening until the road becomes a grand tree-lined boulevard. Behind the palms, clusters of mud houses start to appear, and they too became closer and closer together until they arrive at the city's suburbs—and then they are driving alongside the city's magnificent fortifications. Everything in every direction is the same deep, vibrant terracotta.

There is a stirring in the back as Cassy slows the Jeep down to turn into the old city through a gap in the towering wall. Beccy has made Leen lie down on the rear seat, and she has been asleep for much of the journey.

"We are going to look for a hospital, Leen," Cassy says over her shoulder. "And a consulate or embassy."

As soon as she says it Cassy knows it is a mistake. Leen has lied about her name and nationality. Cassy has also noticed something else—the children's passports have been tampered with. She can't say how, exactly, but she recognises a forgery when she sees one. She hasn't mentioned it to Beccy. She has been waiting for Leen to wake—for one final attempt to provoke some more information. It might be her last chance.

They turn into a crowded street full of open-air cafes and drive along slowly looking for a place to stop. Cassy has decided they need three strong cups of coffee and directions. There are many small side streets, some closed to traffic and filled with cafe tables, occupied mostly by Moroccan men. Then they pass a row of slightly smarter restaurants, and Cassy spots an empty space.

Unfastening her seatbelt, Beccy says to Leen, "We'll get you into safe hands before long."

Leen looks shocked. "But... I am coming with you. Let me stay in the car, please."

"You need help—more than we can give, I'm afraid," Beccy says firmly but with gentleness. "It's the best for you. There's no other option—we're leaving the car here and flying back to France."

Leen doesn't like it. Panic rises and it looks like she might slip back into silence or worse. Cassy seizes the moment before it is lost.

"Where are your children, Leen? Did you leave them behind in Essaouira?"

There is a pause while she takes in the question, and then lets out a gasp, clutches her head, and shouts, "I do not have children! I do not want to have the children. Take them away, no... no... no, please. Don't let them make me do it! Help me, please... oh, please, please... God help me!"

The outpouring is intense but brief and ends in an empty silence.

Cassy leans to whisper in Beccy's ear, "Right. Hospital first…"

She is interrupted by a bang behind her and looks round to find that Leen has jumped out of the Jeep.

"Which way did she go?" Cassy shouts, scanning the street.

There are people everywhere and Leen is nowhere to be seen. Someone sitting at the nearest cafe shouts something and points to the street running down the side of the cafe.

"We can't leave the Jeep, Becs," Cassy shouts, starting to run. "Stay here—whatever you do, don't leave the Jeep."

By this time the whole restaurant is watching. Cassy dodges shoppers, tourists, chairs, and waiters, and turns into the side road and stops. A large truck is blocking the entire lane and sweaty men are heaving boxes of vegetables down and stacking them on the road. She squeezes past and curses as she steps in a stinking puddle of fetid rubbish. She clears the truck and looks around. A few people are standing further down the lane but there is no sign of Leen. Cassy runs on a bit further, sees a lane leading through to another of the side roads leading back to the main street, and takes it. Leen has vanished. Cassy runs up and down four or five similar roads and back into the crowded main street. It is getting darker by the minute. Breathless and dripping with sweat, she returns to the Jeep, torn between sadness and guilt.

"She's gone" is all she can manage.

"Oh, Cassy... the poor wretch."

Back in the Jeep, Cassy puts her arm around Beccy's shoulder and Beccy reaches a hand up to touch Cassy's. For the second time in as many days, Cassy's eyes well up and she feels the warmth of tears on her face. She is thinking of the sadness of Sami's arthritic mother, and now, Leen's mother. She might not even know that her daughter is still alive. Cassy wonders how much longer she will be.

Then she gasps.

"Shit."

"What?" Beccy pulls away, looking out at the crowd, thinking Cassy has spotted a new predicament. But Cassy is staring into her open rucksack.

"It was on the back seat. I had an envelope in my rucksack containing thirty thousand U.S. dollars in hundreds. It's gone—and you didn't leave the vehicle, right?"

Chapter 24

July 2000
Central London

CASSY IS SITTING in the kitchen of her London home with the rain thundering against the window and an even greater storm engulfing her dangerously overloaded mind that is suddenly numbed with shock.

On the computer screen in front of her is a reply from Etienne Giraud, an organised crime tsar with the French police, heading an intelligence unit based in Marseilles. They had spoken once before on a French–Egyptian antiquities case, and she had emailed him only half an hour earlier, following an email sent to Ashi asking him, in cryptic terms, to tip someone off in the French authorities about Leen—or Janice.

"No information for the Moroccan group you ask me about. But one of the names gets a hit, perhaps. This man you called Sami, if he is the same one, he is found dead a week ago. Same name, same parentage—French father, Moroccan mother. I think it is he. There is a murder investigation. That is all I know but I will tell you if I hear of more. I do not think this is of interest to me, unless perhaps you think it is. You will let me know if it should be...? A bientot. Etienne."

Her first rational thought is what to tell Beccy. She is due back the next day, having extended her holiday to visit English friends.

The implications will bloody terrify her. The man we drank tea with has been killed and it can't have been more than a couple of days after we were in his bloody house.

A picture of the arthritic old lady shakily carrying a tray to her prodigal son and his guests flashes through Cassy's mind.

Numbed, she selects the email she had just finished writing before Giraud's reply had sent her into shock. She stares at it trying to focus properly and hits "*send*."

"*I'm working on a museum theft case and need anything you think might be relevant on a sectarian group we think has a U.S. base. Ukiah, north-west of Sacramento, not far from you—and Yakima in Washington state, about a hundred mile southeast of Seattle. Maybe other locations, too. They're probably doomsday groups and may be into Atlantis sort of stuff. Could also have a touch of Islamic mystics—don't ask me to explain.*"

Jerry Mathias is Professor of Criminology at the University of California Los Angeles. She had once stayed at his house on a palm-fringed coast with a fabulous view over the Pacific. The girlfriend had been away and they had ended up making love in the sand dunes. He had once held a similar post to Etienne in the FBI until becoming an academic. Academics in investigative work form a tight network.

***

Things get steadily worse the next day. At 9 a.m. precisely, the phone in Cassy's office rings. It is Nigel Buchanan, beside himself with fury.

"What in *heaven's name* to you think you are doing, Dr. Kim? You want to run your own show behind my back? Well, let me make this bloody well clear. One more rush of independence and you're *finished*. And I don't just mean with this project or with Five. I mean everything. Don't think that I couldn't ruin your career forever. In fact, you may just have gone too bloody far this time."

She starts to say something but he is on a run.

"No excuses! This is serious—more serious than you can possibly imagine! I've got half an hour at lunchtime and I want you here, on the dot, twelve noon. My office in

Carlton House Terrace. Half an hour, do you hear? And it had better be good!"

The phone goes dead and Cassy recoils, pondering her recklessness, and suddenly thinks of Ashi. Only Ashi could have told Nigel about her visit to Morocco—the timing is too much of a coincidence. Despair turns to anger. She snatches up the phone and dials Ashi's home number. There is no answer and she slams the phone back down. Her rage turns towards Nigel and she throws herself into a chair to prepare her defence. If she only has half an hour with him, she had, as he said, better make it good.

***

Whether it is to emphasise his authority or just that he hasn't had time to find somewhere else, Nigel has summoned Cassy to his personal office. She arrives at the reception desk and is escorted to an elevator by a prim young woman bulging slightly, but Cassy notes, not unpleasantly, in a lime-green suit. Nigel's room is tucked away in a corner next to a public lecture theatre built in the style of all hallowed Victorian institutions in London. She is led through a smallish door, partially concealed by the panelling of the corridor, and down a narrow, ill-lit passage which seems to follow the outside of the curved lecture hall. It comes to a dead end at a distance she judges to be level with the stage on the other side of the wall. Two doors face her. It is the oddest of approaches to the office of a man of influence. She guesses that it must have been a service corridor for the stage and the rooms before her would be the technical room and an anteroom for speakers or performers. Her approach has been noticed, for the first of the doors suddenly flies open.

It doesn't look as though his mood has softened.

"*Inside*, Kim," he snaps. "I have half an hour precisely."

She steps in and he slams the door shut behind her. The secretary's footsteps hurriedly retreat back along the wooden floor of the passageway. If this had been a service room it is now transformed beyond recognition into the inner sanctum of a man of purpose and self-obsession. Nigel Buchanan carries an ordered but flawed attitude—everything about him is, on the surface, well-defined, down to his neatly proportioned sandy facial features and trimmed eyebrows. A thick-pile red carpet gives the room something of a living room feel. Or is it the dressing room of a drag artist? Then, as she takes in the massive antique desk with its green leather inlay and the floor-to-ceiling bookshelves on two sides of the room, she realises that it is a gentleman's library. On reflection, it is not too over done; he has implemented the metaphor quite well. But not perfectly.

"Well?" is all he says without asking her to sit.

He is half-standing, half-perched against the desk. It seems to be a favoured pose. She is standing in the middle of the room with no props for comfort. Determined not to be intimidated, she looks around and says, "Mind if I sit?"

She underestimates his anger, for his face turns the colour of the carpet as he shouts, "You *have* to do things your own way, don't you, Kim? Yes, I *do* bloody well mind if you sit down. This is as *serious* as it gets! Are you suicidal or what? We're talking about your *career* here. Not just with us. The Yard. University."

He pushes himself off the desk, storms over to a chair, and plants it next to her. Then he marches back to his desk and resumes his perched position.

"Go on then!" he said. "Sit on it, but it's twenty-five minutes now. Right?"

"I won't need that long, Nigel," she says, shaken by the attack but mastering a calmness designed to emphasise his lack of it. "It's all rather straightforward, really."

"Try me," he said through gritted teeth.

"The *Cleito* email I told you about... it also contained a tip-off. A delivery—an exchange—here in London. In Epping Forest—a few weeks ago. I traced one side to a suspect living here—American student. The other side I traced to a town called Essaouira in Morocco. I had already booked a Euro-trek with my cousin so decided to pop over to Morocco while I was in Spain and take a peep."

The red patch on his neck brightens a touch and Cassy quickly adds, "Just a look-see. No risks. Nothing out of keeping with a laid-back holiday in the picturesque Berber kingdom."

"Say what you want, Kim—you know you disregarded bloody protocol!" He is shouting again.

"No, I did not," she says, managing a sweet smile. "I was just doing what I've been doing for many years. It's something of a *habit* as I'm sure you'll appreciate—I observe, I pick up tidbits of information, I collect pieces of a jigsaw—of several jigsaws. Then, at the right time, to save people like you a lot of bother and mental exertion, I pass it on to the professionals. That's what I'm paid for at the Yard. It's what I do."

"But not with *this* job!" he explodes. "That's what you are *not* bloody paid for. You are *not* paid to go snooping around on foreign soil. You work for *me* at the moment and *I* run you and you have *no* idea what nearly happened out there!"

She waits for more, but he is looking at the bookcase and thumping a clenched fist on his leg in slow motion as if summoning up self-control.

"So why employ me to look for a sect interested in Noah's Ark, then complain when I take some initiative and strike gold?"

He doesn't answer, but looks down at the fingernails of his right hand and burnishes them on his sweater, assuming a slightly calmer pose. "A name?"

"Belinda Ryan," she says. "PhD student. Department of Peace Studies. London University. Been in the country between three and five years."

He purses his lips and nods, and then asks, "And are you going to tell me how you traced her?"

"I saw her make the drop."

"You *saw* her?" He raises an eyebrow. "Then followed her?"

"Through the London traffic? No. I worked it out by sleuth and lucky guesswork."

"What was dropped?"

"A box."

"What kind of box?"

"A wooden box—a Moroccan wooden box."

"Size?"

"About half the size of a small briefcase."

"Containing?"

Curiosity has taken the edge off his anger.

"I didn't get time to examine it—someone came for it."

"What sort of someone?"

"An North Asian. Male, muscular, late thirties, ninety-five kilos, one-point-eight metres."

"But you had enough time to establish it was Moroccan."

"I traced the marquetry later."

"So a marquetried box. Be specific, Kim."

"It was heavy, solid wood, and empty, but I think it had a false base. It could have contained anything—your guess is as good as mine."

"What did you find in Morocco?"

"More boxes. Nothing of any significance, as far as I can tell."

"Nothing else?"

"Nothing else."

"Are you sure 'nothing else'?"

His probing is now oddly reserved.

He's giving me an unspoken order not to talk about whatever else I might have found. Like Ashi closing me down when we talked about Gunther.

There is a silence and he wanders over to the bookcase and casually pushes a book back in that has been poking out. He turns and sees that Cassy is watching and looks curiously self-conscious.

"How was the holiday then?" he says, running a hand along the neatly lined-up spines and leaning to blow at some dust.

"You should take one," she says.

He presses a button on the phone. The interview has lasted less than ten minutes. As footsteps approach, Cassy says, "Belinda Ryan's an assassin. They found a body in the forest—I saw that happen too. I wouldn't pull her in yet, though—she might be useful."

It was a measured attempt to earn some credit.

I know I'm good and I know he knows I am too.

He looks thoughtfully at her for a moment then looks at his watch and says, "Noted, Dr. Kim. It seems that you are as good in the field as you are in your laboratory."

"By the way," she says, "how did you know I was in Morocco?"

"American Express billing information," he said casually and opens the door.

The lime-green assistant escorts Cassy back along the passageway and out of the building. Exiting onto Carlton House Terrace, she walks towards the grand gate that leads onto the Mall and up towards Buckingham Palace.

Cold passion stilled.

That was the title of the book Nigel had poked back into the shelf. It was an orderly library and the slim well-worn paperback had stood out from the neatly lined-up spines of the hundreds of other volumes. The eye is invariably drawn to differences more than to similarities. The title is familiar but Cassy can't place it. *Cold passion stilled*. She ponders on it and starts down the short flight of steps that leads from Carlton House Terrace to Admiralty Arch, the monumental gateway to the Mall. She walks through St. James Park, and then cuts across into Green Park and then Hyde Park. Following the Serpentine Lake towards Lancaster Gate station, she catches a snippet of conversation between two suited young men seated on a park bench and discussing an engineering algorithm used in financial derivative modelling. She thinks of the computer program that had taken her two eighteen-hour days to complete—a complicated code-breaking routine to unlock the secrets of the Essaouira tape.

She had finished writing it the day before and left it running all night to work out the structure of the tape's invisible information. It had taken her a final three hours before breakfast to finally crack it. Cassy Kim now knows what Sami's mysterious package contains, although she doesn't yet understand its significance.

On the black and gold iron railings that encircle London's Hyde Park, young artists occasionally gather to hang their own exquisite handiwork. Every possible genre is represented and walking along Park Lane or the Bayswater Road on these occasions is a kaleidoscopic commentary on art history. Cassy is passing a section of railings covered in expertly crafted reproductions when she stops and examines a picture painted in rich greens, blues, and reds. It contains an abstract sheep's head with a huge eye staring across the canvas at the caricatured face of a capped-headed man. In between are three small figures, Russian peasants, a man with a sickle, an upside-down lady, and another woman milking a cow. Marc Chagall's *I and the Village*. Cassy has seen the real thing in the Museum of Modern Art, New York. It is a puzzle of a masterpiece. Chagall had painted it in 1911 when Russia was in the midst of the turmoil that led to the Tsar's abdication in Pskov six years later and then to the Bolsheviks' coup d'état. The painter himself had been safely ensconced in Paris and the painting is understood to be a montage of his metaphoric memories of Russian village life.

Two things make the connection for Cassy with Nigel's book. One is the Russian Orthodox church sitting among the clouds at the top of the painting. The other is a memory that the period prior to the Russian revolution was marked by terrible persecution of Russian Jews.

Cold passion stilled. It was a novel Cassy had picked up from a stand at Newark International Airport once on her way to Washington. She had missed an early evening connecting flight because of a hurricane in Florida and ended up sleeping on an airport bench. She had given up trying to sleep and went and bought the book from an all-night store. It was a strange novel by an unknown author, translated from Russian and very short; and if she remembers correctly, the subject of heated debate among critics. She seems to recall it had won some sort of literature prize.

It comes back with vivid clarity as she looks at Chagall's Russian peasants. Military authorities had sealed off a Soviet research settlement in Siberia during the height of the Cold War following a spillage. Several hundred workers had been fatally contaminated by a virus and left to die in isolation. A few scientists were present at the time of the accident but most had mysteriously gone to Moscow a week before. Most of the workers were drawn from a Jewish community deep in rural Ukraine. The only act of compassion from Moscow was to order in a team of army medics who travelled by helicopter from the nearest barracks to hold a weekly clinic dressed in barrier suits. That, and allowing in a Hebrew-speaking Eastern Orthodox priest. He had volunteered his services in an act of extravagant self-sacrificial mercy and made the journey on his own from the nearest town two hundred kilometres across the snow, arriving half-dead. It was the priest who was really the subject of the book. The embittered settlers had at first spurned his generosity but with time, cold and sickness weakened their resistance and they thawed to the priest's medicine. Most of the story recounted his successes in exhorting the men to die to their anger and other passions. Cassy is surprised how clearly the magic of the book comes back to her. *A man who has died to himself and his passions cannot be touched by any deprivation however small or large: for him, no disappointment or crisis can have any greater or lesser effect on personal peace than an unexpected success or a fortune won.*

As she recalls the quote, a now-familiar stirring of her emotions suddenly joins the memories. The implied association leaves her puzzled. The emotions summoned by the powerful poetry of the Russian tragedy are unnervingly similar to those generated by Sufi Isa's words. Their messages are spookily similar, now that she thinks about it—the priest and the Sufi—and the effect the same.

There is no doubt in her mind that Nigel had been reading the book—and that he hadn't wanted her to see it.

She steps closer and peers at the painting hanging on the railing. A superb reproduction. Post-impressionist images of reality placed awkwardly but with precision. A crude dotted line from the sheep's eye to the peasant's, demonstrating that it is not only the visible that can be visualised—the impressionist's realm of light-bathed reality but embellished with multiple layers of hidden perceptions. Conflicting modes of representation, making the point that we understand the world around us through variable symbolic conventions. It was a point first made by Plato. The Greek philosopher is on Cassy's mind. Even the Siberian priest had quoted Plato on the matter of abstinence in intimate relationships.

Cassy walks a little along the Bayswater Road and then turns back into Hyde Park and makes her way towards the intermittent waves of choral singing. She looks at the date on her watch.

A Baroque Summer.

She takes the path that leads towards the open-air stage and as she gets nearer, recognises a melody from Handel's Messiah.

"Thus says the Lord, the Lord of Hosts. Yet once a little while, and I will shake the heavens and the earth, the sea and the dry land, and I will shake all nations; and the desire of all nations shall come."

Second *Recitative* of the first *Part*. By the time she comes to the edge of the crowd the singers are on to the next *Aria*.

"... But who may abide the day of His coming, and who shall stand when He approacheth? For He is like a refiner's fire."

She squats on the dry grass next to an elderly couple sitting on a rug with a prim wicker basket containing afternoon tea.

"Would you mind?" she asks, pointing to a small pair of theatregoers' binoculars lying on the rug.

"By all means, please do," the man replies in a refined New England accent.

He picks up the glasses and offered them to her. "We've heard the Messiah every year since we've been married, haven't we, dear?" he says, turning to his wife.

Cassy nods and smiles. "Part of the great historic tradition, then, since its first public playing in Dublin, 1742."

He beams at his wife and says, "Well, dear, we're in luck here! This young lady is an expert." He turns to Cassy to insist, "Please... join us and sit down. You can tell us all about the great English performances—do you know this choir? There's plenty of rug, isn't there, dear?"

His wife nods politely but gives Cassy a suspicious glance, taking in the short summer skirt Cassy is trying to manoeuvre modestly as she sits down next to the husband. Cassy puts the glasses to her eyes and scans the stage. One by one she moves along the male singers, gets to the end of the row, and then starts back again. She stops at a singer right in the middle of the second row, distinguished by his shock of receding sandy hair that has a ginger sheen under the stage lights: the organist and children's violin teacher from the church in the forest.

Despite her American companions and the hundreds of other little clusters dotted around the field, the open-air auditorium and the remoteness of the stage makes Cassy feel quite alone. The run-in with Nigel Buchanan has steeled her resolve at one level but shaken her confidence at another. At that moment she has a premonition that her confidence, ever fragile, is about to come under fierce attack.

The stage, a hundred metres or so away, begins to distort into the Chagall reproduction. The billowing curtain framing the top of the stage is the clouded sky. Abstract mountains cover the rear wall. A criss-cross iron lighting gantry hanging down just below the curtain becomes the church with a little cross on its roof. The singers are the Russian villagers and the two great patterned blue silken side curtains are the sheep and the peasant man staring at each other across the stage. A straight line formed by the back of the stage construction becomes the artist's childish line of sight between the man and the sheep. The sheep transforms into a boat, a great wooden Ark, sitting high up a mountain in the clouds. The capped man is Sufi Isa and Cassy is the tiny peasant woman painted upside down.

Cassy had thought she understood Isa, but what she has found on the Essaouira tape has made her re-evaluate.

Then, in her hallucination Isa becomes the priest in *Cold Passion Stilled* and she recalls a bizarre twist to the story. As well as a lifetime of aestheticism, another experience had prepared the priest for his final and fatal mission. Although Russian Orthodox priests are permitted to marry, this one had never considered the prospect and neither would he have had he not been ordained—for women held no attraction for him. After a few months in the forsaken outpost he found that many of the men's affections were in a state of turmoil, faced with the prospect of a protracted demise with no intimate human consolation. He recognised the problem and he knew how to deal with it. He had never questioned the virtue of chastity and he never thought of administering any other advice to his new flock. Cassy remembers now that it was here that the book was at its most controversial for the critics couldn't make up their mind what to make of the author's powerful writing. Some rejected it for its moralist tone. Others thought it beautiful in its imaginative representation of male tenderness. With compassion born of secret personal suffering he challenged attitudes and beliefs that suppressed gentler, more feminine graces and taught an isolated, rejected male community how to become vulnerable. Ironically, the book had achieved almost cult status among the gay community.

What was Nigel doing reading an obscure novel like that? Perhaps it was only the tidiness of his bookshelves that had concerned him.

Cassy's mobile phone intrudes on her confused thoughts. The American lady shoots her another distrusting look as Cassy jumps to her feet and walks away to talk in privacy. It is Ashi's number. Before he has a chance to speak, she is laying into him.

"What the hell are you playing at, Ashi? Nigel Buchanan summoned me to his office. He threatened to sack me. Ruin me. He told me they traced me to Morocco via my Amex card but I'm sure they were only following a tip-off—you're the only one who knew I'd been there."

There is a short silence before he says, "Calm down, dear. I didn't tell him you had been in Morocco but I'm not surprised he's cross with you. It's one thing to ignore the *Obergruppenfhurer's* warnings; it's another to get yourself onto the European police forces' international Wanted List."

"*What?*"

Even as he said it Cassy has another premonition—of what is coming.

"You mean he didn't tell you? Perhaps his source isn't as informed as mine. Perhaps he's saving it up. The Moroccan police are looking for two women: an Asian, aged about thirty, answering to your description, and another, late twenties, who I strongly suspect answers to your travelling companion's. It's only a matter of time before the British police get drawn in—the French are already helping the Moroccans. I should pack your bag, old girl."

"What are the two women supposed to have done?" she asks, knowing what his answer will be.

"They were the last people seen with a local man before he was murdered—the man was from a small coastal town called Essaouira."

Damn! The police must have interviewed Sami's old mother.

"Any more details?" Cassy asks, free-falling into a pit of despair.

"They have eyewitnesses who saw the murdered man get into the girls' Jeep as they left town."

"*Scheisse drauf*! Where was he found?"

"Somewhere on the mountain road between Essaouira and Marrakech. Shot—in the feet, hands, genitals, and head, in that order. If I'm not mistaken, Cassy, old girl, you've been well and truly stitched up."

Chapter 25

ON THE SCREEN in front of Cassy and Beccy a counter ticks over: 1002, 1003, 1004... telling Cassy that her program is at work searching through data she has transferred from Sami's tape to a powerful computer Cassy sometimes borrows in a little-used lab of the Engineering Faculty. Since Ashi's shattering revelation, she is avoiding her regular haunts while she decides, or is told, what to do. Under the pretence of giving Beccy a surprise, they had packed two suitcases and moved into an apartment in Chelsea that Cassy had purchased with cash a year earlier but never lived in.

In the stuffy underground room in an annex of the university's Engineering Building, Beccy insists Cassy takes her through the discoveries step by step. Cassy has not told her about Sami and is finding it difficult pretending that nothing has happened.

"A computer tape contains nothing but a stream of ones and zeros," Cassy starts.

"I can cope with that."

"So, we need to experiment with interpreting the pattern of ones and zeros until we come up with something that looks meaningful."

"Makes sense," Beccy says, staring at the numbers ticking over. "And these tell you how many times it's gone through looking for something?"

"Exactly."

"So what's it searching for?"

"Letters. Letters, arranged together to form words. The ones and zeros—bits—are organised in blocks of eight, sixteen, or thirty-two. The blocks are called bytes."

"I remember from school."

"If you see a word on your computer—your name, for example—it might have been stored as five bytes each made up of eight bits. The B would be stored as the pattern

1000010. In the binary method of counting that makes the number 66—the code for B. The code for E is 69, 67 is C, and 89 is Y. So the sequence 66, 69, 67, 67, 89 spells Beccy—so long as I know that the sequence of forty bits should be interpreted as letters. My program reads the ones and zeros in blocks of eight and says... let's imagine this is text written in the English alphabet. It records the letters it finds and remembers a whole long sequence of them, and then it checks the letter sequence against a dictionary of English words. If the letters spell a string of recognised words— bingo, we've discovered that the tape contains text in English."

"Why not just stop when it's found one English word?" she asks, screwing up her face.

"If you ask the program to interpret the data as English letters it will always give you English letters. It might be a digitised photo on the tape with the bytes recording the colour or shade of each dot making up a photo of the Alps. But if the program read the number 35 it would tell you it's found a letter C—quite wrongly because the 35 really represents a shade of blue, say. A digitised photo interpreted as English will give thousands of English words purely by chance. What you're looking for is meaningful sentences that couldn't have arisen by chance."

"Right." Beccy says, "Monkeys, typewriters, and Shakespeare, and all that. So what if it's words but not English?"

"Each time that number clicks over," Cassy says, finger on the screen, "it's gone through the millions of digits on the tape, interpreted them as letters from one particular alphabet, and looked up the letter patterns in the dictionaries of languages that use that alphabet. Then it records how many recognised words are found and how many it found adjacent to each other. In some languages it can even recognise meaningful grammar."

Beccy gives Cassy a considered look.

"Okay, you're a genius, but what did you *find?*"

"Hold on and you'll see. It takes about ten minutes to check through all the major languages and give them each a probability related to the number of recognised words it finds in that language. There will always be one language with a much greater probability than the rest, and that's the one we're looking for! Here we go..."

The counter shows an almost completed search. A second later, the screen is filled with words in a script of elaborate, predominantly rounded letters. The words are interspersed with numbers.

"Russian?" Beccy exclaims. "Cool! What does your friend Isa want with a Russian tape?"

"The Russian is just initial information at the start of the tape—a *header*. It gives detail about the data that follow, which turn out to be a remotely-sensed image."

"Like a satellite image? Of what?"

"I'll let you form your own judgement. I've translated the Russian but it doesn't actually tell us much—it looks as if the very front of the tape has been cut off. There's nothing to say how big the image is, what shape it is, or where exactly it was taken."

"Enter the code-breaker!"

"The way to make sense of unknown image data is to play around with the image dimensions—width and length—until you see something that *looks* meaningful. So we're into looking for meaningful shapes rather than meaningful word patterns this time. After the Russian text, there's about one hundred million numbers on the tape. All I can make out from the header information is that each number represents two metres on the ground. It could be a very thin strip of the earth's surface five thousand kilometres long and eighty metres wide, say, or more likely something nearer a square of twenty by twenty kilometres. The only way to find out is to play around and see what the image looks like."

"And you knocked up a program to do this automatically? You're a geek."

"It's all in the number of continuous lines and the percentage of uniformly coloured areas. A square digital photo reconstructed as a rectangle with the wrong dimensions is grainy and full of fragmented and offset lines and patterns—like an analogue TV image with a bad signal. As soon as you arrange the dots in the correct dimensions, all the lines join up; the areas of similar colour coalesce and you get something you recognise."

"Enough of the science—let's see it!" she says, linking her arm in Cassy's with a squeeze.

Cassy is trying to concentrate but all she can think of is an image of Sami, bound and shot, lying in pool of blood. Beccy's exuberance makes it worse.

She types a command at the bottom of the screen. The Russian script disappears and an image starts to form slowly from the top, coloured in green and brown hues.

"It turns out to be a long strip—fifty kilometres by four. What does it look like to you?"

She leans forward peering closely and says, "Mountains? And a flat plain?" She sounds disappointed.

"I'd agree. Take a look at a more detailed section."

Cassy types another command and waits as the screen refreshes itself with another image. This time the terrain is rugged and presents a more interesting picture.

"Still mountains," Beccy says, "although it's looking more like a real map. Look—you can see valleys, and what's that? A deep gorge?"

"It all seems to be the same," Cassy says. "Rugged mountainous terrain abutting a flat plain."

"Nothing else?"

"It would take forever to look at the whole image in this detail, so I designed a little software robot to look for anything unusual—shapes that are different to the predominantly natural shapes you see in front of you."

"And?"

"Have a look..."

Cassy retrieves the results saved from her earlier session—a smaller image occupying about half the screen and showing a similar mountain terrain in much greater detail.

"Mountains with buildings—or steps? It's an Egyptian monument—are there mountains in Egypt? Or an Inca city in the Andes. This one's like the front bit of a boat." She prods the screen. "But with steps leading down to some more buildings? Carved out of the mountainside, maybe?"

"That's what it looks like. There's one problem, though."

She raises her eyebrows.

"They're *submarine* mountain ridges. These buildings are under the sea and if my guess is right they're quite far under. If the tape's header information is correct, this is a seafloor image taken by a Russian submarine back in the seventies."

Beccy sits back and mouths a silent "No way."

Tracing the building-like structures on the screen with a finger she says, "It makes sense. The Essaouira cult... submerged civilisation, Atlantis. But it can't be genuine. Can it? It would be a world-shattering find. The tape would be priceless."

They sat in silence, staring at the submarine map before them.

"The Soviet Navy or antiquities department might have had their own reason for keeping it a secret," Cassy says.

Beccy turns from the screen to look Cassy in the eyes. "And we've absolutely no clue where this was taken? What part of the world, even?"

"No co-ordinates and no description—it looks like that information got cut off the tape."

"So what was Sami doing with it? I thought he'd graduated from Greek mythology to Sufism. You've met his friend in Bangkok—what would he want with it?"

Sufi Isa's fifth and final sign and here I am reading its runes.

Once again Cassy thinks about how it was that she had taken the initiative to seek out the Sufi when he apparently had plans to summon her, and how it had been her initiative to travel to Morocco when it looked as though he had something there waiting for her. Panic starts welling up. But as it does, it is as quickly engulfed by an equally overwhelming sense of resignation, the rollercoaster emotion that plagues her with increasing frequency. Cassy has no idea what to tell Beccy—none of it makes sense.

"Can we look at a bit more of it in the same detail?" Beccy asks. "It's absolutely fascinating."

Beccy's naïve enthusiasm is suddenly too much for Cassy. She buries her head in her hands, considering for a minute telling Beccy about Sami. But she draws back. She doesn't know herself what it means and what she should do, so what can she say?

"Sorry, Beccs, this is getting to me. Yup—more in the same detail. Here we go..."

Cassy retrieves a detail of the bottom right corner of the big image and expands it. An undifferentiated picture fills the screen, like a flat plain. They scan it together in silence.

"See—nothing," Cassy says and scrolls up along the edge of the image strip.

"What's that?" Beccy asks suddenly.

The terrain is similar but cutting into the plain from the image edge are three separate broad curved lines.

"Looks like part of a meandering river channel," Cassy says. "Look, if you extended this bit off the image it would curve round and meet up with this other one... there…"

"Do rivers flow under the sea?" she asks.

"I've heard of submarine canyons running down the continental shelf, but not of meandering rivers. Only mature rivers meander. The curves form as they carve a sluggish course through flat floodplains. Let's see if it appears again," Cassy says, scrolling up further.

It doesn't and neither are there any more surprises. They sit in silence with the bottom corner of the image on the screen.

"What's that bit there?" Beccy asks for the second time, pointing to the very corner of the map. Cassy screws up her eyes and peers closely. There is a very thin line, perhaps two or three dots wide on the screen, with an irregular pattern of colours. She hadn't noticed it because at first glance it looks like the image margin. She zooms in until each individual dot becomes a square, two or three centimetres across.

"It's a pattern but not part of the image," Cassy says. "Just a bit of noise at the end of the tape, I guess."

"It's text or numbers," Beccy pronounces with authority. "It's more information like the Russian you found at the beginning. Your text-finding program stopped when it came to the image data and missed the bit at the end. If image files have *headers* why wouldn't they also have *footers*?"

She was right, of course, and Cassy feels foolish for having missed it.

"You're the genius," Cassy says, her weariness disappearing as she pulls up another window to search for the interpreter.

In a few short minutes some Russian words and a sequence of numbers appears in the second window.

"You're more than a genius, Becs—you're beautiful!" Cassy flings her arms round her, kisses her on the lips, and presses her head close to hers as they look at their discovery together. "It's a geographical co-ordinate. Universal Transverse Mercator system—one of the more common systems for locating points on a map of the globe."

Cassy peers more closely and then adds in a more subdued voice, "The bad news is it's only half there—we've only got half of the co-ordinate. We've got its position in relation to the Poles but we don't know how far east or west of the Greenwich Meridian it is. It looks like half the co-ordinate's been replaced with a sequence of spurious numbers."

"But surely you can do something with it?" Becs says, disappointment showing all over her face.

"Think of a line running round the earth like the equator," Cassy says. "We now know which line to look along but not where it is on that line. The equator's an awfully long way round."

She looks at the screen again and then back at Cassy and then up at the laboratory wall where a large, faded Atlas of the World poster hangs.

"But you'll be able to fix something, Cassy dearest. I know you will. That's why you've got the tape, isn't it?"

As she says this, she jumps up and runs a finger down the graduated lines criss-crossing the two-dimensional rendering of the globe. "What's the co-ordinate?"

Within minutes there is a red line irreverently drawn on the map from one side of the world to the other. Their mysterious underwater image was taken somewhere on a line that runs through Cape Verde Islands off the African Atlantic Coast, hitting the Americas at Guatemala and continuing across the Pacific. It passes through Manila, Bangkok, a point just north of Madras in southern India, and hits the east side of Africa in Ethiopia before returning to Cape Verde.

Chapter 26

October 1999
Rotterdam, Netherlands

HIS NAME IS Miguel Silva and over a period of twenty-five hard working years the short-statured Portuguese shipyard worker with thick black hair cut short by a loving wife but too wild to tame, has, step by step, made his way up the lower rungs of management in Europe's busiest container port. Among his other responsibilities, he now has the job of making the weekly audit of transhipments. At the age of fifteen, he had run away from a children's home in Porto and ended up working as a deck hand on a small line that did the northwest Atlantic coastal run, up to the Dutch port. He had left the line five years later and settled in Rotterdam after discovering that he had got Angeline, a pretty Surinamese prostitute, pregnant. They are now happily married with two children doing well in university and with a modest home half paid for. Not a day passes without him thanking God for lovely Angeline and his good fortune.

He makes little grunting noises as he professionally scans the computer screen showing a list of ships arriving and leaving and another showing several columns of numbers. The numbers identify the off- or on-loaded containers associated with each ship, and tell him whether the off-loaded ones are in store or have been transhipped to another vessel, rail, or road transportation. There are other details too, including the name of the finance company issuing the letter of credit that guarantees a container's contents and a reference number for the letter, the customer, and the purchaser. The data are stored on a computer in the port's main IT hub but the software that manages the logistics accounting is still full of glitches after several years and millions spent on it. Monthly summary printouts under different headings such as origin, destination, volume, transhipment fees, shipping line, value and content often seem to bear little relation to what the old hands on the ground know to be happening. The centrally stored figures eventually tally he presumes, but are of little use as a management information tool to those closer to the daily action. A weekly manual scrutiny of the data was his suggestion and he had been given a pay rise for the idea after he had uncovered ten serious data input errors in one month—mostly incomplete transhipment records that had produced totalling errors. On the basis of that little success, he had managed to convince the port's Director of IT that he should be given access to the main database to make corrections when he found obvious inconsistencies. But when he had suggested that maybe he could sit on what they called the "user group" when a London-based firm of IT consultants were hired last year to make yet another major review of the port's management accounting systems, he was ignored. He could see all sorts of ways in which the flow of data between dockside offices and central office could be made more reliable and user-friendly, but his views had not been sought. The fact that his old-fashioned system of manual checks, corrections, and weekly reconciliations had reduced errors seemed to be lost on the Director of IT.

Miguel scrolls down another page of the listing, gets halfway through it, and then makes an unusually loud grunt. Ismail, sitting next to him with broken biro in hand, checking off numbers on a hand-written ledger, looks up at the screen.

"Odd," Miguel mutters to himself. Then, turning to the young man, he says, "That's a new one. I swear this system gets worse, not better. How much do they pay those fancy IT consultants over there?" He nods in the direction of the imposing office building that houses the port's senior management, across a dock and visible through the window.

At first, Ismail makes no response. Miguel occasionally makes such comments. Then, feeling, perhaps, that one is required, he leans over to read the row Miguel has his finger on.

"What is it?" he asks in softly spoken Indonesian Dutch.

But Miguel just grunts to himself again. He throws a glance at Ismail and decides that it is too much effort to explain the loose connection of thoughts that has intuitively registered as wrong. Also in the back of his mind is a faint hint of deja vu—but he can't quite put his finger on it. He hits a button that brings up another table and cursors down until he finds the entry he is looking for. He toggles between this and the main table a few times, and then gets a third list up and sits staring at it for a moment.

One more grunt and a shrug of the shoulders tells Ismail that Miguel is ready to continue. The official figures tally. It is not the normal kind of error—but then there is that odd feeling of having seen something like this before.

He quite likes the young man. A bit too quiet and deferential, perhaps, when doing this job. But Ismail has a reputation among the men for being rather too enthusiastic—pushy, even—like when he had asked to work with Miguel on the weekly reconciliations after the elderly colleague who had done it for years had dropped dead one day. Now that he thinks of it, Miguel finds that strange. Like there are two sides of the boy's personality that don't add up. But he is reliable with a pen and ledger, and accurate on the screen. Miguel has even occasionally let him do the weekly check on his own—when he has been too busy himself covering for someone off sick, or covering for a sudden vacancy—like last week.

It is later that night in bed, with an impassioned Angeline wrapped around him, that Miguel suddenly sees what it was that had registered as out of place in the pattern of figures and it all comes back. He grunts loudly, pulling himself away from his startled wife and sits on the bed shaking his head in amazement. She looks up at him uncertainly, wondering what she has done wrong.

NOAH'S ART 257

It was the letter of credit that was wrong.

Since the growth of international trade in the Middle Ages, and probably before that, moneylenders have played an important role in the shipping trade. All trade relies on trust, but some risks are too great to assume without some formal kind of guarantee. When a seller of some good or other puts it onto a ship for a buyer in another part of the world, who may not receive it for several weeks or even months, a problem arises in respect of payment. How can the producer be sure that the buyer will pay as soon as the goods are received, or that he will pay at all? And if the buyer is shipping great quantities, then that means weeks or months without either the goods or the payment in his possession. A buyer, on the other hand, is unlikely to want to wire payment for goods at the time of embarkation since he cannot be sure that the goods will turn up at the right port at the right time and in the right condition. So all kinds of financial systems have emerged over the centuries to cover these risks, including insurance and letters of credit. A letter of credit is drawn up for a seller by a bank or specialised finance company and guarantees payment for the goods once they are on board ship. Sometimes the finance company pays the seller upfront—at the time of embarkation—paying something less than the price agreed between seller and buyer in the expectation of taking the full price from the buyer after final delivery. The finance house assumes the risk of a breakdown in trust between the transacting parties and effectively becomes the owner of the goods while they are at sea.

That is why the names of the companies issuing letters of credit are stored in the database displayed on Miguel's computer screen. And it is the name of one of those that he had checked off earlier that day that had caught his attention.

There were three things wrong. The first was the duration of the letter of credit. The official record showed that it covered the content of the container in question for the full duration of its journey from the port of Casablanca in Morocco to New York, including two weeks' storage in Rotterdam while waiting for the on-going ship. But his dockside manual records suggested that the container had been put on a lorry a day after being taken off the small coastal vessel that had brought it up from Casablanca. When he had checked the onward shipment it was as though that transhipment to lorry had never taken place. The official database showed that the container had been put on a Korean ship bound from Rotterdam to New York. If he was right, the container that came up from Morocco either wasn't actually on the ship to New York or it had been switched.

The second thing wrong was the company issuing the letter of credit. It didn't exist. This he knew because when he had first started in the docks he had, in his enthusiasm to get on, decided that he would learn all that he could about the transhipment industry. As he progressed in his responsibilities he expanded his knowledge through visiting the city library, collecting trade magazines, and all manner of information, which to Angeline's mild annoyance he kept in the corner of their living room that he called his "office." Among other things, he had built up his own record of companies operating in the so-called "trade finance" industry. He had become very knowledgeable about them and prided himself on his up-to-date knowledge of newcomers, closures, and take-overs. So when, years ago, he had come across a company with the same name as the one he had seen on his screen earlier in the day, he had investigated it—without result.

He could find no mention of it in the trade finance press. Its trading address was given as number 30 Heneage Street, London, and he had written to that address pretending to be an investor and asking for an annual report or any other public information. No reply came. He had a cousin who worked in a restaurant in London's Soho neighbourhood, and he had asked him if he would mind calling in at the firm with the same request. Heneage Street turned out to be a narrow road of two-storey Victorian houses in the East End of London, now occupied by an assortment of ethnic businesses. Number 30 was a Kurdish restaurant. The only other thing he can recall his cousin reporting from the visit was that on the restaurant's exterior wall was a faded mural of a great wooden sailless boat riding monstrous waves.

The third thing wrong was that he seems to recall—although the memory is very hazy—that there had been a similar suggestion of an inconsistency in the shipping record that had first introduced him to this mysterious trade finance firm. He had been relatively new in the job and had assumed it was his mistake. In any case, back in those days, the management information system was even worse. The official records came printed on long continuous printouts of faded green that could hardly be read. He had had no choice but to assume that the official record was correct.

The thing that now startles him most as he takes hold of the hand that Angeline has tentatively placed on his knee, is that, if he had worked it out correctly, that first incident had happened in back in 1979—almost exactly twenty years ago.

Chapter 27

August 2000
London

"*I'M SENDING YOU a link to a secure computer at ESRE. This geo-informatics company is a market leader and has links to just about every significant project going on at the moment including NASA, oil exploration companies, environmental agencies, airlines looking for lost planes—you name it. An old friend Professor Longas is close to the ESRE Board and owes me a big favour. He's cleared the IPR so no legal issues. The database is state-of-art gravity measurements from ERS-1 and Geosat spacecraft with some fancy geoprocessing. The radar altimeters on the satellites measure variations in the earth's gravitational field and these are combined with depth soundings from ships to estimate seafloor contours. It's a good technique. The spatial resolution is not so good—about one kilometre—but it might be of use. Take a look. What's your project?*"

Malcolm MacFenn's advice had been spot on.

The difficult bit was working out how to take the two hundred-square-kilometre Essaouira strip and match it with every possible two hundred square kilometres on the fifteenth parallel stretching from Cape Verde right round the globe and back. Since Cassy didn't know the orientation of the strip she had had to rotate it three hundred and sixty degrees at each one-kilometre point on the globe's circumference to search for the match. Altogether it was a massive computational task that took ten hours of continuous computing, after asking several people she knew for a favour and eventually calling one in on the University of Hong Kong's state-of-the-art Super Computer.

It turned out that there were three different two hundred-square-kilometre strips in the NASA seafloor map that had a close match to the Essaouira image within the bounds of tolerance Cassy had specified. Two had relatively low correspondence probabilities; the other one was an order of magnitude higher and indicated an exceedingly good fit.

***

"Cassandra!" It is Ashi. "You had better know—the French police are about to make a formal request to Scotland Yard. They want to *eliminate the two women from their enquiries*. You know what that means. What are you going to do?"

Cassy had reluctantly answered her mobile, having ignored it all day. It is the last thing she wants to hear and snaps back, "What the hell do you suggest? Take a trip to Paris and tell them I'm a maverick MI5 consultant?"

"Tell them the truth, Cassy… unless you really did kill the Moroccan."

"Not remotely funny," she says. "And risk being taken in for questioning? I could do without that at the moment, even though it should be easy to prove our innocence."

"How would you do that?"

She is not so sure and the silence conveys this. Finding Leen would help.

"I'll wait until they bloody find me. Meanwhile I'm going to try and find who set me up. Buchanan won't help me if the police ground me—the mood he's in, he'd throw me to the sharks. I'd appreciate a bit of moral support, Ashi."

He is clearly not minded to break whatever protocol is guiding the conversation for all he says is: "Don't go getting yourself into deeper trouble, Cassy dear, and whatever you do, don't try sneaking back into Morocco. The British Embassy in Rabat won't bail you out—they took exception to someone impersonating one of their officials."

"Like I said, Ashi—moral bloody support."

She slams the phone down, realising that extricating herself might be harder than she thought. She dials Beccy's number.

She is still in bed in her Paris apartment and Cassy gets straight to the point. "Beccy, we're in trouble."

"The Moroccan, Sami? I already know, Cassy."

"What? How the hell... who told you?" Cassy is thrown.

"Leen, the Dutch girl."

"Thank God for that," Cassy says in obvious relief. "We can go to the French bloody police with a witness."

"Yesterday evening," Beccy continues. "I had a manic phone call about midnight. I tried phoning you but you were switched off."

Cassy had been avoiding the phone the day before too.

"She's on the run and scared for her life—*seriously* scared. She was hiding in a Catholic monastery but she's on the run again."

No witness, then. Cassy's heart sinks.

"She was more together than when we last saw her, but terrified. After she left us she persuaded someone she knew in Marrakech to let her sleep on the floor for a few days, and then made her way back to Essaouira. Things seemed to have turned sour in the community after our visit. Sami was already dead. They'd had what she referred to as a visit from the Mafia, and police from Rabat were sniffing around. Or maybe she meant that they were the Mafia. Some of the sect members had disappeared and a rumour was circulating that we had given Sami a ride to Marrakech airport. Leen didn't stick around to hear more. She said there were some desperate people doing some desperate things. She *walked* over a hundred miles to this monastery. She's talking local conspiracy stuff—seems terrified of the police. She says the local lot are in with the cult leaders. What can we do for her, Cass? There's got to be something."

What can we do for ourselves? More to the point.

"Is there any way you can avoid getting hauled in by the Gendarme for a few weeks? I'm surprised they haven't already come asking questions. There are European police looking into Leen's case, and that means looking into the sect as well. If we innocently disappear for a while, with any luck our accusers will be discredited by the time French and British police catch up with us. But when they do catch up with you, Bec, just don't mention the tape."

The bloody tape.

Cassy suddenly realises that the tape implicates her with the cult in a way she would find completely impossible to disprove. Who would believe that it had come as a total surprise?

"I'm leaving in ten minutes, Cass. A taxi's taking me to the station and I'm staying in a friend's remote *gite* on the Spanish border. He's on sabbatical in the States for a year and I have the keys. French academics disappear frequently—they all have country homes in the mountains or by the sea."

In the end, it will all come down to Leen. Hardly a reliable pillar of defence, but she's all we have.

***

There are two objects on the brand new and unused kitchen top in Cassy's secret London flat. With Beccy's departure Cassy has retrieved the macabre old Iranian photo. Next to it is an opened Times Atlas of the World, sporting a big X in bright pink gel pen in the middle of the Gulf of Aden. The highest match in her image-fitting programme placed the Russian seafloor image bang in the middle of the Gulf, just off the tiny Yemenese island of Suqutra.

She is going through the tape discoveries made with Beccy. The building-like seafloor objects could always be a hoax, of course. It would have required someone with her sort of expertise to mount it. The match is surprisingly good. The Essaouira image actually lies neatly perpendicular to the line of latitude, as if the Russian submarine had steered a precision survey path. Cassy would have done the same if she were directing a systematic under sea survey in search of something. The image on the tape would be one of many similar strips that fit side by side, perhaps with an overlap for stereo mapping.

But why would someone go to such lengths to fabricate such a deception? And why remove half the locational co-ordinate?

Cassy is not convinced that it is a hoax.

Another possibility crosses her mind: that they have found the remains of a massive piece of mineral engineering machinery. She has looked at the objects many time over the past few days and convinced herself it is possible. The time would fit—the Russians had made the survey in the late sixties, which was when there was a rush on manganese prospecting, according to Malcolm MacFenn. Then there was the manganese nodule in the forest.

Beccy had immediately made the connection with Atlantis, which was an obvious conclusion to jump to, given what they had found out about the Essaouira cult. Besides which, it looks much more like ancient hillside buildings than anything else. It is because of these doubts that Cassy finds her attention focusing not on the man-made object in the image but on the other feature that has puzzled her—the river meander on the seafloor. If that was fabricated too, why not make it a bit more obvious? Besides, she can think of even less reason for that hoax.

"Submarine canyons are what you're after. These are extensions to big rivers that carve their way right down to the deep ocean floor. Imagine a section cut through a piece of the earth's surface, starting from the top of the Rocky Mountains and dropping to the deepest part of the Pacific Ocean. The profile starts off steep as you come down the mountains and then flattens out to the continental platform where most of us live. Then it dips a bit for up to a mile or

so offshore—the continental shelf carved by waves that form beaches. Then a continental slope drops down steeply to an average depth of about three miles."

Cassy has followed Malcolm's description with a pen, tracing the imaginary profile on a piece of paper. She had sent him a second email asking if old river channels can be found on the deep ocean floor.

"At the bottom of the continental slope, there's another platform a lot like the continental platform that humans inhabit. It's called the continental rise. Deeper than this, the ocean bottom drops off in places to their deepest depths— up to five miles below sea level. It's a curious symmetry. If this is why you were interested in the NASA imagery, take a look at the massive canyon carving its way down the north coast of Japan. Once it has tumbled down the continental slope it meanders its way across the floor of the two-mile deep Sea of Japan.

The upper and lower platforms are about equal in area. The upper one occupies about twenty-nine per cent of the earth's total surface and the lower platform about twenty-four per cent. Both have delta formations where they drop down to further depths. The Congo River is a good example—three miles under the sea it has a second delta on the edge of the lower platform that looks just like the current delta on the African coast.

Back in the fifties and sixties there were dozens of theories about seafloor rivers. Best one is very simple—the earth's water periodically changes from ice stacked up on the continents with empty oceans, to sea to ice and so on. That now seems to have been debunked."

Cassy puts down the printed email and leans back in an exquisitely carved expensive Indonesian teak day bed, with the label still hanging from a carving detail, wondering why the Russians hadn't publicised their find. She also finds herself wondering who had discovered the tape in some dusty ex-Soviet archive—and who might now be fighting over it.

***

It isn't often that Cassy takes a London taxi, but she is wearing a favourite little black dress and feeling unusually extravagant. The taxi turns into Fleet Street, London's traditional newspaper quarter, and comes to a halt outside an elegant seventeenth-century limestone building. St. Giles is one of the few historic churches in the capital to have retained its own professional choir. And a choir of some reputation it is, drawing the crowds for lunchtime and evening performances as well as for its calendar of sung religious services. Tonight is a tickets-only charity recital of a rare Italian oratorio with an exquisite mezzo-soprano solo.

Cassy Kim only listens to three kinds of music: contemporary Korean pop, 1980's English punk, and pre-nineteenth-century European sacred. She has often snuck into the rear seats for a performance at St. Giles.

Marten, her Dutch friend, had introduced her to the genre at a time when she needed something more satisfying and possibly more mature than pop or punk. He is also a fan and, although far from agnostic, is as equally at odds with the context as Cassy Kim.

Marten had once been a Priest in a Dutch Lutheran Church but had converted to Islam during a period of study in northwestern China. Cassy's immediate reaction when he had confided this to her was that it was just as well since he would make a bloody awful ambassador for the Lutherans.

During the course of their short relationship, Cassy had learnt of the legendary student stories about his antics when he had taught theology at The University of Amsterdam; and she had once met up with him at a high society party in Hong Kong where he had fallen over drunk and refused to get up. She has noticed that he treats his new persuasion in much the same way as he had his former one but with somewhat more respect. It is as though he has decided to swap one set of rules for another and is enjoying the new ones slightly better.

Cassy enjoys the look Marten gives her and the disappointment he tries to conceal when she introduces him to Oghel.

"Trojan attire or genuine conversion," Marten whispers, flippantly stroking the side of her Muslim-style headscarf as they file into the Church.

"*Praat geen poep*," she mouths back, reminding him that he once introduced her to the creed of Dutch obscenities.

In reality it is neither; she has taken to various mild forms of disguise when she goes out, just in case the French police have come to London looking for her.

Marten takes her arm and draws her closer. "He's so young and innocent. Have you enticed him to bed yet?"

She responds with a forceful elbow jab in his ribs and turns to watch Oghel, who seems genuinely interested in the old building.

Oghel didn't hear Marten's comment but takes note of the brief exchange. He is touched that Dr. Kim invited him to join her at the concert with her old friend. He knows he is playing with fire, but feels compelled to see things through and this is a pleasant development. Marten worries him, though. He has researched his background on the internet. Why does a Christian priest convert to Islam and show so little respect for either faith? The singing starts and Oghel closes his eyes to shut out his distractions.

***

When a tentative wave of clapping signals the end of the first movement, Oghel leans close to Cassy and asks a question about the choir. Her senses bristle as she smells his skin and she wonders again what inner thoughts and disciplines give him such outward poise.

An austere discipline exudes from the cold stone of the church and she watches his eyes explore the architectural and ceremonial artefacts. As he is looking up at the great round stained-glass window, Cassy catches a flash of blue in his iris. A starburst reflection of the mid-evening summer sun filtered through the deep royal blue of the Virgin's robe. A warning to keep away from the sacred.

Would you come to bed with me, Oghel? She adds thrill to the thought by mouthing it silently to him while he is contemplating the glass Virgin.

For Cassy, the question is not fantasy: it had happened once before—with Zach. The coloured window reminds her of the church in the forest. She shudders at the thought.

There was something weird about that place.

Something about its stained-glass window is nagging her. The storm, the lightning, Adam and Eve. Adam and Eve in the Garden of Eden, against a backdrop of mountains spewing great torrents that wind their way down to water Paradise.

Four of them…

As soon as the choir has made its aloof way out and their well-spoken host has invited guests to place cheques in baskets carried by two ruffed choirboys, Cassy beckons to her companions and makes her way over to a huge bronze eagle-shaped reading lectern. It bears a great leather-backed Bible lying open with two red silk bookmarks laid carefully down the centre and hanging over the edge. Like a great sea turtle lying on its back, issuing arterial blood—symbol of the sins of man, desecrator of the planet and renegade earth-curator. Cassy momentarily thinks of the suicide eco-terrorist and wonders what creed the Human Extinction Front follows.

Oghel and Marten join her.

"Welcome to the only place where Fleet Street editors kneel in front of anyone willingly," Marten says. "The newspaper guilds and unions keep this place so marvellously. They pay for the choir—think how much it costs to employ those angelic singers on full-time salaries."

Cassy interrupts. "Actually, Marten, I want your help here." She pats the Bible lying in front of her. "I was possessed with an irrepressible curiosity during that last song. You used to be a man of the cloth: tell me, does the Bible mention rivers flowing in the Garden of Eden?"

He looks at her as if she might be about to tell a joke. Then, when nothing is forthcoming: "Sure," he says, shrugging his shoulders and gesturing with his hands. "Let's turn to the book of Genesis." He steps up to the lectern and assumes a pose that must once have been second nature to him. He even has the slightly affected inclination of the head and elevated eyebrow.

"I'm bloody serious," Cassy says, giving away the urgency she is feeling. "What does it say about rivers?"

"Hardly appropriate language, dear girl. There were four. The Tigris and the Euphrates and two others."

"Two others?" She is still agitated.

It is Oghel who answers. "The Pishon and Gihon," he says, looking from Cassy to Marten.

Marten turns to face him in obvious surprise.

"I say! That's very good, Oghel."

Oghel says nothing. He is looking at the Virgin again.

"*Pishon*," Marten reads from the page he has just turned to, "*flows around the whole land of Havilla, where there is gold.*" He pauses for effect and as he does, Oghel takes up the recitation. Cassy and Marten both turn and stare in amazement.

"*And the gold of that land is good; the bdellium and the onyx stone are there.*"

His eyes are still fixed on the stained-glass image as he recalls the words from memory, with poetic intonation.

"*And the name of the second river is Gihon. It flows around the whole of Cush. And the name of the third river is Tigris; it flows east of Assyria. And the fourth river is the Euphrates.*"

Marten and Cassy look at each other and at the other guests, who are looking at Oghel.

"And the Lord God planted a garden to the east of Eden; and there He placed the man whom He had formed. And out of the ground the Lord God caused to grow every tree that is pleasing to the sight and good for food; the tree of life also in the midst of the garden, and the tree of the knowledge of good and evil. Now a river flowed out of Eden to water the garden; and from there it divided and became four rivers. Then the Lord God took the man and put him into the Garden of Eden to cultivate it and keep it."

He looks around to the sound of clapping and blushes. A small group of concertgoers standing near the lectern had stopped to listen to Oghel's enchanting recital.

Cassy, too, is transfixed, but not just by the poetry. An extraordinary montage of stained-glass cameos suddenly appear before her with glimpses of the themes connecting them, fading in and out of focus and looming large and then small; then vanishing like shadows of insects flying around a tropical ceiling lamp. She needs to get home quickly and look again at the seafloor map she downloaded from NASA.

Chapter 28

YOU CAN SMELL it if a stranger has been in your house. Cassy is paying a visit back to her Docklands home. There seems to her to be no other obvious signs of the intruder. She treads cautiously along the entrance hall and then goes from room to room, switching on the lights, standing quite still in the doorways and slowly surveying the familiar patterns of furniture and belongings.

There is a transaction slip lying next to the fax machine where it had been automatically spewed out. A transaction slip but no fax message. She looks on the floor but finds nothing. What message has been taken? The slip has a fax number at the top and tells her that two pages had been received at 20.36 hours. She recognises the country code and the number—it is from Thailand, from Chavalit. She had faxed him from her new apartment yesterday and asked a favour. The intruder had come sometime after eight-thirty—a half an hour after the concert in the church had started.

Then she noticed that a pile of notes that had been lying next to the computer is missing and that the computer monitor is switched off. She always leaves it switched on.

***

"Let me show you something," Cassy says.

It is Friday afternoon, and she has asked Oghel to join her in the old image lab in the Engineering Department's basement. They are both standing in front of a glowing map and Cassy is watching Oghel's reactions. As far as she can see, only Oghel and Marten had known that she would be going out to the concert at eight o'clock. The burglary has undermined her confidence in her own judgement and she needs to find it again. Unreasonably, she desperately wants to get rid of her doubts about Oghel.

"The four rivers flowing into—or out of—Eden," she says.

Cassy has done some homework.

"Pishon is the first, and flows, as you told us so eloquently at St. Giles, 'around the whole land of Havillah.'" She pauses, watching him.

"Havillah," she continues, "is thought to refer to the southwest area of the Arabian Peninsula. Modern-day Yemen. But there is no river *flowing around* Yemen. Not unless you look where no one seems to have looked before—on the seafloor of the Gulf of Aden."

She windows in on that section of the seafloor image, magnifying a curving shadow that flows out of the Red Sea, for a while hugging the base of the Arabian continental land mass three miles below sea level. It had been part of this that Beccy had spotted on the Essaouira image.

Oghel clearly doesn't know what to make of it. He looks at Cassy as though about to ask a question. He looks at the screen and then back at her.

"And this is the River Gihon," she continues, pointing to the canyon that starts from the coast of Ethiopia and zigzags its way eastwards through the rugged undersea mountain chain running along the middle of the Gulf of Aden.

Oghel follows the line Cassy traces on the screen and sits there in thought.

"Gihon, flows around the land of Cush," Cassy says, "and Cush in ancient Near Eastern literature is… guess what? The name for modern-day Ethiopia."

Oghel peers closer at the image on the screen. The subject is beyond their normal sphere of conversation and he is obviously awkward.

"The word Gihon means *to gush forth* with energy, power, or great turbulent movement. Just look at that undersea canyon Oghel and look at what must have been its source—a ravine carving its way down from the Ethiopian highlands, forming the V-shape coastal topography of Djibouti, and then carrying on right down to the seafloor."

He looks but still says nothing.

She changes tack. "Tell me, Oghel, and excuse me for asking so directly—what line of Islam do you follow?"

Straightening himself up and turning to face Cassy, clearly caught off-guard, he asks cautiously: "Is that what this is about? My religious affiliation? I am not Muslim. I am Syrian Orthodox. A persecuted Turkish minority. Sometimes it is easier to let people assume I am a Muslim." He smiles something of an apologetic smile.

It looks to the shocked Cassy as though it might have been a relief to get it out in the open. The honesty and vulnerability she glimpses in his eyes as he says it suddenly and unexpectedly lifts her weight of doubt. His revelation seems to change things quite fundamentally but Cassy isn't at all sure why or how. She considers for a moment where to take the conversation next but finds herself simply saying, "Now look further east."

She moves the image across the screen to reveal the Persian Gulf, shallow with sediment deposited from the delta formed jointly by the Tigris and Euphrates.

"Where the Persian Gulf enters the Arabian Sea, there once would have been two steep submarine canyons taking the Euphrates and Tigris down to the deepest parts of the ocean floor. All big terrestrial river systems have them. But the canyons from the Euphrates and Tigris have been covered by the sediment spilling out from the silted Persian Gulf. From the undersea terrain, the canyons would have been channelled sharply to the southwest, flowing in a direction that puts them on a convergence course with the Pishon and Gihon, which are flowing into the Gulf of Aden from the opposite direction. The meeting point of these four channels—two from the east, two from the west—is on the floor of the Gulf of Aden, in the centre of two great circles of smaller fragmented undersea mountains, one inside the other and separated by a circle of deeper seafloor—an ancient sea within a sea. An extension to the outer of these circles emerges above the surface several hundred miles to the west as the small Yemeni island of Suqutra."

"Eden on the seafloor?" Oghel whispers hoarsely, transfixed to the computer screen.

"Isa's Eden," Cassy mouths, under her breadth.

Isa's final sign.

After the fifth sign the end will come.

How did he do that? Will me to travel to meet Sami and collect the tape? Did he implant some subliminal hypnotic instruction during the session in Bangkok?

After a while silently contemplating the significance of the image before them Cassy asks, "Why the secrecy about your religion?"

"The history of orthodox minorities in Anatolia is not a happy one," he says, shrugging his shoulders. "There is deep prejudice—and still persecution. I tell those who ask. There is no reason to tell those who do not."

"The Turkish government gave you a scholarship," she says.

"Concessions are good publicity. Still, I am grateful."

"You have always lived in Turkey?" She takes advantage of his mood.

"My childhood was spent in monasteries and churches in eastern Turkey. My... my father. He is an Orthodox Priest with close affinity to a holy order."

"A monk?"

"Almost a monk."

"Orthodox monks can marry?"

"Priests may. Rome tried to unify eastern churches and tried to spread celibacy. We suffer persecution from all sides, you see, even from other Christian quarters."

He pauses for a moment and then says: "Celibacy is a voluntary discipline in our faith—as it was with the early church fathers. It is embraced with joy, for a lifetime or for a season."

NOAH'S ART 275

He smiles a smile with a hint of sadness. "I have to go now," he says.

Is it for life or for a season for him? I hope very much that it is only for a season. If it falls to me to cut that season short, I accept my destiny.

Chapter 29

CHAVALIT HAS BEEN to see Isa as Cassy asked him to, and has the following to report:

"*Mr. Isa send his severe greeting. He go tour and come back to Bangkok for short while. He write this for me to send you.*"

Fortunately Chav had sent the missing fax to the new apartment as well as the house. The next bit is in far better English than Chav's, indicating that he had copied it carefully.

"*Wisdom never tires. Patience liberates; everyone who is hasty comes surely to poverty. I am still waiting, Dr. Cassy. We will wait patiently together. Your destined role will come; meanwhile, continue to put on wisdom. The path of life leads upwards for the wise. But be careful, please. There is one who pretends to be rich but has nothing; another pretends to be poor but has great wealth. Whose sister would you be, Dr. Cassy? The one who guards his mouth and preserves his life, the one who opens wide his lips, comes to ruin? Even a fool, when he keeps silent, is considered wise; when he closes his lips he is considered prudent. Prudent action rewards the wise and foolish alike. I have been worried about you, my new friend.*"

Cassy reads it again. An encouragement to grow wise while she waits for her destiny, and a muted warning. There are two more lines from Chav:

"*You into this stuff, Adjan Cassy? He seem to be you friend. He become your abbot? Next time you come to Bangkok I take you for bottle of Mekong! Sawat Dee Khun Krup.*"

Cassy laughs. Then she goes serious. Isa doesn't know that Sami has given her the tape already and probably therefore doesn't know about his death.

The fallible prophet. Perhaps only charlatan prophets appear infallible.

***

First came the repeat burglary, next the repeat assault. This time it is delivered in person. Cassy has travelled to the university by a circuitous route and dropped into her office to organise things for a period of absence. She has not decided whether to continue hiding away in her apartment or go somewhere farther away. On the corridor opposite her office is a utilities cupboard where the building's trunk cabling and heating ducts pass between floors. Inside is enough room for an engineer to perform an inspection without messing up the carpet in the corridor outside. As she had opened the door to her room the pressure adjustment had caused a slight movement in the utilities cupboard door. She had noticed it out of the corner of her eye; it was usually fastened shut. A minute later there is a knock on her door. As she turns the handle, the assailant knocks her violently backwards as he forces his way in and slams the door shut behind him. Winded and staggering to keep from falling, Cassy is grabbed by the neck and pushed up against a filing cabinet, the angular handles digging painfully into her ribs, making her eyes water. She squints down at the muscular, dark, hairy forearm protruding from the rolled-up sleeve of a ribbed army sweater. His face is covered by a fatigued balaclava.

"*Well, domkop?*" she manages to whisper while gasping to breathe, her verbal violence still switched to Dutch. She is not going to let someone else conduct an interview in her office.

"You're in deep shit, right?" It is a mixed Middle Eastern London accent.

"Looks that way," she whispers through the restriction around her neck, blood pounding in her ears. "*Klootsak.* You'll be the one in deep shit if you don't loosen your grip."

"Shut the hell up and listen!" he hisses, spraying her with saliva that smells of tobacco, and tightening his grip. "I've got a message that you're not allowed to ignore. Listening? You have a six-figure number someone else wants. You been doing some naughty things with bank accounts, professor? Shame on you. Well, you better stick to bloody teaching, right?"

She wants to laugh but instead feels herself spinning into a faint. As consciousness fades, her thoughts are that someone is onto her secret hobby. But then it registers that her offshore bank accounts have eight-figure account numbers.

"You put it on your internet home page tomorrow where it can be seen by the whole bleedin' world and then wipe it off again the next day. Got it? It better be clear and it better be the right number. I'm not allowed to kill you but I got a lot of scope for messing you up –and I know where you live."

He turns his head, still holding on to her, and looks around the office.

"You must have a lot of valuable things in this room," he says with a snigger.

She is fading fast, and from an oddly angled perspective that feels like she is hovering somewhere near the ceiling, she pictures papers, books, and files ransacked or destroyed. With the safety of her intellectual property on her mind, she feels an express train driving into her belly, although even as it impacts she somehow realises that it is not as powerful as it should be. Then she blacks out.

***

Oghel is crouched low, with one hand under her head and his face close to hers, listening to her breathing and trying to observe her pupils. They are hidden under those exotic folds of skin and gently with his other hand he touches one of her monolids and eases it up enough to see into the dark pool of night. The action seems to bring her to consciousness. Unsure of what to do, he looks around the room and then at Cassy, lying awkwardly on her office floor. Her upper body is limp and slightly tilted on one side by a twisted pelvis that has landed on a folded leg. The other leg is splayed out at an unnatural angle and Oghel's initial thought is that somehow she has dislocated it. Quite how that could happen in a small office he cannot understand. Realising that he is taking in the shape of her hips, which are accentuated by the way she is lying, he quickly looks away back to her eyes to find that she is looking at him intently, even imploringly.

"Would you come to bed with me, Oghel?"

This time the invitation is fully vocalised, even if it is in a cracked whisper.

"I shall call an ambulance."

"Let me sit up..." She goes to prop herself up with forearms but violently retches and lets her head flop back on the carpet. Oghel, now on his knees, behind her reaches under her arms and around her waist to bring her head onto his lap so that she doesn't choke if she vomits. He kneels there looking into her closed eyes, wanting to touch them again, fascinated by their structure and captivated by their beauty.

Then he notices that in easing her up onto his lap, the hem of her short dress has risen. He wants to look away but he cannot. All he can think of is softness. The black dress, a thin high-quality woollen fabric with the feel of mohair and buttoned down the front from neckline to hem. One side of an exquisitely laced piece of underwear, the colour and waxy texture of jasmine petals, is laid bare; and escaping from under the lace in the crease of her thigh, a few jet-black curls. He is transfixed and disorientated. The thoughts accompanying his wildly stirred emotions, as far as he can monitor them, are not so much lustful as thoughts of wonder. The softness of the dress, the lace and the milky silk; the softness of the skin in the delicate valley at the top of the thigh and of the angle of the gentle rise disappearing under the hem of the dress. Why should a simple image, a juxtaposition of a few surfaces and shapes, have such an overwhelming affect on him? What does God make of such beauty that he has created? What am I to make of it? Whether it is an automatic defensive mechanism learnt from years of mortifying the senses or a cunning rationalisation of the untamed mind to help him dwell on the sight a little longer, he finds himself looking not at a half-dressed woman but at an artist's still life. The angle of the thigh crease and the opposing angle of the hitched-up hem; the fine mohair against the coarser but silky-soft pubic hair; the natural sheen of the skin against the tightly woven lingerie sheen; the delicate curves in the repetitive pattern of the lace and the curves, at a different scale, on the body; the black, the white, the dark but at the same time light Asian skin.

Then the artist's composition is gone and he is ashamed. He feels a light tug at his sleeve and looks down into Cassy Kim's wide-open, beckoning eyes.

He sees into her vulnerability and understands. He wants more than ever to rescue her.

***

The next day Cassy is sitting in a red-carpeted room tucked away behind a dark-panelled lecture theatre. Staring at her is a curious Nigel Buchanan.

"So you sustained a bruised neck that could have come from the gallows and a bruised cheek bone all by falling off your bike. There's something about that bike of yours—I should get rid of it." Then, with a sigh: "Oh well, if you say so. Let me know if you recall another explanation."

Moving on from the unexpected distraction: "Change of tactic, Cassandra, young lady! You're to be taken into confidence."

"Oh?"

"You may remember Banton?" he says with an apologetic smile. "Now Sir Michael, no less."

The name brings on a dull nausea as Cassy recalled the short but very unpleasant disciplinary interview after she had hacked into her line manager's account at GCHQ.

"He's running this thing?" she asks with distaste.

"Of sorts."

"He wants me taken into confidence? I'm staggered."

"You're a good forensic scientist, Cassandra, and you are proving to be a good investigator too. We're glad we hired you."

"That's the nicest thing anyone's said to me all year."

"Even if you are cursed with the self-destructive tendency of a lemming in heat and seem to have little respect for my authority."

"That's unfair. I always respect superiors when they make good decisions."

"Very droll," he says, scratching the side of his nose then putting a hand through his hair.

"We may not like the way you've gone about it, but you've given us our first result on the Noah's Ark air disaster link. Two, in fact. Everyone's agreed that it would be best to stop the play-acting."

"Play-acting?"

"The French Police have asked to talk to you about the murder of a Moroccan gentleman you were seen with. The Moroccan authorities have put together a strong case with signed witness statements and it's all looking rather sticky. The inspector who's handling it at Scotland Yard is not being very co-operative with me—as you know, they're very sensitive to Europe at the moment—and we need to do something about it."

"You're asking me to turn myself in? And tell the truth or lie?"

"That's precisely what I *don't* want—any of that."

"So what *do* you want?"

"I want you out of the way for a while," he says, putting his diary back on the desk and folding his arms.

"This thing is big. *Very* big... and we're not having you jeopardise it. I'm not prepared to lose you—so that means we've got to have an agreement. Banton's approach was to throw you to *les loups* and watch you squirm. You're replaceable as far as he's concerned. But he's not the one that has to get the job done on the ground, is he. You've got to realise how serious this is, Dr. Kim. You were *royally* set up in Morocco—those sworn witnesses aren't loopy hippies from the cult you chased to Essaouira. They're respected citizens, including a wealthy businessman and a senior police inspector."

The revelations were at the same time comforting and discomforting. Her assailant yesterday had understated it. *I'm in very big shit. And that means I have to rely on little shits like Nigel and pathetic ones like Leen to save me. Perfect.*

"We're talking big corruption. It's the worst of both worlds. Big-time organised criminals plus weirdo cults. That equals danger *plus unpredictability*. I read economics at Cambridge, Dr. Kim. Organised crime might be a nasty business, but at least it's predictable. You get there in the end because you understand the opposition. They are profit maximisers like most of the rest of us—it's just that they don't operate within the same constraints as law-abiding citizens. These other guys are from a different planet—who knows what their goals are? Even with political extremists, in the end it usually comes down to power over material resources. There are cults and there are cults, Cassandra. This one looks as though it's off the scale—it's subtle, it's big, and it's in big-time partnership with big bad money."

She sits staring at him in the eyes through lowered curtains, as though testing out his words, taking in the picture he has drawn.

"Could the cult have supplied a mercenary suicide plane bomber?" she asks.

The passenger on the AIA flight from the Sufi base in Georgia.

He returns her stare for a moment as if considering how to answer.

"That would be one possibility," he says uncertainly, but his body language indicates that he doesn't want to discuss detail. He doesn't seem very adept at moving off-script.

Then, back on track and assertively: "There's more than one government working with us on this and we can't risk any more unilateral covert expeditions."

He pauses, as if waiting for a response, and then says, "Understood?"

She doesn't answer, but sits silently planning her next move. *The one who guards his mouth preserves his life; the one who opens wide his lips, comes to ruin.*

"So what's the plan?"

"I want you out of the way somewhere—far enough away to slow down any action by over-zealous British detectives and fastidious French diplomats. Nowhere in Europe, obviously. But somewhere where you can carry on life reasonably normally—you have university responsibilities to see to. Your caseload at the Yard has been handed over to one of your colleagues."

"Handed over?" she says, caustically. "How long *out of the way?*"

"Maybe we can wrap this up in a month. Six weeks, perhaps. There's a delicate operation going on right now—I mean right now—and I don't want the Moroccans thinking we've sent an operative onto their territory without consulting them first. It could completely foul things up. My guess is that you are a fall guy in some sort of internal corruption game playing. I can't imagine the case against you will stand international scrutiny, but it might get someone off the hook over there. A failed case against a foreigner seeking revenge for a sister lost to a brainwashing cult might give the Moroccan prosecutor enough reason to drop an investigation he doesn't want to pursue."

"The girl they call Leen? They claim I'm her sister? That's as absurd as the murder allegation."

"The Moroccans have obviously decided on something like that."

"Well, that makes a defence simple. It shouldn't be beyond the wit of French detectives to check birth certificates and DNA."

"No one can check anything until the girl turns up."

She chooses not to tell him that Leen had been in touch with Beccy.

"So Rabat are hosting a multinational sting against the Essaouiran cult who they've discovered are into un-cultish things?" she says to elicit more.

"Hardly willing hosts, but yes, you could say that. It wasn't easy to agree the protocol—governments don't like foreign operations on their soil. If they knew you were on our pay roll they'd call us around the table again for an explanation and we'd lose the moment. It might take a year to organise something else—or we might not get another chance. We're not even going to let you talk to the British and French Police just in case something slips out."

Then he leans forward and says very seriously: "Four more weeks and it wouldn't have mattered if they'd pulled out in a huff—but not now. It would cost lives, Dr. Kim. Your bloody independence might already have done that."

It is below the belt and she resents him having said it. She suddenly has the ghastly thought that Sami might have been an agent who'd infiltrated Isa's outfit in Bangkok as well as the Essaouira sect. She feels nauseous.

"The deal is, you disappear completely for the rest of the summer and talk to no one. That includes your Turkish boyfriend. How is he anyway?"

"He's not my bloody boyfriend," she says, affronted by the intrusion.

"Well, watch your back, Dr. Kim, that's all I'll say. We don't want any casualties on that front."

He picks up his diary again—a nervous habit of his she has observed.

"So do we have an agreement?" he says.

"Can you keep the French away from my friend Beccy until things are sorted?"

"Done," he says. "They've already been slipped a false identity for her."

"In that case, fine. So long as you don't mind exiling me to Thailand."

"Fixed," he says, opening the diary to produce a thin blue and red piece of paper about the size of a chequebook.

"You only get away with it because you've been such a good investment so far—you had better keep it up."

She takes the airline ticket from him and flips it open to read the date on the red carbon form.

"Tomorrow night?"

"Like I said, there's a very delicate operation going on right now—and I'm under a lot of pressure."

"Thanks. How about an official letter to my university Vice Chancellor calling me on urgent business to the British Council in Bangkok?"

"Went in the post first thing this morning. Like I said, you're good at this—we're on the same page."

Standing up to tell her the end of the interview was approaching, he adds: "There's one more thing, Dr. Kim. I'm not a fool. I know you think I am, but I can live with that. I don't want you going anywhere near the cult's Bangkok headquarters in the next two weeks—the Americans are responsible for that part of the operation. It's not as sensitive as the Moroccan situation at the moment, but the same principle applies. We're working in a multinational context and there are rules to be adhered to. If trust starts to break down it becomes more difficult to get the job done. You're a bright girl; I'm sure you understand.

Oh, and in case you're wondering at my naivety, there's a reason for letting you loose in Thailand."

She raises an eyebrow waiting for more.

"Like I said, you're a bright girl—work it out for yourself."

As she walks out of the door she asks, "The second result? You said I've given you two."

"Oh yes. The man shot in the forest and his killer. They are linked by a network we knew had a presence in London."

"Russian?"

"Core of the organisation is an old guard ideological outfit strong in Moscow and several European cities. Trotskyists. They're Trotskyists. At least they used to be. In Russia, the origins of criminal fraternities don't matter too much. The ones that started with non-commercial ties like this one can be more difficult to break into."

***

In the lightened mood of a gap-year traveller leaving routine and examiners behind her, Cassy watches a revolving backlit advertising case display a picture of a gold Rolex watch laid on black velvet. It slowly changes into a bottle of perfume designed from frosted glass in the shape of an elegant but headless female torso, and then changes again into a supermodel dressed in a dark blue ball gown. The modern stained-glass windows of the shopping-mall cathedral portraying their own blend of myth and reality. She looks at the shops, arcades, and cafes lining the corridor that faces passport control in Heathrow's Terminal Three, and raises a hand to wave at Oghel. Then she turns to go.

It is good that you go, Cassy Kim. Dr. Cassy Kim. It will give me time.

Say to wisdom, "you are my sister", and call understanding your intimate friend; that they may keep you from the adulteress, from the foreigner who flatters with her words.

On the ride to the airport Cassy had asked Oghel what his name means.

"It is Persian for *wisdom*," he had said.

He had let her kiss him on the cheek as she had turned to walk through immigration. A "thank you" for looking after her when he had found her on the floor. A "thank you" for the hope he had given her by worshipping her exposed body.

Later, her reverie in a corner seat of the business class lounge is broken as the public address system announces *last call for Thai International TG911 to Bangkok—would the last remaining passengers please make their way through to boarding at gate thirty-six? Boarding for this flight is about to close.*

She heads for gate thirty-six, gnawing over Nigel's last revelation. The Trotsky connection has abruptly re-shuffled the puzzle for Cassy Kim. The Ark-obsessed Sufis have a base in a remote small town where Leon Trotski allegedly confiscated priceless archaeological Ark treasures; one of the passengers killed in the AIA air disaster came from the same town; two weeks before the disaster a message about the same flight was received by a Russian student with an interest in Ark history; and Belinda Ryan, red-haired assassin, is linked to a Trotskyite Russian Organised Crime gang.

Chapter 30

September 2000
Koh Samui, Southern Thailand
19:38:00:
PILOT: GOOD EVENING Bombay. Here is AIA706 making intermediate Fix on runway 2.

Air Traffic Control: Good evening AIA706. Report your Final Approach Fix. Air pressure is 1009.

Pilot: Report FAF pressure 1009.

Air Traffic Control: AIA706, negative light system right hand side of runway, left side is OK. Note runway edge light interval is 120 metres threshold and runway end light interval is 6 metres, caution barrier 400 metres from runway 2.

Pilot: AIA706 thank you.

19:40:11:
Pilot: AIA706 Final Approach Fix.

Air Traffic Control: AIA706, Control Tower not in sight of plane, visibility is only 1500 metres, please check your wheels are down. You are cleared for landing on runway 2. Surface wind 310, degrees at 5. Caution please, runway is wet.

Pilot: Thank you. Cleared to land runway 2 AIA706.

19:41:14:
Air Traffic Control: AIA706, is runway in sight?

Pilot: Not yet. Negative 706. Feeling dizzy. Handing control to co-pilot.

Air Traffic Control: Roger AIA706.

19:41:32:
Co-pilot: This is the co-pilot. Runway in sight AIA706.

Air Traffic Control: Tower has sight of plane now. Visibility improving.

19:42:17:
Co-pilot: AIA706 something's not right here. I've got problems. I'm going round.

Air Traffic Control: What's up AIA706? Roger, go round again. What will you do next?

19:42:49:

Co-pilot: Left turn to final runway 2 at 6 DMU. Now maintaining 2000 feet. I'm having difficulty seeing the instrumentation.

Air Traffic Control: What's your problem AIA706? Repeat, what's your problem?

19:47:14:

Air Traffic Control: AIA706 request position please.

Co-pilot: Tower from AIA706, is it raining at the airport? I'm coming in manually.

Air Traffic Control: It is raining lightly.

19:49:31:

Co-pilot: AIA706 Final Approach Fix on Runway 2.

Air Traffic Control: AIA706 you are in sight. Cleared to land.

Co-pilot: Hold on Tower, vision is blurring. Pilot out of action. I'm going round again. Not sure what's happening here. Auto landing switched off.

Air Traffic Control: AIA706, you are in sight, repeat you are in sight. What is your problem? What will you do next?

Co-pilot: I can't see the runway, something's wrong... I can't see... please stand by...

Air Traffic Control: AIA706, repeat, Tower can see you, visibility improving at 3,000 metres. What's wrong?

Pilot: AIA706 going round again. No. Take that back.

19:51:3:

Air Traffic Control: AIA706 please confirm whether you will attempt to land again.

Co-pilot: Roger. Coming in now.

Air Traffic Control: AIA706, check wheels, cleared to land runway 2, surface wind 290, degrees at 3, caution runway wet. Well done, you OK?

Co-pilot: No...no. Struggling. But am landing, runway 2. Approaching now. Wait, I can't see the runway. I can't see anything. Emergency situation. May Day. I'm going out. God help us! Oh sh...

***

The plane had exploded. Accident investigators were of the view that it would have missed the runway and crashed anyway had it not been blown in two first. Cassy scrolls to the beginning of the report on her laptop and reads through the transcript again. Nigel Buchanan had emailed it to her to go with the passenger list he had given her previously.

The initial investigations showed that the automatic landing instrumentation had been switched off by someone in the cockpit, and that both pilot and co-pilot had reported severe dizziness and loss of concentration. A ground-crew member had reported an uncharacteristic comment from the pilot as he had embarked, and there was talk about hypnotically induced suicide. Newspapers had carried interviews with professors of psychology and the paranormal, and psychiatrists and hypno-therapists had been wheeled in front of TV cameras. The view now widely held is that some kind of hypnosis had been tried but that a more conventional backup plan had been resorted to at the last minute. Panic had rippled its way through the airline industry.

Cassy calls up the flight's passenger list and cursors through until she comes to Akhalkalaki. The town in Sufi Isa's photograph. A psychic suicide terrorist working for criminal overlords? A hapless cult member wasted by ruthless cult leaders? She ponders over the other significance of this small town in the far corner of the old Russian empire. Leon Trotsky.

She types two words into her internet search engine: "Lloyds Register." The place to go if you want to find out anything about any major disaster—or near-disaster—in recent history. Reading the tragic flight data transcript she has made a tenuous connection with another airline incident that happened over forty years ago on a flight from Jordan to Tehran. It is just a thought, but is worth following up on.

She looks out of the open door of her thatched beach bungalow and judges the time by the sun's shadow. Packing up the computer, she slips on a loose shirt and jumps over the veranda to the soft sand below.

During her time in Bangkok with Joy as a teenager, she had become friends with the children of a coconut-farming family from what was at that time a lonely beach called Lamai on the island of Kho Samui in the Gulf of Thailand. With the proceeds from the first wave of travellers, the eldest son had been sent to study business management at the London School of Economics and on his return had mortgaged the family assets to buy up his neighbours' plantations. The economics were simple: as soon as there was enough surplus, it was reinvested in a new hut. At some point it had all changed. Higher spending holidaymakers brought in higher receipts; space under the palms ran out, and outside investors provided capital to build upwards.

It was hard to find, but when she eventually located what used to be the sleepy row of wooden houses, it all came back to her. The bungalows and coconut palms were gone, replaced by a small town of hotels, discos, shops with massage parlours upstairs, and a village square with a "traditional" open market that she doesn't recall being there in the old days. Chamlong was as delighted to see her as she him. He has survived prosperity well and immediately took her in a Jeep to a tiny cove around the headland and to a well-preserved village of old-style bungalows.

"My contribution to sustainable tourism. You may stay for free—for old time's sake."

That was three weeks ago and her enforced holiday is halfway through—all being well. She has developed a daily routine, working from midday to midnight with a break for noodles early evening. In the mornings she swims over the coral reefs or walks through the forest trails, heavily covered against insects, and has twice helped Chamlong and his teenage sons with their re-thatching project.

It was not primarily work or relaxation she had in mind, however, when deciding to head south from Bangkok. Just over the water, two to three hours' boat ride away depending on the seas, lies the town of Surat—home to the Sufi brothers' southern retreat.

Before leaving London she had put the six-figure Universal Transverse Mercator grid co-ordinate onto the internet as instructed. *Let whoever it is do whatever they want with the seafloor find.* She knows what she is going to do with it.

After three weeks she is ready to make the trip over to Surat Thani and steal the march on Sufi Isa. Chavalit has left a message for Isa in Bangkok telling him that she will see him in his southern base. Cassy will catch the old coconut boat first thing the next day, and is due to meet Isa in town at midday. This will be the third time she has taken the initiative on a meeting that Sufi Isa seems to have planned in his dreams. Perhaps Chav was right—perhaps Isa is becoming her "Abbot." She laughs out loud at the thought and knows that the laughter betrays her unease.

***

It isn't the old coconut boat that she boards, but something that looks like an aircraft fuselage with no wings or tail and with the top flattened into a kind of upper deck. It is the strangest sort of ferry, with room for thirty or so people seated inside and about the same number lying on the top. Most of her fellow travellers are young backpackers shunning the airport to Bangkok and living dangerously in the footsteps of their trail-blazing forebears. Living dangerously they certainly are for the only thing that keeps them from sliding off the roof is a thin metal rod fixed to the roof-cum-deck. The journey is uneventful apart from a large turtle that almost has the boat capsize as the backpackers move to one side of the roof to watch it.

Cassy is lying on her back, using her daysack as a pillow with feet firmly wedged under the rail and dozes into a fantasy in which Nigel and her university Provost have exiled her to one of the uninhabited islets drifting past. A change in engine noise wakes her—immediately followed by raucous shouts from Thai fishermen and the sound of a boat coming alongside. The bronzed Nordic god lying next to her has rolled over, perhaps in his sleep or perhaps not, to use her outstretched arm as a pillow. She is pleased—he was why she had chosen to travel on the roof. She is just wondering how to retrieve her arm when she hears a voice she recognises.

"Hello, Dr. Cassy." It comes from somewhere near her head, just over the side.

She is momentarily disorientated but cannot mistake the gently rounded North Iranian accent with its self-deprecating undertone. She pulls her arm away and sits up, embarrassed.

"Isa? You caught me by surprise..."

He is looking at the Scandinavian boy still asleep next to her.

"It's not what it looks like, okay!" she laughs. "It's good to see you again..."

She stops mid-sentence, stalled by the same welling up of emotions that has plagued her recently.

"Very good. It's good to see you." She begins again, aware that she really means it. "Do you come up or do I come down?"

"My friends have brought me to pick you up," he says with patriarchal grace.

There are more shouts as the captain cuts the engine to an idling pace and then without warning, Cassy is manhandled off the side of the ship by two glistening sets of muscular forearms.

They speed away in a *hang yaaw* or long tail boat—a sort of gondola implanted with a converted truck engine turning a two-metre long outboard propeller shaft.

"What's happening?" Cassy shouts in Isa's ear at the top of her voice. He doesn't even try to answer, but points towards the approaching land and to what looks like a small sandy cove a little way along the mangrove coast from the river mouth that leads inland a few kilometres to the provincial town of Surat Thani.

Ten minutes later one of the two fishermen and a young boy, who has been riding on the precarious bow, have jumped into the crystal water to ease the slim craft up onto the sand through shallow breakers. It is a glorious cove, up current from the nearby river mouth and free of estuarine mud—a collection point for a dazzling mix of granite sand and fine shell fragments. There are several other small *hang yaaws* beached and in the middle of the cove, a small jetty of weather-beaten grey planks resting on a rickety superstructure of wooden poles. A brightly painted fishing boat is moored to one of the poles and another is being built in a small clearing between the palms. There is obviously a fishing village behind the trees.

"So you've come to see me again, my friend," Sufi Isa says, grasping her hand and leading her across the scorching sand into the shade. A path disappears through the trees towards glimpses of wooden houses beyond.

"You have this effect on people," she says, surprised but liking the quickly developing rapport. "I've been waiting for the summons—what happened?" She laughs, easing her hand out of his. It is odd but comfortable—they are like old friends and she makes a quick and reckless decision not to put up a guard.

"And so you took a holiday in the Gulf of Thailand and summoned me instead? Perhaps we should stop this—summoning each other?"

They both laugh and, grinning, he beckons her in front of him as the path between the trees narrows. The houses are three fishermen's dwellings standing on their own in a shady clearing, overshadowed by the tall coconut palms. Smaller mango and rambutan trees form a partial boundary to the compound, and there is a vegetable patch in a clearing between the houses where daylight filters through. The place is alive with children, chickens, and dogs, and the air is full of the sweet and pungent smoke from wood being slowly burnt into charcoal under a mound of old coconut husks. They approach one of the houses, an extensive single-storey construction built of dark hardwood timbers and standing a metre and a half off the ground on stilts in traditional southeast Asian fashion.

The space between the floor and ground is filled with assorted fishing equipment, and dozens of tiny chicks and birds that look like quails are scurrying in and out of floats, lobster baskets, and nets. Isa leads Cassy up the short flight of steps to a spacious wooden veranda that runs along two sides of the house.

"Please," he says, gesturing to a dusty mat. Cushions surround it, and the overall effect, ignoring the surroundings, is not unlike his lift lobby in the Bangkok apartment.

"This is your country retreat?" she asks with approval.

"No, but it shall be ours for as long as you wish to be my guest."

"The owner is one of your followers?"

"The whole village is open and many are starting to understand. A quiet revolution is gestating here... in the hearts and minds of these gentlefolk. The main part of the village is through the trees—there beyond the rocks. This is the house of the Pu Yay Bahn—the village headman."

"But you have your own place in Surat town itself?"

"I do... we do... but I wanted to bring you here—it will be better to talk here."

"Tension in the camp?"

She had enjoyed his free-flowing poetry last time they met, but wants straight talking now.

"A full house, actually."

"Oh," she says. "Why the high drama at sea? You must have been waiting offshore for an hour—we were late leaving the island."

"Maybe it is time to talk more openly, my friend," Isa sighs. "If you have come in response to my words last time, I will have to be honest for I cannot send you away with nothing."

There is a pause while a teenage boy dressed in a pakama—the Thai country sarong—and a T-shirt serves them with bottles of Coca-Cola.

"Odam is here," he says. "With others. They arrived without warning a week ago. In truth I did not want to come south while they are here. My heart reaches out to Odam, for he has truly lost his way. It is dangerous, I know, to be associated with him, but he is my flesh and blood. Whatever it was that provoked this rushed visit of his, I fear that it was not a good thing. No, it would not have been well for you to arrive at the house."

The sting on the Essaouira cult.

"But we were to have met in the hotel," Cassy says. "I don't know where the house is."

"There," he says with a resigned shrug, "I have given away more than loyalty should have permitted. Yes, there are reasons for avoiding town all together—I admit it. But let us say no more on that matter—at least for now. I am intrigued—and honoured indeed—that you should come to seek me out on a second occasion. Who shall start, you or I? You, I think, under the circumstances."

Seated cross-legged on a village headman's veranda in the South of Thailand, bottle of Coke in hand, she begins the next phase of her engagement with the enigmatic sect leader.

"Okay, you gave me a puzzle to solve and I've solved it."

He brightens. "The Sumerian signs? You came here for that reason?" He is clearly moved by the thought.

"You had a task for me."

"Ah!" He sighs again. "Alas, my vision was seen too imperfectly and tainted by my own desires. It is true I had thought the time had come and that you were the one to interpret the last great sign."

He hesitates.

"But?"

"But, my friend, sadly, a curtain has been drawn and I no longer see so clearly. A great battle has started—a battle that cannot be seen but is as real as a battle of tanks and missiles. A dark shadow has arisen to wage the final stages of a great spiritual war. The battle started long ago, of course, as long ago as Eden, but now it intensifies. In the last days, Dr. Cassy, there will be great acts of nobility and goodness alongside great acts of treachery and evil. While some were perpetrating Saddam's merciless attacks against the Kurds, others risked their own lives in acts of great nobility. Good will get better and bad will get worse before the end will come. Both will advance and the battle for the human soul will rage like never before. Evil has won a battle, snatched away some hope for the moment—but it will never win the war, my friend."

"Sami's death?" she asks, hazarding a guess at the reason for his morbid mood and suddenly realising that Sami had not had a chance to tell Isa about the tape handover before being killed.

His expression turns to one of great surprise. He sits perfectly motionless, cross-legged, head erect, hands on his knees and staring at Cassy. Not rudely, but penetratingly— as though he is re-engaging with the vision he thought he had lost, searching, *see*ing. A *seer* at work.

After a while he says quietly: "*So*. You are not just a university professor."

After another long silence, he opens his mouth as if to speak, closes it again, nodding his head, and then says: "Maybe you are not a university professor at all. If so, I am doubly disappointed—this will be a cruel gift you have bought me, Dr. Cassy. But at least perhaps it solves the Cleito mystery for me. I hope not, for if that is the way it is solved, I shall have been bereft three-fold."

She starts at the mention of *Cleito*. He has been avoiding her eyes but now looks into them and says, "Be honest with me, my friend—I do not blame you if you have deceived me. But for me, whose job it is to hear, to see and to warn, I will blame myself if I have fallen to deception. Who *are* you, Dr. Cassy? A British intelligence agent?"

"I'm a scientist," she says simply, "and I've got the tape. Sami gave it to me just before he died."

There is a brief moment while he considers the statement, and then without a word, in what seems like slow motion, his eyes close and he falls flat on his face, still sitting cross-legged with hands spread out on the floor above his prostrated head. He lies there in what for a man of his age must be a tortuous position. Above the rustle of the palm branches overhead, Cassy hears a gentle humming of unrecognisable words.

When he eventually rises to his knees, his face is red and wet and there is blood on his forehead where he has cut himself on the wooden floor. She finds a tissue and leans forward to gently dab at his blooded face. It is an intimate gesture and there is warmth in his eyes as he receives her expression of affection.

"Is this true?" he says. "I was granted faith to believe it but to my shame chose to doubt. It seems too much. I am ashamed—God be merciful to me. He humbles those who follow him lest they think it is their goodness that achieves his plans. I was lowered into a pit of despair to teach me that a man might see in part but it is God who sees the whole."

"You asked me to be honest with you," Cassy says, seizing the moment, "and I will, but I would like you to be honest with me too. What's meant to be on the tape?"

"I will tell you what I believe to be on the tape, Dr. Cassy, but I am afraid I cannot be more specific—that, if I am not greatly mistaken, is your job."

He has brightened again and recovered the playful manner in which he has chosen to administer his seer's authority. He has every right to it, Cassy muses—*he's just apparently pulled off yet another prophetic coup.*

Chapter 31

September 2000
Surat Thani, Southern Thailand

"OUR AILING PLANET is afflicted with putrid abscesses—weeping sores—unhealed and silently deadly. Any one of them could bring about the end."

They are seated in two heavy teak armchairs placed side by side at one end of the veranda. As he speaks, Sufi Isa reaches inside his robe, pulls out a piece of paper, and hands it to Cassy. It is a cutting from a magazine.

"Do you recognise it?"

She takes it and studies a photograph showing a geyser spouting steam, high into the air against a background of forest-covered mountains. In the foreground are mud-pools and a bubbling river, banked with sulphur deposits.

"New Zealand—Rotarua?"

"Yellowstone. When NASA flew an infrared sensor over it, American scientists saw for the first time what was lurking in their own backyard. The sensor showed a circle of heat, more or less following the rim of Yellowstone. The park is one big Caldera—a Super-Volcano. There are only a handful of them and each has enough power to destroy civilisation. Eight kilometres below the National Park there is a chamber of molten magma forty kilometres long, twenty wide, and ten kilometres deep. It is unlike any normal volcano. The molten rock in the chamber is trapped under unimaginable pressure—a cocktail of devastatingly explosive gasses and liquid rock. Eight kilometres is not a great depth. See the trees on the banks of the river here…"

He puts a forefinger on the photograph.

"The river flows into a lake and at the other end of the lake the trunks of the trees have sunk beneath the water. For a long time the park rangers did not understand what was happening until they realised the lake was tilting. The mound you see in the middle ground of the photo is rising at an alarming rate—a swollen skin, bulging under the pressure of the pus below. It cannot be long before the abscess bursts."

"The tape?" she says. Her immediate thought is that he must think that the tape contains an image of Yellowstone or some similar volcano. There had been a photo of a Siberian volcanic range on the wall of his Bangkok apartment.

"We shall come to that. But first I must continue telling you the story of the three young Sufi brothers. You recall our last conversation, I trust."

She nods.

"Following the time on the ice-bound Turkish mountain with Uthman, my spiritual training took me to the holy city of Jerusalem. It was a time of troubling dreams and visions, of terrifying images of the start of all things and the end of all things, of catastrophic turmoil on the earth and in the sky. The world of men and politics was in its own state of turmoil at that time—the Second World War had not long ended…

"Ah…do you want another Coke, Dr. Cassy?"

She follows his gaze to a tiny girl, who can't be much more than four, who has crept up silently behind them. Cassy notices the affection in Sufi Isa's gaze as the child carefully tucks an empty bottle under each arm and toddles off. He looks upwards to the blue sky sparkling through slats of coconut fronds that are starting to move in a freshening wind.

"*When the female infant buried alive is questioned— for what crime she was killed; when the scrolls are open; when the world on high is unveiled; when the blazing fire is kindled to fierce heat; and when the Garden is brought near: then shall each soul know what it has put forward. When the Event Inevitable comes to pass, then will no soul entertain falsehood concerning its coming. Many will it bring low, many will it exalt; when the earth shall be shaken to its depths, and the mountains shall be crumbled to atoms, becoming dust scattered abroad."*

Cassy looks questioningly. "Your dreams in Jerusalem? Isa and the end of the World?"

"The quote is from the Koran. Part of my calling is to carry the Koran's warning about the final judgement to my generation and its children. But you are right. While the Muslim tradition has Isa returning to earth to implement Sharia law across the whole world and condemning those Christians and Jews who refuse to convert to Islam, I saw something of the Christians' interpretation of the same event during my restless nights. The dreams were both awesome and terrifying."

A loud cracking noise somewhere overhead interrupts him and a dead palm frond, broken at its stem, comes crashing to the ground not far from them. The wind is picking up quickly. Blue sky has been replaced by the dazzling silver-white of light tropical clouds.

"It was later, while at university, that I came to understand the full significance of these words."

"What did you study?" He had not said anything about this period of his life before to Cassy and the thought of him at university intrigues her.

"Minerals engineering," he says, pronouncing the words precisely and slowly nodding as though extracting thoughts from some quarantined memory bank.

She looks surprised, trying to imagine this otherworldly ascetic in a laboratory or on an oilrig. Then she thinks of manganese nodules and the mysterious structure on the seafloor image.

"During my studies I saw something that puzzled me greatly. It was a curious fact to me that the distribution and manner of occurrence of many of the world's mineral deposits and soils can best be explained by the action of ice. I do not mean the relatively minor extensions of the polar ice caps that one reads about in school geography books, but truly global ice ages with ice sheets piled as high as they are on Antarctica and covering all the continents at the same time. It is not an orthodox belief these days. But believe me, Dr. Cassy, underneath the two miles of ice covering Greenland, I predict that one day someone will find a canyon on a similar scale to the Grand Canyon. If the ice sheet above quickly melted, nothing about it would tell you that it was once covered by ice. I believe the Grand Canyon was formed as a great ice sheet over North America melted."

The hair bristles on the back of Cassy's neck. *I was right about the tape. It is happening again—events falling neatly into place according to what he had seen.*

"Leaving the oceans empty in all but the deepest parts?" She develops the thought for him and, suddenly making the connection, adds: "How violent would a Caldera's volcanic eruption have to be to trigger a volcanic winter on a scale sufficient to produce a new ice age—a global ice age, even?"

Sharp eyes fix on hers, as if searching for the source of these questions. Then, nodding in silent conversation with himself, he moves his gaze outside, following the clouds now being blown along at a ferocious speed not so far overhead.

"Not far from where we sit, the island of Krakatoa once dissolved in a series of explosions that dwarfed anything the Russians might have thrown at the Americans during the Cold War. Five cubic miles of pulverised rock were blown seventeen miles into the sky and taken around the earth by the winds of the upper atmosphere. It took two whole years to fall and the following year was called the *year without summer*. Thirty years later, Mount Katmai in Alaska erupted filling the sky with dust for months and causing a twenty per cent drop in sunlight in the summer of 1912. The explosion that formed Crater Lake in Oregon filled the atmosphere with ten cubic miles of debris, and the one that formed Lake Tobra in Sumatra pulverised five hundred cubic miles of mountain. It would have darkened the skies for hundreds of years."

"And how does Yellowstone compare to Tobra?"

"It is not dissimilar in size."

Another loud crack and an accompanying thud, followed by a crash, dramatises his words as a palm frond narrowly misses the veranda roof.

"But enough of these ideas. I am an empiricist, Dr. Cassy—how about you? It is evidence that interests me more than theories."

"The tape?" she asks for a second time.

There is an intensity of expression in his face that mixes childish anticipation with fear of disappointment. It seems that he has staked a lot on this tape, perhaps over many years.

He's kept talking because he's nervous of what I might tell him.

"I don't think you'll be disappointed," she offers gently, touched by the glimpse of weakness. "How long have you known about it?"

"The tape? For some years now. You are right—I am undoubtedly anxious. But only for my own sake. If it is not as it was said to be, I am wounded for the hope I wrongly invested in it but as determined in my mission."

"*As it was said to be?*" she repeats. "Someone told you what it contained?"

"My brother... Odam does not always keep the most honourable of friends. Please do not tempt me into further disloyalty, Dr. Cassy—he is my brother. I may choose to portray him in a certain light if I think it will help his soul, but I may not talk about him at another's behest. This is the way of brothers in the Middle East—you will understand."

She nods.

"One of the many small communities Odam shepherds is on the Atlantic Coast of Morocco." Isa frowns as he says it. "You know about this already—you are... were... acquainted with Sami. The community was re-fashioned from a group whose earlier spiritual endeavours had drawn it to the myth of the sunken continent, Atlantis. It is not surprising to me that they had fallen on hard times. I do not fully understand the form of their beliefs but they were, I think, a modern type of animists, worshipping nature. Odam has many networks of friends throughout the Muslim world and it appears that he... how would you say? Lifted the wretched community from its state of decay. This is the way he works. But as with all things, some good became since there were two from the community who responded to my own Way."

"Sami being one of them."

"Indeed. From time to time I have become aware of aspects of my brother's tainted walk that I would prefer to remain ignorant of. Odam, it seems, had helped acquire for the community certain relics relating to the Atlantis theme—I heard of this through Sami. The cult's leader, who they call Solon, is not completely detached from his former obsession and for some reason, sadly, Odam sees fit to feed it. A rumour of a document kept in a Russian navy museum reached Solon. It was said to describe a tape containing seafloor image data that reveals a collection of structures having the appearance of ancient buildings. Solon somehow got hold of the document and the tape. Sami, who knew well of my own interests, sent a photocopy of the document to Bangkok. I had the Russian translated and had someone check out an identification number that appeared on the document. Bangkok is a very good place for international networks, you understand, Dr. Cassy. It turned out to be something from the former Soviet Union's Naval Research Archives in Leningrad. The Archives are still there but I don't imagine they are very full any more. I hear from Sami that other items had come into the hands of Solon."

Cassy makes a note to let Mal MacFenn know where the rare manganese nodule acquired its catalogue number.

"It was something else, though, that convinced me that this was the sign I had been awaiting for nearly fifty years.

Years ago, it must have been not long after the Russian survey had been conducted I suppose, and while I was still able to travel freely through the Near and Middle East, I once met a man who had heard of such a thing. It was relatively easy for a wandering Sufi to cross the mountainous borders between Iran, Iraq, Afghanistan, and the Soviet Union and beyond, and I would preach wisdom and warn of impending judgement to many thousands of people—sometimes in large crowds, although more usually to individuals in peasant huts. The man was an influential Muslim Muscovite who had worked for the Soviet Navy in some administrative capacity. He was an educated man and engaged me in a long and involved discussion about the end and the beginning of civilisation. We met in an old mosque in the city of Xi'an in China. He told me of an extraordinary finding on a deep seafloor map. When Sami sent me the Russian document, I knew it must be the same thing."

"Did the Muscovite suggest why such an important find might be kept secret?"

Dusk is descending rapidly and Cassy slaps at a solitary mosquito that has already injected its proboscis into the skin of her calf.

"I have wondered about that." Then, leaning forward and pushing himself up from his armchair, he says, "Come. It is time for you to tell *me* some mysteries, I think—I have talked for too long."

"I can do better than tell you. I have the image data on my laptop computer. Shall we go inside before we get eaten alive?"

***

For a while they sit on the floor of a sparsely furnished living room, huddled over a plasma screen, examining superpower imagery in a village headman's simple wooden house. Outside, the dead palm fronds keep falling as the wind strengthens into a storm. She tells him about the missing geo-code and the way she discovered that it was a Russian submarine image; and begins taking him through the steps she had taken Beccy through. They take a break when the Pu Yay Bahn and his eldest arrive, each with a tray of colourful and fragrant dishes.

"You bear the deprivations of a refugee well," she says as their hosts leave them alone again.

"It is, as you say in England, bittersweet," he replies. "I have, in truth, been in exile from freedom many years now—long before finding a haven in this country. My words are controversial and unwelcomed in many communities. I have made many enemies over the years. But it is not wise to ask what might have been. The man who looks back or only looks forward is not a happy man. A rich man may be poor because the one act that would lead him into true happiness has become beneath him in his arrogance. A man of little means might have great wealth because he has found his purpose and is granted the humble resources to fulfil it. In these terms I am both at peace and wealthy."

"I admire you," Cassy says. "What happens when you're caught off-guard? Even great Sufis must have their off-moments."

"I once had a family," he says. "A wife and a child."

She looks shocked.

"What happened?"

"My wife died in childbirth."

They are seated at a thick-timbered meal table and he stares silently at the empty dishes. As the silence prolongs, Cassy gets up and walks over to the corner where the computer lies on the bare wooden floor, plugged into a socket dangling from exposed wires. She kneels down and types a few commands, hoping that the personal intrusion hadn't offended him.

"I apologise, my friend," he suddenly says, peering into the gloom towards her and then rising stiffly. "A few moments of melancholic indulgence from time to time are enough. Come, let us continue—I am, as you English say, all ears!"

He squats next to Cassy and insists on the full detail. It is obvious to Cassy that he keeps himself well-read on matters that interest him. He is totally enthralled with an excitement cultivated by years of anticipation. Leaving the real puzzle to last, she shows him the continental context of the undersea object's location: what looks so much like four great inundated river courses converging towards a point on the floor of the Gulf of Aden; two rivers flowing from the Red Sea and two emerging from the Persian Gulf.

"This is at a depth of fifteen thousand feet?" he whispers as she shows him a close-up of the Pishon River curving around the southwest edge of Arabia and tipping out of the floor of the Red Sea to join the Gihon River gushing forth from the Ethiopian highlands. Together heading east in a vast undersea canyon.

"Eden?" he muses. "In the Hebrew language, *Eden* is also the term for a *construction socket*—sunk in the ground to take the foundation of a building. Could we be looking at the sunken foundations of the world, Dr. Cassy, birthplace of humanity and its civilisation?"

"Perhaps. You believe so?"

"When copper-helmeted divers were being sent down at the time I was an engineer, what could they be expected to see that they were not looking for? Visibility is close to zero down there, even at very shallow depths. They were not geographical explorers but highly paid repairmen, mending cables and servicing bore holes. Now it is the age of the robotic-submarine, but the same may be said—even more so, perhaps. Computers only find what you ask them to find, do they not? A mini-submarine investigating a shipwreck would not know if it were sitting on an ancient beach. Nor would it be likely to discover a submerged cliff nearby. It is a vast uncharted world down there and the technology is only now being created to explore it with the detail that would reveal its biggest secret."

"Let me show you the real marvel," she says, calling up a picture of several rectangular shapes with the gap between two of them looking for all the world like a flight of steps.

"I have seen the marvel—is there more?" he says, looking at her but clearly distracted by his own thoughts.

He leans to peer closely at the new image on the screen, examining it for some minutes. Then he straightens again and turns to gaze out into the tropical night. The strong winds have blown the clouds away as quickly as they came.

"It just could be, couldn't it?" is all he says.

"It could also be a ship broken up," she replies, "or mining equipment, or an unrecovered aircraft from World War Two or a later disaster. There have been at least two documented commercial air crashes in the Aden region, as far as I know."

"I do not know of any mining equipment that looks like this," Isa says.

"We could check with international sea salvage charts."

"It would be possible. But it will not be necessary."

"It would make your case more convincing."

"My case?" He smiles. "That presupposes that I had thought to use this knowledge"—and he gestures to the screen—"for some persuasive purpose."

"Isn't that why you wanted the tape?"

"Only to persuade myself perhaps. It is enough for me to have seen in my dreams, believed and then seen a little evidence. That is quite sufficient. I do not need this for any other reason; certainly not to convince others. They will not be convinced of the coming judgement by this"—he gestures to the computer again—"nor by my wild theories, wrong or right, imagined or revealed, nor by any other material evidence. I am a prophet, Dr. Cassy. That is my life's work. It is the spirit of prophecy that convinces—spirit speaks to spirit, mind talks to mind. A discussion of the intellect will help someone *see* only if the spirit is open and willing. No, what we have before us might only be of value to those who would believe anyway. Even for them it might be of no consequence because the matters we have talked about are too big for most of the faithful. Most true believers are, by nature, simple in disposition and not greatly taken up with the big debates beloved by men of the world. No, I have seen enough, I do not need to see this again. The structures are of some fascination but the location and the rivers are a better gift, a more precise and authentic sign. There—it is much more than I had hoped for, even in my most hopeful dreaming."

He gets up from his squat and wanders over to the veranda to stand illuminated by the broken light of a half-moon filtered through swaying trees.

Cassy had imagined various reactions to her revelations, but not this.

"Isa you are quite incomprehensible!" she says girlishly, jumping up and walking over to join him. "I've never met anyone like you before." She slips her arm into his, needing to show some physical sign of affection.

As she does so, he asks, "The path of *meekness,* my friend—are you familiar with it?" Moonlight reveals laughter in his eyes.

"It's not a word I use very often," she admits. *Never, actually.*

"Having power to do something but happily restraining from its use. It is not the same as weakness; it is love put into practice by the strong. Gentleness is, I believe, a more usual rendition in the English language. Knowledge is power. I could do all manner of things with what we have here—as could you, Dr. Cassy. I choose not to. Its purpose for me is completed. *Resource sufficient for the purpose.*"

"Then why all the fuss about acquiring the tape?" she asks, her exasperation not entirely rhetorical.

"Acquiring? No. I have no more right to it than whoever secured it for my brother Odam. Why did I need to borrow it? Only because of the vision. The Muscovite's story was of an ocean survey that contained compelling evidence of men once living on the deep ocean floor. But God meant to show me the rivers. And you have been his angel. This is the wonderful way of Allah. I have seen the sign—now the tape can go back to where it belongs. My words will carry new authority, perhaps. And through them, God willing, more will be saved from the judgement to come."

"I suspect Odam wouldn't share your views," she says sombrely. "The tape is of unbelievable value if it is what it seems to be." They stand there, her arm linked in his, both looking out into the night.

"You are wondering if my brother planned to make some personal use of this marvel. The tape was certainly no act of friendship towards the leader of the Essaouiran sect. Part of a deal, perhaps, but I cannot imagine what the Atlantis dreamer would have offered my brother."

You haven't met Leen. She shudders at the thought of what Leen and others like her might have done as part of a deal for ancient undersea relics.

He continues his thought. "I am certain from Sami's account that the tape was Odam's doing—as with the other relics. If it was for money it was not for money's sake. You see, Dr. Cassy, my brother, like me, is not interested in the lifestyles that others crave riches to secure. He is a man of simple tastes and lives the life of an ascetic. I *know* my brother, Dr. Cassy—he is a spiritual man and judges his progress through life by his own visions and dreams, as do I. He is not touched by the seductions of material wealth. We are of a kind he and I... in that respect."

"Some pursue power as hungrily as others pursue wealth," she suggests.

"That may be so," he says and a change in his intonation tells Cassy that it might be as much as he will say on the matter.

It is growing late and there is a burning question Cassy needs to put to him before they retire.

"What did you mean by the *Cleito* mystery?"

He turns to look at her at the same time as the single bare lightbulb hanging from the veranda ceiling comes on. There is a noise and Cassy turns to see a pretty teenage girl clearing the empty bowls from the meal table. A mass of suicidal flying things gather out of the darkness to swirl around the light in chaotic orbits.

"I promised honesty," Isa says, "but some things it would be unwise... too dangerous, I think... to tell you."

Then he nods one of his knowing nods and says, "Now I see. I have wondered about you, Dr. Cassy—whether you are truly a scientist or something else. Now I believe that you are indeed a professor... but I see that you are also something else as well."

She waits for more but it seems that he has finished, and his gaze wanders to the moths.

He sighs as though having made some difficult decision and says, "Since you have brought me a gift, I will give you one in return."

With that, he releases himself from Cassy's arm, turns and pads softly across the wooden floor, placing a fatherly hand on the shoulder of the girl as he passes and disappears through an open bedroom door. A few minutes later he returns, clutching a book with both hands.

"I do not know your full purpose in seeking me out," he says, "but I shall entrust this to you. You have served a divine purpose once—you may yet do so again."

As he speaks, he carefully wraps the book in a plastic supermarket bag and ties the bundle around with a length of fishermen's yarn, and then puts it in another bag and seals it up with tape. The act seems deliberate and to have a sense of finality about it, as though in the careful wrapping and sealing he is putting a close to something, sealing up forever something that is now past.

"After you depart this place you will probably not see me again, my friend. I shall leave Bangkok and shall disappear for a while. For a long while, perhaps."

Chapter 32

THE FOLLOWING MORNING Isa is waiting as Cassy emerges from the primitive shower—a plastic bowl and a large concrete water trough—and leads her by the hand onto the veranda where a group of bare-footed children are squatted giggling around something in one corner. They silence and part in respect as Isa approaches, revealing an enamel washbowl.

"For your amusement," he says, grinning. "I think that your spirit is searching and here is a test—a child's lesson."

She says nothing, happy to be played with, and kneels down amongst the children.

"I've been up early collecting mud from the paddy field. Look—a model of the earth."

It is a deep white enamel bowl, chipped with use and half full of a grey-brown sticky clay.

"The mud is the molten rock upon which the earth's continents and ocean floors float. And look: here is a continent."

He takes a thick block of wood from a young child and rests it on the mud. It had been roughly chopped to a shape that filled about half of the bowl. On top of the wooden block he places a large flat stone from the beach, and on top of this he places another layer of paddy clay, spreading it out evenly and then down the sides of the stone and wood as if icing a cake.

"And here is a bit of the ocean floor," he says, taking another flat beach stone from the child and placing it on the mud floor of the bowl next to the iced cake.

"There: the ocean floor and the continents towering miles above. The stone and mud on top of the continent are the sediments laid down by rivers and lakes."

"But no water," Cassy says, playing along and cupping her hands lovingly over the ears of a small girl who has snuggled up on her lap.

He claps his hands playfully and one of the older children runs into the house while the others giggle again. She returns with a block of ice and with her mother, following close behind, laughing and shouting to someone in the other house.

"The entire volume of earth's water, Dr. Cassy. Locked up as ice and stored on the great continental mountain ranges. Look. This is the ice sheet that sat on the American continent. Watch closely what happens."

With that, he carefully places the block of ice on top of the continental mud cake. As he does so, some of the sticky mud that coats the top of the wood is squeezed up from under the ice to form a raised clay mound between the block of ice and the edge of the continent. At the same time, the continent—wooden block, stone, mud, and ice—sink further into the mud at the bottom of the enamel bowl.

"There—I have just created the mountains that ring the edges of all the earth's continents. The Rocky Mountains on one side, the Appalachians on the other. Remember, I was once a mining engineer! The mud and sand laid down by rivers and estuaries and in lakes and inland seas and squeezed to the edges of the ice sheets by an unimaginable weight would join the older sediments squeezed out by previous ice ages and now solidified into great mountain chains of folded rock. The highest mountains such as the Andes and the Rockies are on the side of the continents where the prevailing winds would pile the most snow to create the thickest areas of ice. The mountains are exuded like wax under an old-fashioned seal."

"Where were you when I laid the foundation of the earth! Who stretched out the sea's horizon? On what were the earth's Edens sunk? Have you ever entered into the springs of the sea? Or have you walked on the floors of the oceans? Have you ever caused the dawn to know its place; that it might take hold of the ends of the earth and the wicked be shaken out of it, and the earth is changed like clay under the seal, standing out in clear relief?"

"A song from the oldest creation poem in the world," he says, "from the Hebrew's book of Job."

He is in his element and, like the children, Cassy is drawn into his world.

"See, too, that the weight of the ice has made the continent sink into the molten layer of rock beneath the earth's crustal rocks. Now we wait to see what happens when the ice melts. But first, let us plant a *garden* on the ocean floor."

He says something to a serious-looking boy aged about ten, who, by the state of his hands, looks as though he had helped Isa collect the paddy mud earlier. He scampers away and returns with a fistful of leaves, still deadly serious.

"Go on," Isa says gently in Thai, and the child scatters the leaves carefully on the ocean floor under the shadow of the ice-capped continent.

"Eden in the socket of the earth. A garden planted for the enjoyment of a God-fearing humanity. And watch…"

He nods to another boy who opens a clasped blackened fist to reveal a small piece of half-formed charcoal roughly fashioned into the shape of a boat. The young ark-builder places his workmanship among the leaves on the ocean floor.

"…the Ark—built by a man who was foolish enough and wise enough to prepare for what was about to come," Isa says, placing an arm around the boy.

"Now come, it is time for breakfast."

***

Breakfast is a plate of noodles cooked in the coconut oil that flavours everything in maritime Southeast Asia, and decorated with the tiny dried anchovies that give fishing villages in that part of the world their distinctive smell.

It is time for some manoeuvring. Cassy needs to be in Surat Thani town the next day and Isa's hijack to the fishing village has disrupted a carefully laid plan. As much as she is enjoying his company, she has a more risky appointment to make and timing will be everything.

"I had hoped to catch the early morning ferry back to the Island," she says as casually as she can. "Perhaps I'll walk into town this evening and stay in a hotel."

It is also an open challenge to him to give more away about his reasons for intercepting the ferry.

"There is no need," Isa says without looking up, a spoonful of noodles poised at his mouth. "I have arranged a boat for you already. It will take you out to the ferry in the same way as it met you. You are my guest—all is taken care of."

"You are keen to keep me out of town."

"If that is so, then I have my reasons," he says with a mouth full of rice noodles.

He calls to one of the children on the veranda and asks how the ice is doing.

"Which you will not divulge."

"That is so."

"What if I were to go anyway?"

"I am sure you would not repay hospitality with recklessness," he says with a twinkle in his eye and another spoonful of noodles in his mouth.

They sit looking out over the tranquillity of the simple fishing community. Turquoise sea flashes through gaps in the coconut trees, the temperature already over thirty degrees at eight-thirty in the morning. The wind is still strong and clouds are on the horizon again. Nearby one of the young boys with them earlier is standing on tiptoe trying to hang washing on a line he can barely reach. He looks over at the Sufi and gives a childish wave.

"They love you," Cassy says. "Do you mind me asking what happened after you wife died?"

He didn't answer immediately.

"To my own child, you mean?"

She nods.

"He survived the birth and I looked after him for almost two years. I was living in Uzbekistan in those days. They were difficult times. Difficult, but touched with blessing. I was not a *young* father and it was a time of increasing persecution. One of the women devotees nursed the baby—I could not have managed for as long as I did without her help."

He picks up a battered aluminium teapot and pours two glasses of naam chaa—a tepid creamy flavoured Chinese tea.

"After two years I made the most difficult decision of my life. I had to leave the city and the region I had made my home, with no idea where I might go next. There were threats on my life—a great and hostile backlash unleashed against my work. The life of a wandering holy man in backward regions can be a treacherous one. I have always faced opposition, but at times the skies have grown intensely dark about me and it has seemed that nowhere is safe to go. The greater the reception by the spiritually hungry and materially impoverished, the more violent the reaction from others. In truth I do not blame those who oppose me. I am indeed a poor cleric judged by their standards. If it is an indictable offence to teach others to follow the path that has brought me joy and freedom then I plead guilty and deserve judgement—death, even. But how could I subject my son to such a life? These risks are my own choice and should not be borne by those who have not chosen them. Many depended on me—including parents with their own young ones. They needed me—the more so with the storm clouds of persecution approaching. I could not abandon them."

"The woman devotee took the child?"

"No, she was as devoted to a life of suffering as I. She offered but it was not right. No—I had a dream. In it, I was instructed to offer my son into the custody of someone who would love him as his own. The next day the devotee came to see me, distraught, having had the same dream. There was a man in the city whose wife could not bear children. He was the instigator of much of the local persecution against me and was behind an attempt to have me arrested on false charges. His hatred had enslaved him and I feared for what he would do next—he was a powerful man and his venom had spread throughout the region. His wife, however, was a kindly soul from a noble family and I was moved with compassion for her. It was this couple that had appeared in our dreams."

"You gave your son to a sworn enemy?" Cassy said incredulously.

"The offer was made in public and in a way that made him accountable to the entire community for the manner in which he would take care of the precious gift. In any case, with a mother like his wife I knew I had nothing to fear. The crowd that watched—there were many present—was stunned to silence as you are. You disapprove?"

"I... well—well, no, not disapprove. How could I? It's such an extraordinary thing to do. How... how could you bring yourself to hand him over?"

Memory of the turmoil that had engulfed Cassy like a tsunami when Joy had told her that she was an adopted orphan suddenly returns and her emotions well up.

"I was possessed by an overwhelming love for the man and for his wife. Fear for my son's safety under my own protection was not unfounded. There had been one attempt to bomb my community's compound. One family had been hacked to pieces as they slept in their beds and there were threats to search us out wherever we went. I think I would have kept him if there had been a way. Possessive love would have been selfish love—divine love came to my rescue."

"Unbelievable," she murmurs, shaking her head and wiping an eye.

"Love empowers to do the unthinkable—to give away what cannot be kept to gain what cannot be lost."

"Did you see him again?"

"My son? Once, at a distance, on a pilgrimage. But an earthquake took him not long after that. He perished with his adoptive father. I do not know what happened to the goodly mother."

"I'm very sorry."

"Our little model should be ready by now," he says, and prises himself from his chair.

As they make their way along the veranda he calls out and the children come running to join them again.

She takes his hand, becoming one of the children.

"Now let us see if the paddy mud has performed its role obediently—I have played this little game before, you will not be surprised to hear."

They gather around the bowl, grandchildren happily playing their grandfather's favourite game.

"There, Dr. Cassy, what do you see? Tell me."

She squats with the kneeling children and looks closely at a devastated world, emphasising the wonder on her face for the sake of many eyes trained on hers.

The ice has almost gone from the top of the continent but for two small patches. What had been the lower platform containing the Garden of Eden now contains an ocean of water lapping at the shores of a continent rimmed with a broken chain of paddy mud mountains. Inside the mountains is the footprint of the now-melted ice cap. There are gaps in the mountain rim where the melting water has washed some of the mud away and beyond the gaps, distinct channels in the thick mud slope leading down to the now submerged ocean floor.

"A brilliant model," she says, laughing with delight and snuggling up with the three little ones now nestling against her.

"Oh—and look at Nooh's Ark!" she squeals. "Even more brilliant!"

The little piece of boat-shaped charcoal is resting high and dry, settled precariously in a gap in the mountain rim of the vanished ice cap. It is not on a peak, but is well above sea level. He watches her take it in. Without the weight of the ice the continent has risen, regaining buoyancy in the mud that represents the earth's molten crust, lifting the boat that had been floating on sea, high into the mountains.

"*Very* clever," she says as the children start clapping gleefully. Then, putting on the manner of a schoolmistress and addressing Isa, adds: "Totally obsessive. But very clever."

They are suddenly interrupted by a chorus of excited yelps, and three puppies come skidding and scratching over the polished floorboards towards the happy scene. They land in a heap amongst the laughing children and then, seeing the bowl, leap to it and proceed to drain the world of water. The climax couldn't be more dramatic and Cassy finds herself laughing uncontrollably with the rest of them.

Then as Isa comes over to her and takes her hand to help her to her feet, she is overcome. Instead of rising, she falls back to the floor, face in hands, shaking with emotion. The children gather round, first laying tentative hands on her heaving back, and then one, and then another, thrusting both arms around her neck and kissing her cheeks, her neck, her hair, trying to make her better. But the heaving becomes heavier and the fast-rewinding soundtrack of a lifetime of hurt becomes louder and painfully disinhibited until she is shamelessly sobbing her heart out, covered by a mountain of childlike love.

***

"You have achieved your purpose in coming to see me?" Isa asks.

Cassy and Isa have wandered down to the beach and found a shady rock to sit on.

"I came to deliver what Sami gave me," she says in all honesty, her eyes still red and puffy. He had said nothing, merely standing patiently and watching until it was over.

She had lain there, semi-prostrate, caressed into eventual silence by the hands of the children.

"Yes. But I trust that you will be able to take back something of... of greater personal—or professional—interest, in return for your troubles? What will you do with the tape and its secrets?"

"What do you suggest?" she sniffs, her emotions still on the edge.

"You will think of something."

"What if I let Odam have it?" she suggests, watching him closely. She adds, "What if I already have?"

He sits motionless, looking out to sea.

"There would be a certain fairness in that. But it might not be the wisest course to take."

"If I was threatened with violence it might be very wise."

He looks round at her, concern written on his face. "I am sorry..."

"It's okay," she says, in danger of welling up again at his kindness. "I recovered. Who knows whether it was Odam's lot or not? Someone knew I had the tape and guessed why I had it. But I would like to know the truth just in case someone comes back. Did Sami steal the tape from Odam?"

"Sami intercepted it. We waited for it for almost a year. Sami got there first when it eventually came."

"I see. So they know as much and as little as you. How might they have traced the tape to me? They broke into my office—my house too, earlier." Now she is crying again and Isa closes the gap between them on the rock to put a comforting hand on her shoulder.

"I am deeply sorry, Dr. Cassy. I do not know—what more I can say? If it was indeed my brother I can only apologise, though that is no consolation. Perhaps you were followed from Essaouira? Perhaps the answer lies in another question—how did you come to be in Essaouira in the first place?"

She sniffs again, pulling herself together and sitting upright to look him in the eyes. It is her turn to be evasive. "How about you, Isa? Have you achieved *your* purpose in coming down from Bangkok to meet me a second time?"

"All but one," he says. "But come, let's wade through the water to the boat."

It is one of the small fishing vessels she had seen the day before, about seven metres long with a narrow wheelhouse at the front to protect a lone fisherman from sudden tropical squalls. Behind this are the bare boards of the boat's hull with a thin wooden walkway running along each side to a single seat across the stern. A colourful plastic awning is stretched from the wheelhouse to two poles lodged in sockets at either side of the stern rail. They sit down on the rear bench and Cassy smoothes the excess water from her sodden shorts.

She seizes the chance to ask another question that she has been saving for the right moment.

"You've told me why you were interested in the Essaouira tape and we've talked about Odam's interests. What about your other brother—Nooh?"

At the mention of Nooh, Isa sits up straight and almost falls off the narrow bench and overboard. Cassy instinctively grabs his hand to steady him, and then decides to keep hold of it.

He sits blinking in the sun for a moment and places his other hand on top of hers. His eyes are moist and there is an expression of pain in them.

"Now that does surprise me, Dr. Cassy—from a woman of your genius for uncovering secrets. Nooh, my brother... alas, he is no longer with us."

He cups her hand in a gesture that is both spiritual and intimate, and then pats her knee.

"His life was tragically taken by an errant brother—and with it, the lives of other good men too."

She is thrown.

"But... in your apartment in Bangkok. Wasn't that...?"

"Ah, of course. I assumed you came armed with a full briefing. I do apologise for misleading you—quite unintentionally—but I am delighted to know that you are not omniscient, my mysterious academic friend. It makes me feel much more secure. The Nooh you met was a fellow devotee after the same persuasion, but influenced rather too much, I fear, by Odam. True, he is a brother, but alas, not my blood brother. A Sufi in the Nooh Brotherhood but not Nooh, third of the Sufi brothers."

"I'm no expert," she says trying to find the right words, "but I think you will find there are many who suppose they know about your movement but do not know this fact."

She is thinking of Marten's years of research into the cult.

"That Nooh has passed on? This does not surprise me," he says. "For better or for worse, the three Sufi brothers are something of a legend. And like all legends, the popular image is built on a mixture of fact and fable. From the very earliest stages of our pilgrimages, we had to adopt a vagrant and elusive lifestyle. An inquisitive person could be forgiven for not knowing for certain that Nooh has departed us. Here you see me living as if with my own family in a remote village. It is truly my home. Before the well-meaning United Nations officials hid me away in Bangkok, this is how I lived—this is how we all lived. Camouflage becomes second nature to the permanently hounded. Odam has undoubtedly used this for his own ends. Even I still disappear when the time suits. I spend a good part of the year wandering, staying where I am welcomed, moving on when I am not. When it gets too difficult I retreat to the apartment you have already seen—or somewhere else."

The Imaginary Brotherhood—it was the title of a great Uwaysi epic Marten had told Cassy about—a brotherhood of Sufi teachers and disciples communicating beyond the grave.

So. Odam and Isa are locked in some sort of schismatic cold war but bound by fraternal loyalty, and Nooh's dead.

She cannot say why, but the revelation leaves her disturbed. Perhaps it is the discovery that she had wrongly interpreted an important observation. If one, why not others? A chill shivers its way down Cassy's spine in spite of the oppressive heat. She reaches over the side to scoop up a handful of warm sea, letting it drain through her fingers on to the dry boards and rubbing wet salty hands over her face.

This is all too surreal and you need to keep your wits about you, Cassy girl.

Chapter 33

IT HAS BEEN a stormy crossing back to the island of Kho Samui. The overcrowded cabin is heavy with the smell of wet bodies gently steaming in the tropical heat, and travellers, luggage, and clothing are strewn over the wooden seats like flotsam on a beach. The boat now lurches as it crashes against the jetty. Cassy watches the crew through rain and oil-smeared windows shouting as they set about securing a rope to a thick wooden stake half worn through with years of use.

Above their cries there is another shout—from within the boat. Someone is calling her name. The voice is urgent and she peers into the noisy cabin trying to see who has come to meet her. She spins round as someone tugs violently on her sleeve to find Pichit, the son of her bungalow-owning friend.

"Pichit! Nice to see you but... what's the...?"

Grabbing her wrist, he pulls her down towards the boat's floor so hard that she falls over cracking a shoulder on one of the seats.

"Keep here, Adjan Cassy—man out there are look for you. Here... come back to engine room."

With that he drags her, half-crouching, half-running to the rear of the boat where an open door leads into the engine space and then out through another door to a narrow strip of deck and a rusted stern rail. There is no one else in the engine space—her fellow travellers are filing out of the cabin by a short flight of steps up to the small bow deck and scrambling onto the jetty or negotiating a precarious-looking plank. Those at the rear of the queue are staring at the spectacle of Cassy's exit at the other end of the boat.

"Who's looking for me?" she shouts above the deafening growl of the engine, out of breath and nursing a throbbing shoulder.

"Man, two or three man, come ask around island for you. Last night you bungalow done over. We know this mans—gangsters. They come from mainland—not from my island. They not Samui."

"What should I do?" She was not prepared for this.

"We think of something already, Dr. Cassy. You good friend of family—we take care of you. No worries. Stay here."

He jumps over a gap in the engine room's floor filled with dark oily seawater and disappears out of the rear door. A second later he is back.

"Come," he says, gesturing urgently. "I have boat—mans not see this side of ferry. Keep near floor, please."

He is out of the door again and Cassy at his heels. Outside he vanishes over the side. Without stopping to think she follows him, half-jumping, half-diving from the engine room door to the boat's side and slipping under the inadequate guardrail overboard. She lands in a heap on the floor of a large rubber dingy with a powerful outboard motor. She is about to say something when a heavy sheet of netting is thrown over her.

"Stay, please." Pichit's urgent voice comes from somewhere above her. "We get out of here. You be think about where you want go. You have to go from Samui. They know you come back."

Twenty minutes later the engine suddenly cuts and they glide to a smooth halt. There is a bump as though arriving at a jetty. When Cassy pulls back the netting, however, she finds that they have moored to a large offshore cruiser, and she recognises Pichit's father's new toy—a million dollars' worth of Sunseeker. The clouds are low in the sky and visibility is poor so that she can't make out where they are.

"Here—we get this for you," Pichit shouts, throwing a bag over to her. He is at the wheel in front of a dazzling array of instruments.

"Most your stuff taken. This bag a present. You know what they want? You got something belong to them?"

He grins conspiratorially. She is an old friend and he is giving his loyalty without questions. Cassy has not had to think hard about where to be taken. Pichit tries to dissuade her but she is insistent. She needs to return to Surat Thani—back where she has just come from.

It is two hours before Pichit reduces the throttle and steers them south towards land. so that they complete the last few kilometres hugging the mangrove-swamped coastline east of the river mouth that leads up to the town's port. Cassy has asked him to drop her somewhere where she can find transport to Surat's train station, located fourteen kilometres outside the town. They turn into a small creek carved through the mangroves and eventually come to a village where the wooden houses seemed to be growing out of the saltwater swamp like the mangrove trees that surround them.

"My friend with taxi live here. He drive you, no worries," Pichit says as he cuts back the engine and guides the launch towards the tiny landing stage.

It looks to Cassy a most unlikely place to find a taxi. As they make their way from the jetty, however, along a roughly laid raised concrete walkway between the houses, the remote fishing village transforms into a grubby transport stop along a highway. The traffic noise had been drowned by the noises of the sea. Three or four of the houses nearest the road have been turned into eating places, bedecked with coloured lights and Coke signs, and on the other side of the highway part of a coconut plantation has been cleared as a truck park. Pichit goes over to one of the restaurants and talks to a pretty girl about his own age. She looks over at Cassy and then points away up the road.

"He out in taxi now," Pichit says when he returns. "You stay here and eat—we eat together, then he come back. He expected soon—my cousin." With a wink he added, "You like meet my other cousin—he your age and handsome. I buy Mekong; you forget bad mans. Mekong no worries, eh?"

***

An hour later Cassy is seated in the back of a battered taxi, approaching Surat's tiny rail settlement behind a tour bus that is choking her with filthy diesel exhaust. Pichit's cousin seems oblivious to the health hazard and makes no attempt to pull back or close the windows. As they pull into the rail town's single street there are two coaches parked in front of the station building. The place looks like a Wild West film set—a two-dimensional single row of wooden shop-houses and cafes, the station opposite and a quiet muddy road running between that would have been dusty but for the recent rain. It is still only three in the afternoon but the sky is darkening and a full-blown tropical downpour seems imminent. It is not just the weather that threatens. Cassy can sense something isn't right even before her driver mutters under his breath, "Nu nu pow," and shakes his head in a disapproving gesture.

"*Nu nu pow?*" she asks him in imperfect Thai. The Thai language has five tones so that the word *nu* can have five different meanings depending on the intonation. Pow, she thinks, means holy. *Holy mouse snake? What's he seen?*

"Man at cafe," he answers in Thai, pointing across the road to a bearded man sitting at a cheap Formica-topped table, mostly covered by the newspaper he is reading. "Bad snake."

He says no more but Cassy gets the picture and does some quick thinking. They have pulled up in a space between the two buses and are out of view from the cafe. Her driver is alert and she guesses Pichit has briefed him. A train sits on the line, stretching for what seems to be ten carriages in either direction, and Cassy sees the bright colours of backpacks on the platform. As she watches, some of the travellers start to spill out onto the street and gather around the buses. She can hear someone speaking French and then someone shouting something in German, followed by a chorus of laughter. The train would have come south from Bangkok or north from Butterworth in Malaysia. She wonders which is the better escape route. It takes her a minute to decide on a plan and a backup. She fishes out a wad of five-hundred-baht notes and stuffs several into her driver's hand. Grabbing his arm, she says in a slow and emphasised Thai: "For the ride. More if I come back—wait here until the train leaves."

Scanning the scene, she can see no sign of other watchers so thrusts the taxi door open and is about to jump out when the heavens open. She reaches back into the taxi, throws another note on the front seat, grabs an umbrella that is lying on the back seat, and points to a pair of sunglasses and baseball cap wedged between the driver's sun shield and the car's roof. He gives a toothy grin and passes them back to her.

With a bag slung over each shoulder, she runs to the station building, umbrella pulled low and disguised in a Chicago Bulls cap and a pair of gold-rim aviator style sunglasses circa 1970's and unmistakably provincial taxi driver. The tourists are boarding the buses and some are waiting in the shelter of the station building. She runs over to this group and mingles, making her way to a position where she can view the street.

The watcher is in his late twenties, perhaps, wearing a buff Middle Eastern style tunic, with a short dark beard on the end of his chin. In one hand he is holding an umbrella and in the other a cell phone. A newspaper is now tucked under one arm. He is no longer sitting at the cafe but is walking towards the coaches. He must have seen the taxi come in and is coming to investigate. The waiting travellers stand under a canopy extending the length of the station building and some have wandered back into the main station entrance to get out of the rain. She slips into the forecourt and looks around. A young Spanish couple are panicking at the station's only opened ticket window, rummaging through bags for something. Underwear lie scattered at their feet and behind them stands a small line of agitated travellers. It seems as though the train will soon be leaving.

Cassy spots what she is looking for and crosses quickly over to a green counter between the ticket office and the platform. Behind the counter are several banks of heavy metal shelving units and on them, rows of dull coloured suitcases with brightly coloured smaller bags scattered between. She reaches into her money belt, calls to the attendant who is seated behind the counter with her back to Cassy, and hands over a scrappy piece of yellow paper.

"*Song song kaaw hok*," Cassy says urgently, spelling out the number with a smile. *Two two nine six* is the number on the left-luggage ticket Cassy received by post the day before she had left her island hideaway to meet Isa. Chavalit had done a good job.

She had phoned him with an unreasonable request but he had agreed without questions. Among Chav's friends in Bangkok's vast criminal fraternity was a trustworthy young Chinese-Thai man with Surat connections and a fine record of sophisticated but undetected burglaries. Cassy had supposed that all tabloid reporters long enough in the tooth had such friends, and was proven right.

Five days ago the young man had come down on the overnight train, and three days later he was back in Bangkok. Chav had given the envelope containing a short note and the left-luggage ticket to a courier who had put it on the lunchtime flight to Kho Samui Airport where Cassy had been waiting to pick it up two hours later. She was pleased that it had worked so well, but still didn't know what she had managed to catch in this elaborate trawl. She was about to find out.

"Name *Kha?*" The girl attendant says in a gentle Thai lilt.

"Sam King," Cassy answers.

Chav had suggested a name that would not seem unusual for either a Thai or a *Farang*—foreigner.

She screws her face up as she examines the name written next to the number in her book.

"Saam Kriang?" she says sounding puzzled, then gave a giggle and placed a hand over her mouth.

"My friend write in Thai language. It look like Thai name. Wait, please; I get your bag."

As she walks towards the back of the shelving units Cassy examines the luggage, most of it probably left by travellers taking a break in the Singapore–Malaysia–Bangkok train trek to spend a few days on the beach. Cassy hopes it won't be one of the heavy suitcases—Chav had not got a description of the baggage before he paid off his friend. She has no idea what to expect.

An outburst of shouting draws her attention back to the ticket hall. The Spanish couple has emptied the entire contents of a huge saffron backpack, and three loud-mouthed Londoners who have joined the back of the queue are shouting obscenities. Cassy soon has more to worry about than feeling ashamed of her nationality, however—beyond the ticket queue and directly in her line of sight, a man in a beige shirt with a beard is looking at her. It is not the man with the newspaper and he has a piece of paper in his hand. He looks at Cassy and then at the piece of paper and Cassy interprets the gesture immediately, taking in the implications. She is the subject of a manhunt and they have a photograph.

Shit. This is serious.

She quickly turns back to the counter, relieved to see a smallish grip bag being handed to her. It is a cheap red nylon one with black strapping wrapped around to form handles. She slaps a few notes into the girl's hand, looks back, and sees that the man with the photo had gone. The Spanish girl is sitting on the ground crying and the English boys are now at the counter. She dashes towards the train where doors are banging shut and spots a father with a buggy and two young children struggling to open a carriage door.

Running over to him, she grabs his arm and shouts above the noise of the train: "Let me help."

The door is stiff but with a foot on the fender it springs open. As it does, she catches the reflection of two bearded men who have stopped and are staring at Cassy ushering the children into the carriage. It buys her a vital few seconds, and the train shunts abruptly as the locomotive engages gear to pull away. Jumping in behind the family and slamming the door, she turns to see her pursuers talking. They look at each other, at the piece of paper, and then back at the carriage. She is closer to them this time and there is no mistaking the black smudges of a photocopied portrait photo. She turns her head too sharply and one nods to the other as they both start running towards the slowly accelerating train, heading for the next carriage towards the rear.

Outside, a guard shouts in Thai: "You! Get in or get off."

There are heavy footsteps on the platform running to keep up with the train as they struggle with the door. A bang tells her they have got it opened, and realising she has to act immediately, leaps across the carriage and wrenches the handle of the door opposite. Caught by the wind, it flies open, almost taking Cassy with it, unsteadied by her shoulder bags. The rolling stock is old and the carriage is the type with a central aisle passing through a series of elaborately partitioned seating units that turn into couchettes for the overnight part of the trans-national journey. The chromium and wood structures supporting the pull-down beds means that no one but the startled father has seen her rash antic.

As she stands perched on the footplate and struggling to close the door behind her Cassy half-whispers, half-shouts: "British police. Thanks." With that she clicks the door into place and jumps. The train is still travelling slowly enough for her to hit the gravel running and she falls to a crouch as she gains her balance.

It is a single-track line with just the one platform so there is no one but a few water buffalo grazing in recently harvested paddy fields to see her emerge from the accelerating train on the wrong side. By the time the last carriage has passed she is breathing almost normally and assumes the air of the one or two other travellers who are wandering near the tracks while waiting for their connection. Cautiously she makes her way over the track and back into the station. As she turns into the concourse, she sees that the last of the disembarked passengers are boarding the buses. The bearded man she had seen when she first arrived is standing with his back to her by the main doors in animated conversation on a cell phone and watching the travellers board the coach. Her first thought is for the content of the red bag slung over her shoulder.

What the hell is in it? There's got to be a similar group waiting for me at Kho Samui jetty. This is a big bloody operation.

Her second thought is how to get away from the station. The man's gaze moves from the bus to scan the ticket hall and Cassy slips behind one of the station's red brick pillars. Adjusting position, she finds his reflection in the glass of an advertising hoarding. He tucks the phone into his breast pocket and stoops with cupped hands to light a cigarette, turning against the wind as he does so. She takes her moment and makes a controlled break for the coach. The engine is running and the driver has his hand on the brake. The door is still open and she has one foot inside when the watcher turns back to look at the bus. She has thrown her bags up the short flight of stairs and jumped in as the doors hiss shut behind her. The man frowns as the bus pulls out into the road, takes a step forward, and then starts running, not towards the bus but towards a row of cars. The phone is back in his hand and Cassy realises that she needs to get off the bus as quickly as she had got on it.

Her guess is that there will be another team covering the ferry port—which is where the coach is heading. She could try jumping out in Surat town before they get to the port but the car will intercept them before then. They are two minutes out of the station and into open countryside when the coach slows right down to take a sharp turn over a narrow bridge. Cassy is seated in the front row immediately above the door and instinctively grabs her bags. The bridge is built over a small tidal river and as they turn she spots two long-tailed boats moored to the muddy bank a little way downstream. A fisherman sits nearby, chipping at something. Pulling some money from her shirt pocket, she thrusts it at the driver.

"I need to get out quick, right here! I've left something behind at the station."

Whether he has done this many times before for disorganised travellers, or whether he is quick to read money, he simply shrugs and presses a button. He doesn't even stop as she jumps. The door has hardly hissed shut behind her when she hears the sound of a car racing towards the bend. There is a waist-high concrete wall on either side of the bridge and over the wall, a tree-lined bank leading down to the river. The trees make the corner a dangerous blind spot and give her a split second to throw herself, with her belongings, over the wall as the car slows to take the bend. Tyres screech above her as it negotiates the bridge and speeds away after the coach.

***

She is left with the silence of the river. A Mynah bird with a bright orange beak whoops tunefully in the tree and a chinchock lizard answers with a *cack-cack-cack*. She takes in the peaceful rural scene and feels strangely elated—hidden away in a river cutting under a rambutan tree and several kilometres from town. If the car stops the coach and discovers that she has got off, it is most likely to return to the station. She reasons that she is best off where she is.

The fisherman working downriver doesn't seem to be going anywhere, so she turns her attention to the bags. First she takes an inventory of the items Pichit's father salvaged for her. There aren't many, just a few clothes and a novel. She stuffs them into her sturdier overnight bag and checks that the computer and phone aren't damaged from the dive over the wall. Then she places the left-luggage bag on the ground, opens the zipper and peers gingerly inside. It seems to be stuffed with a bundle of thickly woven fabric like furniture upholstery. With difficulty she pulls it out and sees that it is a shoulder bag of the sort carried by monks, hippies, and wandering clerics of all creeds. The thick fabric is well-worn and looks very old—like something from a Middle Eastern antiques market.

What would a monk's bag be doing in a safe?

Chavalit's friend had taken two days to locate Odam's secret hideaway. His instructions were to locate the premises, take a look around, and to bag up anything of interest—particularly papers and documents. It was a bonus that he was an accomplished safebreaker. He had found nothing lying around the place worth taking but had found a safe and deposited its contents in the left-luggage office at the station. He was an honest enough crook to admit that he had taken half the U.S. dollars he found in the safe as a bonus.

So this was it. A wandering Sufi's travelling bag.

Well, let's see what's in it apart from U.S. dollars.

She slaps an ankle as something bites and a giant red ant falls to the ground. Then she sees they are all over the ground and jumps to her feet, brushing more from her legs.

The wood-chipping sound has stopped. She decides to head for the boat and examine her find later. There are plenty of trees along the river to give her cover if she hears the car approach. She squeezes the stolen bag and the belongings rescued from the bungalow into her daysack, and kicks the empty bags into the undergrowth.

A few minutes later she is being eyed with curiosity by a boatman who, by the look of it, has just finished splicing in a replacement piece of wooden decking.

"Hire boat for one hour?" she says in Thai, producing three of her diminishing supply of purple notes.

His face gives nothing away as he glances quickly at the notes in her hand then continues with his silent assessment of her. The he nods and mutters, "Krup. Dai Krup, dai. Aw pay nay?" *Can do, can do, where do you want to go?*

***

Less than an hour later they emerge from a small creek into a large river and Cassy's heart sinks. "Surat?" she points.

"Krup, Surat," he says nodding.

She bites her lip. He had told her the creek led into the sea. Emptying into the river means they are heading right through the town and its small fishing port.

"Keep to far side of river away from Surat port and head along coast," she says in Thai.

He looks at her with suspicion and then nods towards her shirt pocket.

"Two thousand baht, okay? Twenty minutes along coast."

He looks up at a darkening sky.

"Fon tok."

"Yes, I know it will rain," she says, "but boats float in rain. Keep next to mangroves."

"Okay, three thousand," she offers, quickly sensing she may lose him.

He nods. "We try. Can take cover."

Ten minutes later they are approaching the town's port. Perhaps because of the ominous sky, there is little activity on the water. She moves forward and wedges herself in the recess created by the boat's curved bow. It affords some invisibility at river level but a watchful sentry looking down from a jetty would see the figure trying to pretend she isn't there. She looks down the narrow boat to her helmsman at the other end. There is nothing between them to hide under and nothing she can do will make her look like a second Thai fisherman. She can only sit out the ordeal. They approach the main port area and she sinks deeper below the gunwales. They pass the ferry jetty and several fishing vessels wedged up in dry docks.

Nothing happens. No shouts. No outboard motors suddenly starting up. They leave the slipways behind them to head into the widening estuary towards the open sea. Cassy wipes sweat from her eyes and scans the mouth of the river from which they have emerged, but is hardly able to make it out because of the strange quality of light. It is neither rain nor mist but it has the same effect, like looking through air heavy with transparent moisture. Turning back to the open sea, she is met with a shocking darkness. It is a foreboding sight with no horizon visible. She is about to move back to the stern to talk to the fisherman when she hears a high-pitched whine of another vessel travelling at full throttle. Light, as well as visibility, is rapidly failing, and she can now see nothing. When she tries to orientate herself to place the direction of the sound, she realises that there is nothing but the boat's direction to tell her which way is sea and which is land. All distinction between sea and sky is gone. She stares at the sight, trying to adjust her eyes, but the green-grey water just continues on up into the dark clouds. It is a solid wall of rain and will be upon them in seconds. Suddenly, through the shadow of the engulfing gloom she can just make out the form of the other boat, its bow crashing through the uncannily smooth water towards her.

"Leow saay!" she shouts to the helmsman—*keep to the left!*

He is heading in that direction anyway, following the side of the estuary that leads north, up the Gulf of Thailand past Isa's village. Then she changes her mind. They will put two and two together—they might even be waiting at Isa's village already. She scrambles down the boat to the stern and is almost alongside the boatman when two things happen almost simultaneously. First, a gunshot rings out across the water quickly followed by a dull thud a foot away from her and a flying splinter of wood. The fisherman flinches, looks around wildly, spots the shadow of the approaching boat, and looks at Cassy in anger. Second, they hit the wall of rain. One second the sea is smooth and there is no rain; the next, they are enclosed in a zero-visibility squall that has the appearance of a massive waterfall. The noise is deafening and the impact of the heavy raindrops hurt.

Cassy pushes her bag as far as she can into the triangular bow deck and shuffles herself carefully to the fisherman to shout in his ear in Thai. "Change direction! Other side of bay! We gonna sink?"

He shakes his head and points to his feet where a small bilge pump is hard at work, not quite keeping up with the incoming water. He scowls at her and reaches with his free hand for a plastic bucket.

"Five thousand baht!" she shouts, desperate for him to keep going.

He leans on the heavy pivoted outboard engine that also acts as a tiller and swings it round in a great arc until they face what seems to be the other direction. There is no sound other than the ear-splitting thunder of rain on water and wood. If the other boat were three metres away she wouldn't hear or see it. He lets the throttle out and they plough their way further into the unending waterfall.

***

From thirty thousand feet the barren mountains of eastern Iran look like rippling beach-sand after the tide has gone out. Brown and undulating, they go on and on with rhythmic regularity, diminishing to the south before dropping below the Arabian Sea. To the north they grow into the craggy peaks of Kurdistan, and beyond that, to Azerbaijan and Georgia.

The boatman had landed Cassy at the same place Pichit had used earlier that same day, from where she took a taxi to a tiny provincial airport in the neighbouring province—the suggestion of Pichit, who she had called from the restaurant where she had earlier waited for the taxi to Surat Thani station. From the airport, she had taken a domestic flight north to Chiang Mai, near the Burmese and Chinese border and transferred to the first international flight, which happened to be bound for Singapore. She had stayed the night at Changi Airport hotel and the next day caught a Singapore Airlines flight to Manchester via Bombay. She was being ultra cautious. She didn't want to shake off the tail in Asia only to be picked up again in London.

It was in Singapore that she made contact with Nigel Buchanan. What he said brought the last ramparts of her familiar world crashing to the ground. She would be met at Manchester Airport and taken to a safe house. She would be moved out of her Docklands home, which was now under protection—MI5 would take care of the arrangements. The cauldron could be boiling for many more months and she has been assessed as being at the highest risk. She will not be able to go back to work at the university for the foreseeable future.

"What the hell did you do out there?" he had asked incredulously.

"The feeling is you've stolen someone's crown-jewels and in the process flushed out all kinds of nasties. The Thai Embassy's been on the phone asking if we know anything they don't about what's going on, both in their underworld and a suspect Islamic terrorist network in the Muslim south.

I've got security brass from six bloody nations queuing up to talk to you. The university and the Yard have agreed to two year's leave of absence—you're being lent to GCHQ. Of course you won't be needed in GCHQ—you never did fit in. You're stuck on this case now, Cassy, old girl—sorry, you've become too important for too many people."

She looks down from her business class window seat at patches of snow on the highest peaks of the Caucus Mountains. Further south are the distant mountains of eastern Turkey. Ararat is down there somewhere reaching five thousand metres above the surface of the Caspian Sea, just visible. That's about halfway up to the plane's cruising altitude. She tries to picture Ararat's anomaly—a dark shadow trapped in the ice and perched above a perilous precipice.

Just like me.

Opening the new Prada travel bag purchased from Changi Airport, she carefully takes out the small article she has not stopped thinking about since removing it from Sufi Odam's rather more ancient and modest travel bag. It is a small book bound in heavily embossed, faded leather, and resembling the nineteenth-century pocket Bibles found plentifully in London's secondhand bookshops. It is secured by an elaborate brass clasp. Inside are just ten pages of thick card, each with a cut-out oval window surrounded by hand-painted floral designs. It is an antique photo album. The first five pages are empty but the remaining five each hold a single photograph, the first four of them, sepia portraits. There are two women and two men, all somewhere in their twenties perhaps and judging by their dress, photographed in the first decade or two of the twentieth century. There are no captions but she has formed an opinion about who they might be from the other items she has found enclosed between the gilt-edged pages.

Two faded letters, each a single page of elaborate handwriting in curly Cyrillic script, flowing at an amazingly constant angle, and both signed with the same name. It was on the flight from Chiang Mai to Singapore that Cassy had discovered the significance of this particular part of her haul from Odam's safe—after remembering there was a Russian translation programme on her laptop, installed after discovering the content of the Essaouira tape.

The letters are signed *Leib Bronstein* and both are in the nature of a father's parting treatise. The first, written from Alma Ata in Kazakhstan bears the date November 1927 and is addressed to "My forsaken but beloved daughter Nina." It reads in translation:

"I am asking you to visit me here in my remote exiled home. I do not deserve your attention, I know, but I cannot conjure up regret for my actions in earlier years; only for the suffering that you have been caused on account of your father. I wish to relieve myself of Roskovitsky's infernal treasure. It is too threatening to be contained in the small travelling case I carry always with my luggage. And yet I cannot bring myself to destroy it. I believe that you have a predisposition more suited to resolving a tormenting puzzle that has caused me sleepless nights during a whole decade of my life. I fear that time is short."

The second letter is similar in tone but written to "Leon, my last remaining child." It is dated ten years later—1937.

"It has been hard to bear the deaths of three children. Must I lose you too? Enemies are at my door and I fear we shall not see each other again. Mexico would not be such a bad place to die. There are some private papers—and other things. I have deposited them in a well-concealed place near to the beloved farm—my home in exile. Among them are letters that show how happy I was with your mother. Cherish them. There is something else. That secret scourge of restless nights; tormentor from the Torah; shadow of doubt from the ancient past. Yes, I have lain to rest Roskovitsky's secret. Perhaps you might destroy it. To my shame, I could not."

Cassy's memory of modern Russian history is rusty but she has reason to recognise two of the names in the letters. Leib Bronstein was a Russian Jew and prominent partisan who assumed the name of his jailer when escaping a Siberian penal camp in 1902. He arrived in London later in the same year and then returned to St. Petersburg in 1917 to join the October revolution and became Lenin's first minister of Foreign Affairs. His assumed name was Leo Trotsky.

Lieutenant Roskovitsky was the leader of Tsar Nicholas II's ill-timed expedition to Mount Ararat.

Then, turning to the last elaborately crafted page of the old album, she contemplates the image in front of her. From a much later period, a black and white photograph of two identical twins, born March 1st, 1996, and standing proudly side by side, confident of their heritage and wearing with dignity the authority invested in them by their country and by the wider world.

Kuala Lumpur's Petronas Twin Towers: the tallest buildings in the world. Photograph dated September 11th, 1999.

PART IV: Results

Chapter 34

September 2000
London's East End and Kent
WOLVERHAMPTON AND WALSALL *Hairdressers Academy ladies second place, 1970.*

The certificate is fixed to the wall in an elaborate frame of carved flowers painted bright orange and yellow. The whole place is a charade. Cassy is cautiously re-establishing a lifestyle back in London, and that includes a visit to Dai on the Fringe. Is it a mocking statement about the hairdressing profession, or is he really proud of his 1970 achievement? Perhaps it is a reminder of his humble beginnings, for the next one indicates his rapid rise to success:

L'institute de la coiffure, Belgique, premiere place, femmes, 1971.

The certificate collection has appeared since Cassy was last in the shop. Maybe they aren't even his.

In which case I love his cynicism even more.

The seriousness of her predicament had sunk in when Nigel Buchanan handed her a five-figure cheque to refurnish the new apartment she had been given in Deptford, on the opposite side of the River Thames from her Isle of Dogs home. She has not been into the university and has all but cut herself off from life before her reckless mission in Surat Thani. It feels dangerous to be back in Dai's, but since she has no idea how dangerous it might or might not be, she makes the visit anyway.

It is two weeks since a black Cherokee Jeep met her from Manchester Airport. There had been a de-briefing in the boardroom of an architect's practice in central Manchester, which took most of the following day but was no chore. Early the next morning she had been taken back to the airport and put on a flight to New York, where the same questions were asked in a disused airline office on the first floor of arrivals at JFK Airport. She was on a return flight within ten hours. Two days later she had been handed the keys to her new apartment.

The next engagement in her role as forensic scientist on secondment to Her Majesty's Intelligence Services is tomorrow—at Ashi's farm on England's beautiful south coast. She has no idea why it is at Ashi's, nor what is on the agenda—Ashi has refused to talk.

She has held off trying to contact Oghel for as long as she can, but last night, after a full bottle of Valpolicella, she had succumbed. He has not yet replied.

"Ever read *Cold Passion Stilled*?" Cassy asks as Dai lightly brushes a freshly cut strand back over her ear.

"Now *that*," he says with emphasis and prodding the air with his scissors, "is my kind of book. A miniature masterpiece. Why, my sweet?"

"No reason," she says nonchalantly as he takes her hand and helps her out of the chair.

Still holding her hand, he leans close and although she is the only customer in the shop, whispers, "Those Iraqis you were asking about—I think I have something."

"What sort of something?"

"One of my males saw an old acquaintance recently—three weeks ago, maybe four. They studied Islamic history together and then were in the same Iraqi army unit for a while years ago. He thinks he went on to weapons research at one of the places we bombed in the Gulf War. That's how the conversation came up—we were discussing whether anyone actually worked in those places."

"Recently come to London?"

"My customer spotted him in a restaurant on the Mile End Road but didn't make himself known."

"Any idea which restaurant?"

He tilts his head back and looks at her down the end of his nose. "No, but if you'd like, I could tell him you want to know."

"Can you find out his religious affiliation?"

"Ah! I had forgotten—you are interested in mystics. Now there's a thought. They were from neighbouring Sunni villages."

"Your customer and his old army friend? Anything more specific?"

He turns down the corners of his mouth and nods slowly as if considering the significance of the connections.

"My customer is *Naqshabandiyya*."

"How do you know that?" she says, giving away more of her surprise than she meant to.

He takes a step back, folds his hands, and surveys her like a man considering buying a sofa or examining a wall he's just painted.

"You know, my beautiful friend, I think we've been wrong about you. You're not a normal woman of the Force, are you?"

Naqshabandiyya Sufism, she recalls from her session with Marten, is closely related to the more esoteric Uwaysi order.

She hurries along the Whitechapel road past the East London Mosque, deep in thought about the gift Isa had given her as they had parted. It is a hand-printed Arabic book, the first chapter of which she has had translated. Cassy knows now that there is more than a literary reason for Nigel's interest in the obscure Russian cult novel that she had spotted on his library shelf.

A vintage Routemaster red bus pulls up at traffic lights, and Cassy waits until it is rolling forward again and jumps on to the open sided silver platform, grabbing the handrail. She scans the pavement as the bus pulls away but can see no sign of anyone interested in her.

Twenty minutes later she hops off at the Quaker headquarters on Euston Road and makes her way, via a circular route, to a University College London building and a public-access computer lab. She has not heard back from Jerry Mathias in UCLA since talking on the phone about the Essaouira cult and emailed him last night to see what he'd come up with. Cassy needs to go to the debriefing tomorrow one step ahead of whoever might be there.

"Cassy,

Sorry for the long delay—not forgotten, just busy—but also an interesting one. I'm still working on it—you'll see why. You were right about the towns—Ukiah and Yakima. Asked around old colleagues working the west coast and found something that could be majorly significant. Get this. There's been covert monitoring of person movements at these two cult centres along with many others and I did some bio-data checks on visitors. There have been similar studies across the U.S. and Europe for two or three years now—under a US–EU accord on counter-terrorism. Not sure what's happening out there, but something big seems to be brewing. I did some cross-referencing and there's definitely something going on. I don't know who else has spotted this. Take a look at the data coming out of these studies—it's public domain for people like us. I wrote a little search program to look through the visitors monitored at hundreds of sites across the globe—by agents earning extra pocket money on days off. They record numbers and age–gender–ethnicity profiles from observation. There's some richer data where it's been possible to track back to immigration records.

I found a flurry of networking among a bunch of cults that have no known connection up till now. One pattern of profiles could definitely be Islamic fundamentalists—can't say what flavour, I'm afraid. They've been spotted visiting about ten small cults in the U.S. One visitor is Caucasian, middle-aged, male and slim—sometimes moustached. If it's the same man—looks like it could be—he sometimes travels with another man, and sometimes they visit a few weeks apart. Possibly also a woman—hard to tell. The matching also pulls up a late twenty-to-early-thirty-something, Mid East or Med but not Arab man, and an older woman, probably Arab. Then there's an older Mid East man too. Always on his own but, like the others, often a few weeks before the Caucasian. If we've picked these guys up at ten places, my guess is that they could have visited twice that number of independent cults. It's an amazing set of data—the patterns stand out like roses on a fish counter. You'd love it.

If you want the names—cults, I mean—I can let you have a list. Sorry—there's no bio-data on these visitors. It's never been possible to track the profile to an immigration record. I guess that makes it even more worrying—how can a bunch of conspirators rove around the globe undetected? You'd think there'd be a traceable record in one of the countries. You've got the Sacramento and Seattle towns already. Here's the name of the others. I'll send more when I've completed the analysis. Hope it helps. Breakfast's on the table—ciao."

A list of towns follows. Instinctively looking over her shoulder, she takes it in, wondering how many fish shops in California are decorated with roses.

***

"So let's go through this bit by bit," Nigel says, sounding impressively assertive.

It is hard for an Englishman to be convincingly self-assured in the presence of a six-foot-four, blue-eyed lantern jaw from Washington. The American's city affiliation was the only introduction when Cassy was eventually ushered into the musty smelling and darkly panelled living room of Ashi's historic farmhouse. Apart from Nigel, Ashi, and the man from Washington, there are three other men in the room: Michael Banton, Nigel's line manager, grim faced with small eyes set in leathery skin; a silver-haired Brit; and another holster-toting pin-up type who hasn't been introduced and has kept silent so far, apart from offering a minor point of information. He is slightly olive-skinned and could come from anywhere. Cassy places him as a Hispanic New Yorker.

"You'll have a chance to report on your discoveries later," Nigel continues. "Right now, we want to go back to Morocco."

He clears his throat.

"Dr. Kim," he says, more formally than seems necessary, "you're here to listen to the storyline and match it against your own intel and interpretation. Feel free to chip in, ask questions, and suggest alternative narratives."

Thanks very much, my favourite MI5 Praat geen poep.

She looks around at the familiar surroundings and sees Ashi shift uncomfortably in his chair. He isn't enjoying the performance.

Why here, Ashi? What haven't you told me?

The man from Washington opens the "narrative."

"Some things you won't know, Dr. Kim," he starts, nodding to her with a more successful combination of efficiency and civility than Nigel had managed.

"Just after you left for Asia, we moved in on Essaouira. We only just held onto the Moroccan's co-operation and had to move before relationships deteriorated any further."

Banton interjects with a blustered: "You almost bloody blew it, Kim—I want you to understand that." He pauses for breath but the American gets in first.

"Sure, your timing wasn't good, Kim, but we had an uncooperative local police chief who Rabat were up against all the time—least, that was their line. Guess that just showed the depth of the problem. Anyway, it was messy, but probably had to go that way—the cult's founder leader, man they called Solon, was shot-up. We're still deciding if it was a Moroccan policeman, a cult member, or a suicide. We weren't the only ones with high velocity rifles."

"Any other casualties?" Cassy asks.

Banton scowls.

"No, no others. Sixteen lost souls rounded up for questioning and most deported back to their embassies for repatriation. The general consensus is that the core we were after had ran—possibly a week before we got our men in place."

Nigel again. "We think they went south over the border into Western Sahara. A well-connected fugitive can get to anywhere in Africa with the Tuareg tribesmen—they're dispersed throughout the region right to the Kenyan coast and all gateways beyond."

"Or by sea?" Cassy suggests, more reasonably she thinks, drawing another glare from the bulldog.

"Or by sea," the American repeats, although it sounds as though the idea has already been dismissed.

"Who were you expecting to find at Essaouira?" she asks, partly to tempt Banton into apoplexy, but also because she wants to hear the official line before she is asked for hers.

"Well now," the American says, "I guess that's where we'd be interested in your views later on. As for the bigger picture..." He checks himself and looks round the room at the others present for assent.

The silver-haired Brit who, by his demeanour, Cassy takes to be either Banton's superior or perhaps someone senior in MI6, nods but says quietly, "*History*, yes. No issues of deployment."

One thing she has picked up from the dynamics so far surprises Cassy: Ashi is obviously in on this at a high level. She doesn't know whether to feel hurt or reassured.

"Of course," the American echoes, "it goes back a very long way, Kim—a *very* long way. This will surprise you. It should sober you too."

He gives her a suitably sobering look and holds her eye contact for a second. In the silent communication, Cassy imagines that she sees something of puzzling complexity. There is deadpan, high-stake seriousness in it, but also a hint of something lighter—humour, even, as though this might all just be an act. Perhaps it is just his professionalism—this being what he does every day.

"A group of governments have been tracking something for almost fifty years," he continues. "It wasn't until the early eighties that we were quite sure it was a single group. You know the term *nakbah?*"

"Jewish occupation of Palestine after the War. *Catastrophe* in Arabic," she replies.

"1948—a long time ago. Amongst the young rebels who started a resistance movement was a young teenager known as the *Holy Kurd,* although no one knows for sure if he was, in fact, a Kurd. He was an outstanding and tough leader known for his ascetic lifestyle, idiosyncratic beliefs, and an ability to bewitch men into submission. He was also obsessed with the Islamic prophet Nooh. The Ark, the Koranic flood story, judgement—the works. His fringe position in the world of Islam didn't matter in the climate of a guerrilla war, and he flourished for a while alongside young Yasser Arafat and the others. That's all we know from that period—he apparently disappeared into obscurity. While Arafat was building *Fateh* from his Tunisian exile it seems that Asmir—that was the name given him at the time—was building some sort of power base of his own. Accounts of a wandering mystic with a liberal but extreme vision, uncertain agenda, and fearsome powers of persuasion started coming in from all parts of the Muslim world. The stories pointed to the same person or group but were too imprecise to generate meaningful intelligence. We're talking mid-1950's by this time, Dr. Kim—parts of the Arab world had hardly blinked at the West at that time, yet alone looked us in the face over a negotiating table."

The 1950's.

On an impulse, Cassy asks the American: "Was Winston Gunther one of yours?"

She could have taken her clothes off and broken into a belly dance—they all sit with mouths open in stunned silence. All except Ashi, who is looking down trying to avoid her gaze.

"Sorry," she says quickly. "History but not matters of deployment, right? Don't worry, no one told me—I guessed. I'll forget about it. Anyway, he's been dead a long time. No one's at risk."

No one answers, but they don't have to. She catches a flicker of pride in Nigel's face and a shadow of outrage on Banton's.

The American has gathered his thoughts and makes the official response to the wild card: "Ahem. I'd like to follow that one up, Dr. Kim, but it's out of bounds, however long ago. The case is still open. That's the point. I should have an answer prepared, though, if I were you—for when we come back and ask how the hell you know about Gunther."

He is either being very unsubtle or very subtle—telling her that she is right without breaking protocol. Cassy recognises the brainless decorum of multi-government collaboration. She has seen the same slavery to rules of verbal engagement in the various Interpol forums she has had the misfortune of having to attend.

"Anyway, Kim, it's a bit of a hazy storyboard from 1954 right up to now. There have been occasional accounts from places as far apart as the western Sahara and western China and everywhere in between. All painting the same kind of picture."

He is being artfully subtle—1954 is the date of the Tehran photo. She guesses it will have been lost on Nigel, but Banton reacts with a pained and angry expression.

"The Islamic states have had their own investigations going on, of course," the American continues. "They like it even less than we do. But even they, it seems, can't pin him down or conclusively pin anything on his movement."

"What's he accused of?" Cassy asks.

The American purses his lips.

"The Arabs don't like the corruption and religious dissent he stirs up. We don't like it because we know he has links with organised crime and international terrorism. And then there's the current situation."

"Current situation?" He had paused as if to allow her to ask the question.

"Osama Bin Laden," he says.

"The Saudi dissident. What's the situation?" She is clearly being permitted to ask and assumes that it is the next level up from Nigel's initiation briefings earlier in the year.

"Extensive networks coming to light, increased activity in the Afghan training camps, and a hint of some *major* imminent threat. We thought it was going to be a millennial hit. New year 2000 came and went but the intel keeps coming in. We don't know what's going on, but everyone's looking at the Islamic fundamentalist threat in a new light."

"Which means cranking up the investigation of Asmir and his Noah network."

"Precisely, Dr. Kim. Bin Laden's a young upstart compared to this one."

"You must have something on Asmir's criminal connections," she says, thinking of the girl in the forest. "Organised crime must be easier for Americans and Brits to infiltrate than underground mystical movements on the Islamic fringe."

"You'd think so, wouldn't you?" he says. "But it's a blurred picture: corruption in business and government that seems to correlate with Asmir's movements; commercial guilds that have come under his influence blowing apart six months later with an embezzlement scandal; a big fish about to be netted, suddenly getting released by a local judge and we discover a prophet Nooh link; arms shipments to the PKK Kurdish Workers Party; payments for arms vanishing in areas known to be under the movement's influence. But no hard facts, I'm afraid—until we come to the Essaouira group, that is."

"And two plane disasters, each with a tenuous Noah's Ark connection?" she adds.

"And two plane disasters," he repeats solemnly. "Other assassinations too—religious and political. None of them verifiable. There are those who think someone's planning something much bigger than anything else we've so far seen in this genre of terrorism. Everyone's on tenterhooks but no one knows who, when, or where. Although Bin Laden is in the sights, we think it's just as likely to be Bin Nooh's guys. So everyone's looking at everything we've got. All angles. All networks. All possible threats. It's like we're about to enter another Cold War, only the opposition's just a bunch of fanatics spread across the globe in any number of semi-anarchic networks. No one really knows where to focus. Where to dig. The plane crashes with the Noah's Ark connections sent the auto-intel buzzers going off in bureaus all around the world. All eyes are suddenly focused on the many brotherhoods and movements thought to be associated with the *Holy Kurd*. We're sure many have been mistakenly associated with Bin Laden."

"Enter the forensic Ark expert."

He nods. He has been leaning forward in the faded green tapestry chair but now leans back, hands behind his head and legs outstretched, showing off shiny black Agency-compliant shoes.

"Actually, Dr. Kim, it's worse than I've made out; we're not certain we even know his real name or identity. He was known as Asmir once—in one place at one time. He's a shadow, a gust of poisoned wind, a *noire* Mid Eastern Pimpernel with the ability to merge into the background. Virtually invisible. We don't understand what drives him, what his objectives are, and we can't predict where his influence might turn up next or what he might be planning next."

At this, Cassy notices the other American look up from the carpet in a manner that indicates he might not agree on that point, as if it is something they had been discussing earlier. Or maybe the man from Washington is exaggerating the mystery and his colleague is impressed with the tactic.

"The one thing that all seem agreed upon," Washington continues, "is that his link with organised crime is not for the money. We don't think he's making money to finance arms for a network of underground terrorists. Money and arms we could find. And if he were stowing either away somewhere we'd have uncovered his networks years ago. So big problem—no certain name, no reliable bio-data, no hard evidence linking him to anything, no motive. Just a shadow—a rumour, almost."

"And that," Banton storms in again, "is the reason we bloody bought you in. Somehow, I can't for the life of me see how, you've got closer to him than anyone has ever done in recent years. I hope you realise your responsibility, Kim."

Closer to him? What does that mean exactly? She has a disorienting sense that she is going to be shocked by whatever is coming next. And she can't quite tie up what she has just been told with what she knows. They are either unbelievably uninformed, or they are playing her a counterfactual *narrative*. It must be an interrogation technique.

"May I ask a question about the Bangkok connection?" she says, addressing Nigel. He had all but told her once that Isa's apartment was under surveillance.

"Go ahead—that's why you're here," answers the American.

"I take it you all have a report on your desks somewhere about Kurdish Sufi refugees in Bangkok? There are—or were—three brothers: Isa, Odam, and Nooh. Isa's details are on a United Nation's data base in Geneva—you must have dug that up."

"Go on," says the American.

"He was resettled in Bangkok by UNHCR and keeps in some kind of regular contact with his wayward brother Odam—who I assume is your Asmir. That doesn't quite tally with the picture you've just painted. You're talking about a phantom, riding the night air without trace for fifty years. I'm saying the U.N. found a flat for his brother along Sukhumvit Road in Bangkok, not that far from the British Embassy. I was in his flat for less than two hours and discovered many things about Isa and his brother Odam, including the fact that the Brotherhood has a base in Surat Thani in southern Thailand. It took a minor crook from Bangkok to locate that house and empty its safe. Am I missing something?"

"Why do you assume that Odam is our phantom Asmir?" the American asks abruptly.

Cassy hasn't even stopped to consider the alternatives—it seems so obvious, piecing together what she has learnt from Marten, Sufi Isa, Sami, and Leen in Essaouira, and now the Agency man from Washington.

"It's bloody obvious. Because Sufi Odam has links with Morocco—other similar groups too. Because he keeps bad company and because of the account his brother gives of him."

It is a petulant answer.

"Your view, I think, is very much influenced by your friend Isa's," the American says.

Friend? The comment alarms her like the accusation of "*getting close.*" She had made an effort to conceal her affection for the old man during the initial debriefings.

"You're suggesting Isa wrongfully maligns his brother's reputation. For what purpose?"

"What about the third brother?" the American asks. "What if the man you call Nooh is Asmir the phantom?"

"That might be impossible."

"And why is that?"

"Because it seems he's on the other side of the great mystical divide—dead. Murdered by one of his own."

The American's eyes lock on hers for a moment then he turns to the elderly British man who hasn't spoken more than the one line so far, and then at Nigel, and then back at Cassy.

"Go on, Dr. Kim."

"There's a Sufi brother in Bangkok that people might think is Noah, but he's not one of the three blood brothers. He's one of Adam's stooges."

There is silence while they all consider what she has said. Then the American speaks: "Let me be frank with you, Kim. Our problem is this: the only Sufi brother anyone has ever actually seen for many years is the one you call Isa. There have been no verified sightings of the one you call Nooh—not for at least thirty years. Some *rumoured* sightings, but nothing corroborated. As for the brother you call Adam, or Odam—there was evidence years ago that he moved from Kurdistan to Morocco but no one in the Rabat Immigration Department seems to remember ever having interviewed him, and there's no immigration file on him there nor in any other country where he's been reported. Again, there are rumours of his movements dating back over the decades—all of them like your own account of Odam. The few people admitting to have met him have only ever talked to him in a darkened room or from behind a blindfold. It seems to be one of the ways that he's constructed an aura of fear and mystery around himself. No one seems to have seen him face to face."

"No one? Ever?" Cassy is dumfounded.

"Historians have analysed the reported sightings, stories, and other rumours, and can track them back to the same Sufi guerrilla involved in the early Palestinian resistance. A lot of effort's gone into it, believe me."

Cassy wonders how much of Marten's research has been funded by Intelligence bureaus.

"So what are you suggesting? Nooh's not really dead? There are two corrupt mystics fronted by a Mr. Nice Guy? What do the intelligence boffins of the world make of it all?"

"What do *you* make of it, Dr. Kim?" the American asks slyly, as though she might be part of the conspiracy.

Cassy doesn't answer. The American turns to the others and says, with something of a sigh, "I guess her story confirms our position from a different angle."

"Has anyone interviewed Isa in Bangkok?" she asks, somewhat incredulous at the way the conversation is going, and feeling the blood pressure rise in her neck.

"Of course," the American says dismissively, "but he says nothing—it's been the same with every attempt, whichever government tries to speak to him—he always denies knowledge of his brother's whereabouts. U.N. protection cramps the style of some of our allies who might be inclined to try more persuasive methods. There has been at least one successful attempt by a Middle Eastern country to kidnap Sufi Isa. He resisted torture and the U.N. High Commission for Refugees managed to rescue him. He was even protected by U.N. security for a while."

It is more than Isa had told Cassy, but it is consistent with what she had observed. Reluctant family loyalty tied to deep disapproval. When the chips were down on the torturer's table, Cassy can well imagine Isa counting it some kind of perverse duty to pay the price for his brother's folly. But he had more or less told Cassy that Odam was in Surat Thani. Perhaps this was, indeed, their first specific lead. It must be what Banton meant by getting closer to Asmir than anyone else. Then a thought hits Cassy. The first hint of doubt.

Was Sufi Odam, in fact, at the house in Surat Thani? Isa was very evasive about why he didn't want me in town.

"I believe Isa's account," she says, emphatically—combating the thought, which is deeply disorientating. "He's straight—I'm quite sure of it. He distances himself from Odam because he disapproves of his brother's beliefs and friends."

As she says it, she realises that she is not as sure as she had been a few minutes before. "Anyway, he's imbued with Middle Eastern blood-thick loyalty—I'm not surprised he's held out."

By now she is acutely aware of how unreasonable she is sounding. She is giving too much away of that "closeness" that she had developed with the beguiling elderly seer in the house full of children.

They look at each other again as if trying to make up their mind how to break something to her. Nigel bounces in: "So let's brainstorm Cassandra's first question—how is it no one's ever been able to track a lead from the Bangkok refugees direct to the missing brother—or brothers?"

It is an amateur performance compared to the American. She looks from one to the other, waiting.

"We have a theory, Kim. We'd like to see your reaction to it. It happens to be shared by the Saudis too."

She had misjudged Nigel—he had been setting up the American to come out with his theory.

"Okay," she says warily. "Isa's either lying or ignorant and I don't think he's a liar."

"We'll see about that," the American says.

He looks at the others again, and then looks her in the eye. "There's only one of them. The three Sufis are a fabrication. A fantasy, a brilliant decoy. An alibi woven over fifty years of artful conspiracy. Your friend Isa is a brilliant and dangerous international conspirator. A callous religious terrorist and genius tactician of the first order."

Chapter 35

Kent, England
September 2000

THE IDEA IS devastating, and five pairs of eyes watch as Cassy reels under its impact. She no longer knows what to say and sits, lips tightly shut, trying to contain a crushing meltdown in orientation, struggling to mentally rework the data collected over the past months, unable to string one thought to another. All she can think of is a picture of Sufi Isa playing with children in the fishing village. The clip freezes with him placing a hand on the shoulder of the pretty teenage girl.

Just as she is about to submit to whatever short-circuiting is going on in her brain and the humiliations that will follow, anger replaces confusion. A great wave of defiance rises within. The more she replays what has just been said about Sufi Isa, the more infuriated she becomes. Like a parent who has just been told some awful maligning story about their child.

It is then that Cassy suddenly realises what is happening. She realises that she is sweating and that her face, while blank and expressionless with shock, is twitching erratically in several places.

They are observing me.
This is a test.

She might be an expert witness giving evidence from her observations but the real object of the debriefing is much subtler than that. It is her reactions that are being recorded as evidence.

She suddenly comes to life, looking around at the blurred staring faces, wondering which one of the two unintroduced panel members is the psychologist. Of course, it must be the olive-skinned one. She wonders whether he is pay-rolled CIA or is wheeled in for jobs like this one—from a university office like hers, perhaps.

She had sensed the scrutiny of course, but had not understood it until now.

The man they called Asmir stands accused of being a master of duplicity and manipulation and she has been summoned to test their theory. A hint from Cassy of inordinate loyalty towards Isa and the psychologist would tick a box and one of the purposes of the interview will have been achieved. Then a more humiliating thought comes.

Her banishment to Thailand for the summer was an *experiment*, and now they are examining the results.

This is a laboratory. I am an experimental subject.

***

Cassy does not know what happened, but she suddenly finds herself coming to, as though she has slipped out of consciousness for a brief moment. Only she can't have, since they are all still there in exactly the same positions, watching her. A degree of lucidity returns with a pump of adrenaline, and she quickly sees the weakness of her position. Before her is the covert intelligence of two world powers and from what has been said, they have been on the case for years. Decades. How many hours had she spent with Isa? Hardly a couple of days in total.

In what must be a reflex against complete internal meltdown and public humiliation Cassy, still dazed, goes on the offensive. "So what bloody changed in Essaouira?" she asks, looking around angrily, challenging anyone who might choose to answer. "What was that all about?"

The American looks at the elderly Brit. "Hugo?"

Hugo nods protocol clearance.

"Essaouira stood to give us the best evidence we've had so far. The FBI intercepted a hot import in October last year: weapons-grade uranium in a container arriving in New York. It bore resemblance to similar finds in Europe and Asia. Three years ago there was a haul of about the same quantity in Italy—Sicily—and, back in 1993, another in the holiday town of Los Gigantes on the island of Tenerife. That was the same year that the Indonesian government intercepted an identical shipment in Jakarta. Last November local police made a routine raid on an eco-community in a place named Caliente in the Nevada desert. It was a regular check for incriminating computer documents—eco-terrorist plans, targets, those kind of things—but they took the back off a computer that didn't work and found a smart electronics device that looked like it might have been modelled on circuitry in our W-88 warhead design. The sect leader whose office it was in had disappeared before the raid. The device is naturally being linked with the uranium in New York."

"The uranium—it was connected with the man killed in the car crash in New York last spring?" Cassy asks quietly.

"You were briefed about that?" the American says, looking surprised and turning to Banton.

"She was briefed on the Iraqi visitors we had in London at the same time—but that was all," Nigel adds as if covering his back. "The bulletin would only have contained the press story."

Regaining more of her wits, she notices that Nigel fails to mention that he had also given her the classified report on the case. The report had made no mention of uranium, however; she had just guessed about the connection.

Her minor achievement acts like another shot of adrenaline and some of the resignation recedes.

"So where was the container in New York bound for?" she asks, addressing the American, hearing her voice as if listening to someone else.

He looks from Nigel to Banton before turning back to answer. "The container itself was due for transhipment to San Francisco, but evidence suggests the uranium might have come to New York just to get shipped back across the Atlantic."

"Back across? Where did it come from originally?"

"The ship came direct from Rotterdam but transhipment documents in the Netherlands indicate that it probably originated from a small cargo vessel that sailed into Rotterdam from Morocco. It called at three ports there before heading north to Europe: Tarfaya, Agadir, and Essaouira."

Suddenly, from nowhere, her full sensibilities rush back with crystal clarity and she knows that she has pulled through, at least for now. She has not been duped.

You're the ones who have been bloody duped.

She takes the picture in. Dormant but lethal WMD arms dumps scattered in Europe and Asia, another in West Coast America and a shipment in New York that could have been bound for any destination. According to the list Jerry Mathias had given her, unidentified Middle Eastern visitors had recently visited sectarian communities in Santa Cruz, capital of Tenerife, and Catania in Sicily. The same visitors had been to another community located less than a half-day's drive from the small town in Nevada. She wonders if the Americans have done the same analysis as Jerry. Why would they have?

"We are working on the theory that the uranium and the American weapons technology found in Nevada were bound for Europe," the American says, as if to forestall any further speculation.

"For what purpose?" Cassy asks, knowing she won't get an answer.

"Damned impertinence! You'll *answer* questions, not ask them, Kim," Banton barks.

Ignoring him, Cassy says, "So Odam's using his networks to help smuggle arms—and Essaouira was a base. And you'd not picked up the trail of anyone who had escaped the Essaouira sting until I filed my report from Singapore?"

"You got it," says the American, also ignoring the simmering Banton. "We know for sure that at least four people left Essaouira in a hurry just before we hit it."

The revelation draws a sharp glance from the senior British officer.

"But we've no evidence to say that Asmir—aka Odam, Isa, or Nooh—was one of them. The next thing we hear is that you're reporting Odam has turned up in the South of Thailand and all hell's let loose. Another source—as close as we'd got to Essaouira until you—was down, so you surprised us."

He pauses and then adds, "But you didn't actually see Odam, did you?"

"You didn't know about the base in Surat Thani until my phone call to Nigel from Singapore?" Cassy asks in reply, partly goading, making it clear that she finds it hard to believe.

There are more glances across the room, and then the American says, "We've had the Thai authorities look into the matter. They've found a house in a village very near the town, which seems to have been rented for a long time by an extreme wing of a local Thai-Malay fundamentalist group—it's empty most of the year."

"A bolt-hole," she explains. "One of many—scores, perhaps, dotted around the world."

"The locals are saying nothing," he says.

"I suspect it would be the same in a dozen other countries," Cassy says. "Have you interrogated the Essaouiran cult members yet?"

"Those we picked up were either too brainwashed or brain-dead to talk—or plain terrified. They'll talk eventually, of course—at least those who've not gone over the brink. But we don't really expect to find out much more about Asmir."

"Because he rarely visited in person and only talks in darkened rooms?"

It was the man who the American had called Hugo who answers. "It looks like he only ever met with Solon."

"Who's now conveniently dead. So your phantom's slipped away into the darkness again, but this time, it seems, he left without some of his belongings. Are you going to tell me what you made of my little haul?"

Cassy had passed the stolen bag and some of its contents to the reception committee at Manchester Airport and not heard of it since. There had been other items in the carpetbag along with the antique photo album: fifty thousand U.S. dollars in high denomination bills, and two Middle Eastern passports. She had heard from Chavalit in Bangkok that there had been a pile of passports in the safe. His burglar friend had been disturbed and left the building in a hurry, stuffing everything he had found in the safe into the bag. The bag had caught as he climbed a tree to scale the compound's wall and its contents spilt on the ground. He had jumped down, grabbed as much as he could, the bundles of dollars first she imagined, and resumed his professional getaway.

"The passports are good fakes," the American says. "We've had them checked and we're waiting for the Syrian and Turkish authorities to come back to us from their records. The woman's has been used a lot and we can get a pretty good feeling for her movements over the last six years. The man's is new and doesn't even have an entry stamp into Thailand. You say there were others? Pity—they're much more valuable than the dollars."

"But no positive identification?" she asks.

"No—not yet," he says, with a little hesitation, "– but we're hopeful."

There is a movement from Hugo.

"We're puzzled about something, Dr. Kim," he says. "We can't see why fifty thousand dollars and two passports would stir up such a reaction." Hawk-like eyes fix on Cassy's but there is a trace of humour in his voice—the same ambiguity she had sensed from the American at the start of the interview.

The American comes in again. "You have a theory, Dr. Kim. We would very much like to hear it."

***

There is silence in the room.

"It's just a theory," she begins uncertainly.

She shifts uneasily in her seat. Calmer than a few minutes ago, strengthened by the way the conversation has turned, but confidence still deeply shaken.

"The cult is split down the middle," she says, annoyed at how reticent she sounds. Even as she says the words, she sees how weak it will sound. But something has engaged that won't back down. She will defend her analysis and hold onto her sanity whatever the outcome.

"Sufi Odam has his own obscure agenda, which could be stereotypical Islamic terrorist's, but is likely to be more complicated—a mission of vengeance and of corrupting the corrupt with some arcane religious justification that most good living fundamentalists wouldn't recognise. And as you described, he's in league with big-time crime. He flits around the globe using his powers of persuasion and access to funds to win over small sectarian groups. My guess is that he strikes deals with their leaders, promising them money—and in the Essaouira case, stolen ancient treasures as well—in return for assorted favours. He's a broker. A callous and manipulative broker without morals."

"You describe Asmir well."

It is the olive-skinned New Yorker, nodding understandingly in a way that confirms her suspicion that he is a psychological profiling expert.

"He probably has several bases that he retreats to when he's not travelling," she continues. "One is the house in the South of Thailand. Another is in a small town in the ex-Soviet Republic of Georgia. Akhalkalaki."

Eye movement in the room signals interest and several pens scribble down the name. That bit is new.

"One of the passengers in the sabotaged American International Airways flight was listed as coming from Akhalkalaki," she says. "There's a photo of the town on the wall of the Sufi's Bangkok apartment. My first thought was that Odam had supplied a contract suicide terrorist from the Nooh Brotherhood. There are plenty of impressionable cultees out there who've followed their leaders beyond the point of rational thought and sensibility."

"But you no longer think so?" the American asks.

"It could be. But there's another possibility."

"Which is?"

"Odam overstepped the mark with one of his customers. He stole something from one of his criminal partners but underestimated its value and the fallout that would follow. The American plane attack was a gangland revenge against Odam's group."

More glances around the room.

"What could be so valuable?" Hugo this time.

She clears her throat for effect.

"Two hand-written letters from Leon Trotsky about hidden Noah's Ark relics and one photograph."

She decides not to add "*... and possibly a priceless computer tape stolen from the Soviet Naval Archives*," because she is still not quite sure how that fits in with her theory.

Mouths drop open and all eyes are on her lips. She becomes more emboldened.

"One letter is to his daughter Nina; the other to his eldest son Leon. They appear to confirm that one of the first things Trotsky did as Stalin's Foreign Commissar was to confiscate the records of an archaeological expedition the Tsar had dispatched to a site fourteen thousand feet up Mount Ararat. Rumour at the time said that Trotsky executed the expedition's couriers who were taking the reports and relics back to the Tsar. The details were lost in the aftermath of the revolution and the story faded into fable. It appears from the letters that Trotsky carried the treasure with him for years and was increasingly troubled by it."

"You've seen the letters?" Hugo asks dryly.

Not waiting for her reply, or assuming it to be a rhetorical question, Nigel asks, "Are there diehard Trotskyists for whom that revelation would be significant?"

"Perhaps not anymore," Cassy says. "But it would be highly significant for ex-Trotskyists turned lawless capitalist adventurers. Imagine the value of genuine Ark relics, if there are such things." Turning to Hugo she adds, "You are right—there were other items in the carpet bag."

She picks up her rucksack, unzips it, and carefully takes out a small guilt-edged photo album with faded embossed leather binding. Opening it, she withdraws two neatly folded letters and hands the album and the letters to Hugo, who has got out of his chair to formally receive the submitted evidence.

"I've already had them authenticated," she says. "I traced a Trotsky expert on leave from Lomonosov Moscow State University and working at Cardiff University. I expected your boys to be following me to Wales last week."

There is an awkward silence, as if each is waiting for someone else to respond. Eventually the American looks around at the others and says, "Well, we hired an archaeologist—what did we expect?" Then, turning to Cassy: "Good work, Cassandra. Brilliant work. Well, I'll be damned. She's wasted in forensics," he says, turning to Hugo.

They are all out of their seats and gathering around the sepia photos and the Cyrillic scrawl of the legendary Eternal Revolutionary when, without looking up, Hugo asks a question that has them all facing Cassy once again. "Why *that* plane?"

"The American flight?" she says. "My guess is that the passenger from Akhalkalaki was Sufi Nooh. The Trotsky gang took their retaliation at the highest level. He probably had a whole retinue of devotees with him."

Then as an afterthought, her concentration still recovering, she adds, "Oh, and there's one other thing you should see. There was something else in Trotsky's photo album."

Reaching into her rucksack again, she brings out the photo of the famous Kuala Lumpur skyline.

"What would Sufi Odam be doing with a photograph of the Petronas Twin Towers?"

Chapter 36

Central London
September 2000

"WHAT DID YOU find in the Victoria and Albert Museum?" Oghel asks Cassy as they come to a stop in front of a large three-dimensional relief map of the world's ocean basins, empty of sea; their giant mountain ranges, vast plains, and rugged faultlines exposed. She had asked him to meet her here at London's Natural History Museum. Like most of her journeys these days, she had come a circuitous route with plenty of double backing—and today, in and out of three museums.

Oghel explores the fine details of Cassy's face in the reflection from the glass cabinet housing the map. The corners of the eyes are as he remembered them but even more exquisite. He can tell from the reflection that she is studying his face, standing side on, observing him as he looks at the map. He can even see that her eyes are wandering to and fro across his face, just as his are across hers. Does she know?

"It has an exhibition of apocalyptic art through the ages. 'With the breaking of the Seventh Seal comes the Seventh Day. Welcome New Heaven. Eden re-created.' I was trying to solve it. It's a riddle."

The line from the Sufi cult's website has been occupying Cassy, who has been educating herself in the ideas of Biblical and Koranic prophecy in an attempt to better understand Sufi Isa's grand vision of the future.

She watches Oghel staring at the denuded Atlantic Ocean, his eyes wandering over the exposed features.

"You brought me here to talk about the Garden of Eden? You have a fascination with it, I think," Oghel says thoughtfully.

"I have a fascination with you, Oghel, and your understanding of Eden mythology. Can I ask you about your father?"

"It is not my father who taught me about the Garden—it is my uncle."

***

"Tieguanyin. Iron Buddha tea. The best in China, they say." Cassy pours Oghel a cup of the fragrant brew from a French press that a waitress has just brought to the table. She had paid for a pot of tea but said she just needed water and passed the vacuum-packed sachet to the girl at the service counter. They are seated in a cafe hidden away on one of the museum's upper floors.

"The man I call father is my adoptive father. I love him greatly. I think I have told you he is a priest—a Syrian Orthodox *Cor-Episkopos*. I grew up in the town of Mardin in the southeast of Turkey—there are four Orthodox churches remaining, serving a community of about a thousand Christians. We are a small minority now. At one time the Syrian Orthodox Church had six hundred thousand monks scattered from Europe to India. Syrian Orthodoxy has married priests and unmarried monks including the Bishops. A married priest like my father has to wait for his wife to die to be ordained a Bishop. He cared for me with my adoptive mother since I was a young child. My true father, I never really knew."

"Do you know anything about him?"

"My natural father? He was a wealthy man—a Muslim, originally from Central Asia."

"So you are not really Turkish *or* Syrian?"

"Sometimes I do not know what, or who, I am. My real father, I am told, was an unusual man. He was killed in an earthquake when I was six years of age—there was a great earthquake that demolished the Turkish town of Van in 1975. Four thousand were killed in one night. I only have a very faint memory of him. After I was born he became friendly with Orthodox monks travelling through Central Asia. After his wife—my true mother—died of an illness, he travelled, taking me to Syria and southern Turkey. I think it was a kind of spiritual search—a pilgrimage—although I don't think he can have known where he was going. We stayed for several months at the great Saffron Monastery south of Mardin, the town that became my childhood home. We moved to Van a few weeks before the catastrophe. He took me back to the monastery one day while he was doing some business in Van, and that was the day that the earthquake struck. I never saw him again. It seems that no one in Turkey knew where he had come from and that he had told no one from his original home where he was going. No relative came to Mardin from Central Asia to look for me. It was a lonely and sad time for a small boy. I couldn't understand why no one came. Looking back, I think that he must have alienated himself from his home community—maybe his family also. Perhaps it was his fascination with mysticism—I think he was quite a prominent Muslim at one time. My adoptive father once told me that my natural father had been profoundly influenced by a wandering Sufi."

"I would like to meet your adoptive father," Cassy says, thoughtfully.

"I would like you to meet him, though you would have to travel to Turkey. For a short while I remained at the monastery, being looked after by the monks. They did not go to the authorities for fear I would be taken away. After a while, arrangements were made for me to be taken in by the priest and his wife in the nearby town. They had lost their only son while he was a baby. They have been good parents to me."

"Your uncle. You mentioned your uncle."

"You will have to forgive me, Dr. Cassy, for not having the clearest knowledge about my family, but you will understand from what I have said. I have not had... my upbringing was not a normal one."

"Neither was mine, Oghel. I think that is one reason I like your company so much. We have something in common." She reaches out and touches his hand.

"It is not easy for a Syriac Christian to get a good education in Turkey—especially an immigrant and an orphan with uncertain nationality and parentage. I had always been aware of a family member in the background. But my adoptive father never mentioned him and still claims no knowledge beyond his existence when I have asked since. Then when I was eighteen, I received a letter and then a large sum of money—from someone who said he was my true father's brother. The money was to pay for a university education. It was not only the money—he had made arrangements for me to study at one of the country's best universities. We did not know what to make of it—there are all manner of corruptions in the part of the world where I grew up. The money proved to be real and the numbers on the bills were not registered as stolen. We waited a year before banking it and following up the university place."

"And that was the only contact?"

"There was one other occasion. He sent me a long poem. More a treatise than a poem, but very beautifully written—like a song. It was about the start and the end of the world. *Silence in Heaven* would be the translated title."

Cassy's thoughts are in high gear, motoring faster than she can register them, running round and round in wild circles. It makes no more sense than it had before—much less, even—for the obscure connection is as tortuous as it is tentative. But it is there nevertheless.

I think I've known it for some time, but now I'm sure of it. Oghel is part of the Imaginary Brotherhood.

"What are you thinking about, Cassy?" Now it is his turn to reach out and touch her hand.

There is no way she can start to explore her questions with Oghel. Sometime in the future, perhaps, but it will have to be the right time, and she has other questions she needs answers to before then.

Slowly, she turns her covered hand upwards to face his, clasping it into a ball; then delicately, and aware of the sensuousness of the movement, opens it up like a blossoming rosebud, massaging his palm from the centre out until her fingers are touching his, fingertip to fingertip. There her fingers wait submissively until, with a gentle encouragement from her, a subtle signal, skin against skin, she allows his fingers to explore the inside of hers until they are completely intertwined.

"You are very lovely, Oghel," she says quietly, looking up into his eyes. "It can't have been easy. Does it still hurt?"

"My childhood memories? Yes. The thought of a grandmother, grandfather who didn't come looking? Yes."

"But you have forgiven them."

"Forgiven? Yes, the only true healer."

"Could we... can you... I mean... you have taken some sort of religious vow?"

"I still have feelings."

Their intertwined fingers play against each other in search of tighter intimacy.

"You are in a religious order?" Her fear expressed at last.

"Not fully. A novice, I think you call it. It happened while I was at university—and it was my own choice. I have received so much—everything in fact. Nothing I have of any worth is my own doing—all is a gift from Heaven. It was the happiest of decisions."

"Until now?" she dares, despising herself for asking.

"It is possible to entertain regrets without being regretful."

"But you've not signed up for life?"

"Had I done so already, I would be inhuman not to explore the emotions of regret. But exploring them is not the same as submitting to them."

"You mean this is an experiment to see what it feels like?" The idea hurts.

"Not an experiment," he says, shaking his head. "Maybe I am like a teenager. I am a mature man but I have not had to explore such emotions before. My devotions from childhood have been towards God—I know it is hard for you to understand. There are still some of us like that in the world—not many, I have come to realise. I am a foreigner in more ways than one, Dr. Cassy. Although my father is a parish priest, my upbringing was monastic and in many ways of a different age. I am studying for a doctorate in a technological subject, but innocence has nothing to do with knowledge and intelligence—it is a matter of the heart..."

He stops, staring at something behind Cassy. She turns to see what it is and sees that he is looking at one of the sculptured shapes adorning the wall of the cafe—a roughly hammered metal bowl in a complex mixture of distressed bronze and galvanised iron.

"A bowl poured out," he says.

"A matter of the heart?"

"I have the answer to your riddle, Dr. Cassy."

"My riddle?"

"*With the breaking of the Seventh Seal comes the Seventh Day. Welcome New Heaven. Eden re-created*," he repeats. "I have studied the apocalyptic writings in the Bible and the Koran. The Seven Seals. They unfold the closing down of a corrupted earth. The Seventh Seal is the final curtain—it follows a great cataclysmic upheaval. When the Sixth Seal was broken, *huge hailstones about one hundred pounds each came down from Heaven upon men; and men blasphemed God because of the hail, because its plague was extremely severe. And every island fled away and the mountains were not found. And when the Seventh Seal was broken there was silence in Heaven for about half an hour."*

More of the poetic mantra Cassy had heard in St. Giles.

"Creation finally completed after a long and patient wait. Six days God laboured in the first stages of creation but he rested on the seventh, waiting. Rested, not stopped. There are only six complete cycles in the creation poem of Moses—the Genesis account. Six days of creation each defined by evening and morning—darkening and brightening, *cooling and warming*. I think, Dr. Cassy, that perhaps water was God's creative tool and that the earth was shaped by repeated cycles of ice ages. It is just a theory, but it is a simple and beautiful one. On the Seventh Day in Genesis, the day of rest, no evening and morning is mentioned. The seventh cooling and warming are yet to come and only after the last global freezing will the sun rise on a finally finished creation—a New Heaven and a New Earth. Eden once again on the ocean floors. God will have finished his rest period and will be ready once again to dwell with men."

"The poem sent by your uncle?"

He nods, looking up at the bronze bowl again, as if it helps him remember.

For the first time in their growing friendship, Oghel sees Cassy as an East Asian. As she elegantly pours more tea he pictures her dressed in a simple Korean kimono, kneeling on a dark wooden floor, performing a traditional tea ceremony. He tries to imagine some image or other from the childhood that she cannot remember. Then because he cannot do that, he tries to picture her in his childhood.

She is the young girl he had once caught a glimpse of playing hide and seek with her mother in the great Saffron Monastery.

Chapter 37

"STARBUCKS LANGHAM PLACE at five-thirty?"

"Yes, that will be nice," Cassy says.

The phone clicks before she can put the receiver down. It is one of Ashi's contacts. They have used the method once before. Last time the diversionary rendezvous had been a Café Nero in Kensington High Street. It is a mild attempt to mislead anyone who might be listening in. The meeting place is the same, whatever the coffee house.

An hour and a half and three changes of Tube trains later, she walks up the steps of St Paul's Cathedral in London's commercial heartland. Adjusting her eyes to the darkness inside, she spots Ashi, leaning against the wall in the south aisle separated by tall arches from the main sanctuary—a great cavern curving elegantly upwards to its domed pinnacle. High above, tiny figures peer down into the chasm from the tiny circular viewing gallery.

"Don't tell me," she says, "you're taking over as my *controller*, Banton's died from heart failure and gout, and Nigel's been promoted."

Ashi gives her a rueful smile and holds up both hands in his favourite gesture.

"It's not how it seems, Cassandra. I'm sorry for what's happened. I know what you must be thinking about me. I wanted to warn you before the meeting at the farm."

"Hey, its okay. I'm used to it—you're under orders."

"It's not okay, Cassy. Not really. There are some things I just can't say, but I had to see you—I've become truly worried about you my dear friend."

Friend? You were an observer, I was the experimental subject.

"Neither of us," he continues, "you nor I, are a real natural at this game. The trouble is that we're both too good for our own good. It's a dangerous line—playing games with the Intelligence services. Especially when you've compromised yourself. Was that an *act* at the debriefing? You didn't exactly try to hide your admiration for your Sufi friend."

"What's going on, Ashi?"

"It's a big project—bigger than you probably think, even after what you learnt at the farm."

"When did you get involved?" She tries to disguise the resentment.

"First? Early eighties sometime."

"Bloody hell, Ashi—early *eighties!*" The revelation is deeply shocking.

"It's got a lot hotter recently—first the American airline Noah thing, and then everyone's getting their knickers in a twist about Bin Laden. There's more chatter out there this year than ever before. Your picture of the Malaysian skyscrapers went down a treat. You'll be heading over to Langley in a few weeks' time. They'll be wanting to know everything about your raid on the Sufi's southern Thai base. And you had better find out the name of the guy you hired to do the raid—they'll be wanting to talk to him for sure."

"A target?"

"Petronas Twin Towers? Who knows? Everything should probably be considered a potential target. Malaysia's a Muslim country but the Towers are as potent a symbol of Western decadence as anything in Manhattan. GCHQ is scouring through communications data tagged to Jemmah Islamiyah cells in Malaysia, Indonesia, and Singapore."

"You're special advisor to MI5 as well as Interpol?" she asks, making sense for the first time of Ashi's unexpected post-retirement job.

"That, and more early morning starts for the 8 a.m. Virgin flight to New York than I care to remember."

Then she suddenly sees that the contrivance was even greater than she had imagined. "They engineered it, didn't they? Intelligence had you finished at the university. You agreed to it? That's way beyond the call of duty, Ashi."

She thinks about it for a moment and adds, "And now it looks like I've joined you by the same route."

"Almost, but I think you had more going for you in the university—you got taken out for your own protection."

"Meaning?" she asks defensively, sensing an oblique reference to Oghel as well as the more obvious threats.

"Meaning you're a wanted woman and the enemy seems to know a lot about you."

"The enemy?"

"An Islamic fundamentalist network, local mafia in three countries, Russian organised crime... who knows who else? We really are in the dark with many of the details. We're pretty sure it's not Bin Laden's network. No, our guy's something quite different. It's just as they said: a phantom rather than a commander, and a shadow rather than a network."

"So was I given the full story?" Her voice raised in anger.

"It was hardly my fault that I got taken on board before you."

"I'm sorry—this is difficult, as I'm sure you can understand. So what *can* you tell me, Ashi?"

"To watch your back with your student."

"Is that official?"

"No, of course not—why do you think I asked you here like this?"

"I failed the test at the farm debriefing, huh? You thought so too?"

"Yes. The *test*. Was it that obvious?"

"Blindingly. The only trouble was I realised too bloody late, didn't I?"

"They've been scrutinising your friendship with the boy as well as with the Sufi."

"Were *you*?" Again, defensively, and with anger; then, sensing a chance to prise some information, she adds: "Why should they be interested in Oghel?"

"I'm sure you've worked that one out for yourself, old friend—why do you think?"

"Oghel's a complex young man," she says evasively.

"Perhaps he's dancing to several tunes."

"He's caught up in something he doesn't understand—an innocent pawn."

"As I said—we're worried about you."

So now it's "we" who are officially worried.

"You think Oghel's under Asmir's influence?"

"We have evidence."

Blood rushes to her head, thumping in her eardrums, temples, and neck.

"We know that he's linked up somehow, and that makes it significant when you try contacting him out of hours. They're watching you and I don't want to see you compromised in that area too."

"Maybe I have my own reasons for courting an attractive Turkish researcher."

This draws a look that can only be described as despairing.

"Then I'd strongly advise you to think carefully about how far you push it. The stakes are too high to be playing your own little game on the side."

"So what are you suggesting?"

"Stop calling him. Nigel knows you tried the other day and he's watching closely. You've no idea how odd you sounded at the debriefing."

Cassy is sobered into silence.

Then, knowing that she has to deliver something that will make them take her seriously, she pronounces, "Oghel's connection with the Sufis—it's his uncle."

She scores. Some of the condolence goes from Ashi's face.

"Uncle?"

"He has a mysterious unidentified benefactor. He says it's an uncle. It could be any one of the three Sufi brothers. I've got my own theory."

"You really believe there's three of them, don't you? It had better be good. Otherwise, don't even think of telling Buchanan. Then again, if it *is* good, you'll be under even closer scrutiny. You really are convinced Sufi Isa's as pure as snow, aren't you?" he says with a slight shake of his head. "And you weren't alarmed by his powers of persuasion? We could all see the effect at the debriefing."

She doesn't respond.

"Be honest with yourself, Cassy. I know how this sort of person works. I should hold back on Oghel's uncle for now," he says with a sigh. "I'll not report that one."

So he is here under bloody orders after all.

She is surprised he let it slip. Their secret rendezvous is a ruse—another method of taking observations on Isa's handiwork, only using a more personal approach. It has worked—he has prised out a new piece of intelligence: Oghel's "uncle." Nausea and loneliness engulfs Cassy.

They sit in silence by an elaborate painting hanging on a stone pillar. A crowd of tourists approach.

"Possibly the most famous religious work from the Pre-Raphaelite movement," the guide begins. "Holman Hunt's most iconic work. As you can see, it depicts the resurrected Christ standing at a door that is barely visible for the weeds and overgrowth. He holds a lantern in his hand to signify the light he brings to the human condition and the door is the door to a man's heart. It was inspired by a letter written to a first-century church in what is now Turkey..."

Cassy stands up at the mention of Turkey and moves closer to listen.

"... And pictures the Christ standing outside a believer's heart. His knocking demonstrates an insatiable desire to enter the human soul and bring joy. But even the pious lock him out. The overgrown garden is the sin that entangles and corrupts even the most religious amongst us."

Cassy looks up at the weeds, the trees, and the darkness of the garden, and something bothers her. She sees a form, but can't quite identify what. Something has registered somewhere in her memory, but too deep to readily recall.

The guide stops and takes questions, and she turns to Ashi. Cassy wanders back to sit next to Ashi. "Lesson for today—never completely trust the overtly religious. It's an idea Trotsky would have been happy with. I wonder why *Roskovitsky's treasure* bothered him so much."

"He had a Jewish upbringing," Ashi replies. "You can never really shake off those early influences."

She gets up again and re-joins the tour, trying to imagine Ashi as a boy with his Persian father. She stares at Hunt's finely detailed Christ. All of a sudden it is Isa she sees in the painting. And then, by some slight of the light or imagination, the image flickers and she sees a dark shadow behind him—an alter ego, an emptiness, a sinister form not quite Isa but not obviously something distinct. Then she loses it and only sees Isa, warm, charming, and benevolent. The darkness appears again, this time as a monster, suggested by the weeds that surround Jesus, and then Isa is on his own again. Like a Pre-Raphaelite hologram it continues its trickery until Cassy has to shake her head and rub her eyes to break the visual confusion. The experience is physical—more powerful than a mere flight of imagination—and leaves her short of breath. She quickly turns and sees that Ashi is watching her with a saddened expression on his face. It is obvious what he is thinking. She turns her head for another look at the painting—to convince herself that her mental state is normal—and is relieved to see only the artist's depiction of Jesus. He looks sad to her—the sadness of being shut out and misunderstood by those who call themselves friends.

As she walks away, with a shot of adrenaline that sends her pulse pumping far too fast, she suddenly realises what it was that she had seen in the painting. She runs back, pushing through the startled tourists and stares up at the picture. Ashi looks on for a moment and then, with a shake of the head and heavy sigh, turns and walks towards the exit.

"The forest! That bloody plastic sack in the tree—the heavy one that wouldn't move!" She is shouting and some of the tourists move cautiously away from her, staring.

"Ashi! Quick," she calls out, running to catch up with him. "We need to see Nigel, or the MI5 or 6 guy with the silver hair—now. Immediately, I mean."

Chapter 38

London's Epping Forest
September 2000

BY THE TIME Cassy arrives at the copse of beech and oak trees it has already been cordoned off with blue-and-white-striped tape. Two vans and three high-speed police cars are parked in the road that leads back to the bikers' cafe, lights still flashing. The sirens of at least two others approach along unseen forest roads. In the cleared scrubland a helicopter squats, its blades slowing to a halt—it had landed as Cassy pulled up in her black Escort RS Turbo, which is parked on the grass behind a police van. The sliver-haired senior British official is talking with a man in army fatigues and three more soldiers appear from the other side of the copse from the direction of a well-camouflaged military vehicle. It is an impressive gathering mobilised at such short notice; it has been only two hours since Cassy phoned Nigel Buchanan from the steps of St. Paul's.

"Ah, Cassandra, glad you showed up." Cassy turns at the sound of Nigel's cheery voice. "It would have been awfully embarrassing had you not."

"You obviously had your doubts."

"Let's just say I had a call from our friend Ashi just after yours," said with a condescending smile.

"But you took me seriously." She gestures towards the security operation unfolding in front of them.

"It's on stand-by three hundred and sixty-five days a year, my dear. Whatever our worries about you, we couldn't risk logging a call like that and not passing it on through the proper channels. So here we all are. It had better be good."

Nigel looks over his shoulder and calls out, "Ready to go, Hugo?"

The silver-haired man is clearly in command and beckons Cassy over.

"Hello again, Dr. Kim. More your cup of tea, I imagine... than being quizzed by a panel of mealy-mouthed officials, I mean."

"Actually I'm more of a desk person," she lies.

Hugo is beckoning over a military officer who has just stepped out of the helicopter.

"All right, we want to get this over as quickly as possible—we don't want an audience, do we? If you'd like to show these boys the tree, Dr. Kim, they'll take over. Just lead them to it and then come straight back if you please. Okay, lads, over to you."

Two mounted-policemen have appeared and are holding a conversation with a group of riders just along the bridle path. Behind them the path is closed with more blue-and-white tape.

Cassy nods to the soldiers. "Straight through here, bang in the middle of the copse."

Ten minutes later, Cassy is standing at the edge of the trees again, looking along the overgrown path with Nigel, Hugo, and a police inspector. The soldiers are about fifty metres away but their fatigues make it difficult to see what they are doing. Nobody speaks as they wait.

A shout breaks the tension, followed by a muted thud of army boots running on soft forest soil.

"Nothing doing, sir," says the leader as he emerges from the path and crosses the road to address Hugo.

Think hard—you're right, but they've put it somewhere else. What would you have done?

By the time the incriminating eyes gather around Cassy she has an answer.

"It's been moved," she says, throat tight with nerves. It is a weak start but she has to convince them. A movement to her left distracts everyone for a moment and Banton gets out of a dark green Jaguar. It is not what Cassy needs. Nigel and Hugo walk over to the car, and the soldier who had returned from the tree shrugs Cassy a silent gesture of solidarity.

Everyone looks around at the second shout. There are more boot thuds, walking quickly this time, not running, and two other soldiers emerge from the path holding between them what appears to be a plastic bin—smaller than a domestic dustbin but similar in proportions and moulded from heavy-duty rubber or plastic.

"No doubt about it, sir, it's a dump of some kind."

Cassy looks at Banton then at Nigel and Hugo.

"Nice timing," she says to all three, producing a sweet smile especially for Banton.

"It was sunk into the half-hollowed-out tree with a sealed lid over the top and leaves on top of that," the soldier explains. "The lid was well down into the trunk so anyone feeling around would find just a shallow pool of piss water like most of the other trees in there. There was a plastic lining—like in a garden pond—over the lid and tucked up into a cut in the tree walls. A lot of care went into designing it, sir—a long winter night's work, I should say. The bin's quite dry under the artificial pond."

"Very good." Hugo gives an appreciative nod to Cassy. "Well, what have we got?"

"Nothing in it, sir," they both answer together.

There are glances as everyone ponders what that might mean.

Turning to Nigel, who knows the details of Cassy's earlier forest find, she interrupts the silent conference: "Would *you* leave the bin's contents there if you knew that someone had blown its cover?"

"I thought you put the wooden box back where you found it." Hugo is the quickest off the mark.

Everyone looks at Cassy.

"She took something else from the dump and didn't return it," Nigel says, looking apologetically at Hugo, clearly flustered.

"Okay, we can deal with that later unless it's got a bearing on the current situation," Hugo addressing Nigel sternly. "What are you getting at, Dr. Kim?"

"Three possibilities come to mind," she says, quickly thinking on her feet. "First, they didn't have time to dismantle the dump or thought it too risky. Of course, there's always a chance that the people who might have wanted to remove the evidence got removed themselves—but hold that one for the moment. Second, it's an old dump and the people who've been using the tree-pond recently don't know about it or don't care if it's found. Third, there are two different interests at work here. The pond gets used for day-to-day exchanges or holing up goods for short periods, while the bin is for deep-cover stuff and is used by operators at a different level. Maybe merchandise gets moved between dumps from time to time."

As she says this, she moves over to the bin to take a closer look.

"Do you mind?" she asks one of the soldiers who'd carried it from the tree.

He looks at his superior, who nods, and Cassy turns it onto its side and squats to examine the base. It is coated in a thick scum of decayed leaves and bark, and she picks up a stick to scrape it clean. She finds what she is looking for—embossed letters running round the edge of a raised circular area in the centre of the base. She feels it with her finger, wipes the debris off, and leans closer to read: "Made in Newcastle, England, 1969. There we are—deep-cover storage."

There is triumph in her voice: "Abandoned or empty at the moment but sitting here silently for thirty years. My gut feeling is that there's another one not far away."

Looking at Hugo, she says, "Are you authorised to re-deploy this lot to another site?"

He looks down his nose at her as if peering over the rim of a pair of spectacles.

"Do you have somewhere in mind?"

"About two miles away. It might take a while to identify the right tree, but I'm pretty sure of the location."

***

It had taken less than an hour with ten policemen, three soldiers, and four specialised sniffer dogs with their handlers. There had been plenty of other finds in the unusual tree ponds of the lopped beeches surrounding Boudicca's ancient forest camp: a Coke bottle circa 1940, a rusted army knife, evidence of romantic encounters, several pieces of World War Two shrapnel, a handbag, and the skeletal remains of several small mammals. Eventually there had been an exuberant shout as a young policeman prodded his stick into something that didn't feel like rotted wood. It was another concealed plastic bin container—only this one had not been empty. Carefully wrapped in waxed canvas, they had found a sealed, old-fashioned tin box, the kind that biscuits used to be sold in. Inside the tin had been found a book.

Two of the dogs had also picked up a positive scent. The dump had at some stage been used to store explosives and contained traces of a compound used in the manufacture of a chemical warfare agent.

***

At three o'clock precisely a lime-green secretary politely ushers Cassy down the narrow corridor and knocks at the door tucked away at the end. Nigel greets her with guarded civility and invites her to sit. Hugo and the two Americans from the previous meeting are in the room but thankfully there is no sign of Banton or Ashi.

"Well, Dr. Kim," Nigel starts, "we've had a little discussion after the drama in the forest and there are a few more questions my colleagues would like to put to you."

The American nods a greeting. "A lot's changed since we last talked Dr Kim."

She acknowledges with a nod.

"Perhaps you can tell us precisely how you discovered the forest dump."

She repeats the story.

"*Cleito* mean anything to you?" the American asks her.

"Apart from being the mother of Atlas, no."

"And that's all? You just got the email message out of the blue and nothing before or since?"

"Nothing." She is not going to tell him that Isa had referred to the Greek character.

"You're sure you don't have anything else to tell us on that matter? You've no idea at all who tipped you off?"

"No idea at all."

"Let's come to the meeting at the Bronze Age fort," the American says.

She repeats what she can recall of the conversation she had overheard in the forest.

"We've had the American biker woman in for questioning," Nigel says during a pause.

"You found her?"

"When she eventually returned from a rather long holiday."

"And?"

"She's not admitting anything and we've got little on her apart from your accusation—and the body. But the body's produced no incriminating evidence. We want to keep quiet and watch her for a bit longer but she isn't moving—she's frozen. Some of us..." he says, looking for a second at the American. "We needed to get some hard information pretty sharpish."

"Nothing at all on her?" Cassy asks, finding it difficult to believe.

"Nothing directly from *her*." The American takes over again. "But we have quite a bit on her background: an organised crime connection in the family as thick as Mississippi mud. A New York Russian immigrant clan. It's not only children of the respectable professions who study for their doctorates these days, you know. We traced a bank account she uses in London and others in New York and Moscow. So we're waiting."

"The Trotskyite connection?"

"Buchanan told you about that? Know much about ROC?"

"A little."

"There are four types of ROC groupings. The *Vory v zakone*—historically the Russian criminal elite. They're professional common criminals and grew into strong organisations during the Gulag era. Then there are the alliances between corrupt former or existing Communist Party members, government officials, and businessmen. Ethnic groups like the Chechens, Georgians, and Armenians form a third pool. The fourth is made up of the criminal associations that form around shared experiences and backgrounds. Some form around sports clubs; others around old ideological movements. At the last count there were about two hundred and thirty major organisations all together. About twenty of them are based on what started out as hard-line communist groups. Three of these have strong Trotskyite roots."

"*Belonging* matters more than purpose," she says, thinking of the Essaouira cult.

"Those with a residue of ideological purpose mixed with their criminal activities are often the most ruthless," the American adds.

"They're diehard believers?"

"Possibly. Possibly not. Trafficking to finance Trotsky's perpetual revolution or perpetuating memories to justify their trafficking. Who knows? Maybe the political stuff's just a habit. Or entertainment."

"So you've got her bank accounts," Cassy says. "Sounds like a result to me."

"Yes, but the trail stops there, as far as links with the Sufis are concerned. We've no idea who else uses the accounts. She's been drawing on a large sum deposited just before she arrived in London, which has also been debited from the U.S. Another large sum went in about a week after your forest meeting—deposited in London. But she's maintaining it belongs to a relative who's financing her studies—which, knowing her family connections, could well be accurate. Our guess is that it's one of a number of accounts she runs in parallel with the same cover story. Each is used to launder one or two big payments. Whoever was meant to draw on the money you saw handed over in the forest is sitting tight. It's a blank at the U.S. end at the moment, I'm afraid."

"How about starting from some other parts of the network and working back?" Cassy says, knowing that she has them in her hand.

All eyes fall on her as she pulls out a sheet of paper from her rucksack.

"Check this out. It's a list of towns that are home to a collection of assorted New Age, doomsday, and eco-cults. They've nothing in common other than they've been visited in the last two years by the same team of interlopers—one of whom is a Middle Eastern or Mediterranean woman. She could well be the owner of the passport I brought back from Sufi Odam's base."

No one speaks, waiting to see if there is more.

"The list comes from analysing patterns in one of your data sets," she says, smiling at the American. "Small independent groups like the one in Essaouira—looks like Asmir—Odam—or his followers are out on a corporate take-over spending spree."

The American takes the list without saying anything and scans it. An eyebrow rises as he gets halfway down the page. He passes it to Hugo, turns back to Cassy and, looking at the floor, says, "We are aware of a... a possible connection with one of these towns. Would you mind telling us where this list came from, and why the hell you haven't passed it to Mr. Buchanan before now? We're all getting just a little tired of your game playing."

His voice is steady and threatening, and he looks up to await her reply, face empty of expression and unmoving.

"One of your ex-employees. A professor in California—ex-CIA cryptologist. We're a close-knit community. It's public domain data for people like him. Your guys have access to the same data, it's just that they wouldn't have known what pattern to look for."

"And you did?" His coldness now laced with more than a hint of annoyance.

"It's taken a while for the pieces to fit into place. There's another lead you can work from in Bangkok. That's what you hired me for, wasn't it? Looking for leads, mapping networks, analysing patterns." She smiles at Nigel, whose initial briefing patter she is quoting. "All the things I'm good at doing."

"Keep going, Dr. Kim, we're hearing you." Then to Nigel: "We're running over—you need to cancel your next appointment."

When his gaze returns to her, Cassy continues, "Get the joint Thai-British vice squad to bust an outfit that goes by the name of East West Ecumenical Children's Aid Foundation. It has an office on the ground floor under the Sufi's Bangkok apartment. Whatever else they discover there, they'll find links to a video shop in an eastern suburb of Bangkok that's hopefully already been raided by British detectives. Between them they run a child-trafficking outfit, which I suspect they use to supply child abuse networks in the West and the Middle East. Sufi Odam's lot supplies the child traffickers. I've met one of them."

"You're too bloody clever, Dr. Kim. Why haven't you come out with this before?" Nigel is angry and shouting.

"For one thing you would have used it to seal your case against Isa before I've finished my job."

"But now you've come to your senses?" There is satisfaction—relief, even—in the American's voice.

"The case is already sealed," she says, her voice dropping to reveal the resignation she has already given into.

I am about to give you the firmest evidence yet for Washington's bloody three-in-one theory and you can stuff it up your Agency-issued arses.

Cassy now knows for sure that she will soon be facing Isa across an extradition courtroom.

"Meaning?" asks the second American cautiously and looking at her as though observing something of some significance.

"You need to have this." She says it with a sense of deep resignation and resentment.

She reaches once again into her rucksack to produce a book. It is the book Isa had given her as a gift as she left him in the south of Thailand.

The drama is interrupted by someone knocking on the door.

"Wait!" shouts the American, as if interrupted at the climax of a movie. Then he looks at the door and motions to Nigel to respond anyway.

A secretary silently places two gold cafetieres with china cups and saucers on a coffee table and quickly leaves, shutting the door behind her. The coffee table sits under a gilt standing lamp by the bookshelf. Cassy glances at the place where Nigel's own copy of *Cold Passion Stilled* had been. There is no sign of it this time. It is neither protruding nor stacked back in the neat row of paper spines. She is quite sure where it had been. The Russian cult novel is no longer there.

Nigel moves over to play host with the coffee and the American nods to Cassy.

"Continue."

She takes a deep breath.

"You want to prove that Sufi Isa is your Asmir? Well, here's all the proof you need. The last time I saw him he gave me this book. It's in Arabic but I had the first chapter translated. It's the same book as the soldiers retrieved from the forest dump a few days ago: *Cold Passion Stilled*."

There are deep and considered intakes of breath around the room. The American rises to his feet, clasping his hands together so that his knuckles click, and then walks over to the desk and picks up a phone.

Nigel is staring distractedly at his bookcase.

***

Thirty minutes later, Banton and two others join the party in Nigel's office. Extra chairs have been brought in. The man is in his mid-thirties, wearing an anonymous suit and haircut and the woman in her fifties is smartly dressed, but looks more like a homely grandmother than a security official. Neither is introduced to Cassy as she is ushered back into the room, having been taken to another room while they discussed her revelation. An old-fashioned-looking tape machine had also appeared—the sort used in official interrogations.

"Go ahead, Dr. Kim. Let's hear what you have to say." The American opens up stage two after Cassy is seated, pressing the button on the recorder.

The upholstered chair she had been sitting on before the break has been given to the woman and Cassy is now perched uncomfortably upright on a wooden seat that has clearly been brought out of retirement from a store cupboard somewhere in the old building. She wipes a finger along the dusty rim.

Whether it is the build up of tension under examination or the extreme mental dissonance she has just experienced in being forced to accept the American's theory about Isa, she finds the hand that she has just used to measure the dust with is shaking. Not much, but enough to make her wary that something is not right. Unwisely, she tries to calm the neurological attack by concentrating hard on an image of Isa on the veranda with the small children at his feet. As she does, something like an electric current seems to pulse from the front of her head down her spine and she physically jerks. It is real enough to make her look round for the person who had assaulted her with some kind of interrogation device.

The hand is still shaking and she sees that it has been noticed. She grips the seat of the chair hard with it and focuses all of her energy on composing herself to talk. Another sensation suddenly overwhelms her—a welling confidence, the resigned defiance of the martyr. A conviction that she is right whatever anyone else might think. With it returns the otherworld serenity she had experienced under Isa's words, and then the emotional soundtrack to the image—an overwhelming desire to be far away from Nigel's office, from her life in London, to be with Isa and his grandchildren.

And it is from this psychological location that she restarts her account.

"My guess is that the book—*Cold Passion Stilled*—is used for messaging in some way. Maybe it's an identification signature like a Freemason's handshake or it's an old-fashioned encryption manual. Isa gave me a copy because he guessed I had connections with you lot. A gesture of gratitude for my help. Perhaps also a reluctant move to finally rein in his brother. You're going to use it to prove your theory; I say that it proves mine. Why would he give it to me if it was his deepest secret?"

"Gratitude for what?" Banton snaps suspiciously, ignoring Cassy's counter foil.

"For archaeological services rendered to his grand cause. I seem to have given him his life's ambition—the location of what, for all the world, looks like the site of the Garden of Eden."

A knowing look passes between the two Americans. Banton just snorts in derision.

"The tape from Essaouira?" the woman asks,

"You know about the tape?" Cassy is visibly shocked. She has told no one about it apart from Beccy and Oghel.

"Grow up, Kim," Banton snorts again.

"Why would Isa want to have his brother closed down after all these years?" the woman asks.

"Because Odam went too far. Because members of his sect got assassinated along with a couple of hundred innocent men, women, and children on the AIA plane. Because the stakes are getting too high. Only so much can be covered by filial loyalty."

Then the American from Washington shakes his head and assumes a look of purposeful gravity.

"We looked into your theory about Nooh and others from the group being on the plane. We have another interpretation, I'm afraid, Dr. Kim. You have the victim and villains mixed up."

"Oh?" Now the side of her face is numbing as the neurosis spreads.

"The passenger list. From your report on the assassination in the forest we have now made some connections. My colleague here," he says, nodding to the woman, "is an ROC expert with the Israelis."

Cassy looks at her, mentally adjusting the assumptions she had made about her.

"You were right that the AIA flight had a party of underworld characters on board," he continues, "but it wasn't Odam's lot: it was the Trotskyites. They were on their way to secure an important deal with the Mumbai Mafia. It was quite a party—no less than nine members of the Trotsky gang died when AIA706 exploded above the Bombay runway. We think you may have something, however, with the idea of a suicide bomber on board from the Noah Brotherhood's Central Asia base."

Cassy feels like retching. She suddenly knows with sickening certainty that she has been utterly wrong about Isa. They have their case in a bag and it was she who delivered it.

But being ever the fighter, Cassy Kim digs down deep to find something to rescue her from complete humiliation and comes up with: "Asmir had a bash at suicidal mid-air psycho-terrorism once before."

"How was the Noah's Ark toy bomb psycho-terrorism?" the American asks.

"Much earlier than that." Cassy looks him in the eye. "Get someone to check back on Winston Gunther's first attempt to fly to Iran from Jordan in 1954. You'll find that the BOAC plane he was on narrowly escaped disaster. You'll find an investigator's report saying that the pilot confided uncharacteristic suicidal tendencies to his co-pilot just after take-off. The co-pilot took control, restraining the pilot as a precaution, and took the plane back to Amman."

She had obtained the air accident report from archives at Lloyds Register.

It is the Israeli woman who responds. Speaking in a slow eastern Mediterranean accent she turns to Hugo: "It is so. This is our theory too. Some of Asmir's followers seem to practice the occult—or perhaps it is hypnotism. It is the way with some Uwaysi Sufis. It appears that the art has been honed as a tool of crime and terrorism—as with their ability to manipulate minds and command allegiance even to death. I would like to congratulate Dr. Kim."

She nods at Cassy slowly as if to set an example to the others.

"Dr. Kim," the Israeli continues, "has been taken in by Asmir, yes, but this is what we expected, no? She has given us what we need. She has been a very productive asset."

Cassy is giving all her attention to calming down, measuring her breathing and focusing on a spot in the middle of the carpet. The word *expected* sends a shiver down her spine but she keeps on focusing.

For a moment, no one responds. Then the Agency man from Washington clears his throat: "We'll need to pick up on some of these issues. I've got a room booked tomorrow morning at the U.S. Embassy for a meeting that I can cancel. Let's all make it for a seven o'clock breakfast."

Nobody declines and no one else speaks. Finally he stands up, and as he does, everyone else does likewise.

Nigel ushers Cassy out, closes the door behind them, and then marches off purposefully along the dreary corridor towards his secretary's desk with a "This way, Dr. Kim, please."

Before she takes a step, she hears a low mutter of several animated conversations breaking out at the same time in the room behind her. Above the other voices the Israeli woman is saying to someone: "We'll need to move quickly on Miss Kim's friend—you have my approval to haul him in."

Cassy takes a few steps so Nigel can hear that she is following him, and then moves closer to the corridor wall that runs along one side of Nigel's office. Keeping close, she can still hear conversation. The muffled voice of the American is saying: "There are some loose ends that need to be tied up first. We're planning to make a move next week. Departure routes will be covered from Monday. We'll leave things undisturbed here for a few more days."

Then Nigel is calling back down the corridor after her.

Shit. They're going to move in on Oghel. I've got to warn him.

Cassy is sweating as she comes to the secretary's desk. Nigel is stooped peering at a letter being held up for him to read and Cassy walks straight on past him towards a waiting area where three corridors converge round a corner, and then hurries through some swinging doors, finding herself in another passageway. Then she breaks into a measured run, pulling out her cell phone and finding Oghel's number. She rounds another corner and is blocked by a group of young males talking loudly and laughing—coats over arms, ready to go home at the end of the day.

"Sorry, I'm lost. What's the best way down? I need the rear exit," she asks, trying to sound normal but breathing heavily.

There is more laughter as one of them hooks an arm in hers and winking at his jeering colleagues says, "Follow me, my dear. I'll take you down with pleasure."

Chapter 39

Central London
September 2000

A SLOW-MOTION tear drifts down alabaster skin tracing a graceful parabola. Mesmerised, Cassy watches the drop of wax spill into a moist pool at the foot of the church candle and raises her eyes to Oghel's. His face is the colour of the candle in the subdued light of her living room and almost the same complexion. Her pedestalled sculpture in her museum.

They are in her own apartment—her secret one.

She had called Oghel as soon as she was out of the British Council Building by the back door that opened directly onto the Mall and given him a coffee shop and a time later that evening. She was somewhat surprised that he had turned up, even more so to see him with an overnight bag. Silently she had led him a few blocks via a circuitous route, to her secret hideaway.

Mozart's "Requiem" is playing in the background. Two emptied bowls face each other either side of a low, Korean-style dark wood table. Apart from the two simple ebony stools they are seated on—each a gently upwardly curving plank on two short vertical planks—two Tatami rush mats and a free-standing Korean-style wooden bath, plumbed in through the marble floor as the room's centrepiece, the living room is otherwise empty and pristine.

"We must talk," she whispers after a long silence.

"You're in trouble, Oghel. Don't ask me how I know, but it's serious."

His eyes search hers, exploring her sincerity. Looking around, he tries to interpret the room they are in. Perhaps unwittingly also evaluating her sincerity.

No turning back now. Can this be her home?

"You're being used—a pawn in someone else's game. I think you know it, although I don't think you know why or how."

His attention is back at the table. It is very small table for a large room, making the conversation intimate.

"What has happened?"

"I can't say—just a conversation I overheard. You need to get away, Oghel—immediately."

He believes her. She can see it in his face.

"You may be perfectly innocent but I've a feeling that won't help. If you've been stitched up, then it's been done convincingly and it's going to take time to undo. You may be exonerated eventually, but right now you don't want to be around, I'm afraid. Is there anywhere you can go for a while? I'll sort things out with the university for you."

"How bad is it?" It is said without surprise, as though it is confirmation that he requires, not an explanation.

"My guess is that you'll be picked up by intelligence agents from any one of three countries in the next few days and whisked across the Atlantic into custody. What happens beyond that, I have no idea—only that the stakes are big and your abduction could easily be justified."

"Abduction?"

"Yes, abduction. Something big's going down in the world of fundamentalist Islamic terrorism and you may be Syrian Orthodox but you're connected in some way."

"My uncle? The ones who threatened my father? You have discovered something, Dr. Cassy? Please tell me."

"They're waiting for something. You need to go tonight. And go by a route that will make it difficult to trail. They're not expecting you to run immediately so you should have a chance. Here..."

She gets up from the table, walks out of the room, and returns with a leather shoulder bag.

"Money to buy yourself train and plane tickets and some new clothes and things—it's a present. Don't refuse it." She sits herself down opposite him again.

It is actually more than that—it is a hundred thousand pounds. A contribution to his new life.

"Pack a bag that doesn't arouse suspicion—I'm sure they'll be watching your home. Take a channel ferry or head for a regional airport and catch the KLM city hopper to Amsterdam. You'll find any connection you want from there within a few hours."

"You expect me to go just like that?"

He is looking around the room again, thinking quickly. Making decisions. The apartment is large for Central London; four bedrooms, he guesses.

"What can I say to convince you?" Cassy feels the warm moisture of tears on her cheeks and knows that she doesn't have to search for more words.

Oghel drops his eyes for a moment, and then reaches over the table and takes her hands. "I am fortunate."

Then he quickly takes his hands back, straightening himself as if to emphasise some inner resolve. "You don't have to convince me. I have planned for it. See? I have my bag." He gestures to the holdall lying on the floor by the door. "There are things I haven't told you, can't tell you. I have sensed the danger gathering closer."

"Where will you go?"

He stares at the candle and she adds quickly: "Don't answer that—just go somewhere safe."

"I have somewhere. Somewhere very remote and very quiet." He smiles a distant smile.

In his mind is a mountain, a flowering valley, and an ancient building.

"Have you ever been to Morocco?" Cassy asks.

"I have been there—twice. To a Catholic monastery in a fortified earthen-walled town at the foot of the High Atlas. Taroudant is the name of the town. There has been a monastic community there since early French colonial times. There are only a few brothers left now."

"I thought you were Syrian Orthodox."

"A broad-minded one."

Cassy wishes she hadn't asked the question, but it is too late to go back on her trust. She is in love with an innocent Oghel.

"Whose idea was it? To visit Taroudant, I mean."

"My adoptive father's. He organised the first trip for me."

"I must ask you about your father, Oghel—your real father. I know it's a painful subject, but I want to talk about him."

"You know something about my real father?" His eyes search her face, trying to see behind it.

"It might well turn out to be about your real father. But there's something I need to put to you before we go any further. I'm sorry if it hurts."

He is sitting upright on the stool as if bracing himself, and Cassy leans forward.

"Why do you think the relatives of your real father didn't come looking for you after he died in the Turkish earthquake?"

"Travel restrictions? A family rift?" There is no conviction in his voice.

"What if it was both of those, but also because you were no more his natural son than you are the son of a Syrian Orthodox priest?"

His jaw sets rigid and he grips the edge of the table.

"I found out something," she says solemnly. "I believe that the man you call your real father took custody of you at an early age—with the willing consent of the man who is truly your blood father."

He remains in silent submission to her words, looking down.

Whatever she will say, I know that it is right. I have been drawn to her for a purpose.

"There are other possibilities—but this is probably the best. If I'm right, your natural father is still alive."

"Alive?" This he hadn't been prepared for. "Now? Where? But... why would...?"

"Why would a father give up his son?" Cassy sees Oghel, the abandoned little boy. And having seen it, she realised it has always been there—a tender vulnerability barely below the surface of the deep straw and green-blue universes that are now pleading with her.

"For your own good and with honourable motives. He was a hounded man, constantly threatened with violence and always moving on. He couldn't allow you to suffer the life he was committed to."

"My mother is still alive too?" he asks in a tone that tells Cassy he is prepared to believe her whatever she says without question.

"She died in childbirth. I'm sorry."

"But if this is true, it was so long ago—surely he would have made some kind of contact..." He stops what he is about to say.

"Your benefactor uncle," she says. "The possibility has crossed your mind over the years?"

"Yes, of course, but there is no reason to imagine an explanation like this. Why would my adoptive father conceal the truth? He would not lie. And why would a real father send money to his son pretending to be an uncle?"

"Why should your adoptive father have known the truth? The wandering pilgrim with a young son befriended by monks in the local monastery was no doubt just that to him. And the uncle who makes occasional contact—what reason would your adoptive father have to doubt that claim?"

"I cannot imagine how you have investigated my past in such a way, Dr. Cassy, but please tell me what you know: is my benefactor my *uncle* or my *father?*"

Without letting her answer he says, "You think it is my father."

"No. I'm convinced your natural father doesn't know you are alive. I think it really is your uncle—your real father's brother."

"My father doesn't know that I am alive and I don't know he is alive—and yet his brother sends me large sums of money? What sort of a family is this, Dr. Cassy?"

That is one bloody good question, Oghel, my sweetheart.

"Your natural father thinks that you died in the earthquake along with the man he entrusted you to. The man's wife died of an illness long before that time, and their respective families had washed their hands of him and his adopted son because of his wayward religious convictions. He had rejected the orthodox Muslim beliefs he had once served zealously. If your real father had ever enquired of the family, they would have told him you were both dead—out of spite, ignorance, or perhaps in a metaphorical sense."

"But if he heard a rumour that I had died in an earthquake he could have come to Turkey to make sure—to search among the survivors."

His eyes flash and she sees a little boy's confusion and anger in them.

"He was not welcomed in Turkey and his movements—at least his official movements—were restricted and still are. All the more so now."

"He is in prison? Where?"

"Not quite. He is in exile. A refugee now living in Asia—in Thailand. He is an influential teacher—a Sufi by tradition but a free spirit that marks him out as a dangerous threat to many Muslim authorities, including more orthodox Sufis."

His jaw drops and he stares beyond her at the floor.

The tragedy of Oghel's life suddenly overwhelms Cassy and tears start to flow silently.

Given away to an enemy who became compelled enough by that generous act to seek after Isa's hybrid and errant *Way*—and the enemy with tragedy and irony, in death bequeathing the love-gift to Syrian Orthodox parents unknown to Isa. It was even possible that the man had taken

Oghel to Turkey in search of his real father—to return him perhaps.

There is a long silence. Eventually he says, "You have met a man giving this story? And made the connection with my own story? It is too much of a coincidence. Can it be true?"

"I think it is true, but I cannot explain the coincidence. There is no coincidence—the improbability is too high. I'm sure of it—no coincidence, just scheming. You are being used in some way, Oghel—as I am too. Don't ask me to explain because I can't—I'm working on it, but I don't understand what it all means. Somehow, the reason why you came to London to study with me is tied up with the reason for me travelling to Asia to meet this man."

"And I am to disappear just like that, leaving my past exposed and unresolved?"

"You must ask the Syrian Priest some questions you've never asked him before."

"I could visit the man you think is my real father..." He clasps the bag she has given him.

"That would be the very worst thing you could do at the moment, Oghel, my dear," she says, looking at him tenderly.

"He's in trouble not only for his beliefs but with the international intelligence community too. He's been under surveillance for years—you wouldn't believe how long this goes back. But right now, with whatever is going on in the Islamic terrorist community, everyone with any connection to any secretive fundamentalist Muslim network is a suspect. If you try to make contact, you'll confirm everyone's suspicions. And by the nature of the conspiracy he's suspected of, it might be a long and painful process to disentangle yourself. In any case you won't find him. He's gone walkabout."

"Walkabout?"

"He's a wandering holy man—a very successful one with a large flock to look after."

He pushes his lower jaw out and looks at the ceiling, his eyes full.

"What do you know about the man who sends me money, Dr. Cassy?"

"Your father has, or had, two brothers—at least some say so. I think I believe it."

She is watching him very closely but can see no flicker of guardedness.

"There are two accounts about one brother. He may be dead or he may be alive but not in communication with your father. He may be your benefactor, Oghel—his name is Nooh."

He flinches at the revelation.

"I know more about the other brother but it is not pleasant. His name is Odam—Adam. It would be best not to talk about him. He also could be your benefactor but I hope he is not. He is in contact with your father but they do not see eye to eye. They are bonded by blood loyalty but if that were not the case they would be arch-foes—they are as different as light and dark. It is a unique family, Oghel."

"It is this brother—Odam—who is in trouble with the authorities?" he asks. "And he has implicated the others because of their loyalty—and implicated me?"

He is as quick as ever on the uptake.

"It's a little more complicated than that. That would be an accurate summary of the way I see it. No, the authorities are convinced the *three brothers* are a myth—constructed to protect…" She hesitates. "A masterfully ruthless religious terrorist. They think that the brothers are three faces of the same man. That's why you need to get away tonight before they can take you in."

He sits in silence and Cassy gets up, walks around the table, and places a hand on his shoulder, standing looking beyond him at the wooden bathtub with petals scattered on the flat wooden rim and spilling to the floor.

"Wait here," she says without looking down at him.

Moments later she is walking from an open bedroom door, slowly, purposefully, across the floor, bare feet on soft limestone. She has changed into a plain white knee-length silk sarong, wrapped around and secured by a double roll at the top. Behind her ear is a single young rose stem. The rose is red and the stem has been shaved of thorns. On one side. On the other side, some of the thorns have been removed but others, the ones protruding at oblique angles have been left in place.

Not far away, a car pulls up at traffic lights and one of the passengers struggles to open flat a piece of paper that has a number scribbled on it.

Oghel's total senses are anaesthetised. He cannot move.

Cassy is standing behind him and Oghel can feel the warmth radiating from her body. *She is very close.*

Slowly and methodically, she lifts her hands as if to place them on his shoulders, pauses, and then takes hold of the top of her sarong and gently unrolls it.

Placing her hands back on his shoulder, there is a flash of white as the sarong drops to the floor.

The car pulls to a halt at the elegant entrance to an upmarket riverside apartment block. The door is flung wide and one of the passengers jumps out, looking up and down the street, and then beckons to the other. Slamming the door behind them, two figures run across the pavement into the revolving door of the lobby.

Oghel can hardly breathe. He has not looked round since Cassy left the table and then the room. He has monitored her soft walk back across the floor, felt the warmth of her presence and then the swish of soft fabric falling to the floor. Her hands have moved from his shoulders, reaching down, stroking the hairs on his chest and feeling the buttons at the top of his shirt, undoing one, and then another and another until, reaching down, cheek against cheek, she gets to his jeans. A small tilt of the denim anchoring the brass stud is enough to release it from the buttonhole and, with a little gentle nudge at the fly, nature does the rest. On the way back up, her hands brush lightly against his nipples as she explores the breadth of his muscular chest. Then she is stroking the hairs on the back of his neck and spreading his opened shirt wide to reveal manly shoulders.

I do only what my father tells me. Can you really want me to throw so much away? He is whispering under his breath.

She holds her breath to try and catch what he is saying.

He seems to her to be calling someone's name:

Arumim... Arumim. Don't abandon me, Arumim. Arumim. Forgive me.

Cassy is standing naked. Stepping out of the fallen sarong, she moves forward further, pressing her body to his. Then, cupping her breasts, she gently lifts them so that they rest either side of the beautiful neck she has just prepared for them.

She is quivering inside but perfectly still on the outside. In the small of her back is tattooed a simple solid black diamond with a small question mark in the centre in red gothic font. Her life: a black box; her origin: unknown; the reason why she is as she is: unknown; what she is looking for: unknown. And above the black diamond, a ship. An ancient wooden ship, riding huge waves. The image is criss-crossed with angry streaks of red that match the colour of the question mark, like a chaotic fiery hail storm bombarding the boat from all directions. Only they are not painted pigment but gaps in the tattoo. Angry scars from a rope that has eaten into young flesh. One scar, more curved than the rest and coming from under her left arm, gives shape to a hint of a rainbow, which the artist has understated in the selection of colours.

The Ark had been Zach's idea not long before they recklessly married. The Ark was how they had met. The Ark was his solution for covering up the scars of her unknown childhood. It is why she still loves him despite him having abandoned her.

In the lobby of the apartment building, a piece of paper is being held up against a keypad mounted next to a glass door that leads to a solid brass elevator shaft studded with decorative ceramic pieces.

Cassy Kim is having a rebirth experience. It has never been like this before. Ever. She is denuded of her physical covering but is experiencing an emotional and spiritual denuding. Kissing Oghel's head, she glances down and sees what she has desired to have so much.

Mystery fountain of life. Will he turn or will I have to gently encourage him? I am ready for your child, Oghel. The child that I never was.

Then a thought from a cross-wind:

I will carry Sufi Isa's grandchild. I will be part of the Nooh Brotherhood.

Oghel's senses are strained to maximum pitch. His cheeks are burning against the softness and firmness of Cassy's breasts. He is surprised how heavy they feel—one more than the other, perhaps. And they smell of freshly opened rosebuds. Perhaps there is a hint of honeysuckle too—the honeysuckle of his childhood monastery garden. The smell of the young girl playing hide and seek with her mother. In his peripheral vision her nipples are large and effused and her areole dark.

One effortless one-eighty-degree movement will change his life forever. God has brought him to this point, but can he see it through?

A nightmarish vision interrupts the engulfing softness. In a sickly yellow glow of a solitary dim bare lightbulb, he sees himself seated at the end of a row of men, all perched on stools like his and all naked. Dripping with sweat, their muscular young bodies hung forward shamefully, their energies spent. They are looking at him scornfully. His is the only stool turned away from their tempter.

Then the inner voice he has heard so frequently recently.

Have you sufficiently died to your self-serving ways that you would willingly give up all that I have given you? Will you obey if I ask you to give up your self-righteousness to unite with a prostitute, as I asked of the prophet Hosea of old?

All Oghel can think of is the weight of Cassy's breasts on his shoulders and the picture that has replaced the nightmarish vision of the brothel. It is of Abraham on Mount Moriah being asked by God to put the son of promise to the knife. Isaac to the Jews and Christians, Ishmael to the Muslims. A symbolic killing. Or was it a ritual killing? It was a killing of Abraham's claim over the gift of God. A giving of the miracle son back to the one from whence he came. And with it a giving up of the hope of promise fulfilled—the lineage that will be as numerous as the stars of the sky and that will bless the whole of mankind.

What will I be left with if I give up all that you have given me? Will you rescue this woman? Is she worth that much?

Then he feels the tears, first dripping onto his shoulder, then running down his chest and forming a wetness that slowly works its way down to mingle with his own.

Only it isn't tears. With alarm he sees that it is blood. As he eases himself from Cassy's bosom and spins round to see what is happening there is a muffled shout from the direction of the front door followed by someone ringing the bell repeatedly.

Cassy looks around the room, disorientated, awakening from a trance, and Oghel is staring at her naked form.

"Stay here," Cassy whispers, bending to gather up her sarong.

She hurries out of the room, pulling the door shut behind her, and hears more muffled noises from the landing outside the apartment. Whoever it is has their finger on the doorbell now. Wiping her eyes and pressing her face to the tiny spy-lens, it takes her a split second to take in the scene, and she flicks the deadlock, grabs the handle, and turns it. The body leaning against the outside of the door forces it open and falls in a crumpled heap at her feet.

"Leen?" Cassy says in shock, looking up at Beccy.

"Cassy!" She stands, staring for a minute, taking in the sight. "What's happened? The blood –there's blood on your head—and your dress…"

"Its okay, Becc; really, it is."

Beccy leaps over Leen and buries her head on Cassy's shoulder. They both now have blood on their faces. "You've got to help. It's desperate, desperate! I didn't know what to do. She phoned me yesterday in Paris saying she was in London. I tried calling you. I jumped straight onto a plane. She's freaked, but won't let me take her to the hospital or police or phone them—she turns violent when I try, but she agreed to come here. I'm so sorry—I know this place is meant to be a secret but I couldn't do anything else. I'm so sorry, Cass." Now Beccy's tears are flowing with Cassy's blood.

Beccy lets go of Cassy and drops to her knees, putting a caring hand under Leen's head. Cassy looks over her shoulder, wondering what to do about Oghel, and then looks at Leen curled up into a foetal ball.

"She got worse and worse in the taxi."

Cassy manages to get the front door shut and squats down with Beccy to examine the pathetic heap. Apart from longer hair she looks much as Cassy remembers—but for the heavy dark patches under her eyes, and the smell. She looks and smells filthy.

"She's been living on the streets?"

Beccy nods, sniffing. "She's been on the move for months. God knows how she made it back to Europe. From what I can make out she's spent most of the time in Spain before making her way here. She says she came to London to confess."

"Confess what?" she asks, knowing full well what is likely to be plaguing Leen's wretched mind.

At that, Leen lets out the same heart-rending groan that they had witnessed in Essaouira. Cassy looks back towards Oghel again.

"The children," she sobs, still half-curled up and face pressed into the antique Persian rug that is the only object in the empty marbled hallway. "It wasn't my fault; they made me do it. I love children, I love children, you must believe me, I love them..." The pitiful voice trailed into uncontrollable sobs.

"Come on," Cassy says to Beccy, positioning an arm around Leen's limp form to lift her. "Let's get her onto a bed."

She lets them help her off the floor and support her through a door into Cassy's bedroom. As they manoeuver her onto the bed she catches Beccy's eye and silently mouths, pointing towards the living room.

"Oghel's here."

Beccy takes in the bloodstained white sarong and makes questioning eye contact for a brief moment before getting on with the task in hand.

Beccy is kneeling beside Leen, stroking her forehead.

"The children," Cassy says to Leen, kneeling at Beccy's side. "Tell me about the children."

"They made us do it," she sobs.

"They?" she asks gently.

"The old man."

"Solon?"

"Solon and the others. We were trapped."

"We?" Beccy joins in.

"We all did it—all the young girls. They would have killed us—we had to."

The sobs give way to heavy breathing as she tries to gain control.

"Have you spoken to anyone about this since leaving Morocco?" Cassy asks.

She shakes her head violently from side to side and Beccy whispers, "I don't think she's really talked to anyone since then. Not *really* talked—she's just been surviving."

"What did they make you all do, Leen?" Beccy asks.

"Take the children—to Europe." She is sitting up now and blinking tear- and sweat-filled bloodshot eyes.

"From where?" Beccy asks.

"Ukraine… mostly Ukrainians. Georgians and Armenian too."

"You took them to Europe?" Beccy continues.

"And Asia—they gave us passports and papers," Leen says, her voice cracking. "Passports that said we were the children's mothers. But we weren't."

"Where did the children end up?" Cassy asks, getting down to make eye contact and holding her breath against the foul stench.

She thinks of the sinister German man with thick black glasses in the EWE-CAF office on the ground floor of Isa's Bangkok apartment building and feels sick.

There is a noise in the hall and Cassy senses Oghel's presence at the open door. She jumps up, exposing a breast as the sarong catches. Her left breast is completely covered in a tattoo of rosebuds in the process of opening into flowers. Hidden beneath them is the shadow of a skull. She quickly covers herself and rushes to stand in the bedroom doorway. An instinct makes her wary of allowing the two sides of her own personal mystery to come together. Oghel has already looked at the bed, however, and Cassy has seen his eyes take in first Beccy and then Leen. He withdraws, stepping quickly towards the front door.

"I think I must go now," he whispers. "See, I have my bag."

"Drugs?" he mouths. "You will need to phone for an ambulance?"

Cassy doesn't hear his words. She looks at a light about to be extinguished. She wants to hold him, to rescue him, to run away with him. Instead she lays one hand on his shoulder and leans to gently touch his cheek with hers. They hold their restrained embrace for a second that seems much longer, and then he is gone. With no further words he has opened the door, bag slung over his shoulder, and stepped out. She stands watching as he disappears down the stairs.

She spins round as a terrifying shriek comes from the bedroom; it is followed by a loud crash and the breaking of glass. Cassy slams the front door shut and runs back to find Leen on the floor again, with Beccy hovering, not sure what to do next. Leen is chanting, mantra-like, incoherently, over and over again. Even before Cassy can distinguish the precise sounds that make up the word, she knows what it is. It is her own mantra that rings repeatedly in her mind as she goes over and over the endless, seemingly insoluble puzzle that has engulfed her life.

"Cleito! Cleito! Cleito!" Leen is chanting with a dull, mindless horror.

***

As Cassy steps back into the bedroom, Leen whips round with hatred and fear in her eyes. She leaps to her feet with an unnatural strength and lunges towards Cassy.

"Cleito!—I saw him. Cleito. Cleito…"

***

Leen's face distorts into something that resembles a fierce dog and she growls as she lunges. Cassy dives aside as Leen flies past. There is a framed photograph in Leen's hand. The glass is broken and there are rivulets of blood on her wrist. She turns in the hallway for a moment, looking back into the bedroom and then at Cassy, and then twists round as if seeing invisible eyes staring at her from the other doors leading from the hall.

"We can't escape," she says, dropping her voice and shaking violently.

Then, turning on Cassy with the dog's face reappearing, she screams, "Why do you keep a photo of him in your bedroom? I thought you were a friend. You are the same as the others. I always knew. You've been tricking me. Ugh! Her too."

She spits towards Beccy and snarls and as she does, backs towards the front door like a cornered animal. "You slept with him like the others, didn't you? Huh? I can see it—I'll show you, I'll show you all..." She turns and with the same unnatural force wields the metal photo frame against the glass sidelight window that borders the front door, following it through with her fist. Cassy turns her eyes as Leen twists her arm again and again in the jagged glass, and hears Beccy retch behind her.

Before either have time to react, there are heavy footsteps running up the stairs two at a time and a man's voice calls out: "What's happening in there, Dr. Kim? Open up the door *now!*"

It is vaguely familiar, and when Cassy releases the latch, two dark-suited men barge in. One goes straight to the impaled Leen, pulling a pair of latex gloves from an inside pocket as he crouches down; the other shouts a call sign into his in-ear phone and asks for backup and medical. Leen is bleeding badly. Beccy has Leen's blood on her hands and Cassy's on her cheek. Cassy's head is still oozing where the rose thorns she had carefully prepared had embedded into her scalp as she pressed against Oghel's crown.

"What is it with you, Dr. Kim?" the agent asks as he fiddles with a button on the back of the earpiece. "A handsome young man comes in a taxi, you spend two hours with him alone before two young ladies turn up in a second taxi. Then there's screaming and you're all covered in blood. I take it she did this to herself... or is your man friend a psychopath? Where is he anyway?"

Thank God. Oghel got away unnoticed.

All Cassy can think of saying is: "Tell Buchanan we've found Leen."

"And loverboy? Who's he?"

She is sure the watcher must know the answer to that already.

But it is no longer Oghel who is on Cassy's mind; it is the other man in her life.

Zach. Her ex-husband, the husband who had walked out on her and whose picture she can't remove from her bedroom. Cleito? Surely there can be no connection—Leen is confused. She is seeing ghosts from her miserable past. Cassy gingerly picks up the silver-framed photo, its glass smashed and the picture of Zach smeared with Leen's blood. A ghost from her own past swoops upon her and as it takes her in its embrace she stumbles.

Beccy catches her and says in a hoarse whisper: "Zach?"

"Zach," Cassy echoes. "I've just seen it all very clearly."

Chapter 40

Kent, England
March 2001

THROUGH TURBULENT EDDIES of mist emerges the outline of a classical building. Slender colonnades topped with a triangular portico, and then the silhouette of a man. The cloud thins for a moment to reveal Ashi's aristocratic Persian profile. He is sitting cross-legged on a tiled bench, the mosaic fresco of a minaret behind him to one side and classical Doric columns to the other. He looks very much at ease between the two cultural references. Cassy has tracked him to his health club. It is the time of reckoning.

"Cassy?" he exclaims uncertainly, peering through the steam. "Good God, girl, you could give a man a heart attack! A ghost from the past in a polka-dot swim suit."

It is almost six months since Cassy last met Ashi—at the debriefing meeting that had shattered what remained of her professional self-esteem. She had learnt not long after that he had been promoted and gone to Washington to work with his American counterparts.

Oghel had also stepped out of her life at that time. He had left her apartment after the Leen episode and vanished. No one had seen him since. There was just a scribbled note left on the Korean stool where they had so nearly consummated the relationship that had been snatched from them. Isa too had disappeared—as he had told her he would. The Thai police had agreed to classify the search for him under their counter-terrorist programme, for which they receive U.S. funding, but he was nowhere to be found. Leen had recovered from the suicide attempt but had deteriorated badly and is now a permanent inmate in a secure psychiatric unit in a quiet suburb of Brussels. Cassy has received a letter offering a research fellowship financed by the Home Office that carries enough funds to keep her independent of any other university commitments. Her security risk status has been downgraded. Another letter, signed by Banton and requiring her signature, has bound her to secrecy about all matters arising from her involvement with the intelligence agencies—*past, present, and future*. No one said what this phrase means, but Cassy knows that she has not seen the end of it.

It has taken half a year to pluck up the courage to confront Ashi. Cassy had once been on friendly terms with the housekeeper at the farm, and had managed to establish that Ashi was due home from Washington for a week, en route to somewhere in the Middle East.

Cassy sits, legs tucked to her chest defensively, in a corner on the opposite side of the steam room from her one-time lover, friend, and confidant.

"I have to talk to you, Ashi. Sorry if it makes your life difficult, but it won't be half as bloody difficult as mine has been for the past year."

With too much time to run through the many competing explanations, she has drawn a few conclusions about her personal involvement in the Noah Brotherhood affair and wants to put him on the spot.

"I know about Zach," she announces as an opener.

The steam room suddenly becomes even quieter. Ashi is holding his breath.

"We thought they had lost him," he says.

"They?"

"The Israelis. You know about him, but you don't know who he was working for? I'm surprised they haven't told you. There's no reason why not now. The Americans were questioning his loyalty."

"He worked for the Israelis?" she says, trying to contain her astonishment.

"Works. They'd lost touch with him. Well before the Essaouira raid."

"He's a Mossad agent? How long..."

She stops, not wanting him to answer the question. She considers the revelation.

"They recruited him when he was in London working with you. 1993, it would have been. An obvious target. MIT and Cambridge graduate, multiple languages, and working on a classified project with the Brits and Americans. I'm surprised we didn't get him first."

"You never told me," she says, at a loss to know how to express the numbing sensation spreading like a quick-action anaesthetic.

"I didn't know. Not then."

"You should have bloody told me, Ashi."

"I couldn't—you know that."

He was right, but she hated him for it.

"But you're telling me now."

"About his involvement in Essaouira? No—you're telling me. It was one of the world's best-kept secrets. There were only a handful of us who knew. Nigel didn't. I'm not even sure about Banton."

"When did you find out?" she asks.

"About Zach? Not long after he moved into action."

"You briefed him on the Noah Brotherhood? Set him up with a believable history of cult involvement?" It was a guess.

"That and more. The Americans often came to me for that sort of thing in those days—where the Middle East or Pakistan was concerned."

"And now you work for them?"

"It's a secondment."

So Zach broke his relationship with me to infiltrate the Essaouiran end of Odam's operation. A joint venture—Americans, British, and Israelis. Screw you, Ashi. Screw you all.

She has lost the energy she had waited so long for in preparing for this confrontation, and tucks her head into her knees.

Not long after she had last seen Ashi, she had recalled Isa's account of how he had come to hear of the Russian naval survey and how the tape had suddenly turned up on

Odam's shopping list for Solon. The ensuing thought had made her physically sick.

"You helped Zach research the story of the Muscovite Muslim and the Russian submarine image?" she says from between her knees.

He doesn't answer immediately, and she wonders if she's completely missed the mark.

He lets out a long sigh, which has the effect of clearing some of the steam between them. He is gazing distantly into the be-fogged room.

"I'm sorry they had to do it to you, my dear. It was a pure piece of opportunism. Zach chanced upon Isa's Muscovite story when he was with him in Bangkok, visiting the Sufi with some of the others from Essaouira. It was not long after the sect was taken over by Asmir's envoy. I think the ruse was Zach's idea originally. He saw how obsessed Isa was about Eden and the seafloor. Isa told Zach about his *final sign* of the approaching doomsday he'd had in a dream in his youth. Contriving the sign seemed a perfect way to get someone very close to him. Believe me, everything else had been tried. It was a long shot, but there was not a lot to lose, and it wasn't a very expensive operation as these things go. We had a completely unorthodox enemy and had the creative thinking team in to help us dream up an unorthodox tactic."

Her stomach knots at the sudden and unrepentant disclosure of callousness. She hugs herself more tightly. The conspiracy was even more complete than she had imagined.

"The Americans were just about ready to take him out. Asmir—your friend Isa. If he's still in the land of the living he can thank Mossad he's still alive. If it weren't for Zach's plan, he'd have been dead two years ago. The Israelis had been insisting for a long time that Isa is a front for Asmir, not Asmir himself. If that was so, liquidating Isa would have made matters even worse—we'd have had only shadows. Zach's plan was the last chance. The last in a long list of unsuccessful covert actions."

"And the American's three-in-one theory?" Her voice is tight.

"Intelligence from a workshop of Islamic sect researchers hosted by the Saudis in late 1998. The Americans quite suddenly became aware of the rising threat from Bin Laden and were frantically trying to map his network of ex-Mujahedeens. That's when the Nooh Brotherhood rose towards the top of the list. Before that workshop I don't think they had much of a clue."

"And I confirmed their theory for them so they could finally take Isa out?"

Cassy can see the three-in-one theory more clearly now than ever before. Asmir's schizophrenic charade played masterfully over half a century. It would help explain why he had never been caught. At any one time, only one of his personas being acted out in full flesh and blood with the other two taking their respective parts in a carefully managed shadow play. Asmir, wooing the world as the winsome Isa. Nooh, exiting centre stage to make way for him. It had been a strange turn of phrase that Isa had used when talking about his brother Nooh: Nooh's life was *taken by an errant brother.* Something else Isa had said comes back, too. It is a reference to Odam during their journey to the airport after their first meeting.

One day he will rise to extinguish the light—brother against brother.

A metaphorical extinction—a fading of Sufi Isa to give way to Sufi Odam?

Cassy has become too numbed to the whole affair over the past six months to be angry anymore. But what Ashi is now disclosing is stirring things up. *Contriving the sign*, Ashi had said.

"The tape that arrived in Essaouira was fabricated?" she asks.

"Not the whole tape, just the ruins of Atlantis. It was a good piece of work, don't you think? The image tape itself was the genuine article from Russian Naval archives. Having heard about the Muscovite's rumour, it didn't take too much effort to verify that there was, in fact, a Soviet Navy collection of curios—although it turned out to be kept in a mothballed museum in the Arctic port of Archangel, not the main archives in St. Petersburg. We considered fabricating an entire image, but once we'd discovered the Russian original, we thought it would be neat to use it. It was cheaper than paying the Royal Navy, anyway—they offered to extract a suitable image from our own Trident submarine surveys for a ridiculous fee. All we had to do was to hire a minor Russian crook to steal the thing and then later to replace it. The operation probably only cost five thousand quid."

What breathtaking bloody nonchalance. "So if you had the original tape, what did you need to fabricate?"

"The CIA image lab couldn't find anything unusual on it."

They obviously hadn't been looking for undersea rivers.

"How did the tape get into the hands of the Essaouira sect?" She is now looking up, becoming, to her own disgust, a measure intrigued by the artfulness of the plot.

"Zach made up a story about bumping into an expert on Russian museums—one of the 1960's music-loving tourists visiting their little village. Zach spread it around that intrigued by the community's Atlantis beliefs, the tourist had mentioned a collection of curios amassed by the Russian Navy. The collection included a tape containing a mysterious seafloor image. Zach told Solon that the Russian had come across a document describing the tape when doing some archive research and had given him details of where it could be examined if members of the sect were interested. Solon fell for it immediately and put the tape on his shopping list when one of Asmir's stooges next came to broker a deal with the Russian gang that's been using the cult. It couldn't have worked better—we received a report of a break-in at the archive within three months of Zach telling Solon about it. Our guys had only just replaced the doctored tape and a fictitious official document describing it. It was a beautiful operation which also turned out to be a neat way of tracking the cult's criminal connections in Northern Russia."

"Korean sardine fishermen," she says.

"Sardines? You don't miss a detail do you, Cassy?"

"So the tape was stolen from the archive, doctored by the CIA, and returned," she says in wonderment.

"Temporarily removed well before Zach spun his yarn to Solon, but as I say, we were almost caught out by the speed of the response. Our crook in Archangel only got it back in its dusty box and the document in place the week before Asmir's guys turned up.

"We were all a bit disappointed not to find anything on the tape—I'm sure the sniff of ancient mystery helped speed the project through the bureaucracy. But the CIA image lab had a great time designing a bit of Atlantis."

"And once everything was in place, Zach tells Isa that I am the only person in the world who can interpret the tape, find its location? I think he might have told Solon too. It wasn't only Isa who was waiting on my analysis."

"Zach was acting with the noblest of motives."

At that, Cassy wants to walk over and hit him. But she hasn't enough energy to do anything but sit hugging her knees.

"Why did Zach tip me off about the forest rendezvous?"

It was the only explanation she had been able to find for the Cleito email.

"Now that, old friend, is a puzzle to us all. It wasn't in the plan and it meant that you were viewed with the greatest of suspicion throughout. We had this wonderfully sophisticated plan in place and had just set it in motion when all of a sudden you had some sort of inside knowledge about the Sufis. You discovered them before you were meant to. The Americans think Zach panicked into sending an emergency warning—about something of great immediate importance. WMD in London, perhaps. If he had his own reasons for not wanting to contact his Israeli masters, it doesn't surprise me that he thought of you as an alternative."

For a fleeting second, the thought touches her vulnerability, and the anger that has been constricting her like an icy sarcophagus momentarily melts as she pictures Zach at a moment of crisis thinking of her. But it is only momentary. The weight of the treachery returns with even greater impact.

"The wooden box," she says. "I found in the tree—it was heavy, and I'm sure it had a false base. It could have contained a weapon component."

She suddenly sees very clearly how it might have been with Odam's—or Asmir's—operation. She still cannot bring herself to think of it as Isa's. Multiple layers of fronting and deception.

The renegade Iraqi agents in East London would have been part of the supply chain.

"My own conclusion," Ashi says, "is that it was a momentary inspiration on Zach's part to perfect his plan. He had the idea of giving you a lead that would let you make your own approach to Isa. He was familiar with the Sufi website, of course, and the words it contained, and he emailed you a clue he knew you couldn't resist following up. If it worked it would be a brilliant finishing touch to the charade, making both you and Isa feel as though some inexplicable propulsion—the hand of God—had drawn you to each other. And don't tell me it didn't work—just look at what happened to you. Zach engineered your almost-conversion to Sufi Isa. That's got to be a counter-terrorism first."

"Screw you, Ashi." But she only whispered the curse into her knees.

"Zach was based in Essaouira at the time—he hadn't always been living with the cult—and we know that he had occasional access to the internet when he found himself alone in the office of one of the Essaouira businesses linked to the cult. I suspect he had such a chance on the day you received your *Cleito* email but was interrupted."

"Why might he have wanted to avoid contact with the Israelis?"

"We think he didn't trust the Mossad officer running him."

"So I jumped one step ahead of your prize-winning bloody plan by collecting the tape from Sami, and Zach jumped one step ahead of it by introducing me to the Bangkok Sufi. We'd make a good team," she says sardonically. "What if I hadn't found the Noah Brotherhood's website?"

"There was a plan to get you to Bangkok to meet Isa and get the tape anyway. That's why Buchanan was so upset when he found you'd been there already. He didn't know Zach had been infiltrated into Essaouira. He just knew the basic game plan with the tape. You caught everyone by surprise—and aroused no end of suspicion. You can imagine the sort of things people started thinking. They'd been hatching a covert action plan of the highest security order and all of a sudden you seemed to be ahead of them on not one but two counts: Bangkok and Essaouira. It almost blew the project out of the water. The Americans and Israelis accused us of running our own sideshow without telling them."

Cassy's mind is spinning, trying to take in the immensity of it.

"You're getting too hot in here, my dear," Ashi says, observing her expression, which is actually paler than when she had entered. "It requires practice to endure Turkish steam. Let's get out before you collapse on me."

He carefully lifts one leg out of his semi-lotus position and gingerly takes some weight on it before beginning to unfold the other. But he stops and looks up as Cassy leaps out of her corner, strides over to stand right in front of him, hands on hips, and then slaps him on the face, hard. Then again. And again, and a fourth time.

Having taken his punishment like a man, he leans forward to nurse his bruised cheek. It is then that she brings a knee up to smash brutally into his face. Ashi falls back under its force, smacking his head on the tiled wall behind him and then slumping onto the bench. He is making a strange wheezing and gurgling noise and she realises that she has broken his nose. He raises himself on an arm and she is shocked to see that he is afraid.

"Was Oghel Zach's idea too?" she demands.

"I'm sorry, Cassy," he says, breathing heavily and holding his blooded nose, "but there have been compensations that you might thank me for…"

She stands there for a moment glaring down at him, and then turns and goes back to her corner.

Instead of walking out and calling security, he continues talking in a nasal snuffle. It is a measure of his guilt that he is willing to bear the mistreatment. It is his confession and penance.

"The Israelis discovered Oghel years ago. They were tracking bad money and found it in his bank account. They pieced together a picture from interviews with the Syrian Orthodox authorities in Turkey and local sources in Oghel's hometown. They followed the trail to Central Asia and found a family that had adopted him from a wandering radical Sufi. No one doubts where the money comes from, but nothing's ever been proven." He paused, as though testing the response.

"Go on," she says, now commanding the conversation from her corner, not retreating.

"By getting Oghel close to you at the same time as getting you close to Isa, we reasoned we could flush out our bad guy from two directions. I had the idea when I heard Oghel had studied computer science for his first degree and graduated top of a class of two hundred but couldn't get a scholarship for further study."

"*You* had the idea?"

"Like I said—sorry that it had to happen. National security and all that." He winces in pain.

"A pincer movement," Cassy says, staring at him, trying to hate him but failing.

"How did you find my secret pad? You must have had an expensive trail assigned to me. Since buying that place I've never approached it in a way that's anywhere near direct."

"The Home Office regularly investigates a sample of cash sales of Central London properties. It would be too costly to do all of them. The checks always throw up a few bad apples. Not that they have pinned anything on you yet. Where did you get that kind of cash, Cassy?"

So, they don't know the full story. Oghel kept his secret.

"Was Oghel working for your lot, the Israelis, or what when he hacked into my office computer?"

"Oh, that was Banton," he says with a snort that could be a mimic of the old bulldog or an attempt to clear his blooded nose. "A typically nasty touch. Sorry, I couldn't do anything. It was designed to bring you and Oghel closer together. Get the young man to try to complete the Home Office's job and track down any illegal cash flows helping Dr. Kim sustain a secret luxurious lifestyle. A bit of pressure so two hard-done-bys would find solace in each other's company. I asked them to go easy on you. The trouble was, I knew it would work. He cuts an impressive figure, does he not? The official theory on your secret stash of money is that you were partnered up with Zach on Mossad pay for a while. Maybe you still are…? Some think so. The Israelis have denied it, of course, so what can be done? At some stage I guess you can expect an interrogation on the subject. Right now you're too fragile and at the same time too useful. Anyway, did you get him into bed?"

"Had anyone got close to Oghel before?" She chooses not to rise to the bait, surprised by how the barb hadn't hurt. Since her consummation with Oghel—which is how she likes to think of it, since for her, that is what it was—she knows that her nymphomania has been less compulsive. She even dares to believe that Oghel may have cured her of the bittersweet handicap she has been enslaved to for as long as she can remember. She rests the side of her head on her knees and looks at Ashi while thinking about that evening.

"You should know the answer to that one," Ashi snuffles. "You could hardly accuse the man of wearing his heart on his sleeve. He's as closed a book as Isa: self-possessed and content in his semi-cloistered world. I think there have been one or two attempts in the past but he's too closed, too intelligent to have casual acquaintances uncover much about his past. It would have been no good hauling him in and subjecting him to the heavy stuff since it was quite clear he had no contact with the Sufis apart from the anonymous money transfers. Believe me, he's been watched like a hawk since the Israelis discovered him. Not a penny of his funds from Asmir has been used for anything other than innocent educational and living expenditure. He's been followed whenever he's taken off on one of his retreats and it's always only ever been just that—the young man seems to need to get away. The people he stays with are always squeaky clean."

"Do they know where he is now?" There is hope in her eyes, her face still resting contentedly on its side on her knees.

"It seems not."

"So not followed well enough when it really mattered." She likes that.

"That was the beauty of it, you see, Cassy. We needed someone to get *really* close—or as close as anyone can to someone who's taken some sort of monastic vows. Getting him over here to study under your tuition was a perfect solution, and fitted in a bizarre sort of way with Zach's plan. There was always a danger of an unforeseen interaction effect, of course—something arising from your friendship with Isa that threatened your friendship with Oghel or *vice versa*. But everyone eventually agreed that the additional dynamic added value to plan. It'll find its way into a textbook one day. The Israelis were pretty sure Oghel wasn't actually in touch with his benefactor—in recent years, at least—and they seemed to be convinced of his religious vows. What they liked about it was the chance for you to probe him about contacts in the past and the probability that something quite unexpected would turn up as you two played your tender dance."

"I suppose I should feel flattered at the role dreamed up by my ex-husband and my ex-lover," she says in a distracted voice.

"Don't take it too hard, Cass—you played a key part in a brilliantly successful operation. It's going to go down as a classic in the new Cold War that seems to be coming upon us."

"Fine. Great," she says, drifting even further from Ashi's hurtful words.

"I've convinced everyone that Isa's the bad guy. A schizophrenic mass murderer. Wonderful. That was the objective of the whole operation, I suppose."

"That, plus hard evidence about the cult's link to the American plane disaster, its agenda and ambitions, and ways of breaking into its unbelievably obscure networks. It was simple and elegant; you've got to agree. And it worked—you came up trumps. Someone's going to get a knighthood out of this, Cassy, and I'm sure they'll find a way of honouring you in time. We could have got more out of it, but you take what you can in this game."

"Where is Zach now?"

"No one knows. He's out there, we know that for sure—but no one knows where he is or who he's working for. The Israelis have tried to pull him in, but he's evasive and has got access to money. It's one of the few unsatisfactory loose ends from an otherwise perfect op."

Then, standing up, keeping his eyes on hers, he asks, "Who was it that debriefed you about Zach?"

"Work that one out for yourself," Cassy says, standing up herself and wrapping a towel around her. "And I hope you get into one hell of a mess for it."

"No one did, huh? You always were a sly old fox, Cassandra dear. I deserved to fall for that one."

"Okay, now we're on the level, tell me this: if everyone knows everything about Oghel and he was set up from the start, why were the Americans planning to swoop in and pick him up a few days after that last debriefing?"

Ashi slung his towel around his shoulders and looked at her blankly.

"It wouldn't have made any sense at all, as far as I can see. You must have got that one wrong, Cassy."

She knew she hadn't misheard the conversation as she had left Nigel's office. But she had got it wrong. The American must have been talking about Isa when he said they would pick up Dr. Kim's friend in a few days. It looks as though she had chased Oghel out of her life for no reason.

Chapter 41

April 2001
Lake District National Park, Northern England

IT IS APRIL and there is snow on the hills. Spring started, but an unusual weather system brought it to a halt with waves of Arctic blizzards. The sun is now shining, but it has been that way all week: first clear open skies, and then thick snow, driven horizontally by sub-zero winds.

Cassy's solitude of the last six months has had an unexpected effect. Her professional judgement has been summarily dismissed; she has been publicly humiliated and abused by those who had once taken her body. But she has found comfort in her own counsel. She is not sure whether it was the conversation with Ashi in the steam room; that had certainly been a turning point, or whether she had really started to change in some profound way through her "consummation." Or was it through her quiet acceptance of a bond with Isa? Perhaps the consummation had been anything but that: more of a washing-away of something.

Whatever it is that has happened inside, she knows that while all the facts are stacked against her, she has decided that Isa is innocent and Washington's three-in-one theory wrong.

She knows what Odam is after. It suddenly seems so obvious, and the revelation is chilling.

"You know why you're here?"

"I've been briefed."

"Airline investigators ruled out the hypnosis-suicide theory once and for all—did Banton tell you that?"

"Of course."

"Did he tell you why?"

"Of course not."

He chuckles. She has grown to almost like Hugo—he seems different from the rest somehow. She wonders what his background is. He looks older than when they had last met.

"The Americans spoke to your friend in California and sequestered his data."

"Oh?" She had imagined they would have done that, but has heard nothing.

"You were right—up to a point. Well done, Cassandra; you're a fine professional. Don't let Banton's goading get to you."

"Up to a point?"

"We haven't yet made a link with the American girl in the forest—but we're still working on it. You can't always rush these things—sometimes it's better to sit and watch. But there are some interesting patterns of financial transactions emerging."

"What about the other groups on Jerry's list?"

"We think we've found an ROC connection with at least two of them."

He looks at her with curiosity and says, "A word of warning, Dr. Kim—you might want to think about guessing it wrong a bit more often. You'll have people suspecting you know something we don't—or that you've picked up some of your friend Isa's mystical abilities."

"What about the contaminated dustbin in the Forest? There's something that didn't work out too well. We got to it too late."

"You've got some damn good qualities, Kim. I'm sorry all this has happened."

His mood has suddenly turned sombre and distracted, as though he is thinking through a weight of unhappy consequences of a decision he or someone else had made, Cassy being just one of them.

"Don't be," she says. "I'm beginning to feel good about myself again. Patronising doesn't help the recovery."

"Glad to hear it. You'll play the part tomorrow, then?"

There is hesitancy in his eyes, almost a pleading. Even people like Hugo need to justify themselves.

"I wasn't talking about tomorrow. I feel good about myself because I know what game Sufi Odam's playing."

He takes a step back to gain a better vantage point from which to examine her. They are standing by a window in a large period conservatory built into the side of an old house overlooking Lake Windermere in England's historic Lake District. He turns to the window, taps the glass as though testing it, and then rubs a hand down the old ironwork window frame, withdrawing it quickly as he snags a sharp edge. A single spot of blood appears on his forefinger and he puts it to his lips thoughtfully.

"Which is?"

"Odam's a broker. He brokers deals between organised crime and a ragbag of independent fanatical cults he seems to have won or bought the allegiance of. The cults get funds in return for services rendered. Money and ancient artefacts channelled to the Essaouiran sect were paid for by a children-smuggling service but every case would have been a unique negotiation. Others will have paid by drug or weapons smuggling or money laundering. Odam's just a middle man."

"So you've said," Hugo says, examining his finger. "Darn clever analysis, Cassandra. The Israelis took years to work that one out. But it's old news. What does he get out of it? That's what we all want to know."

"Influence."

"Over what?"

"He uses the gangs and the cults with equal cynicism—uses his position to manipulate the conditions of the deals."

"In what way?"

"To perpetrate an agenda that's been his quiet obsession for over half a century."

"Moral corruption, political destabilisation, religious assassination? That's old hat too but it hasn't got us very far. It's all there, but none of it points in a single direction."

"That's because all that is just the sideshow—a diversion. His sights are higher than that. Time's running out for him and he's closing in on the ultimate strategy."

Hugo gives her his full attention.

"He arranged for the Essaouiran cult to purchase a quantity of ex-Soviet chemical WMD raw material from the Trotsky gang as part of the payment for people like Leen doing their child-trafficking bit. My guess is that the deal was subsidised by Iraqi dissident agents who thought they were paying the Russians for the goods and paying the cult to ship them."

"Why would Solon want weapon-grade toxins?"

"Malthusian genocide. In revenge for what people like him call *terracide*. Take a look at Jerry Mathias' list. All the groups are obsessed with the idea of revenging a violated earth, the destruction of nature by an out-of-control human species. It's written all over their websites."

"What interest does Odam share with eco-terrorists?"

"For most of them, none at all. Only with the most fanatical, those willing to pay any price."

He purses his lips, nodding thoughtfully. "Shake the foundations of the capitalist West. Push modern civilisation into some kind of reversion. An unlikely—but plausible—partnership."

"That would be a good result for Odam—that's what the plastic bin in the forest was all about. You remember the girl from the Human Extinction Front who shot herself while contaminating the Hamburg water supply? The HEF had suddenly come into big money. But Odam's after more than just shaking up the West."

"And what, do you suggest, could possibly be *more* than a chemical attack on London?" His eyebrows are raised, challenging her for a new insight that couldn't be instantly dismissed.

"A cleansed earth. A *new earth* and a *new Heaven*. Cleared and set on a path to starting all over again. Sufi

Odam believes himself to be a prophet of doom hastening the great Day of Judgement portrayed in the Koran."

Instead of switching off, his interest intensifies.

"He's planted an idea in the minds of a score of the most fanatical eco-cults, providing them with funds and materials, and is waiting to see what they do with it all. He's like a venture capitalist; the cults are the entrepreneurs. He funds, sows a few seeds of inspiration, and sits back to let the various perverse cultish economies take their course."

"An idea?"

"His favourite one, I think, is to detonate a high powered explosive device—preferably nuclear—at the site of an unstable volcano—a Caldera or Super-Volcano would be best—and trigger a volcanic winter. He's reasoned that the science says there's a tiny probability of this triggering a global freeze. Miniscule, perhaps, but a probability nonetheless. He believes that a global ice age will recreate Eden on the new land exposed by receding oceans as icecaps thicken across the globe. The ultimate suicide mission by the ultimate judgement freak. It's something he's been planning for fifty years or more."

***

There is a stunned silence. Then: "The ultimate suicide bombing. Huh? Switching the lights off and handing the planet over to some remnant generation? Good God, Cassandra. You're right. It's plausible. Bloody hell, woman."

"When the Toba Caldera in Indonesia blew seventy-five thousand years ago," she presses in while she has his attention, "anthropologists believe that the volcanic winter that followed reduced the world's human population to five to ten thousand individuals—almost to the point of extinction. The world's major volcanoes are potentially the most deadly but least guarded targets for the right kind of terrorist. It sounds bizarre, but under a severe volcanic winter it would take only a hundred and twenty years for most of the water in the oceans to transfer to ice sheets on the continents. Unbelievable, I know, but true."

Cassy's monosyllabic friend Mal MacFenn had asked an acquaintance at the Met Office long-term climate-modelling programme to run an unusual projection. She had been spooked when she received the answer and was spooked again, repeating it to Hugo. *The one-hundred-and-twenty-year warning*. A period of one hundred and twenty years: the length of time God gave Noah to prepare for the impending flood in Genesis. And one hundred and twenty years for the flood to reverse during a global freeze, re-exposing Eden on the seafloor.

Hugo stands staring at her for a second then turns and heads for the door.

"Hold on. I'll be back." It is said with more earnest than she has seen in any of his performances so far.

She moves to the window wondering what's coming next. The house is set back from the lakeside and perched on a rocky hill. To the left is a field backed by woods, and to the right, a drop to the lake with a view of a youth hostel and its private jetty. It is one of the largest hostels outside London and a favourite destination for overseas students and their families during the vacations. A coach draws up and a line of veiled women and girls bundle out followed by husbands, fathers, and brothers. The sound of laughter and playful shouts floats towards her as the men gather round to pick up luggage. It is a warm and homely scene but strangely set. Cassy envies the women with their menfolk and thinks of the simple fishing village in Southern Thailand.

Hugo returns and joins her at the window, breathing heavily, showing that he has run up the stairs. In his hand is some sort of official report with a "SECRET" chop stamped at the top.

"Malaysians," she says, nodding at the coach party by the lake.

"He disguises himself as a woman like that, did we tell you?"

"Odam, Isa—Asmir?"

"Just a rumour. Plus the passport you brought back and Jerry's data."

"More likely Odam's got a female accomplice—the Sufi sect allows women in its ranks. They have a women's house in Bangkok."

"Maybe," he says, gazing out of the window. "We held our breath a few years ago when the Israelis placed an agent in a house where an elderly Middle Eastern devout was due to be staying. She turned out to be a real woman. It involved an embarrassing moment, I believe."

Hugo laughs at the thought.

"An Israeli agent? Zach?"

He goes silent and stares at the craggy snow-covered mountains beyond the forested shores on the other side of the lake.

"So you've worked that one out too, huh? We suspected as much. How long have you known?"

Ashi had evidently kept quiet after their last conversation. She hadn't expected it and was pleased.

"It was when the Belgian girl did her thing in my apartment. She hadn't randomly picked up the photo of Zach." That was what Cassy had told her debriefers. "It was the photo that sent her berserk."

"I see. And that was the first time you got wind of it? We were worried a few times."

"My taking off to Essaouira?"

"We were priming you to take his place, you know—to become our number one person close to Isa. Zach set you up wonderfully and it was going to work. You wouldn't have needed to move in with them like he did. It wasn't working out that way for you. Much better your way. Quite amazing, really."

"Until I blew it a second time by having Odam's Thai base raided?"

"Within a month you moved from being the perfect infiltrator to being number one on Asmir's hit list."

"You should have told me."

"The Israelis wouldn't let us—they were too concerned for the safety of your ex-husband. And anyway, the way things worked out, you didn't have to know—not at that stage, anyway. Zach was out of action—the Israelis still don't know where he is."

"Do you?"

"I'm afraid not, but we know he's in the field and active."

Cassy is cross-checking Ashi's account.

"Wouldn't I have been compromised?" She recalls Isa's probing questions about her and his cryptic surmises.

"That's part of the beauty of it, Cassandra—don't you see? You were showing every sign of being taken in—coming under his spell. He was letting you get close to him, and that's all that mattered. If he felt he had you under his power he'd enjoy the game—perhaps the more so if he knew you'd come to spy on him. Our task was to keep you close enough on the side of normality to keep you useful to us. That's where the Americans wanted you."

She notices he doesn't say "that's where *we* wanted you."

So the hawks watching me so closely at those meetings will have been pleased with my performance. Patting themselves on their bloody backs. Not only did I confirm their hypothesis about Isa, but I also confirmed the merits of their own callous professional spycraft.

Before Cassy can say something suitably cynical, Hugo says it for her: "You have to have gone through the experience of crossing the line to be a *perfect spy* in these waters."

"Is that what happened to Zach?" she asks. "He went too far over the line?"

Hugo doesn't answer.

"You were throwing me to the enchanter to see what I could glean in the process of losing it? How do you control someone who's partially compromised their analytical powers—or their loyalties?"

"It's not like the old days in the Cold War," he says. "You can't get inside a cult without *feeling your way in*. You can't convince true believers for long if you don't *really* believe."

"The strategy of generals," she says with distaste. "Only I didn't sign up to be expensive cannon fodder."

"That's a bit harsh."

"Yes, it bloody is."

"We try to get them out before they reach the state of your Belgian friend."

"You do this as a matter of course?" Cassy is disgusted.

"It's usually dispensable assets we use for this sort of thing. People who can be turned and run for a little while before it all gets too much and they either go under or back over to the other side. Makes for patchy quality intel but it's often better than nothing. Zach was special, though. This is a special case."

"And I'm special too?"

"You had all the right qualities: maverick, deep thinking, clever, resourceful. You were too good an opportunity to let go. Brilliant forensic scientist with the right background. Failing in your university job because of your love for detective work, and on the margins at Scotland Yard because you're an academic—and an attractive woman at that. We figured we could find a way to help you take the bait once you'd agreed to help us look for Noah's Ark terrorists."

"Thanks for the career break. What now?"

He ignores the question.

"You understand people like these Sufis. You gave a stunning performance at the debriefing at Ashi's farm. Let's face it; you would have done well as Isa's friend. It wasn't just about Isa of course. Isa-Odam-Asmir is the target, but his links with undesirable agencies of one sort or another are so diverse, we had high hopes of what you could bring in. Anyway, I came to encourage you to participate at tomorrow's meeting."

"Yet another conference on East European organised crime links with terrorist groups," she says flatly. "I've got nothing further to offer, I'm afraid."

"I'm not looking for specific intel—we've plenty of that. I want you to ask questions, to put yourself in the place of your friend Isa—or Odam, if you prefer—and think what he would do. We've no idea where the big man is or if he's still alive, but his influences and cronies certainly still are. Something new's come up. I want you to help us *feel* our way a bit further with the evidence we'll be going over. That's how active intelligence works in this field. You had better get used to it."

Cassy considers what he is saying.

"So I'm an experimental intelligence device. Expose me to the facts and watch me extrapolate predictions on the basis of a soul-tie with an Islamic cult leader. Post-modern espionage at its most sophisticated. A cult-sensitive litmus. I'm flattered."

She pronounces it more as a conclusion than an accusation. She doesn't even shout or swear. Perhaps it is a final act of resignation.

All she can manage is, "You're amoral, you know. The lot of you."

"Dismiss and scoff if you want, Dr. Kim, but you've come up with something, and it will save lives. Lots of them, probably."

"What do you mean?"

He taps the report he is holding, leaving a smear of blood on it from his finger.

"Last month two Iraqis, a Yemeni, and two Russians died inexplicably in a mining accident in Russia."

"It was in the newspapers. A gas explosion in a decommissioned copper mine in Eastern Siberia."

"There was more to it."

"Like what?"

"It was fired by methane from agricultural waste dumped in the old mineshaft but the roof caved in because of three huge charges of high explosive very expertly placed along the main entry tunnel."

"Who were the dead?"

"The Iraqis, both ex-Sadaam secret service types, were working for a group based in Islamabad and linked to Bin Laden. One was staying in East London for a while last year—I think you were once briefed about him. He was a chemical engineer with sophisticated munitions experience. The Yemeni was also known to us—Hisham Moustafa. As well as perfect English and Arabic, he had fluent Russian from his days as an undergraduate in Moscow State University during South Yemen's Communist period and passable Mandarin from five years doing a PhD at Beijing's elite Quing Hua University."

"And?"

"His major was in economics and international banking. He was a Mujahedeen leader for four years in Soviet occupied Afghanistan, turned up a few years later as a businessman living in South Kensington, spent a few months in Ulaanbaatar in 1991 helping the Mongolian Government set up the Mongolian Stock Exchange and then in the mid-1990's came on the radar again living briefly with a group of Sufi refugees."

"In Bangkok."

"In Bangkok."

"And since then?"

"Various places around the world, ending up working on an Egyptian passport in a multinational shipping office in the Siberian port of Vladivostok. Looks like he'd been there for about six years."

"And the dead Russians?"

"That, I think, is where you may have hit payday, as our American friends say."

"The Trotsky gang?"

"No—another ROC gang, prominent in the early years after the Soviet collapse, but then dropped out of competition for the usual type of underground business in order to specialise."

"In what?"

"Army surplus."

"Obviously not uniforms."

"Weapons-grade uranium from warheads, live warheads, and small non-nuclear missiles from a major stockpile in Kalingrad Oblast on the Lithuanian border. They also have access to the one hundred and second Military Base in Gyumri, Armenia, and can source from five other smaller sites spread across the former Soviet empire. It's a strategy that gives them source-flexibility and makes them a reliable supplier, dominating the market. The brother of one of the gang members used to be high up in Gosatomnadzor, or the so-called GAN—Russia's nuclear inspectorate. That seems to be how they developed such a powerful market position."

"So two Russian weapons suppliers meet two Iraqi weapons buyers and a Yemeni middleman representing Sufi Odam in a derelict Russian copper mine. Why were they all killed there instead of doing a deal?"

"We found part of the answer to that in a hotel room in the nearest town, fifty miles away from the mine. It's a very remote area. We have a shrewd idea who might have been doing what in the transaction but the motivation has eluded us. But you may have hit on something, Dr. Kim."

He tries to conceal it but there is definitely a smugness as he said it and Cassy senses, with surprise, her excitement rising as he is talking.

"What was in the hotel room?"

"Four more bodies."

"Before or after the mine explosion?"

"Killed the same day. All the deceased—at the mine and the hotel—were part of a group booked on an organised tour of the old copper mine due to happen two days after the killings took place."

"What kind of group goes on a tour of a disused mine in Eastern Siberia?"

"The mine's owner is SIMECHIN, a small Moscow-based copper exploration firm owned by a Saudi Arabian mining conglomerate and recently listed on the London Stock Exchange's Alternative Investment Market for small-caps. The tour was put on by SIMECHIN for professional mining investment analysts from AIM, the London FT, the Shanghai Stock Exchange, the Hong Kong Stock Exchange, and an assortment of private investors specialising in small-cap mining companies. The price of copper's going up fast due to the Chinese, and there's a lot of new prospecting going on around abandoned deposits. The Russians think that whoever planted the explosives was going for a quick and easy indiscriminate kill of the whole tour group. Moustafa and his unlucky companions, however, seem to have made an unofficial trip before the main event and triggered the explosion. That left some of the targets back in the hotel. The guess is that as soon as the killers realised the smaller party was on its way to the mine, they hurriedly dealt with the remaining targets in a more messy way and fled the scene."

"Two separate groups," she says, thinking aloud. "It makes sense. Who died in the hotel?"

"A Moroccan, an American, and two men travelling on Iranian passports. What makes sense?"

"How old were the Iranians?"

He pauses and looks at her pointedly. "One old man, the other in his thirties."

Her chest goes suddenly very tight and her breathing quickens to overcome the restriction.

"That's what we thought too," he says, acknowledging her reaction. "Bound and gagged, I'm afraid, with a bed sheet draped over each head to protect the killers from splashing blood. Then their throats slit."

"Any lead on the killers?"

"The Russian Embassy gave us the hotel's guest list. There are two other Russians that we recognise who checked in a day after the investor group. They turned out to be members of the Trotsky gang. They were gone by the time the police arrived, as were two Central Asians who arrived with the other investors."

"So, four suspects," she says, summarising aloud. "Two Central Asians arrive with the investor group and two Trotskyites arrive the day after. All disappeared after nine people were killed, five in the mine and four in the hotel. Anything else?"

The picture is already complex enough, but she senses that it has to get more complex before she has a chance of spotting the full pattern.

"The shipment logistics," Hugo says. "Russian intel linked a stolen van found abandoned in the hotel parking lot with a container ship due to sail from Vladivostok a week later. The Russian police assume that one party or other was planning to load weapons on the ship, which was doing the short haul to Osaka to pick up High Definition flatscreen TV's, Honda bikes, and car parts, and then continue on to Seattle."

"How did they link the van to the ship?"

"When the van was picked up, they found a map in a glove compartment—map of the docks and a copy of a ship's bill of lading with transaction details for a single container and the ship's itinerary. But that wasn't all as luck has it. The van was stolen a year ago from a truck stop in the Siberian interior and spotted with false plates in Vladivostok a few months later. When the local cops hauled in the driver they were embarrassed to find that it was someone Moscow had under surveillance for international money laundering—Moustafa who died in the mine. Moustafa, it seemed, had bought the van from a legit secondhand dealer so, under instructions from Moscow the cops apologised, let him keep it, and Moscow kept him under surveillance. Although the Russian police haven't admitted it, it seems they hadn't realised who exactly he was. He went quiet on the money-laundering front and the next thing they know, the van turns up in the parking lot of a multiple-homicide scene. Moustafa was on vacation from his work at the time of the mine explosion. He didn't turn in for work on the Monday he was due back."

"So where's the uranium or warheads or whatever it was that was being transacted?" Cassy asks. "I assume it didn't sail to Osaka and Seattle."

"Disappeared. The Russians assume the killers took the spoil but they've traced neither them nor it. The Russians had it wrapped up as one gang plundering another. Nothing out of the ordinary—everyone getting their just desserts. Greedy baddies having a bad fight with each other, most end up dead, the victors disappear. QED. End of case."

"Tell me, was there any evidence that Moustafa had made another trip to the copper mine before it was booby-trapped? He was in Vladivostok for five or six years, right?"

The urgency in her voice startles him.

"It's in the report," he says looking impressed. "The lone security guard cum caretaker who manned a gatehouse at the entrance to the site admitted to having taken a bribe about five years earlier when a group of three mining engineers paid him to have an unofficial look down one of the old shafts. He thought they were from a company interested in bidding for mining rights. One of the men he described sounds like Moustafa."

"Five years ago? What does that tell you?"

"The plan's been in place a long time."

"It's why Moustafa took a job in Vladivostok. He arrives there to work and shortly after goes prospecting in old mines. That means that he's part of something that's bigger than brokering a deal on behalf of some opportunist Iraqi terrorists."

"Moustafa was buying his own stuff from the Russians as well?"

"Let's assume that Moustafa was the broker, bringing buyers and sellers of WDM together, and as part of the deal, he arranges to take delivery of the weapons from the Russian suppliers in some remote spot and to store the goods in a safe place until the Iraqis arrived. That way he controls buyer and seller—a necessary position for a broker. He and others from Odam's network take the weapons to store in the mine. That's what he's got a van for. He needs to bring buyer and seller together within sight of the merchandise, but in a setting that is public enough to discourage any attempt to do anything foolish. The investors' tour would have been ideal for that. Moustafa knew the layout and would have found just the right place to secrete the goods—somewhere that could be reached in a short detour by the transacting parties. They might even have planned to exchange a briefcase or two of cash there and then to complete the deal—or if it wasn't cash, an account number certified by Moustafa and underwritten by Odam's credit and reputation."

"So why did Moustafa take both parties to the mine two days before the tour?" Hugo asks, echoing Cassy's own thoughts. "He got wind of something and rushed to conclude the business?"

"Say that when the Trotsky gang booked into the hotel the two Russian *sellers* got suspicious and pushed to close the deal immediately."

"If Moustafa's van was found at the hotel," she says, snatching the report and rifling through its pages looking for any other mention of the van, "how did he and his customers get to the mine? There must have been another vehicle."

She takes a deep breath as she mentally re-processes the evidence.

"There were two different groups of killers," she pronounces. "It has to be. The four at the hotel were murdered for a different reason and by different attackers than the five in the mine. I don't think the Trotskyists had any interest in the copper mine; they may not even have known which mine the investors' tour was about. All they knew was that Odam was coming to stay at that hotel. Finally he was on their soil and it was their long-awaited chance to avenge their lost colleagues on the AIA Bombay flight. They killed him and the others in the hotel room, but it wasn't they who blew the mine shaft—it was Odam's group."

She has dropped the report and is gripping his arm tightly.

"Odam had someone else working on the case," she says. "Someone closer to him than Moustafa. That person or persons wired the mine. Then, on some pretext Odam ordered Moustafa to organise the transaction early. Odam's other men drove them to the mine, triggered the explosion, and then disappeared. It would have been the two Central Asians. Moustafa must have hidden the payload somewhere in the shaft that was blown, and the Central Asians would have subsequently moved it and wired the shaft. Then they drove Moustafa and the other four to the mine to make the transaction, and left when all five had been blown to pieces. My guess is that the two Central Asians were the two who visited the mine with Moustafa five years earlier."

"Why would Odam have a highly skilled operator like Moustafa wasted along with the Iraqi buyers and Russian sellers?" Hugo's turn to ponder.

"Odam is ruthless. Probably just thought it was neater to clean up the entire operation in one go. Having them all die would also point the finger away from the Noah Brotherhood. Planting methane in the shaft made it look like a genuine accident, with broker and both sides and the payload buried under hundreds of tons of rock."

"Only the WMD had been moved," Hugo says, "and instead of being shipped to Seattle from Vladivostok by

Moustafa, the goods were taken away by Odam's two loyal Central Asian followers. But where?"

"I think it's still in the area—at the site or nearby. What do we know about the copper mine?"

"Uh... I'm not sure we have anything on that beyond a financial and technical prospectus issued by the mining company."

"Where? Where is it? Do we have it here?"

"No—it's back in London."

"Have it faxed through. The best quality ores—copper, gold, silver—occur in rocks formed as volcanic magma that didn't quite reach the surface. Under those conditions, metals that are normally dispersed in tiny quantities throughout a rock get sorted as they flow and when the magma solidifies, they form seams of pure metal. The richest seams tend to be found around ancient volcanoes. Some of those ancient volcanoes are also sites of current volcanic activity."

She lets go of Hugo and turns to look at the bleak mountain landscape the other side of Lake Windermere.

"So Odam found his volcano," she muses.

"And has a nuclear bomb to test his theory," Hugo says.

"If, as I suspect, this mine is located on the flanks of Mount Klyuchevskaya Sopke, then if there's one old shaft, there's a hundred others left over from Soviet Siberia's mining heyday. This shaft probably only had a caretaker at the old guard house because it was being kept mothballed for the right buyer. Mines with deposits more thoroughly exhausted would be left for the bears and bats. There's probably dozens within a few miles of our mine."

The sound of voices passing along the corridor has Hugo looking at his watch.

He exits without another word, leaving Cassy alone in the conservatory. He had no doubt originally planned to contrive casual chats with half a dozen others like her prior to the next day's conference. It was called *steering* a meeting—or stitching it up beforehand. But she had given him much more than he had bargained for.

As she watches, the gaps between the distant peaks fill with cloud. Five minutes later, the tops of the mountains are engulfed. Another snow blizzard is heading inland from the Irish Sea.

Reaching into her shoulder bag, Cassy pulls out a wad of papers. The 1950's Tehran photo is on top. She shuffles them in her hand like a flimsy pack of cards. The wind is picking up as the wall of cloud comes closer. She recalls how she felt in the headman's house with Isa and the children. Something stirs within as she watches the approaching snow. It is almost at the opposite edge of the lake now. The coach-load of Malaysians has stopped attending to the luggage, and they are standing motionless between the bus and the jetty, looking across the water. A party of boy scouts stands further along the jetty, also perfectly still, as if in awed anticipation of what is about to hit them. As she watches, more people flow out of the youth hostel, including kitchen staff with chequered aprons, one with a chef's hat on his head. She fiddles with an old latch and opens the window a crack. Her eyes water in the icy blast but her face warms with a flush of excitement. She looks at the piece of paper in her hand—the Cleito email that has changed her life:

"*The hundred-and-twenty-year warning is about to be given.*"

A period of one hundred and twenty years—the time God gave Noah to get ready for the great deluge.

The words of Isa come back with perfect clarity and, not for the first time, she is overcome by an insuppressible elation, a burst of joy that anaesthetises all contrary thoughts and emotions. She pictured the seer surrounded by laughing children again, and then pictures the stained-glass windows of St. Giles and the little church in the forest.

Perhaps she has crossed the line.

She smiles. She will perform well in the meeting tomorrow. Hugo will be proud of his new intelligence device. She has crossed the threshold—*the perfect postmodern spy*. It isn't only a euphoric joy that she feels; it is a reckless freedom. It feels as though she has traversed some boundary into freedom beyond.

The fearsome wall of cloud is halfway across the lake now and will be upon the house in a matter of minutes.

Isa. How could someone evil give such infectious hope?

It is upon them. First a few stray snowflakes, then a darkening of sky, and then thick, thick white snow. The assembled crowd on the jetty, engulfed in the whiteness, the hands of children and adults too, reaching upwards to feel the soft descending sky. After they have gone, for a while all she can make out is an iridescent emerald green glow from the youth hostel's neon sign. In a field nearby a lone lamb bleats for its mother.

***

Back in her tiny bedroom at the top of the house, Cassy sits on a wide old-fashioned windowsill and wipes condensation from the glass panes to watch the snow gathering on the ledge outside, then opens the window to scoop up a handful. White, pure, and crystalline, she holds it against her cheek, enjoying the numbing pain.

A movement in the corridor interrupts her thoughts and she turns to see the doorknob rotating as someone tries it from the other side. The door clicks open and a hand comes round to ease it open over the thick pile of a newly laid carpet.

"Oh! My apologies, Cassandra—I knocked but no one answered."

"I was far away," she says. "You've come to brief me about tomorrow too?"

"Just came to encourage you to chip in wherever you want."

"Hugo's already done that. I'm touched by all the concern."

They must be nervous about their new intelligence tool—they want to make sure I'm functioning properly.

"Tell me, Nigel," she says, "did the Russians have their own man trying to infiltrate the Noah Brotherhood in the 1950's?"

He looks beyond her towards the window, which has misted up again.

"How did you figure that?"

It had struck Cassy that the Russians might have had their own interest in tracking down a maverick populist leader roving through Muslim Central Asia.

"In 1951 a Russian team claimed to find Ark remains with an Islamic inscription carved in ancient wood. Was that a ruse to flush him out?"

"Gunther was the beginning of the CIA's copy-cat operation," he says. "It was more sophisticated than the Russian's and more successful."

"Not for Gunther."

"No. Not for Gunther."

"Let's hope it will all have been worthwhile," she says.

"It might turn out to be just that, Cassandra. Hugo had a word with me. Read this."

He hands her a single sheet of fax paper.

"Top cover of a technical report by the mining firm," he explains.

She looks at the patchy text, smudged in places, missing in others. Mount Klyuchevskaya Sopke. The volcanic mountains pictured in the photo in Isa's Bangkok apartment.

"You had better be right on this one, Cassy. Hugo is briefing the Minister of Defence as we speak and we expect the Russians to move in troops to search the mines within a matter of hours. You're booked onto the 8 p.m. BA flight to

Tokyo Narita tomorrow night with an Aeroflot connection Narita to Vlad fifteen hours later. They'll also show you the bodies, which are in cold storage—you might recognise some of them."

As his footsteps fade away down the corridor, she returns to the open window and hears voices in the driveway below. Hugo is talking to someone.

"Damn clever, that Dr. Kim. Damn clever girl."

A car door clicks open and an engine starts up.

"Chip off the old block—uncannily like her father. Both of them damn clever. Damn clever. We've done well. Very well indeed."

"Mother was North Korean, wasn't she?" says the other voice, more muffled.

"South Korean, but the North Koreans abducted her as a teenager. The NIS got her back with the help of the Americans and then recruited her. Sad loss—great team."

Cassy thrusts the window open and leans out in time to see Hugo disappearing into the rear of a black Mercedes and an arm of someone she can't see reach forward to slam the door shut as the driver pulls away.

Hugo knew my father. My mother was abducted by North Korea and escaped to work with the South Korean National Intelligence Service.

She turns, grabs her overnight bag, and flings everything into it, emptying the wardrobe in one sweep. She picks up a piece of white silk that has fallen to the floor. It is stained with dried blood running from top to bottom. Her wedding-night dress. The purity she never had, given back to her in pain and blood. A second chance. But her wedding-night partner had disappeared. Unnecessarily. Then she flees the room.

Hugo's conference can go to hell. If they want to fly me to Siberia, they can bloody well catch me.

Cassy Kim has finally been driven to do what she has been avoiding for so long: hunt down her estranged

adoptive mother and force her to answer a lifetime of questions.
###

Thank you!

THANKS FOR READING Noah's Art. If you've become a fan of Cassy Kim or perhaps, like her, have grown dangerously intrigued by brother Isa, perhaps you would be kind enough to spend a few minutes writing a review on Amazon. And of course, tell your friends that Noah's Art is a must-read. Subscribe to Noah's Art website for updates on the Noah Brotherhood trilogy, including sample chapters of the sequel: Adam's Eve: **http://www.noasartthenovel.net/**

Acknowledgements

THANKS TO SO many people who have encouraged this writing project, including Bill Massey, at the time, fiction editor at Headline Press, London, who read an early version; beta reading friends of various drafts, including G.A., Paul F., Jonathan B., Paul J., Andrew W., Maggie W., Malcolm and Franny F., Norman and Caroline A.; the librarians at the Cardiff University Arts and Social Science Library who keep such a rich collection of scholarly books about obscure Sufi sects; Martin G., for a story of a Kabul market mystic; Wendell E. for loaning me a book about Sufi poetry years ago in Casablanca; Andrew G. for *Arumim*; Mark P. for the cosy dinners with Shadow Cabinet members of the U.K. Government; the Chinese intelligence official who gave me a Uigar dagger from Xinxiang Province; and the American geologist authors of a 1970's book about ice-reversal theory "Subdue the Earth" (the cover of my copy is long since gone and I cannot find it in any archive or catalogue). The book intrigued me with its unorthodox theory about global ice ages and regular ice-water reversals and in many ways led to the plot of Noah's Art. The greatest debt is to my long-suffering and ever-supportive wife, who never once complained about my creative indulgence.

About the Author

J.B. DUKES (NOM de plume) is a professor, with positions in two of the world's leading universities. Born in London in 1957 and educated in the U.K., he has lectured, researched, and consulted all over the world. He has two doctorate degrees and is a Fellow of the Royal Society of Arts. He has written and edited eight academic books; has approximately two hundred papers, articles and chapters published in scientific journals, professional journals and edited works; and his scientific papers have won and been nominated for many international prizes. This is his debut novel. He is married to an amazing woman and has an equally wonderful daughter and son.

The Noah Brotherhood Trilogy

NOAH'S ART IS inspired by a book on the history of Sufism that I read as a neo-hippie teenager on a visit to Casablanca; by the story of a mystic that a friend of mine met in a Kabul market place in the 1970's; by the great Cold War spy stories of Le Carre and Len Deighton; and by real life thriller characters I have personally come across in the course of my work. These include an English university lecturer exposed as a sleeper agent for the East German Stasi; radical Muslims of a good and bad kind, including the work-party of Indonesians I joined to help reconstruct Banda Ache months after the 2005 tsunami; and a lecturer at a Malaysian university who was implicated in the 2002 Bali bombings and, as far as I know, is still on the run. It should also be clear that I draw inspiration from the intriguing ancient myth-history and eschatological literature preserved in the Bible, Koran, and other sources.

Noah's Art is the first book in the Noah Brotherhood trilogy:

Noah's Art
Adam's Eve
Isa's Return

Selected Sources and Acknowledgements

Ahmet T. Karamustafa (2007) Sufism: The Formative Period, Edinburgh: Edinburgh University Press.

Harun Yaha Perished Nations, Chapter 2 'Nuh's Flood'
http://harunyahya.com/en/Books/904/perished-nations/chapter/3271

Kabbani M H and Kabbani S M H, 1995, The Naqshbandi Sufi Way: History and Guidebook of the Saints of the Golden Chain, Chicago: Kazi Publications.

Sells, M A, 1995, Early Islamic Mysticism: Sufi, Qur'an, Mi'raj, Poetic and Theological Writings (Classics of Western Spirituality), New York: Paulist Press.

Spencer L and Lienard J L, (2005) The Search For Noah's Ark, copyright EHRC,
http://origins.swau.edu/papers/global/noah/default.html

Bible quotations based on New American Standard Version and New International Version; and **https://www.biblegateway.com**. Some Bible quotations quote selectively or mix different original texts as might realistically be expected of the characters making the quotes from memory.

Qur'an, quotations based on the English translation by M.H. Shakir (1983) published by Tahrike Tarsile Qur'an, Inc., in 1983; and Koran Browse, University of Michigan: **http://quod.lib.umich.edu/k/koran/browse.html**. Some Qur'an quotations quote selectively or mix different original texts as might realistically be expected of the characters making the quotes from memory.

The 1950s alleged discovery of ark remains containing carved references to Muslim prophets:
http://www.oocities.org/capitolhill/parliament/3555/noh.html

The technical part of the computational puzzle to find the location of the object on the seafloor is taken from a real puzzle I once had to solve using unlabelled and unstructured raw data on a digital tape of high resolution earth-observation satellite data from the French SPOT satellite.

Global ice age and periodic ice-reversal theory from a popular book published in the 1970s by two American geologists who I think were named Wentworth and Wentworth. The cover of my copy, along with publisher and author details has long since fallen off. If anyone can help with more accurate bibliographical details, please let me know via Noah's Art Website.

The black-box transcript borrows technical structure from several examples published on the internet (with all due respect to the victims of those sad accidents).

The Popular Mechanics quote comes from an article by Mike Fillon in Popular Mechanics, Dec 96, Vol. 173 Issue 12, p39.

The newspaper story about the Israeli police deporting American members of a Christian doomsday sect from Jerusalam comes from a report carried by a November 1999 copy of the Bangkok Post.

The first two chapters of Adam's Eve, sequel to Noah's Art. Enjoy!

Adam's Eve
by
JB Dukes

Sequel to Noah's Art
(Publication in 2016)

ACCORDING TO SOME Muslim scholars the final judgment of Western civilization will come in 2076. What if the apocalyptic number 666 could be decoded to predict the onset of the 'eve' of Adam's race in the same decade? A strange alliance of interests might arise between those believing they are called to hasten that day by violence. Those charged with preserving national security would know their opponents' end-game but would need a new kind of intelligence device to make sense of the contradictions. One such device has recently been groomed: Cassy Kim. But she is on the run, escaping from manipulative forces on all sides and searching for the unknown past that made her such an effective post-modern spy. What Cassy Kim discovers in *Adam's Eve* will get the world talking.

http://noasartthenovel.net/

Chapter 1

Military compound in North Korea, 20 km from the Chinese border.
November 1979

SILENTLY, THE BOY'S head emerges from a single heavily stained bed sheet and elevates at an incline just sufficient to scan up and down the central isle of the dismal ward. The sheet is his home, his shell, his castle and sometimes, when he sails far away, his boat. Gingerly he slips one leg and then another from the iron framed bed and sits waiting, making sure that the man they call Hobag (호박), Korean for pumpkin, has gone.

Hobag is one of the night watchers and had come six nights ago and unlocked the padlock that chains the boy to the bed. Hobag had been watching him with particular interest for some weeks and the boy had been afraid when he heard movement outside his sheet and then frozen as someone fumbled with the chain attached to his left foot. But instead of doing something unimaginable, the watcher had walked away. It took only a few moments for the boy to realise why. The key-bearer had walked the few steps to the chair that he falls asleep on during long winter nights. The boy knew that it was not just he that Hobag had an interest in.

So he had done what the watchman wanted and what he himself wanted and tentatively took twenty bare-foot steps across the ward to an identical iron-framed bed.

On the first night, he had simply knelt at her bedside. He knew that she had not been asleep; she had not acknowledged his presence, apart from remaining under the sheet and being awake. He could tell from her breathing that she was awake: an acknowledgement of sorts. More than an acknowledgement—he had interpreted it as a conspiratorial welcome. So the next night, after Hobag had repeated the routine with the shackle, the boy had sat on her bed. For longer than he had knelt the previous night. Still she had not emerged from her private space. Only on the third night did she move. First turning under the sheet to face him, then when he next looked down at her after checking in the direction of Hobag's shadow, finding her looking up at him questioningly. It was not a friendly look but neither was it hostile. Just curious.

He looked over again into the voyeuristic darkness. Instinctively, the boy had immediately known why the guard had picked this moment and not any of the other nights over the many weeks and months since his and then her incarceration. He might be young and ignorant of life outside Camp 15, where he had been born and where he had spent the whole of his young life until being moved here, but he is not foolish. He has seen the pattern of comings and goings and understood the bleak rhythm of this latest place of imprisonment. And he has heard the rumours.

Without warning, she had put a hand on the rough nightshirt covering his shoulder and pulled him down into the pillow. Then she had kissed him on the lips. A surprisingly gentle, innocent kiss, like the small girl he had once seen kissing her baby sister before the baby was taken outside to die under a winter night sky—a pregnancy that had been discovered too late for the usual abortion.

Tell-tale whites of eyes in the shadow told him that the guard was now standing.

Now, for the fifth night, the boy draws his freed knee up to his chest and touches the raw skin of his exposed ankle, sucking through his teeth as his finger sinks into pulp. Silently he pads barefoot on concrete that radiates cold like ice. It is twenty paces away but to him it is an adventure to the other side of the great mountain that eternally hides the early morning sun from Camp 15 inmates. His feet are completely numb by the time he reaches her bed. Two nights ago, Hobag had disappeared after removing the shackle. The boy had hoped that this meant he had grown tired of the sport, but now realises that if that were so, the nightly liberations would have stopped. He thinks he understands what the new phase of the game means but he doesn't care. Watched on unwatched, he has made a friend.

He has had two other friends in his entire life as far as he remembers. One was an old woman who shared food with him the day he had been moved to a new dormitory the other side of the putrid-smelling stream that flowed into the Taeolong river that formed the border to the camp. She had been the boy's first experience of kindness. The boy had cried for a whole day after the old woman had died of a fever. It was his first experience of tears of grief rather than tears of pain or anger. The second was a girl, even smaller than himself, in the school that prepared the camp-born children for a life of hard labour. She had been called Hayan, meaning 'white', probably, he thought, on account of her deathly pale skin. This time he was more prepared. He received friendship without giving and even then, told himself that he did not like her. But he had liked her. And he had again, cried himself to sleep after she had died. Death was a weekly experience in the camp—from hunger, sickness or execution. By the age of six, he was used to dodging flecks of brain flying from smashed skulls. The children used to try to identify animals in the patterns of bloodstained sand on the floor of the firing squad yard. He only knew what six animals looked like—dogs, rats, cats, pigs, chickens and horses. You got more points the bigger the animal. One day an older child who had not been born in the camp had pointed to a fresh patch of blooded sand and exclaimed 'Nagta', Korean for camel. Afterward, he had had nightmares of long-necked, humped-back monsters trampling on human heads. His second friend, the kind girl at school, who had stuck to his side without ever saying a word, had dropped her daily portion of cabbage soup and broken the bowl two days in a row. He knew that she had developed something wrong with her hands during a session of hard labour in the quarry the week before. Her punishment was to be sent outside to stand in 30 degrees below zero. With no shoes, coat, hat or gloves and a rag of a dress, without even the dignity of underwear, she probably died within an hour. Like the illegal baby, he was given the task of dragging his friend's stiff little body to the incinerator and had dared to brush his lips against her frosted forehead before leaving her on the ground with two other corpses.

The boy is now sitting on the bed of his third friend. Although he imagines it is Hayan. He knows why she has allowed him into her personal space: she wants him to comfort her.

Chapter 2

Twenty-two years later, Vladivostok, Eastern Siberia
April 2001

WEDGED INTO A window seat at the back of a blue and cream tramcar that could have been in service since the tramway opened in 1912, Cassy Kim presses her face further into the icy glass. Distractedly she wonders how long it will take the skin of her delicately crafted Asian mono-eyelid to stick fast. She imagines the brutishly handsome but foul-smelling driver having to unpeel a passenger from his vehicle when they get to the terminus. Outside, the temperature is below freezing and a light snow has just turned a grade thicker. What had started as an historical time-lapse of neoclassical frontages interrupted by the spaghetti of overhead tram wires, had become a mesmerising blur. As instructed, she had boarded the 315 at the station in Logovaya Street and is now heading along Svetlanskya Street. She is looking for a grey-white limestone building with classical arches that in the photo had reminded her of the Foreign and Commonwealth Office in London's Whitehall.

Her eyes catch a mint-green tramcar heading towards her on the opposite track. It is a number 222, the line she has to catch next after picking up a package from a man sitting in a black Mercedes parked with its engine running outside number 299 Logovaya Street. *Why couldn't they just have sent the Merc to my hotel?* As far as she was told at the pre-briefing in an anonymous London office building off the Strand, her host is the ФСБ—the Federal Security Service of the Russian Federation. The FSB working in collaboration with the local Division of Criminal Affairs of the Primorsky Krai Directorate for Internal Affairs—the Regional Militsiya for Eastern Russia. *Perhaps the collaboration isn't working well.*

Then as the number 222 tram rattles past over a crossing and clangs its vintage bell, a second memory comes back. The blur outside the window becomes a trance as her focus shifts from passing buildings to somewhere inside her mind.

It is not a daydream. It is definitely another memory. Cassy Kim is not sure why she knows it but she does. It must be the smell. She seems to recall that you don't smell dream worlds; but the grey, unlit hospital ward with concrete floor and peeled white painted walls is familiar for the smell of disinfectant, urine and sadness.

The first memory to return had been the clanging. That had been yesterday. It had come the moment she had stepped off the short-haul flight from Tokyo's Narita airport to Vladivostock's Knevichi Airport. The clanging of the number 222 seems to have unlocked some synaptic stronghold, tipping her into another level of uncharted memory.

Cassy Kim has never been able to find a single crumb of information about her life before the age of twelve. Not from her memory, nor from the woman who had the temerity to masquerade as her mother until that fateful day when the truth of her resented adoptive status was spat out. It had come from Joy's lips like venom that had been poisoning her for so long. Fumbling in her alcoholic anger, Joy had grabbed a dirty wine glass lying by the sink, stuck it under the tap then swilled the water once around her grimaced mouth before spitting it out with force. Three days later, Joy was in hospital and Cassy was in a youth detention centre under observation, having sliced through her adoptive mother's upper arm with a kitchen knife. Passing through her teens and twenties in ignorance about her origins has given Cassy what she regards as her secret weapon. She doesn't care. She is a survivor.

Rather, she *didn't* care. Now she does. After the parting comment she overheard being made by the senior

MI6 officer they call Hugo as he disappeared into the back of a black limousine in England's Lake District.

"Chip off the old block—uncannily like her father. Both of them damn clever. Damn clever."

It had been snowing then too. Much more heavily. As it had in her dream that had now become a memory. Hugo's earth-shattering revelation was less than a week and seven thousand miles ago.

The first memory of the clanging had been just a disembodied sound-track with no imagery. It had jolted her brain like a two-hundred-volt current as she stepped out of the plane onto the air-bridge. She had passed through customs drenched in sweat in spite of the cold. Then last night in the squalid old lady of a building that passed for a four-star hotel, a visual track had accompanied the clanging. Clanging of twenty-four chains against the ends of twenty-four identical iron beds.

Then the smell had come. And then the boy.

She had woken up at that point. When she had first seen the boy, her mind had frozen the picture as if fighting the power of a hallucinogenic drug that had found and unlocked it. Then, slowly, frame-by-frame, it had rolled forward. Just a little. Then it had stopped, and the start and end of the memory fragment was as blank as her early life had ever been. But she now has some clues and she knows that they will help.

There is the book that the man who had unlocked the boy's shackle had always been pretending to read as he watched the children: *Seohwa* (서화), meaning Rat-Fire. She had woken from the dream last night with the knowledge that the book was by the North Korean author Ri Ki-yong, even though she cannot remember the name having been spoken or written in the dream. With an overwhelming sense of excitement she had paced back and forth in the hotel room at 3am playing back a harrowing tale of a peasant woman and daughter being abused by an evil pre-revolutionary landlord. It was somehow connected to the book. That was when she was certain that it was not just a dream. Another memory followed. The guard with a pumpkin face was barking out short, seemingly unconnected sentences from the book to wake up his wards before daylight.

And there was the boy's name. *Yoon*. The name had echoed through the fragments of images as she held her breath, waiting for what might reverberate back.

When the reverberation came, it was a single raw emotion of a heavy, heavy sense of loss, stabbing deep like the knife she had used against Joy. Even as she registered the pain, Cassy had known that those emotions are the real clue to retrieving a lost past. When she had finally stopped pacing the hotel room, she had stood staring down at the iron bed frame, a disbelieving shaking of the head turning into a tremor that became an uncontrollable shaking as she wildly scavenged every detail of the memory. When she awoke later, she had been on the floor and the bed sheet was torn and duck-down from ripped pillows filled the hotel room like snow.

Then she had remembered that snow had been falling outside as they had lain together, comforting each other in a silent, tight motionless embrace. The falling snow had framed the guard's head one night, which was thick and folded as a pumpkin up to the eyes but elongated and narrower above, like an evil squash or gourd. She can't remember how many times the boy had left his bed to make his way over to hers but she knows why he had done it. He had come to be comforted.